ISBN: 1-938798-12-0

ISBN-13: 978-1-938798-12-2

DEDICATION

For Julia, who doth teach the torches to burn bright!

CONTENTS

ACKNOWLEDGMENT

I thank Robert Rimm, managing editor at Arch Street Press,
for his invaluable help in birthing this novel,
giving its pages weight, form and shape.

And as imagination bodies forth
The forms of things unknown, the poet's pen
Turns them to shapes and gives to airy nothing
A local habitation and a name.

MERCUTIO

True, I talk of dreams,
Which are the children of an idle brain,
Begot of nothing but vain fantasy,
Which is as thin of substance as the air,
And more inconstant than the wind, who wooes
Even now the frozen bosom of the north,
And, being anger'd, puffs away from thence,
Turning his face to the dew-dropping south.

. . .

ROMEO

I fear, too early: for my mind misgives
Some consequence yet hanging in the stars,
Shall bitterly begin his fearful date
With this night's revels and expire the term
Of a despised life closed in my breast
By some vile forfeit of untimely death.
But he that hath the steerage of my course,
Direct my sail! On, lusty gentlemen.

William Shakespeare, *Romeo and Juliet,* Act I, Scene IV

A lot has changed from a quarter-century ago or so, when our fair city was best known for graffiti-decorated subways, blasting boom boxes and the faint smell of urine rising from the summer pavement. ...

The dog shit was piled so high in the streets you needed a mountain ax just to traverse the sidewalk—but we liked it. The buildings were so blackened by grime you could barely see them in the dark—but we liked it. The subways were so dangerous you felt you were descending into Hell—and we liked it, we loved it, hallelujah!

Ratner, Lizzie. "The Bad Old Days." The New York Observer [New York] 28 May 2007

CHAPTER 1

Brooklyn Boys

March 17, 1975. Later, they would refer to it simply as "that day." Nando would dream about it; especially he would see the face of Mariel at age 12, and remember the untroubled expression in her eyes before it began.

She had been riding her bike in the sunken concrete schoolyard at PS 13. Built into a steep hill and shaped like an arena, the yard lay 20 feet below street level on one end and spilled out into a small road at the other. She circled the empty basketball court on her purple chopper with a banana seat and high handlebars. Nando watched her from above. He liked to climb up to the school roof around twilight and drink Mountain Dew. From that vantage, he could watch the yard and the surroundings, a mosaic of old brick and tar brownstone rooftops alongside spring planetrees and maples beginning to green. Lying flat on his back, the world would slip away, leaving only the red clouds of sunset afloat above the steady hum of traffic and the rising city lights, embers softly burning within the dusk descending upon Brooklyn Heights.

On the cusp of teenage beauty, Mariel wore a short-sleeved shirt unbuttoned to show the top of her training bra, along with scant shorts that easily revealed her smooth pink thighs. Nando was supposed to be blocks away; he had promised to meet his best friend, Mickey, after school. Instead, when the gang rode into the yard, he was on the roof alone, silently watching Mariel from above.

They entered from the street side, first two, then three more, four more. Nine in all. Riding on choppers like hers, they were Latino and black, some mixed. They came

1

from the projects on the other side of the park separating the Heights from the great untraveled beyond that led to the Manhattan Bridge and eventually to Queens. Three of them had bike chains around their necks, which they removed and swung as they dropped their bikes to the schoolyard pavement and took up positions around Mariel.

The leader, tall and older than the rest, wore a blue-jean jacket with the sleeves ripped away to show muscular limbs, scarred on the forearms and shoulders.

Nando surveyed the surrounding streets. Empty. He thought to run from the roof, to get help, but instead he lay quiet, watching.

"Little sweet white bitch," said the tall one in a high whine. "Come on little sweet bitch." He advanced toward her.

"What's your name?" he said, grabbing the handlebars of her bike.

The blood had drained from Mariel's face. "You can have it," she answered, getting off the bike. "Have it."

"Don't need no fucking bike, little damn bitch," menaced the tall one, emphasizing the word "damn ." "You a cute little bitch."

Mariel shrank toward the high stone wall of the yard surrounding her on three sides. Two gang members blocked the exit. Three stood around her. The others sat on their bikes, one coasting lazily around the perimeter, watching the scene with curiosity and amusement. They circled her like wolves waiting for the kill.

A cold vacuum spread through Nando's loins and stomach. There were too many of them. He had no weapon. He pulled back from the ledge, out of sight, and wished that Mickey were there.

He lay on his back, yelling at the top of his lungs, "*Help! Help! School yard!*" He drew a deep breath and then called out again "*Leave her alone. Leave... her... alone!*" He paused and listened.

"Where is that motherfucker?" demanded the gang leader, the tallest, then in a louder voice, "Ain't no one comin' here motherfucker. Ain't *no one* comin' here."

Silence. The tall one started to cluck and chirp like a chicken.

"Hey chicken-shit motherfucker, come out here, come *out* here, ain't no one comin' here to save your little bitch."

Nando heard a scuffle and shriek from Mariel, followed by whimpering.

The tall one said, "Show your chicken-shit ass, or I'm going to cut up your little bitch."

Nando could hear Mariel crying. His legs and arms seemed to empty of blood, replaced with the dead weight of liquid fear. He thought of Mariel's father, her sister Carmela and brother Eric, and their grocery store two blocks away, where he would sit on the front steps drinking strawberry Yoo-hoo and imagine kissing Mariel when she was just a little older.

He stood.

"I'm up here," he said in the lowest register that his 14-year-old throat could muster.

The tall one had Mariel's arm in his left hand. In his right, he held a box-cutter from which protruded a gleaming razor-blade triangle. He looked at Nando, sized him up, then laughed.

"What you gonna do, little motherfucker? No, no, nothing, little fuckass."

Mariel fell to her knees. Nando searched the roof for a bottle, a stone, anything. He found nothing but an empty can of Mountain Dew.

"Come down here, fuckass motherfucker," shouted the tall one.

Nando stood motionless as dread spiraled through his arms and legs. He knew they would hurt him.

"Come down here, chicken shit, or I cut her now."

He wanted to move but could not.

"All right little chicken shit, *here*!" said the tall one. He reached over and slowly drew his box-cutter down Mariel's right temple. A red line appeared and blood started to drip down her face. Nando's own head began to swim.

Trembling he swiftly clambered down from the roof as his heart beat in his ears. It seemed like the whole world had stopped turning, time slowing to a sickening crawl.

They watched as he climbed down a drainpipe, hands shaking, finally dropping onto the pebbled concrete.

Nando picked up one of their idle bikes by the back frame and started to swing it wildly around, as the pack approached on all sides. Feeling a liquid adrenaline flame in the small of his back, he let the bike fly like an Olympic hammer toward the tall one. The bike hit him in the arm holding the box-cutter, without knocking it from his hand. The tall one let go of Mariel, who wailed while holding her temple. Blood painted her face horror-movie style, soaking through the right side of her white shirt collar.

They surrounded Nando and grabbed his arms and legs, pulling them apart and holding him on the ground. The tall one started to kick him methodically. He struggled and screamed.

As they hit him repeatedly, in his mind Nando heard the old song his father liked to play on their living room stereo:

New York, New York, it's a wonderful town,
The sky is up and the battery's down
The people ride in a hole in the ground,
New York, New York, it's a wonderful tooowwwnnn!

They picked him up and dragged him to the left wall of the schoolyard. The tall one held up the box-cutter again. Mariel had vanished—where, Nando could not see.

"Cut you up, cut you now chicken-shit motherfuckin' little cocksucker," he growled. As the impending violence seemed to inflate spacetime, Nando studied his tormentor, who now appeared magnified, in slow motion. His eyes sunk into his skull, cold and empty. His long face had small patches of wiry stubble around the chin and upper lip. His black hair, greasy and irregular, fell close to a small scar beneath his left eye. His muscular neck carried a faded, five-pointed star tattoo.

Nando wondered where his own scars would be and whether he would die. He thought about his mother's red hair, and breakfast that day, bacon and scrambled eggs. He thought about his seventh-grade teacher Sister Patricia, on whom he had a kind of crush even though no one should think about nuns like that. He felt the box-cutter split the skin on the left side of his chin, as though it were a peach, then a trickle of juice running down his neck. "Where are you, Mick?" he whispered.

Fifteen minutes earlier, Mickey had emerged from the large brownstone where he lived several blocks away on Montague Terrace. Standing at the top of his front steps, he gazed out purposefully over the Promenade, Brooklyn's balcony overlooking the dramatic Manhattan skyline. He could see the adolescent Twin Towers and also the Brooklyn Bridge, the Statue of Liberty, Governor's Island and the sun, that gigantic red ball slowly descending over shimmering New York Bay. The best view in Brooklyn. As his hazel eyes focused sharply, he felt an electric charge of excitement in his gut. He was up to no good.

Two of his fellow miscreants attended him. On his left stood Harvey, a 12-year-old with a rumble of curly black hair and a pointy nose too large for his thin face. On his right sat Eric, slender and freckled, three years older but still too young for the skull tattoos needled on the underbellies of his forearms.

"What have you got?" asked Eric, getting to his feet.

Mickey slipped the canvas satchel off his shoulder and peered inside.

"Let's see…half a mat of firecrackers…15 bottle rockets…two roman candles…and…oh yeah…hmmm…25 M-80s."

"Twenty-five M-80s?"

Mickey grinned demonically.

"Are you gonna use them?" asked Harvey.

"Are you fuckin' kidding me?" smiled Mickey. "We're gonna scare him, not blow off his legs ." The three of them looked into the bag together.

"You're an Irish psycho," said Eric, punching Mickey playfully on the shoulder.

"Yeah," came the reply, "we have to hurry, he'll be here any minute now ." He started to jog down the block, Eric and Harvey following closely.

The street was spotted with innumerable little mounds of dog crap, Brooklyn's own wild flowers. Mickey stopped at each pile for a moment, studying its size, shape and consistency. Finally he selected a nasty heap at the corner of Montague Terrace and Pierrepont Street.

"This is the one," he said with great solemnity.

"Are you sure?" asked Eric.

"Am I sure? Am I sure? I'm a fuckin' dog-shit expert!" exclaimed Mickey. "I saw his wife out this morning with that goddamn Great Dane. Might as well be a cow. I mean, Jesus Christ, look at the size of this."

He unwrapped a square packet of firecrackers, pretty little blue and pink devils, each one covered with tiny white stars. He carefully separated four, two of each color, untangling their gray paper fuses from the thicket.

"That oughta do it," he muttered, before carefully unwinding the fuse on each cracker, expertly scraping out all but a trace of the gunpowder with his thick thumb.

"What are you doin' that for?" asked Harvey, leaning over his shoulder as if Mickey were a doctor performing some medical procedure.

"I'm slowing down the burn, numbskull, like Mission Impossible. So we can get away and watch. You wanna get covered in this?"

"Where'd you learn that?"

"I learned it inside my brain, you idiot."

"Oh."

When finished scraping the gunpowder from the fuses, he twisted them together and pushed the miniature bundle of explosives beneath the center of the stinking pile, careful not to get his hands dirty.

"That'll teach you to let your animal dump on my sidewalk," he chuckled under his breath.

"OK Eric, now go down to Willow Street," commanded Mickey, "and when you see him near the corner, whistle."

"OK boss," said Eric, trotting away giggling.

"Where's Nando?" asked Mickey.

"He's down at PS-13 tryin' to hit on Mariel," said Harvey.

"Damn. He's gonna miss all the fun. He's really got his head up his ass with that Mariel. What's he gonna do, just sit there and stare at her all afternoon?"

"Man, she's a fox."

"Yeah, who'da thunk Eric'd end up with a sister like that," mused Mickey. "Man, she's got a sweet little ass."

Eric's low whistle wheedled from the corner of Willow and Pierrepont, where he crouched from his lookout perch.

"That was quick," said Mickey, digging out a pack of matches from the bottom of his pocket. He kneeled by the pile and waited.

"Light it," urged Harvey.

"Not yet."

They waited.

"Come on man, come on, light it, light it. Mick, *light it!*"

"Not yet… not yet. This has to be timed exact," said Mickey intensely, his eyes drilling into the distance. His heart had started pounding in the most pleasing way.

Tucking Mickey's satchel of explosives as though it were a football, Harvey took off in a run, unable to endure the suspense of Mickey´s dogshit explosive.

"Pussy!" called out Mickey after him. He waited another moment. Another. Another. The pressure built up in his temples as his sweaty forehead glistened.

"OK. Now!" he said in a tense whisper, talking to himself, lighting the fuse.

He turned away, walking casually down the block and looking over his shoulder in time to see Mr. Steele, owner of the offending Great Dane, turn the corner. About 50 feet from the pile, Mickey ducked behind a parked Monte Carlo, watching intently through the back window.

Wearing a pinstripe navy-blue suit with a five-button vest, staring straight ahead through his large tortoise-shell glasses and carrying a leather briefcase, Mr. Steele appeared to be deep in thought, intent on getting where he was going.

Mickey's eyes darted back and forth, back and forth, between the visibly smoking fuse and Mr. Steele, who obliviously stepped ever closer to Mickey's carefully constructed dog-shit landmine.

Come on, thought Mickey. Come on, not yet, just a little longer, just a little longer. Oh God, please. Please. Oh yes. *Yes*.

Step, step, step. Ten feet away, five feet. Three feet away.

Now it seemed to Mickey that time had become infinite. He could not resist. Rather than peering through the back window of the green Chevy, he stood up so he could get the full view.

BOOM!

BA-BOOM!

Mr. Steele was splattered from head to toe in his Great Dane's excrement, little flecks glistening on his cheeks and glasses.

Looking out over the top of his now-speckled spectacles and squinting, Mr. Steele spotted Mickey. Their eyes met as Mickey took in his full expression: shock, questioning, horror… a dawning awareness… outrage, hostility, and at last a giant thundercloud of rage swept over him. Mickey felt like he had painted a Sistine Chapel of emotions on Mr. Steele's too-serious face. It was a beautiful thing to see his masterpiece unveiled.

Dropping his briefcase, Mr. Steele moved quickly, surprising Mickey, who ducked and rolled under the car. Beneath the Monte Carlo, he cursed himself. *Fuck! Why didn't I run?* He knew why. This would be more fun.

Mr. Steele circled him.

"You little bastard. It was you! It was you!" he hissed, bending over to see where Mickey lay beneath the car. "I'm going to drag your little ass out from there… you… you… you're on your way to the cops, you little shithead."

"You're the one with shit on his head," taunted Mickey from under the car.

Spitting and cursing, Mr. Steele got down on his hands and knees and tried to grab Mickey, reaching under and then crawling in the filth along the gutter where the car was parked. Mickey rolled out of reach. *I could run now, but this really is just too much fun.*

Mr. Steele crawled around to the street side of the car.

"You little creep, I'm going to kill you!"

Mr. Steele grunted, sliding on his three-piece suit-covered belly and trying to pin Mickey against the curb.

When Mr. Steele had gotten himself under the car, Mickey crawled quickly toward the front fender like an infantry soldier, rolled out and started to run.

His white button-down shirt—part of the uniform he wore at St. Bart's Catholic grammar school—was now covered in grime. He laughed hysterically, dashing away.

"Harvey! Harvey!" hollered Mickey at the top of his lungs as he flew down Columbia Heights, the stippled blood-orange glow of the sunset over New York Bay falling on his back.

Harvey burst from an alley clutching their satchel of munitions, sprinting behind Mickey as Mr. Steele receded into the distance.

When they had put a few blocks between themselves and their crime scene, Mickey slowed to a jog.

"That was fuckin' classic," said Mickey between huge gasps of breath.

"Did you see his face?" asked Harvey.

"Oh man! Oh man. Now where did Eric go?"

"He probably went to find Nando."

"Come on, come on. We gotta tell 'em. What a riot ." Mickey broke back into a run.

As they sped over the mix of cobblestones, pavement and blacktop, passing the elegant brownstone and brick row houses, Mickey felt fantastic, like his legs were made of metal springs and he could run a thousand miles. The evening air smelled clean and cool in the moist breeze blowing from the East River. He passed his oldest brother Eugene playing stickball where Cranberry Street met the expansive entrance to the Promenade. Eugene saw Mickey and waved heartily with his meaty right hand.

"Where you going, chucklehead?" shouted Eugene.

"Nowhere," Mickey called back.

He turned the corner of Cranberry and Hicks heading toward PS 13, and immediately knew that something was terribly wrong. Eric and his sister, Carmella, were huddled in front of the family store. Their sister, Mariel, lay on the pavement among them, her unconscious face covered in blood.

"What happened?" demanded Mickey.

"They're in the schoolyard, the fuckers, about 10 of 'em," said Eric, holding his sister's pale bleeding face in his hands. "Dad's calling an ambulance ."

"What about Nando?"

"He's down there. In the schoolyard. I think they've got him."

"Shit."

Mickey stood up with black eyes, pulling a large folding buck knife from his back pocket. With a clean downward motion, he flicked open the six-inch steel blade. He started for PS 13.

"Wait," said Eric. "I'll get our bats."

Mickey paused, thinking.

"Get the bats and get Gene. You got two minutes."

Harvey looked nervous, his eyes blinking rapidly.

"Gimme the bag," demanded Mickey.

Harvey handed it over and Mickey grabbed two handfuls of M-80s, sticking them in each of his front pockets.

"Fuckers," said Mickey. "They'll see some shit now."

Shifting Mariel onto his sister Carmella's lap, Eric sprinted in the direction of Eugene.

Mickey ran alone toward the schoolyard with his knife open.

Bending low, trying to remain hidden, he crept toward its high wall and peeked through the spiked fence at the scene 20 feet below.

Their bikes littered the playground, with Mariel's purple chopper tossed to one side. The gang had circled Nando. They were holding him on the ground, too many to count, as one of them, the tallest, stood over him.

Mickey backed away, cursing and looking up the block, scanning for some sign of Eugene and Eric. Harvey would not follow; he felt sure of that.

Hearing Nando scream, he stalked back to the fence.

Damn. Damn. Shit. Fuck. He had to do something now. They were kicking his main man Nando in the chest, again and again. A siren exploded in his head. Now. It had to happen now.

He reached into both pockets and pulled out the M-80s. Fuck. *Start with four.*

He lined them up along the fence and took out his matches. He looked again.

Goddammit! A deadly quiet had descended as they dragged Nando to the wall and the big one got in his face. They were cutting him. *Fuck it!*

Mickey struck a match and lit each tiny bomb in turn. When he got to the end of the row, he grabbed the first one and held it in his palm, inspecting the fuse, now three quarters of the way down. The image of his hand being blown off his arm flashed in his head. *Don't fuck this up!* He waited, and waited, studying his pinless grenade until the time was just beyond right, then threw it in a long arc. It slowly fell and shattered the silence in an escalating BOOM, exploding above their heads.

"Fuckers," he said out loud. An M-80, thought Mickey, shit, it might as well have been a mortar shell. Everyone was deaf now, stunned.

Heaving the other three in quick succession, he felt like the god Thor, throwing lightning bolts.

BOOM... BOOM... BA-BOOM!

On his knees, Nando bled from his chin. Everyone had scattered. Mickey looked up. Eric arrived, then Eugene, all 250 pounds of him seeming to roll forward like a human bowling ball.

Eric tossed Mickey a slugger and they ran down into the schoolyard side by side. Mickey leapt the last 10 stairs and began swinging at everything in sight. He caught one in the back, making him howl in pain. Another tried to get on his bike but Mickey attacked the front wheel, breaking spokes with his foot, then cracking the rim, reducing it to a mess of metal and rubber. The rider, a fat kid no more than 11, ran toward the back of the yard, leaving his broken chopper on the ground.

Eugene and Eric were chasing the others away and Eugene clipped one on the shoulder, spinning him around. He wobbled and fell to the concrete like a clipped bowling pin. Crawling back onto his feet, he stumbled forward and limped into the street.

"You fuckers, *you fuckers!*" yelled Eric. "I'll fuckin' kill you all."

Mickey crouched next to Nando, who was trying to stand up. Stripping off his dirty white dress shirt, and finding a clean section on the back, Mickey held it up to Nando's chin, trying to stop the bleeding.

Nando trembled, clutching his ribs.

"You're hurt bad, you're beat to hell," said Mickey. "Mar..." wheezed Nando, "is Mar OK? He cut her."

"Yeah, he cut her... he cut her bad. Her and you. Her and you. He cut you both."

Mickey scanned the schoolyard. The tall one, the cutter, was gone.

"This ain't over," he said, staring with wild eyes into the distance.

CHAPTER 2

Queens Girls

March 17, 1978. In two columns of bunk beds, less than two feet apart, lay four of the five Rafter children: the girls, Helen, Terri and Colleen, and little Stevie, nearly three years old. Peas in a pod, as their mother liked to say. In the right bottom bunk, Helen lay beneath her middle sister Terri. On the left, Stevie was sprawled in a blissful infant slumber on the bottom berth. Above him, five-year-old Colleen was about to fall off the top bunk again.

The bedroom felt as cramped as a youth hostel. When the door opened, it hit the left bunk bed, and they had to squeeze into the room sideways. No space for a dresser, their clothes lay in a large chest of drawers in the family room, where James, the fifth Rafter, slept every night on the couch.

"How did we get so many of you?" Mr. Rafter made a habit of saying before going to sleep.

"You know quite well," Mrs. Rafter would reply, "and I hope you're satisfied."

Helen stretched, nuzzling her pillow in early-morning semiconsciousness. The shower had been running. It stopped and she heard James slip out of the bathroom. He kept quiet in the mornings so as not to wake their parents, who slept in the other narrow bedroom facing the bathroom in their modest apartment in the Sunnyside section of Queens. *Mom has her hands full with the boys and the girls, and me,* thought Helen as she remembered her image in a family picture she kept by her bed. At 17, the eldest girl and taller than the rest, she was becoming a woman.

On her way into the bathroom she passed James busily polishing his buttons. He was on his way to early-morning drill practice at Xavier, his Jesuit military school. Helen thought he looked impressive all dressed up in blue, with his rifle and its frightening bayonet. James said the blade was dull, but she could see a sharp-enough point to kill a man.

11

For her 10 minutes of morning privacy, she closed and locked the bathroom door. She slipped off her robe and stared at herself in the small fading mirror above the sink. Someday she would have a full-length three-way so she could really see herself, front and back. Pulling off her pajama top, she examined her breasts approvingly. They seemed to be getting larger. Boys stared at them—something new. She admired her clear and smooth complexion. *Like the girls in the magazines,* she thought as she washed her face and then applied cream. Not much time to herself before having to rally the others. Terri was the worst. Terrifically sullen in the morning, she had to be scraped out of bed and prodded like a sleepy piglet all the way out the front door. At least she did not have to bother with James, for he could take care of his own body. Emotionally, that was another story.

James had a case of Irish self-pity coupled with an almost prurient interest in tragedy. Full of every sad story, he liked to pull them out one by one, parading them at the dinner table. Did you know Daniel McCabe's cousin died of cancer? Did you know Aaron McCardle's father woke up dead in his own bed of a heart attack? Did you know Father McCorkle has cirrhosis of the liver? And he's all yellow now? A miserable parade of dark tales marched solemnly out of James' mouth.

Helen did not mind being the one to get the others going before school. It was only fair to let Mom sleep. After all, she stayed up every night to make dinner for Dad when he arrived home hours after midnight from his doorman job at that fancy midtown co-op.

"I have to be up for him, Helen," Mom confided. "If I don't, he'll be off with his pals and we don't want *that* in this family."

"That" served as the uniform pronoun for all manner of unnamable evils. What they did in the movie the children were not allowed to see: "We won't look at *that* ." What they did on the subway, writing on the walls: "We don't want *that* ." Getting pregnant out of wedlock: "We won't have any of *that*." Dropping out from school: "None of *that* for the Rafters."

It was no ordinary Friday. The Xavier Military Ball. Helen had been invited by one of James' friends, not just any boy. He was Colonel of the Regiment, a position of high honor for a Xavier senior, like being first in your class. Tonight, Helen imagined, she would be queen of the small army of good-looking boys. The first lady of the ball, that would be her. It made her smile.

She planned to wear a sleeveless green prom dress that showed off her curvy figure in a way that would make Dad wince, so Helen knew it had to be right. Light and silky, the dress had white feather edging along the bodice and hem.

Staring into the bathroom mirror, she indulged in a minute of daydreaming about her prom date. Charlie Cunningham: a boy soldier, with his shoes all shined like little black mirrors on his feet, the gleaming buttons and medals on this uniform, his broad shoulders, the way he held himself with a straight back and neck, not like the other boys slumped against a wall or street lamp. Helen loved the way he called Dad "Sir" instead of Mr. Rafter. She loved the smell of his Aqua Velva aftershave, his strong chin, friendly smile and straight white teeth. She thought about how she could make him stare at her body by standing just so, and how she could make his face get red by whispering in his ear. She knew he had a strong future in front of him.

As she thought about that future, her mind darkened and belly tightened. Charlie had earned himself a place at West Point. He would go there and she would never see him again. No, she began to edit this thought. She did not know whether she would see him again or not. She might. No, in fact, she might see him on all the holidays, or most. He might write to her often. Yes, surely he would call her every week. No, this was silly, he would not call every week. But he might write to her very often. She stopped herself. *Never mind about the future. They had tonight, didn't they, and the next month?* They had until West Point started. She knew it started in the summer. She should not think further out than two months. She left the worry there, like a pan in the sink needing a soak before scrubbing.

The day inched forward like a midtown traffic jam. The three-block walk to the subway. The 40-minute ride with Terri to Sacred Heart High School. Helen could barely concentrate. In study hall, where she could usually finish all the homework due Monday before the weekend even started, she stared blankly out the window high above the street noise, imagining the evening. Terri was also coming to the ball, presenting both an advantage and a challenge.

Did Terri's date have to be Mickey Shea? They all knew of his bad reputation. Dad said 14 was too young for a prom and James called Mickey a cradle robber. Helen did not know Mickey well. Had seen him once or twice outside Sacred Heart. A good-looking boy with curly golden brown hair and a big smile. Charlie called Mickey a delinquent. Kids said he carried a stiletto knife, the kind with a blade that shot up from the handle when you pressed a button. The priests found it in his locker, but that was the least of it. Helen heard that he had other bad things hidden they never found, like drugs and explosives, and that he liked to play stupid pranks on people, like putting itching powder in their jock straps and squirting heaps of mustard in their sandwiches.

James said Mickey's father was an important doctor who gave lots of money to the school, so the priests wanted to keep him. And with four brothers, the school did not want to lose the whole family. It seemed unfair, to keep a hooligan just because his dad was rich.

But this hooligan had something very important to Helen: a party after the ball where she could be alone with Charlie. They had never been out later than 11. But in a situation like this, Helen mused, an unwritten rule applied, which said that if she and Charlie were at someone's house after the ball—not out on the street, and with adults—then she could call and say, "We'll be home in the morning." This meant that she and Charlie could spend the whole night together. Picturing them huddled somewhere together in the dark, she felt a distressing yet pleasing nervous energy below her navel.

Mickey's party was to be at a *second* house his father had in Long Beach. Helen could not imagine having one house, let alone two. Her mind came at last to the challenge: Charlie and Helen could not go to that party unless Terri invited them, and if she did not go to the ball, then none of them could go to the party.

Helen replayed her dramatic plea to Dad to let Terri go to the ball, along with promises to look out for her and watch out for awful Mickey Shea. "Please, Dad, it will be the only chance Terri and I have to go to the ball *as sisters* ." His forehead had crinkled with suspicion. After all, Helen and Terri did not seem to enjoy doing many things *as sisters*. Charlie himself had promised Dad that he would watch out for Terri, which put him in an even better light. Charlie's blue eyes were so earnest and straightforward, like he was a Boy Scout about to get his Eagle rank pinned on him. Charlie's promise also masked the fact that no one was going to watch out for Helen with Charlie. She felt another tingle of electricity.

She remembered her father's weary, lined face as he had weighed the situation, Terri standing right in front of him, Helen behind her, and Charlie behind Helen. James Rafter Sr. was a stern man with a violent, unpredictable temper. Mr. Rafter believed that good parenting entailed regular thrashing. If he beat you, thought Helen, it was only because he cared. As Mr. Rafter pondered, an icy foreboding settled into his eyes. He understood very well what could become of unguarded girls—his daughters—in the hands of unsupervised boys.

Squinting through a spire of cigarette smoke, the newspaper open on his lap, he looked disdainfully over the top of his reading glasses, first to Terri, then Helen, then Charlie, then back to Terri.

"You're too young, Teresa, too young for all… *this* ." He hissed the word 'this' with a particular feeling of disgust.

"But it's the Military Ball, Dad, the *Military Ball*," said Terri, "and I'll be with Helen the *whole time*. Everyone will be dressed up in their blues, Dad…you've seen how handsome Charlie is in his blues…and Charlie, he's the head boy this year, and…and I want to see Helen and Charlie get all the attention. They're stars of the ball Dad, *stars*. Helen's sitting at the head table… with Charlie… he's there too… and I might never be asked again, you know… I might *never*."

Charlie's blush made his eyes seem bluer.

"And what about this boy, Teresa? This Michael Shea?" demanded her father. "I've never met him. He's never come here to shake my hand. What do I know of him?"

"He's… he's… he's just a boy, Dad, that's all, just a boy," said Terri. "His father's a surgeon."

"A surgeon is he? And what does that matter? Does that matter to me? I don't like what I've heard from your brother ." He pursed his lips and drilled his eyes into Helen's. She could see that he was about to say no.

"Dad… wait… wait. I… I promise you," said Helen, "we'll watch them, Charlie and me, we'll watch over them, you know. It'll be OK, Dad."

Terri crouched before her father and laid her head gently on his knee. He took off his reading glasses and rubbed his eyes with his thumb and forefinger.

"Please Dad," begged Terri, "Please. It will be fine. I promise."

He sighed, his brows furrowed and pinched together in a dark frown.

"Get up girl, get up. Do you think you can charm me, do you? Do you?"

He paused, blinking, and looked sternly at Helen and Charlie, then back at Terri.

"Teresa, look me in the eyes please… right into my eyes… I'll take my belt to your behind if you disappoint me, girl. To the both of you." He paused for emphasis. "I swear it, Teresa. Helen, you as well. Do you understand me?"

"Yes, Dad, yes," said Terri.

"And Helen, are you to accept responsibility?"

"Yes Dad. And Charlie. And Charlie. We'll be responsible."

Charlie nodded.

"Well then," said her father, pausing and sighing deeply, "you may go."

Terri screamed with delight and gave Dad a hug and kiss, but Helen shivered while remembering the cold look in her father's eyes. She could tell that he did not at all believe Mickey's parents were to be at the party after the Ball.

So Terri provided a ticket to the party, but she was set on that wild Shea boy and what if they did something they should not? Terri was not as developed as Helen but she had a sexy girlish way about her, a devilish look in her eyes. And all at 14 years old.

Helen's mind carried on like this through the entire afternoon, moving in a great circle around variations of the same anticipations and worries and musings, as each minute marched past her in solitary confinement dressed as an epoch. Deliverance did not arrive until 6:20 p.m. when the downstairs bell rang in the Rafters' Sunnyside apartment and Mrs. Rafter buzzed in Mickey and Charlie to collect their dates.

Mickey had permission to drive his father's shiny black Lincoln Town Car, a gigantic boat with electric windows and little round portholes on each side of the back seat, making it feel like the inside of an ocean-liner cabin. Three couples were sharing the car: Mickey and Terri, Charlie and Helen, and a friend of Mickey's with his date.

Dad was at work, so Helen's mother delivered the warning to Mickey Shea in her strongest voice.

"Michael Shea," she paused, working to pin his ears back with a stern, motherly stare. "I expect you and Charlie to behave like gentlemen and return these young ladies home safe, sound, and in the state you found them. God help you if you don't."

Mrs. Rafter glanced sideways at Charlie, who had been included in the warning only for the sake of not insulting Mickey.

"Don't worry, Mrs. Rafter," assured Mickey with his gravelly voice, his eyes wide. "I'll take her care good."

Mrs. Rafter knew that Mickey had mixed his words and hoped she understood what he meant. Terri's cheeks flushed pink and her eyes crackled with playfulness; she looked at Mickey with excitement, as if she expected a piggyback down five flights.

Closing her apartment door and leaning back against it, Mrs. Rafter thought of James Rafter, Sr., at the age of 17, and a bead of sweat erupted on her brow.

They burst onto the street. Mickey scooped up Terri in his beefy arms, spinning her around and around, making small circles toward the Lincoln. He whooped and sang a modified version of "Rosalita (Come Out Tonight)":

Spread out now Terri, doctor come cut loose her mama's reins

You know playin' blindman's bluff is a little baby's game

You pick up Little Dynamite, I'm gonna pick up Little Gun

And together we're gonna go out tonight and make that highway run

You don't have to call me lieutenant Terri and I don't want to be your son

The only lover I'm ever gonna need's your soft sweet little girl's tongue, Terri you're the one

And Terri you're the one, that's what I said!

He yee-hawed as he swung Terri onto the Lincoln's front seat. Helen shot an astonished look at Charlie, who did not seem to know what to do except get in the car so they could go. The little Rafter apartment looked out—if one could call it a view—onto the narrow alleyway on the right side of the building, so Mrs. Rafter could not see the evening getting started.

Charlie and Helen got into the back seat, joining Mickey's friend and his date.

As soon as the doors slammed, Mickey roared out into traffic, throwing his right arm around Terri and squeezing her in a playful headlock.

Terri giggled, her face flush.

"Mick, you are gone in the head," she snorted as she wriggled away, getting up on her knees, looking toward the back seat. "He's a madman."

She smacked him on the shoulder, then swung at his head. Ducking, turning to face her, he made a series of squeaking kissing sounds. He started to sing "Terri, Terri baby" to the tune of "Sherry, Sherry baby." These antics carried on while the two couples in the back seat watched with a combination of irritation and amusement, as if the front seat of the car had become a kind of bad sitcom stuck on the TV set.

Helen glanced at the other couple. The boy looked Italian, with thick, wavy hair, and light brown eyes with green flecks. His glance sharp and penetrating, looking lean and muscular beneath his uniform, he smiled at Helen warmly. The slender girl next to him wore a low-cut, cream-colored Baby Doll evening dress. This struck Helen as strange because the girl had barely any bust. The dress hung on her loosely, threatening to reveal her small breasts, which were, Helen hoped, encased in a strapless bra. Her long brown hair spilled onto her shoulders in a way that seemed unkempt, but nevertheless silky and attractive. She wore much less makeup than Terri and Helen, and she had not bothered to hide a long thin scar visible along her right temple. Frightening but also oddly elegant, the scar ran down her temple like a delicate crack in a fancy vase. Her pale blue eyes set above high cheekbones twinkled, alert and lively. Her hand rested lightly inside the boy's right thigh.

"Pleased to meet you, I'm Helen Rafter. You know Charlie, don't you?"

"Everyone knows Charlie, he's Colonel of the Regiment. My name's Ferdinand, but call me Nando. Everybody calls me Nando."

"Ferdinand… that's an interesting name," said Helen. She had been reading *The Tempest* in school and remembered a particular character. "How did you get your name, isn't it from Shakespeare?" Helen was pleased with this effort at intelligent, adult conversation.

"He got it because he's a spic, and his dad's a teacher, he teaches Lit-er-a-ture," said Mickey, interrupting in mocking voice. "He's the only spic lit teacher in Brooklyn."

"It's a Spanish name. My dad is Cuban, he teaches Spanish and drama at Brooklyn Friends, where Mariel goes," said Nando, turning the attention to his date.

"Hi, Mariel Burns."

Helen had known a few Spanish families from church. Nando did not look Spanish to her. A lot of the Spanish were poor, she thought, having just come to New York within a generation or two, like the Irish in Sunnyside. Plus they were brown; to Helen they looked like Indians.

Nando caught the curiosity in her expression.

"My mother's Canadian," he said, "I only speak a little Spanish."

"Here's the only Canadian spic in America," said Mickey.

Helen frowned.

"You should have known Mick before he had his accident," said Nando.

"What accident?" said Terri.

"When he was three, one of his brothers smacked him in the head with a two-by-four and he had to have a brain transplant. They were short on human brains so they had to use the brain of a clam."

"A clam doesn't have a brain," said Terri.

"Exactly, that's why he has to think with his asshole."

Helen burst out laughing, especially because Terri had been used as the straight man.

Mickey laughed too, as did Charlie. Nando looked straight at Helen, right into her eyes, as if to say, "Don't worry about me, I can look after myself."

Mickey then pulled a flask from his breast pocket and took a swig, "Southern Comfort," he gurgled, handing the bottle to Terri, who also took a mouthful before making a sour face.

"Terri!" shouted Helen, imitating her mother's tone of high reprimand.

"Shut up, Helen," said Terri. "I don't scold you when you French-kiss Charlie on the stairs, do I?"

Helen flushed pink and glared at her sister.

"Mickey, my man, be cool, we've got the whole night," said Charlie.

Mickey passed the bottle to Nando and Mariel, who both took a swig.

Nando offered the bottle to Helen, who shook her head and directed a don't-you-dare glance at Charlie.

Nando took another and passed it back to Mickey.

The roles for the evening had been cast. Helen and Charlie were the parents, Mickey and Terri the unruly children. Nando and Mariel remained neutral, sometimes laughing with Mickey and sometimes chiding him to tone it down.

When they arrived at the ball, Helen and Charlie went off to a separate table for the Regiment Officers. Helen soaked in every minute. Charlie received a big award, not for being the smartest boy, but for being the one who most showed the values of the school in everything he did. Everyone stood and clapped for him as Helen radiated pride to be at his side.

He gave a short speech to say what Xavier meant to him and how he would never forget what he had learned, how he would make them all proud at West Point. Dad would have loved his plain and direct words, thought Helen. Charlie did not say anything about her in his speech but she did not expect it because they had been going out less than six months. Then the rector, Father Reardon, came to their table and shook Charlie's hand. Father called Helen the most beautiful girl at the ball. Charlie heard him say it and blushed. And in the glow surrounding being the first lady of the ball, Helen forgot all about Mickey and Terri and whatever they were up to and wherever they were.

Everyone danced and Charlie did not much like it, but Helen saw Ferdinand twirling Mariel around him like they were in a disco movie. *He's a good-looking boy,* thought Helen, *and a terrific dancer. Why couldn't Terri be with someone like him instead of the wild Shea boy? And where had they gone to anyway?*

Helen left Charlie with some friends and went to find her sister. The ballroom had a shadowy, open-air balcony overlooking the street. About 30 couples had gathered outside in small groups, talking and smoking cigarettes, and passing bottles like the one Mickey had smuggled in. Helen saw Nando and Mariel standing in a circle.

"Have you seen Teresa?" she asked.

Nando nodded toward the back left corner of the balcony.

Helen stared. There in shadows, Terri sat atop Mickey, kissing him full on. It seemed that she was trying to suck his tongue out of his face, and she was not just sitting on his lap—she had her dress hiked up so she could straddle him like a horse. Helen approached silently, leaned over and put her mouth to her sister's ear.

"*Teresa,*" she snarled in a penetrating whisper, "you're behaving like a *hoorrr.*" She said 'whore' in her grandmother's Irish brogue. In the best Irish accent she could muster, a manner of speaking reserved for a moment such as this, she continued. "Now get your Irish arse off that boy this instant."

With a smacking sound like a suction cup being pried from a window, Terri disengaged from Mickey and stood up. He had achieved the stage of drunkenness in which motor skills are still intact but social inhibitions have been removed like an uncomfortable pair of pants. He did not understand exactly what Helen had said and, in the dim light, he could not see her expression.

Before he could open his mouth, Helen said, "We're going to freshen up," and whisked Terri away.

Inside the ladies room, Helen pulled Terri into a stall. Then, as she peed, Helen berated her.

"Jesus, Mary and Joseph, what has come over you, girl? What's next? Are you planning to do him in the middle of the dance floor? Do you think the boys here won't tell James what you're doing and do you think James won't tell Dad?"

"We were only kissing," said Terri defensively.

"Only kissing while you hump him through your pantyhose," snorted Helen. "That boy is wild. Do you think you can shut him off like a bedroom light once he's been all wound up? You'll be standing in front of the 8th-Avenue Express if you keep on. And you stink of that disgusting Comfort whiskey. I wish I could take you home right now. You're a shame to me."

Terri's eyes welled up and her lower lip started to quiver. "I'm sorry, Hel," she whimpered.

"He's not a nice boy, Terri. I'm only looking out for you. Behave yourself."

She flushed the toilet and without another word left Terri to compose herself.

The three couples arrived at the Shea family house in Long Beach after 11:30 p.m. The large, windswept house sat two blocks off the boardwalk. Three stories, brick, with huge windows to let in the sea breezes. It had bedrooms above and a first floor with a large family room opening onto a large deck that almost covered a small backyard. Mickey's two older brothers and their friends had arrived much earlier with a gang of friends from Brooklyn. They had a keg going on the deck and a full bar set up in the kitchen. The place had a ragged and tired look from years of extended family traffic and drunken parties.

As Helen entered the first floor, the smell of pot invaded her nostrils. In the corner near a fireplace she saw a group huddled around an enormous bong. So much for parents, she thought. The massive stereo speakers on either side of the room blared Led Zeppelin so loud that normal conversation required yelling. Mickey and

Nando went out on the deck and were talking with Mickey's older brothers, massive boys thick in the neck and shoulders from weightlifting. Eugene had played starting center for the St. John´s college football team. Terri and Mariel, who had just lit a cigarette, were standing off to one side.

Terri swayed back and forth from having had too much to drink. *She will probably soon be asleep in a chair,* thought Helen.

She leaned forward and spoke directly into Charlie's ear. "Let's get some air." Charlie seemed relieved to escape the smoke and noise and crowd that was still building as waves of boisterous teens crashed at the front door every few minutes.

They walked in silence for long time, crossing over the boardwalk hand in hand and heading down to the sands, toward the waterline, where the beach was flat and hard and easy to tread. The clear and still March evening let them walk without feeling chilled as the low tides whispered softly nearby where the earth met the sea. The ocean seemed a vast, formless landscape extending to infinity.

Since they left the ball, Helen and Charlie had each been thinking about sex. She had decided to let Charlie go further with her tonight than ever before. She once let him feel her breasts through her sweater when they kissed on the stairwell in her apartment building. She had let him squeeze her behind when they had kissed in the movies. Once she had sucked a spot on his neck below his collar, leaving a crimson mark. She saw with surprise how much that hickey pleased Charlie. He had inspected it in the mirror and grinned. Several times he had attempted to run his hand inside her thighs and this she stopped immediately. "No Charlie," she had said low in her throat, "I won't be able to say no if I let you." She tried to imply that her own desire would get the better of her, but she did not think he believed her. She had let him stick his tongue deep into her mouth, and had flitted hers past his lips, but did not like it much. His mouth was too wet and it made her feel sick.

She knew that he wanted to press himself against her, saw the longing and desire in his eyes, but would not touch him where he wanted. This would be crossing into some far more dangerous continent. She felt unsure how to draw the line between touching him there and what might follow. *Could you go only so far and then stop? If I touch him at all,* she thought, *wouldn't I have to keep going? And then repeat it whenever he desires?*

What she knew about sex, she had learned entirely from Professor Howard. Not from the man himself, but from beneath his bed. A teacher at the City University, he had hired Helen to work part-time as his secretary after school. He would often give her the keys to his Upper East Side apartment so she could straighten up and sometimes type notes while he was teaching in the afternoon. He had a box under his bed frame. Inside, a dog-eared copy of *The Joy of Sex* lay atop a pile of *Playboy* and *Penthouse* magazines. Helen would whip through her chores and then sit on Professor Howard's bed, enthralling herself with the anatomy of human desire as well as its profane depiction. There on his bed she had intentionally explored her own body, for the first time without guilt or fear of being discovered.

Staring into Charlie's eyes she knew that she could satisfy desire in a boy, but had never actually done it. Passion seemed to her a powerful poltergeist. Unleashed, it could never be recaptured; like perfume from an unstopped bottle, it would pervade everything.

Charlie was also at a threshold. Every day he imagined what Helen's naked breasts might look like and feel like to hold in his bare hands. He daydreamed about being alone with her in his bedroom, imagining the day she would let his hand wander up beneath her plaid Sacred Heart skirt.

But Helen's reality frustrated him. When they kissed, he felt her body tense as if he were her dentist about to check for a cavity. She seemed to be completely unaware, or uncaring, about his desperate longing for satisfaction with her.

At the same time, he felt conflicted about his increasing desire. They attended church together most Sundays, and he felt, as he sat in the uncomfortable pew with her, that she looked at him as someone who always knew the right thing to do and always did it, that she saw him as a superman of morality and chivalry. He would protect her and be a good man, and never satisfy his desire until God himself acknowledged it to be blessed and righteous.

Part of him relished the perception of moral valor; he wore it like another medal on his chest. He was Colonel of the Regiment. He was the winner of the Block X Award for character and leadership. He felt proud that Helen's father trusted him.

But he also hated himself for it. Would he go to war and die a virgin, he wondered, and at his funeral Father Reardon would say he had gone straight to heaven? Part of him—a big part—would rather sleep with Helen there and then, and go straight to hell.

He both admired and loathed himself, making him want to run away fast and far. He longed for a different girl, one who wanted to be bad, and who would admire him for his own badness and sinful lust. He watched Mickey Shea carry on with Terri—who looked a lot like Helen—and felt envy.

These opposing desires warred within Charlie, causing turmoil and confusion in his head and gut as they paced the sands of Long Beach.

"Helen, I've been thinking about the future."

"Yes?"

"I'll be leaving for West Point in July, early in July."

"I know that, Charlie."

"I want you to know something. I mean… we're both so young. I wouldn't want you to think I expect you to wait for me. I mean… I know… I know you'll want to date while I'm there. I mean… I know you'll want to date someone else."

Helen walked silently, looking straight ahead.

Charlie tried to read her silence, but did not know what to make of it. He felt surprised to have heard himself say what he did, on tonight of all nights. It sounded weak and pathetic. He expected her to say, "No, I won't" or "Why are you saying that?" or to protest in some way. He could not understand her silence, unable to see her eyes to read it. He felt stupid and sensed in his gut that he had only said it because she could not or did not want to be with him in the way he needed. He wanted to say, "I want to sleep with you now. Tonight." Instead he said, "I expect you to date someone else." Acid gurgled in his stomach and his teeth clenched.

"What about you? Will you date other girls?"

This seemed such an obvious response and yet he felt unprepared for it. To say 'no' would be like saying, "You can date other people and I will wait for you." This seemed ridiculous. On the other hand, if he said he wanted to date other people, it would be like saying, "I want to stop seeing you." He felt stupid and unsure.

After a long, awkward pause, he said, "I'll be so busy I won't have time to date. I'll just want to focus on my work. I'm just saying we're so young, we both know we'll probably have other experiences." After he said this, he wanted to run into the sea and drown himself.

Helen tried to keep herself from bursting into tears. She now felt more hurt by anyone than at any time in her life. It seemed that Charlie had chosen their most special evening to break up. She had been planning, or at least considering, letting him go further than ever before. She had been thinking about letting him touch her bare breasts or maybe even taking him up to an empty bedroom and letting him touch her, anywhere, and then just seeing what would happen next. Instead, he said he expected her to date other people!

He sensed her anger and hurt, but could not think why. He had done something, said something wrong. But what had he said? Only the truth: They were young and would probably see other people soon. But telling the truth had been a bad mistake.

"Helen, are you all right?"

"I'm fine," she said in a shaky voice.

"Are you sure?"

"I understand."

"What do you understand?"

"About the future." Her voice was cold.

He tried to put his arm around her, but felt her tension; it almost made him shiver. And then it made him angry.

"Fine then," he said, as blackness descended over his mind and heart and gut, the awful blackness of frustrated desire.

"Let's go back," she said. "I'm getting tired."

"OK."

He sulked, but maintained a faint hope that something would change, and somehow, something would happen to sort out this muddle of feelings and badly chosen words.

This something he wanted took the shape of Helen's brother, James, running down the boardwalk, screaming her name, *"Helen! Helen! It's James! Are you out there?"*

Alarmed, but grateful for a distraction, Helen yelled back, *"James, we're here, what's wrong?"*

"Mom sent me over with Uncle Sean to bring Terri home. Only she's gone!"

Terri Rafter wondered what had become of her panties. She knew they were on when she left the ball. Now she found herself in a dimly lit room crouching face down and lying on top of something with one knee on either side of it, with an unexplained absence of underwear on her rear end. Still wearing her formal dress, she slowly regained consciousness, like looking up after being face down asleep in the mud. Her brain felt as if someone were squeezing it on either side; she did not want to move because she felt sure that pain and nausea would follow.

Terri opened her eyes and slowly turned her head to look up. *Oh my God,* she thought, *Mickey.* He was sleeping below her, naked except for a pair of boxers like the kind her dad wore. She remembered vaguely that Mickey had told her to come upstairs because he wanted to put on some casual clothes. He had stripped down to his underwear and then taken out one of those water pipes, like the one they had downstairs. Did they call it a bong? Whatever. It was right there on the night table next to the bed. She had a memory flash of him sucking smoke as it bubbled, then laying back on the bed, coughing. Did she kiss him again? It hurt to remember. She wanted just to lie on top of him and be very still, but where in the name of Jesus were her panties? She peered over the edge of the bed to check the floor.

No luck. Stretching out, however, had made her brain feel compressed in a vise twisting tighter, and this triggered another squeezing sensation down in her bowels. A rumbling geothermal tremor of nausea radiated from the pit of her stomach. *Oh my God, why did I drink so much of that whiskey? Why? I am dying. Mother will find me here bare-assed and whiskey-dead.*

Doubled over, she rested her forehead on Mickey's belly button. Eyeballing his crotch, she could not help but wonder what he looked like beneath his boxers. Her mind involuntarily conjured a fantastical image of Mickey's privates. She thought that it must look like the one belonging to Michelangelo's statue of David. She had studied a copy in a big art book in the Sacred Heart library. It was OK to stare at a penis if on a famous statue. As this strange thought lurched through her mind, another violent surge of nausea broke against the back of her throat. She vomited liberally all over Mickey's groin and also peed on him a little. She felt streams of sweat run on her forehead as the pressure built up in her head. She thought her temples might burst like an angry boil.

The stench of vomit mixed with regurgitated Southern Comfort and a splash of urine pervaded everything. She looked down at Mickey horrified. His vomit- and piss-covered boxers now clearly revealed what had been hiding beneath. She stared at him with a combination of nausea, a tinge of arousal, and relief at having rid herself of the nasty stew that had been bubbling in her stomach: masticated Chicken Alfredo simmering at 98.6 in sweet southern whiskey. Mickey's did look a lot like the one on the David statue.

Mickey stirred a little, groaned and then stayed blissfully asleep. *He looks just like Stevie,* thought Terri from deep within her inebriated and throbbing consciousness. *Just like Stevie in a diaper covered in vomit, waiting for someone to clean him up.*

She looked down at her own dress and saw that vomit had run down the front of it. She moaned, wanting to plunge her head into a bucket of ice. As she tried to stand up, a mouthful of drool dripped over Mickey's chest. She heaved again, this time all over his torso. He continued his peaceful slumber, now covered in another warm vomit bath.

Crawling off the bed, she tried to steady herself. *I have to get out of these disgusting clothes.* She cringed as she pulled the stained dress over her head and stood naked except for her bra. Her head felt like someone had driven spikes into it, while her sense of modesty had been completely obliterated by the irregular waves of nausea sweeping up through her body and crashing as they reached her temples. The bed had still-clean covers on the end of it; she thought she might need to wrap herself in them to leave without her clothes.

She felt she had to wipe up Mickey. "I can't let him wake up like this," she decided aloud. *It wouldn't be ladylike. What would Mom say?* She needed something to wash the vomit off so they could get dressed in something else. Maybe they could share the sheet at the end of the bed. Sure, that would not attract too much attention, the two of them naked under a sheet walking out the front door. The bong Mickey had been smoking was still filled with rusty water. Her head vibrated with pain and she felt confused and sick again. She reached over and poured the bong water over Mickey's chest and groin, wiping the vomit from him using her similarly stained dress as a washrag. The bong water smelled like the sewer. Another bad mistake.

Mickey started to rouse and opened his eyes. As he absorbed the sight of Terri nearly naked, consciousness flooded his brain like a searchlight seeking a man overboard. He stared down at himself and an expression of confusion and loathing swept over his face.

"What the fuck?"

"I'm sorry, Mick. I'm trying to clean you."

"Clean me? Holy fucking shit!"

"Mick, I don't feel… don't feel good, I want to go. I'm sick."

"Mary Mother of God, no fucking kidding, what is all this?"

"Mick, I think I'm going to pass out."

"Oh my fucking Jesus Christ what the goddamn fuck?"

Terri knelt on the floor clutching her stomach as Mickey tried to rub the vomit off his crotch with her prom dress.

At that moment, a knock came on the bedroom door, followed by the voice of Charlie Cunningham.

"Mickey, are you in there? It's Charlie and Helen. And James. And their Uncle Sean is here. We have to go. Have you seen Terri? We can't find her."

"Oh God, Mick, oh God," Terri groaned audibly.

Mickey heard Helen say, "Terri, what are you doing in there?"

"Open the door," demanded Charlie.

Mickey's drunken thoughts simmered in a hot muddy stew of pot, whiskey, beer, and Terri's upchuck. "Uh, yeah, uh, oh, hang on man," he mumbled toward the door.

"Mick, oh my God," said Terri moaning low in her gut and crawling on her knees toward the bed.

Charlie had heard enough and rammed his powerful shoulder against the door. Dislodging the bolt along with a big chunk of the door frame, he exploded into the room.

Helen, Charlie, Uncle Sean and James stood stunned. Teresa Rafter's just-14 bare behind crawled toward the bed as Mickey held her mucky dress, wearing only his filthy boxers, himself bathed in a sauce of vomit, saliva, urine and bong water. The room stank of everything, along with a hint of teenage sexual arousal.

They stood motionless, gaping at Terri and Mickey.

After what seemed to be 10 minutes but was a matter of seconds, Uncle Sean stepped to the fore, deciding that the unfolding scene required Mickey Shea to receive a proper beating.

Sean, the 35-year-old kid brother of Helen's mother, worked construction and bartended at Maggie Mae's, a rough Sunnyside tavern. He often operated the jackhammer at the worksite because of his powerful hands, forearms and shoulders. At the tavern, he "went over the bar" at least twice a month to break up a fight or eject a patron who had worn out his welcome. It was not as heroic as it seemed because Sean generally did not drink behind the bar and his victims were usually hammered out of their skulls. Sean's method was to deliver a massive dose of violence up front to render the patron submissive or even unconscious. He approached Mickey like a combination case: a patron to be first neutralized, then ejected from the establishment. Charlie and James deferred to Sean, in his capacity as the older male, to get the beating started. In the matter of delivering a beating to Mickey Shea, Uncle Sean served as proxy for Mr. and Mrs. Rafter.

Sean grabbed Mickey by his curly hair and slammed his head into the plaster wall near the bedroom doorway. It left a huge indent, and he stood up bleeding from his forehead and both nostrils. Mickey, however, had tangled in numerous all-out fights every year since he was 8. He drew upon all those years of street brawling and mounted an impressive comeback, especially given his inebriation and head injury.

Mickey grabbed the empty bong on the bed, smashing its heavy glass and metal like a backhand tennis stroke into Uncle Sean's face. Mickey then grabbed him by the throat and punched him forcefully in the nose three times. Uncle Sean was not used to this kind of brutal retaliation. He fell on the floor holding his face.

Mickey did not fare so well with the combined attack he then received from Charlie and James. Charlie boxed regularly, and he began to circle Mickey, throwing combination punches at his head while James held him from behind to prevent blocking or swinging back.

While this bloody conflagration shook the bedroom, Helen led Terri into the hallway and unraveled her sister's filthy evening gown, attempting to restore a scintilla of her dignity by making Terri put it back on. In the rush, the gown mistakenly went on backward. Terri looked ridiculous, but Helen felt relieved that the mystery of her sister's missing panties was now concealed to all who might pass by. By this time, the outrage and illness resulting from such festivities had converted Terri into a barely cognizant lump of flesh with no other purpose than to return to the shrunken Queens apartment from whence it came in order to receive its next round of punishments.

In her stupor, Terri did not notice Ferdinand as he ran down the hall past them toward the bedroom. Helen, however, took in what would later appear like a slow-motion picture: his face, his physical presence, the look in his eyes. It was the first time she really saw him. His expression, sober and sharp. His body, energized but not tense; he moved like a predator. He seemed to look past and through her as he darted into the bedroom. She focused on his chiseled features and the scar on the left side of his chin.

She heard blows exchanged. A large crash. A series of grunts followed and James flew backward through the doorway, his head smashing against the hallway wall. He dropped to the floor. A few seconds later, Nando emerged with Mickey over his shoulder in a fireman's carry. Mickey appeared to be unconscious, his face a bloody mess. A trickle of blood oozed from the corner of Nando's mouth.

Stopping in front of Helen and Terri, who was slumped against the wall, Nando grabbed Helen's hand and looked her in the eye. His demeanor was strangely gentle and without malice, as if he knew that Mickey had only absorbed what he had coming.

"Get them out of here. Mick's brothers are coming. You have about five minutes."

Then he disappeared down the narrow stairs.

Helen surveyed the damage. The bedroom was completely wrecked. Blood streaming from his forehead and nostrils, Uncle Sean sat on the floor amid the shambles. Charlie sat on the bed, his hand covering his bloody mouth, as Nando had knocked out one of his teeth. James crawled along the hallway holding his rib cage.

Helen cringed inwardly, fearing this event would become the subject of family stories for the rest of her life. She imagined where it would fit inside the pantheon of the Rafter tales of woe as carefully chronicled by sad-eyed James.

As they drove back in silence to Sunnyside bathed in the blended spectrum of orange street light beneath a beaming silver moon, bleeding and aching both physically and emotionally, Helen thought of their scars, not only the ones that Uncle Sean and Charlie had earned, but the one on Mariel's temple, and also the other on Ferdinand's strong chin.

CHAPTER 3

Finnegan Presents...

September14, 1978. Ian Finnegan sat in his office at the San Francisco Plum, a borderline grimy Sixth Avenue tavern around the corner from Xavier High School, pondering the momentous series of decisions he was about to make. He conducted business from the far right corner of the tavern bar every day between 4 and 8 p.m., except during rehearsals, when the schedule would shift a couple of hours, 6 to about 10.

During his office hours, he usually smoked a full pack of Marlboro 100s, his second pack of the day, drank as many as six beers, and sometimes ordered a sandwich or two. He would also grade papers for his sophomore and junior English students, and plan Xavier drama club's activities for the next days and weeks.

If the day had been very good, he liked to close out the evening by ordering a dry Manhattan. "Just rinse the glass with Vermouth and skip the cherry." One Manhattan sometimes led to two, and then three, which led to a visit with a male prostitute. He tried to avoid the third because it created stress that neither his limited bank account nor his guilty conscience could bear. His homosexuality was something that he worked hard to hide and even deny.

Finnegan understood that the Jesuits employed a pioneering, unofficial don't-ask, don't-tell, don't-acknowledge policy regarding to gay faculty. As long as staff members did not admit in public to being gay, and as long as they did not have sex with students, homosexuality mattered little, even if they were as outwardly flamboyant as Liberace. In keeping with their highly intellectual and devout form of Catholicism, the Jesuits understood that the boundary line concerned action and not what happened inside the brain. Inner homosexuality could be carried like a cross. Rare lapses into overt homosexual behavior, if accompanied by guilt and regret, were only reminders of one's inherently sinful nature—a problem afflicting all of humanity. The general commitment to strive for abstinence amounted to penance. The more painful the penance, the more effective. Thus, Finnegan's experience of a terrible inward longing and frustrated sexual desire that made him consider suicide amounted simply to highly effective penance. In this Jesuitical view, repressed homosexuality could actually be understood as a virtue allowing one to come closer to understanding the suffering of Christ.

Because Finnegan knew all of this implicitly, he found himself accepted within the brotherhood of priests and lay faculty, more gay than straight, who took it upon themselves to turn Catholic boys into Catholic men—indeed, into soldiers.

So it was that Finnegan cultivated and kept his lust inwardly burning as his personal crucible, while carefully concealing it within several layers of disguise. These included a gruff and unkempt outward appearance and manner, a rough baritone register in his voice textured from years of chain smoking, carefully mimicked heterosexual body language, intermittent remarks about the beauty of the female form, the espousal of conservative Republican values including affection for war, the use of "fag" or "faggot" as a derogatory description applied to an effeminate man, and demonstrated competence with a hammer and saw. He also intentionally carried an extra 40 pounds that conveyed a Churchillian quality somehow associated with being heterosexual, no matter how many fat gay people in fact inhabited the earth.

His colleagues considered him a brilliant teacher. A classics scholar, fluent in Latin and Greek, he could read and teach the New Testament in Greek, as well as the works of Ovid, Cicero and Virgil in Latin. He had an encyclopedic knowledge of poetry and drama, especially of Dickinson, Frost, Poe, O'Neill and Shakespeare. He could recite entire scenes—indeed, whole plays—from memory, on demand. To emphasize a point, or simply to impress, he could recall at will almost any poem he had ever read—either a line or, if necessary, the entire work.

Apart from teaching, he had led the drama program at Xavier for more than 20 years. Through careful and painstaking trial and error, he had transformed Xavier Dramatics from just another extracurricular activity into a shining jewel in the crown of Xavier's non-academic offerings. Performances drew audiences of more than a thousand. Complete with realistic scenery, glossy programs, music, dance, period costumes, and impassioned and funny performances, the works paid for themselves and contributed money to the school's budget, even factoring in Finnegan's extra compensation. Parents left the theater thunderstruck at the miraculous transformation of their awkward and boorish children into elegant, convincing thespians. Ian Finnegan felt his miracle was to splice refinement into the personalities of hordes of adolescent cretins. Parents understood and believed that a boy who recites Shakespeare on a stage will never be the same again.

Sitting at the bar, increasingly inebriated, he fancied himself to be Xavier's Prospero, and dramatics his Island, a mysterious place to which wayfarers were drawn, tamed, and transformed into civilized and cultured men. Savoring a mouthful of rye, he indulged in a long rumination about drama's power, the power of collective imagination and creation. Drama bound them—audience, cast and crew—indeed, the whole community. It wove them together in a collective fantasy. He, Ian Finnegan, played the sorcerer behind the scenes, conjuring and chanting; he drew in the wayfarers and bewitched them.

He basked in the state of high anticipation that always came to him at the start of such magic-spell casting. This was a moment of extreme power in which his decisions would transform lives. Tonight, an evening in late September, he would cast his Xavier Dramatics production of *Romeo and Juliet*. His excitement particularly came because he had decided to cast two seniors and an unknown Sacred Heart girl as leads in the play, all having no prior acting experience. This bold move would provoke questions by the other faculty. Yet such controversy elated Finnegan. 'What is that brilliant rascal up to?' he imagined they would say. Could he take average boys, barely thinking and feeling lumps of dirt, and convert them into pieces of shining gold in less than a hundred hours? Yes, he could.

Finnegan felt more confident about his cast than he had about his last 10 productions. He saw something extraordinary in this troika—Romeo, Juliet and Mercutio—that would carry the whole production. They had a special potential that only he, with his director's intuition, could perceive at this moment. He could already see—months ahead—an audience exceeding a thousand in which half were moved to tears, not only by the tragic end of the play, but by the less-well-remembered but equally moving death of Mercutio. And this could only be achieved through an electric connection between the characters of Mercutio and Romeo. He already sensed the seeds of a profound connection between them.

And between his Romeo and Juliet, he saw something extraordinary as well. He could not explain it yet, but could feel the romantic sexual tension they themselves did not understand. It was latent but informed everything, just like the gay lust burning beneath Ian's own mountain of flesh and contrivance.

To play Juliet, he had selected Helen Rafter, an Irish-Catholic senior from Sacred Heart. It surprised Finnegan to see her turn up at the tryouts. He remembered that she had been going with the dashing Cunningham boy, now at West Point. Senior girls whose boyfriends had gone to college normally dropped their extracurricular activities. Her reading had been quite flat until she had paired up with his Romeo; then she had been equally uninspiring—indeed, it had been worse—but not her expression, not their chemistry. He felt something nuclear happening between them. He could build on it, knowing to trust his instincts about such decisions. And physically, ah, physically, he remembered her face and figure. She seemed exactly right. Tightly wound, but stunning with stormy, resonant eyes and lustrous silky hair, she was blossoming—that would be the word used by a straight man of some refinement. A clinician would have said sexually emerging and rapidly so. Any 16-year-old boy would simply have whistled, because Helen Rafter was a glowing, freshly-blown hourglass brimming with gunpowder.

Ferdinand Valdez as Romeo. Where had this boy been for three years? The first thing Finnegan noticed—beyond his looks—was that Ferdinand already knew the lines and only pretended to read them. Finnegan had never, in more than 20 years, seen anyone come to tryouts already knowing the part. He had cornered the boy.

"Ferdinand, you already know the lines for Romeo?"

"I think I know some of them, sir."

"Did you study them?"

"Not really sir, I just read it a few times. I wrote a paper on the play last year for Father James."

Unbelievable! Such an intelligent boy! A likely early admission to Columbia, maybe even Yale, so his counselor had confided. And the way he looked, more handsome than Finnegan's favorite Italian movie star, Franco Nero. But again, Finnegan thought he saw something more, something special, a deep channel running in that head, in that heart. A passionate if quiet intensity. To be with this boy could melt one's defenses.

Finally, Michael Shea as Mercutio. He had come to the tryout with Ferdinand. Now here was a puzzle. Finnegan knew Shea to be a smart-mouthed troublemaker who had been repeatedly threatened with expulsion. If not for his prominent father, who had bought him his seat at Xavier, he would no longer even be a student. Shea was a wiseass, violent brawler. Ian had often separated him from other boys in the lunchroom. He was always in the headmaster's office for some flagrant act of disobedience or vandalism. Last year, remembered Finnegan, Father Flynn had slapped the boy across the face for some saucy remark at an assembly. He had watched Shea's eyes flash. The boy had enjoyed it! Some of the faculty believed that Shea had taken up selling drugs and weapons to his classmates.

And yet, Shea had come to the tryout and really tried, really given the reading his all. *By Jupiter*, thought Finnegan, *he was not half bad.* Inside the devilish Shea, Ian saw a smart boy fighting his way to the surface. Too bad he was already a senior. Shea would have made a great Hal: strapping and loaded with charisma. Finnegan chuckled to himself and imagined how he would take this rake of a boy and draw out the good man within, the one who would make his father proud. He would give this boy some poise, give the parents of this shameless miscreant a memory to last them a lifetime. He, Ian Finnegan, would be the turning point in Michael Shea's misguided life. He would show the world the bright, inspiring Michael Shea, the feeling Michael Shea, the adult Michael Shea waiting to be born. And yes, years from now, when Shea made it as a something or other— Ian hiccupped in mid-thought, feeling his Manhattan work its way further through his brain—yes, someday ages hence, Shea would send him a postcard and say how much it had all meant.

Finnegan sat in the corner of the Plum and fantasized all evening in this manner, picturing each student and each part, himself at the center of the creative psychological storm. The scenery, the blocking, the programs, the music… all conjured in a haze of Malboros, Miller drafts, a Manhattan, a second and, yes, a third. Elsewhere, in Brooklyn, Queens, and all parts of the city holding the prospective cast and audience, he saw the future beginning to gather and organize around him, like a massive weather system about to unleash its splendor and fury.

September 15th. Standing in the lobby of Xavier High School, Helen stared in disbelief at the cast list posted on the wall.

As Romeo . . . . Ferdinand Valdez

As Juliet . . . . Helen Rafter

How could this have happened? She had barely tried at all. So little that Terri had complained after the audition:

"Thanks, Hel," Terri had pouted bitterly.

"What? What do you want?"

"You were as dead as a fish. I've seen you put more effort into reading Mother Goose to Stevie."

"What do you mean?"

"You know what I mean. And if you don't get a part, I won't be allowed to come to the rehearsals. And then I won't be able to see Mickey at all."

"And that would be a real tragedy."

"Thank you soooo much. You don't care at all."

"I said I would try out and I did, didn't I? How can you expect me to enjoy being in the same place with that thug and his sidekick—that Ferdinando—or whatever they call him."

"Nando. And what did you expect him to do, Hel, let James and Charlie kill Mickey that night? Mickey's his friend."

"Terri, I don't want to go through it again. You ruined my life. I haven't heard from Charlie in two months. He's probably forgotten about me and it's all because of you. I said I would audition so you could see him once, just once—I didn't say I would spend every afternoon for the next eight weeks so you could go and have regular vomit sessions with him."

That was unfair, thought Helen, but only by a hair.

"Too bad," she had whispered with finality to pouting Terri. "I'll just have to miss watching you spend every afternoon sticking your tongue down Mickey Shea's throat. And you'll have to miss it too. How sad for us. No more beatings from Dad."

Terri frowned, turning a light shade of scarlet.

Helen hated Michael Shea. He seemed to have no self-control at all. To call the house after what he had done!

She had answered his first call in April, about a month after the ball:

"Hi, I was calling for Terri, uh, is she there?"

"Who's calling please?"

"It's Pope John Paul calling from the Vatican. I'm calling to forgive sins."

"What?"

"It's the Pope, where's your sister?"

"It is not the Pope. Who are you?"

"Well is she there or not?"

"She's not here and please don't call again with your silly pranks."

Helen hung up. She knew that it was Mickey but kept silent. She did not want to talk about that evening or anyone involved in it—except with Charlie—ever again. Even James, who wallowed in every single moment reliving such events, had decided it would be best not to mention it. He had stuffed the episode into the enormous bag of sad memories that he was letting incubate and ripen.

The fiasco had earned Terri a stinging slap across the face from her father, leaving a hand-shaped bruise lasting three days. She had missed school while it faded. Her sentence punished her and Helen as well: she was not to leave Helen's sight between the end of school and her arrival at the apartment. She was not allowed to go anywhere with anyone but Helen, who had also been excoriated for failing to keep a vigilant watch. Helen had not been beaten; she thanked God for that. Her father's temper frightened her. Even Charlie had been shamed. He had thrashed Mickey but that had come too late, and at the expense of a broken nose for Uncle Sean and a broken rib for James.

A month after the first call, the second one came.

Terri and Helen had been alone in the house. Terri answered in the kitchen. Helen noticed her speaking in whispers. She crept up to the kitchen doorway, standing out of sight.

"I can't… No, I can't. You don't understand. I don't want to."

A long pause.

"Oh… oh… yes…."

Another long pause, followed by a giggle.

"Mick, I can't, I can't talk with you anymore. My sister's here."

More giggling.

"OK, alright, no, I, no, Mick…that's it."

Terri hung up.

Helen darted back to the living room and sat on the couch.

"Who was that?" asked Helen innocently.

"Oh, it was, um, just my friend Sarah, she wanted to ask me about school." Terri was a transparent liar.

"Really, what about?"

"Summer reading."

"What's on the list for you this summer, Mickleberry Finn? Or is it The Shea Hunter?"

Terri's face flared like a neon restaurant sign.

"You're an evil girl," continued Helen. "Have you lost your little peabrain talking with that gorilla? Dad will beat us both."

Terri stood for a long while in silence. Then she sat down in an armchair and stared at Helen blankly for what seemed like five minutes. Then she burst into heartbreaking sobs, burying her face in her hands.

Helen sat coldly, but as Terri continued sobbing, she could not help feeling moved. It seemed like Terri was crying not just for herself, but for everyone in the whole world.

Helen knelt in front of her.

"Terri, what is it? What's the matter?"

"Oh Hel," she said, "I am so… I am just so… sad."

"About what?"

"You know."

"No I don't, you tell me."

"I can't stop thinking, Hel… about him." Terri looked up, her eyes red, her face wincing in pain.   "I think I love him."

"Oh you foolish girl," said Helen gently. "What do you know about love? Why do you spill your heart for someone like him? He doesn't deserve you." She squeezed Terri, rocking her back and forth.

"I don't know, Hel," said Terri, plaintively. "I'm all… what's wrong with me? Something's gone wrong in here," she said, pointing to her heart.

CHAPTER 4

On a Fire Escape in August

August 17, 1978. Mickey Shea was dreaming. He had gone to bed like any other night, crawling into the bunk below his little brother Paul, in his room looking out over the promenade to lower Manhattan, all lit up at night. It had been a full day, racing around the neighborhood, playing street ball, drinking a couple of beers with Eugene because his father and mother were out. Exhausted, he drifted off like an unmoored sailboat into a still harbor.

In his recurring dream, Terri Rafter had come to live with him at the Shea house in Brooklyn. He had introduced her to his brothers and mother. Everyone loved her. Sitting at a dinner party, his father came by and put a big steady hand on Mickey's shoulder, leaned down and whispered in his ear, "That's some girl, Mick. She's a keeper."

Terri sat next to him at the big Shea dinner table, a massive rectangular antique that could seat 12. His mother had also looked at him and winked, glancing at Terri.

He and Terri had gone upstairs to his room, and here the dream got weird. He had taken off all of his clothes and lay on the bunk bed. Terri had done the same and straddled him, just like that night in Long Beach. And he knew that her name was Terri Shea now, not Terri Rafter. She opened her mouth and he thought that she would barf on him again, except instead of barfing she sang him a poem in an angelic whispered tone:

Had I the heavens' embroidered cloths,
Enwrought with golden and silver light,
The blue and the dim and the dark cloths
Of night and light and the half light,
I would spread the cloths under your feet:

But I, being poor, have only my dreams;
I have spread my dreams under your feet;
Tread softly because you tread on my dreams.

Mickey knew that he had heard this poem before; he thought it was a favorite of his mother's, by an Irish poet, but he could not remember the writer's name, nor when he had last heard it. After the dream, he could not remember the exact words she had said except for the last lines:

I have spread my dreams under your feet;
Tread softly, because you tread on my dreams.

It echoed in his brain: *tread softly, because you tread on my dreams*. And when he repeated this, he saw the image of Terri's smiling face and her beautiful naked body, which he had only seen once, when it was covered in puke.

Tread softly, because you tread on my dreams. Those words seemed her call to him from wherever she was in Queens. He knew that he had to see her again.

James had told him—warned him—to stay away from her. He had personally come to the Heights to deliver the message, catching Mickey as he came out of his front door.

"Shea, you keep the fuck away from my sister."

"No problem, bud. I'm done being the family vomit bucket."

"You'll be a fucking dead man, you understand me?"

"Loud and clear asshole."

He had called her the very next day—just to show James that he was not a pussy, but they refused to let her talk to him. When he finally got Terri on the phone, she would not see him. But that dream had told him something. It said go. Visit her now.

The thing that moved him was how she had used her own dress to clean the puke off his crotch. It was like he, Mickey, mattered more than her dress. Most girls would not have seen it that way. Most girls would not have used their prom dresses to wipe puke off their boyfriends. It seemed to him like her dress was the heaven's cloth that she had laid beneath his feet. It felt like her puking on him was… a kind of special gift.

And then, he could never explain this, he liked the fact that she had drooled on him and vomited again. It was like being all wrapped up in her, even if she stank.

39

And this too: He remembered the way she had said, "Oh Mick," when she felt sick. Like he was her bosom buddy and would make her feel better. That "Oh Mick" of hers crawled inside his belly and made him want to kiss her.

And another weird thing. He felt this impulse to go and somehow take care of her. He wanted to take her away from James and Helen and her dad and the rest of those fucking Rafters. He wanted to put her in the Lincoln and just drive off with her down the expressway. He wanted to put her in a headlock and wrestle her, then eat scrambled eggs with her, then just sleep with her under a big cozy blanket.

Thinking about his earlier dream had made Mickey want to buy Terri a gift—he did not know why. He had never in his life given any female anything—except his own mother.

It seemed crazy. He went shopping for it, and came as close to getting the right thing as he could, though he knew he probably got it all wrong. What did it matter? How could he give it to her? He could not see her now anyway. It was summer, so he could not meet her after school—there was no school. She would not take his calls.

On waking that August night, one of his cracked ideas popped into his mind. He did not tell anyone, because they would have just said, "Mick, are you fuckin' wacky?" He waited until about 1:30 a.m., stuffed his brass knuckles in the left back pocket of his jeans and put his buck knife into the right front. That felt balanced. He put on his tight black Alice Cooper T-shirt and slipped out quietly.

He jumped in his dad's Lincoln and drove over to the Rafter apartment in Sunnyside. Arriving after 2 a.m., he parked a couple of blocks away under the elevated subway on Queens Boulevard.

The streets were nearly empty; he climbed unnoticed over the spiked fence outside the alley that ran alongside Terri's apartment building. He clambered over a large dumpster along the fence wall and passed a dead, rotting cat lying next to it. The alley smelled bad, trash strewn all over it, with broken beer bottles, some spoiled food, and old yellow newspapers that had been rained on, left out in the sun and then had blown around in the wind. He looked up, and there it was, just as he remembered, the fire escape running up the side of the building.

He counted the floors to her bedroom, picturing the apartment and checking his memory of the layout. That had to be her bedroom window—the one right off the fire escape. She shared it with three siblings, but not killer James, he laughed in his head. Killer James slept in the living room on a sofa bed, Terri had explained that one afternoon at the pizza parlor near Sacred Heart. OK, he would worry about Helen and the others—*What were their names?*—when he got up there.

The ladder to the fire escape was hooked on the second-to-lowest rung so it hung high above the ground. *This was to prevent idiots like me from using it to get to an apartment.* He grabbed a trash can, turned it over, put it under the ladder and stood on it. Still too far to jump. He grabbed a plastic milk crate laying in a corner of the alley, put it on top of the can and stood on that, teetering precariously. If he jumped as hard as he could he might make it. Of course, if the hook bent under his weight, the whole ladder would come crashing down, maybe on top of him.

What the fuck. He jumped high into the air, grabbing the lowest rung of the fire-escape ladder with the tips of his fingers. The whole fire escape creaked and banged under his weight, and the milk carton and trash can tumbled over, making an alarming racket. He hung on the bottom rung of the ladder for about half a minute, wondering whether the whole fucking tower would just rip right off the building. He waited while the vibrations and clattering subsided. The hook and chain that suspended the ladder were taut, but they held. He hoisted himself up onto the escape's first platform, having put the gift for Terri in a knapsack that he carried on his back.

Surprised at how easy it had all been, within a couple of minutes he found himself sitting on the rusty fire escape outside Terri's bedroom window. The many humming and blowing air conditioners hanging out of windows along the fire escape tower had muffled the sound of his passage.

Terri's bedroom window was open a crack. How could he get her attention without waking up everyone in the room? How could he do it without scaring the crap out of them? What if they had a shotgun? What a stupid way to die. He thought of the dead cat he had passed in the alleyway. Hah, another idea popped into his head.

He crouched next to her window and began to meow and whine like an alley cat.

"Meeeooohhhwww, eeeeyooowww."

As he heard himself, he squelched a giggle. If he survived this, it was going to make a great story.

"Meeeeyyyeowwwww."

Then he hissed and made a sound like a cornered cat, "Reeeyyyhowww! Yeeohwww!" *I'm a fucking cat ventriloquist.*

Inside the room, Terri had, by good fortune, been lying awake, thinking about her sad life, condemned forever to be under the watchful eye of her angry older sister. And Mickey, she would probably never see him again. Eventually he would stop calling. *He probably doesn't love me anyway. Could a crazy boy like him love anyone?* He seemed to live from moment to moment just doing immediately whatever floated to the surface of his addled brain.

With all her heart she wished that they could start over, that he could be some other boy in some other family and that they would have another chance. *Why did people have to be so connected to what they had done in the past? Why couldn't they just all agree that the past didn't have to be connected to the future anymore?* From now on, what happened yesterday would be forgotten and every day would start fresh. Was this moment really part of all that had come before it? It did not seem that way. It seemed to stand on its own two feet looking out at a new day full of possibilities that had nothing to do with what had already happened. *People chose voluntarily to connect the past to the future, didn't they? And if they decided just to start over again, they could, couldn't they?*

But the problem was they would not. They insisted that what happened tomorrow must take into account everything that had come before it. If you made a mistake, you had to put the mistake in your personal red wagon and then wheel that nasty, noisy contraption everywhere you went, so it stayed part of you forever, like a rolling billboard displaying mistakes that went in but could never come out. They were always there, trailing behind you, for the whole world to see.

And it was not fair, because the good things you did—no one cared or remembered them or, if they did, only for a few days. For the rest of her life she would be the stupid Terri who vomited all over everyone and lost her panties and made everyone try to kill each other and made Charlie forget about Helen. It was horrible.

Her dark-of-the-night brain was murmuring on like this when she thought she heard a bizarre screeching sound on the fire escape outside her window, mixed in with the sounds of the street—car engines, a horn here and there, the background nighttime roar of the city. The whining sounded like a cat, but it could not be a cat—she had never heard a cat sound like that before. It made the hair stand up on her arms and made her throat feel dry. What was it?

She peered over the edge of her bed to see if Helen had woken in the bunk below. She was sleeping, but lightly. Terri thought that perhaps Helen was dreaming, the way she stirred and turned and moaned softly. She looked at the other bunk and saw that Stevie and Colleen were asleep too.

The noise on the fire escape continued, but faintly, not loud enough to wake anyone. *I can't sleep with that noise.* She edged off the bed, dropping to the floor in her floral-cotton nightie. She approached the fire-escape window slowly and drew back the curtains, which were swaying in the easy humid breeze. She would just shoo it away, whatever it was, a cat or some foul cat-like bird.

She opened the window a little higher and poked her head out so she could see what strange creature was on the fire escape. Before she could say anything, Mickey said, "Shhhhhh. Terri, it's me, Mick."

It was well done. The shhhh sound had startled her, but did not seem dangerous, not the sound of an attack. Hearing her name was startling but not alarming. Her ears picked up the sound of Mickey's sandy voice and then heard him say, "It's me, Mick."

"Mick?" she whispered, staring into the shadows. Was this some kind of dream?

She could not see him at all because he had moved back along the fire escape next to the wall of the building, so as not to startle her or in case it was one of the other Rafters with a gun or baseball bat. It would be hard to shoot or hit him with a bat from that angle, he figured. In a stroke of luck, Terri herself had come to the window.

"I didn't want to scare you," he said softly, "I'm over here." He stepped out into the light from the street, still partly in the shadows of the fire escape.

She stared at him as if she expected at any moment to wake up after a strange dream.

"Mickey?"

"Yeah, it's me."

"Oh." Another long pause.

"What are you doing out there?" she whispered.

"I missed you."

"Oh," she said, as if that explained everything.

Terri stood paralyzed. She thought for a moment. She could not talk to him through the window, but she also could not bring him into the room.

"Can you come out?" Mickey whispered to her.

She pulled the window up a little higher still, then wriggled herself onto the platform level with the window ledge. She said to herself, *Terri Rafter, you are mad as a hatter.* She grabbed his outstretched hand and stood up.

He pulled her toward him, leaning back on the stairs leading up to the fire escape's next level so that they were between her floor and the roof. He put his arms around her and pulled her close to him.

She silently put her head on his chest and leaned her whole body against his. He fell back onto the metal stairs and ignored the pain, focusing all of his attention on her.

She lay against him for long while, feeling happier than she had in weeks, like Mickey was her home and she had finally come back after a long journey. *What a strange feeling to have on a fire escape, hanging out in midair, in the middle of the night.* She stretched up and whispered in his ear.

"Mick, I'm sorry about what happened." Her voice cracked.

He tenderly pulled her face around so that he could look into her eyes.

"Don't you say that, you don't be sorry, not about anything—not about anything, OK?"

Her eyes welled up. She wanted to tell him that she loved him, but could not find the words.

They held each other in the warm nighttime breeze and listened to the sounds of Queens.

Mickey pushed her away a little.

"I have something for you. It's in my bag."

He wriggled the pack off his shoulders and pulled out a plastic bag from within, pushing it into her hands.

"What is it?" she asked, holding the bag.

"It's a dress like the one that got messed up. I looked for it—all over. I think I found the right one, only I didn't know your size. The store lady helped me. I had to guess how small."

Terri squeezed the bag in her hands. If he had given her a diamond pendant it would not have meant more to her, as if Mickey were saying, *I respect you, I want you to be fixed up, I want you to put your dress back on, I want to erase all the bad that happened.* Surprised, that was just how she felt. Mickey, this stray dog, had suddenly become human.

She hugged him around the neck, kissing him tenderly on the cheek, then softly on the lips, in a way that said, simply, Mickey Shea, I love you.

He felt possessed by a feeling that he had never before known, thinking that she had called him all the way to Queens and now he was face to face with her. Only she was channeling something, a life energy. It was coming through her, but was also just her. She felt all warm and alive in his arms, a feeling coming out of her mouth and her hands, like in his dream: a healing warmth, a goodness against the backdrop of a hard city night. *And she is so fucking beautiful, the most beautiful girl on the earth.*

"Terri, I'd, I'm, I..."

She put her mouth to his lips, and he took her hand and squeezed. He opened her hand and kissed her open palm as softly as he could.

She withdrew that hand from his and put it underneath his T-shirt and opened her palm on his chest. She moved it down to his heart and felt it beating inside him, before resting her head under his chin, leaving her hand over his heart. They stayed like that for another long while.

Finally, she pulled back from him and looked up. "What shall we do, Mick?"

"Listen," he said, "Xavier has a drama club, you know, and you could come and try out in September, and I will too, OK? They let in girls from Sacred Heart. And even if we only get small parts, or even if we're just in the background, you know, like the crowd players, we can still meet there. What do you think? No one will have to know that we planned it. We'll both just go. The club meets almost every day."

Terri turned over this proposal in her mind.

"OK, Mickey Shea, OK… we know a bit about drama, don't we?" she smiled at him.

"OK," he agreed. "Good."

September 18th. The dojo on 23rd Street was hot, despite its huge open windows. The worldwide headquarters of Tadashi Nakamura's Seido Karate Organization conducted classes in a vast, empty room with a plain hardwood floor that had been taped around the edges to show where to bow as you entered and departed. Sensei Oliver, five-feet-five inches of solid muscle and blistering speed, tensile and unforgiving as his bamboo pole, stood still in the center of the floor ready to poke the stomachs and crack the fists of the karateka, who were kneeling in rows and practicing their meditation.

Nando was in the first row; his gi and part of his black belt were soaked through with sweat from two hours of drills, kata and sparring.

"Clear your mind," Oliver had said, "and listen only to your breath."

"If thoughts come, just observe, and let them go. To clear your mind, let your thoughts pass as if not yours. When you can observe without judgment, then your mind is clear. Then you can see. Then you are first awake."

He had said this, then modeled discipline for them by remaining in absolute silence and stillness himself.

Nando loved the dojo. Discipline, respect, honesty, and also focus, power and ferocity. He had learned these values here. The key to everything was focus, which came from meditation. Focus created the ability to see what was happening now without being distracted by the past or future or your own desires or fears. Now was the time to practice focus.

He had learned that meditation was not tuning out. It was tuning in, being riveted to the present. His breath was the doorway to the present moment because breath was always and forever in the present. He had discovered that he could not think of his past or future breaths. To think of his breath at all brought him to now. To stay in the now, he had to let each thought pass untouched, unfollowed, without judgment. His mind would clear if he could learn not to interfere with his own thoughts. In this way, his mind became focused; he saw his own thoughts as though not his.

Verses from the Gospel of John passed through his mind. Jesus said that unless a man is born from spirit he cannot enter the kingdom of God. Jesus said that flesh gives birth to flesh and spirit gives birth to spirit. He told Nicodemus that the wind blows where it likes; you can hear the sound of it, but have no idea where it comes from and where it goes. This was Zen. In that way, said Jesus, you cannot tell how a man is born by the wind of the Spirit. Jesus was talking about breath. The breath is the spirit, and you cannot tell where it comes from because it comes from God. God is infinite and unknowable. God is breath. These thoughts washed over him and away.

Mariel suddenly passed through his mind. He saw the scar on her temple and saw her lying on the couch in her living room, reading, in soft purple corduroys and a white T-shirt. He saw her kissing him and naked in her bedroom and in bed. He saw himself entangled with her. He saw her laughing and smiling. He saw her holding his hand. He saw his own scar in the mirror and how their two scars now linked them.

Then Mickey. Mickey with a large bag of pot. Mickey with a pile of money on his bed. Mickey on his 10-speed bike in the neighborhood. Mickey with a black zipped bag in the Lincoln's trunk. Mickey with bricks wrapped in tinfoil in the basement. Mickey snorting cocaine from a buck-knife blade in the Xavier bathroom. He and Mickey together in the projects. Mickey jamming his switchblade into a man's shoulder. Mickey with his eye black and his mouth bleeding. Mickey with blood running from his nostrils. Mickey lighting an M-80. Mickey smoking a joint. Mickey cooking some heroin. Mickey hugging him. Mickey puking his guts out.

He saw his own fists in a blur of punching and blocking as his foot delivered a roundhouse to the temple of a tall Italian man swinging a baseball bat. These images passed through his mind; he let them go.

He saw his mother and father and himself at their family dinner table, his mother smiling at him, dressed in her shiny green bathrobe, her hair in curlers. His grey-bearded father, putting an arm around his shoulders. His father's study filled with old books of Spanish and English poetry and drama. His father kissing him on the cheek. He saw himself in his Xavier uniform. Himself in the Xavier library, writing. He saw his college applications. He saw his rock albums on the cabinet next to the stereo in the living room. Let it pass. Let it all pass.

He saw Mickey Shea give him an envelope stuffed with cash. He saw himself pushing it away at first, then accepting it.

He saw emptiness and a clear blue sky—a spot from the Brooklyn promenade where he could look up and see only the sky, nothing else. He saw the dojo floor, with little puddles of sweat glistening in the afternoon sun. He felt his feet tucked under his ass and his legs, warm but stiffening from being so bent and still. He saw himself in the dojo at 23rd Street and all the people outside in the street at this moment, and all the people of the city of New York at this moment, and all the people across America in this moment, and all the people around the world at this moment. He saw the world spinning, the moon spinning, spinning around the world, and the moon and the world together spinning around the sun, and the sun and moon and world spinning in the Milky Way, and then the whole universe moving and expanding, and an infinite mind, all in this moment. Let it go. Let it pass.

Then Helen Rafter appeared to him reading her part from *Romeo and Juliet*:

'Tis but thy name that is my enemy.
Thou art thyself, though not a Montague.
What's Montague? it is nor hand, nor foot, nor arm, nor face, nor any other part belonging to a man.
O, be some other name!
What's in a name?
That which we call a rose by any other name would smell as sweet.
So Romeo would, were he not Romeo call'd, retain that dear perfection which he owes without that title.
Romeo, doff thy name; and for that name, which is no part of thee, take all myself.

She read the words without sense and kept glancing up at him. Nervous, she blushed pink, and when he caught her eye, she would look away like a sparrow darting from one branch to another. He saw her eyes, startling blue-green like the sea. Her breasts and waist and ass appeared in his mind and he felt a stirring in his groin. He saw the cast list and his name across from the character Romeo. He saw Mickey slapping him on the back and laughing. He observed these images and let them float away, untouched.

He experienced his longing to be with her, his interest in her, his lust for her, his curiosity about her, and he let it all pass as if the thoughts and feelings were not his own and he was standing outside himself, indifferent but observant.

He felt his breath slow and his heartbeat steady, and he felt a sense of power and control and electricity running through all the nerve fibers in his body. He sensed that he could slow down time, and he slowed it down so that every, single, moment, was, observed, completely.

September 20th. "I won't do it. I can't," said Helen as they walked together out of the Sacred Heart lobby.

Terri said nothing.

"You know I can't," Helen repeated. "What's going to happen when Dad finds out?"

From Terri, silence.

"Do you really think James won't tell him?" They were walking to the subway after school.

"Look, Terri, let's suppose that somehow, through a miracle, James doesn't tell them. What's going to happen when they come to see the play and look at the program? What's going to happen then? Hmm, let's see, Dad will turn to Mom and say, 'Is that Michael Shea the same Michael Shea who tried to rape my daughter?'"

"He did not try to rape me, Helen."

"He might as well have. As far as Dad is concerned, if he got you to take your clothes off, he raped you. We know he got your dress off, girl. If he didn't rape you, then you volunteered—that's worse!"

"Hel, we didn't do anything."

"It gets better! You expect Dad to believe that you and Mickey got drunk and took your clothes off and you didn't do anything? Mickey's Irish. Terri, do you think Dad is daft?"

"Yes, I think he's daft. *We didn't do anything.* I swear by almighty God and the blood in my veins, Helen."

This made an impression.

"Look, I went along with the *crazy* audition idea so you could see him *once*, Terri. Now you're asking me to just ignore what happened and act as if James and Dad and Mom are just going to forget it. Explain that to me, girl, how is it supposed to happen? Dad said you're not to see him again. How am I to be in the play with him and have you there every day and just, well—whoops!—forget to tell Dad? Not to mention "Ferdinando," who broke James' rib and knocked out one of Charlie's teeth, remember that? And I'm supposed to play his girlfriend? Terri? Terri?"

More silence from her. They walked down the Upper East Side streets, past the fancy stores and little gourmet restaurants and corner news shops.

Helen looked at Terri out of the corner of her eye. She was all pale and sad and helpless again. *Damn it*, thought Helen, *this is so unfair to me. Why should I give up my life so she can spend afternoons with that boy?* Then her mind wandered to Nando and she felt confused, not as sure of herself. Her mind had a flash of him in the hall that night. Then a flash at the audition. The strength of him, his face, that penetrating look. She remembered how he had grabbed her hand and held it and looked into her eyes. He already knew the part. How did he do that? She was afraid of him. Why was she afraid?

"Terri, if you have an idea, tell me, please."

"Well," Terri started tentatively, "James won't be at the rehearsals, so he won't see anything that happens there."

Helen imagined herself prying Terri off of Mickey every 10 minutes behind the bleachers in the Xavier gym. Not good.

"And you know, Helen, it's a very big honor to be the first girl in the play. Thirty girls tried for that part, Hel—30 girls! From every Catholic girls school in Manhattan. It's a big honor, Hel. Last time they did a play at Xavier more than 1,000 people came. You'll be famous."

Terri knew that this appeal to Helen's vanity would be a strong card to play. She had a great weakness for being in the spotlight.

Now it was Helen's turn to be silent. She imagined herself, the applause. People all around her. Relatives coming up to her, "We didn't know you had it in you, Helen!" If she wanted to do drama later, maybe this would be her start. Maybe she would be an actress? Maybe she would be discovered and get on television? She imagined herself as the subject of a fashion magazine interview, "My first role was Juliet." She let this thought linger for a minute and then the practical, no-nonsense Helen rushed back to her mind to dismiss this line of vain and ridiculous speculation.

"What about Dad?"

Terri ignored this question and continued, "That Mr. Finnegan, he's the most respected high-school drama coach in the city. He's brilliant. He has the whole play memorized, you know. Has had for years, since he was a boy himself. He can tell you if you missed a word without even holding a script! He only does this because he loves children so much. He could be a director in Hollywood if he wanted to. He turned down being a Broadway director, several times."

With the exception of Ian Finnegan's photographic memory, this was an utter fabrication, but it sounded terrific. Terri looked with pleasure at the doubtful, worried expression on her older sister's face. She could see Helen weighing the cost of walking away from such an enormous, prestigious opportunity.

Terri knew, however, that to finish her task would require inventing a strategy that would address James and her father. The key was their mother. Even though she was only 14 years old, Terri knew that if Mrs. Rafter extracted consent from her husband, then he would not interfere. Such was the power of the female head of the family, especially if she still shared her bed with her husband. The key to Mrs. Rafter's approval was only to show her that Helen had accomplished something enormous, and she should not be deprived of this glory just because the evil, awful Mickey Shea had wiggled his way into it, too. This idea had to be followed up with the suggestion that Ian Finnegan was a perfect Irish guardian of righteousness and that nothing unseemly could ever have the slightest possible chance of taking place on his watch. In this way, for Terri and Mickey to be at a Xavier drama rehearsal together would be as if they were all together in heaven seated at the Rafter supper table under the watchful eye of Mr. Rafter, with Saint Peter himself at James Sr.'s right hand.

"You have to explain to Mom, Helen. You have to tell her that you had *no idea*, none, that they would be in the play, and now they are, but you don't think you should be cheated of this chance to improve yourself because I made a mistake. You've suffered enough already."

Terri beamed inside, because with this, her spell was finished. She could see Helen's mind churning and coming to the very same moral calculus. Helen Rafter would rather be damned than let her stupid little sister steal her future from her. Nor should those two awful Brooklyn boys be given the chance to upset her honors. Why should she give up the part she had earned with her brilliant reading?

Helen said nothing the rest of the way home. But as they descended the stairs from the elevated subway at their stop in Sunnyside, Helen winked at Terri, pinched her side and smiled.

"May the cat eat you, girl, and the devil eat the cat," said Helen.

Terri grinned, mischief visible in her eyes. She thought of Mickey, of his roguish smile, and of the warmth inside his beefy arms.

CHAPTER 5

The Players

September 25th. King Finnegan's court had opened for business. His subjects were a motley assortment of 13- to 17-year-old Catholic boys, and a smaller number of girls about the same age. Chattering in their thick New York City accents and representing all five boroughs—they had gathered on the fourth floor of the school in a large classroom that had an amphitheater's raked seating. Finnegan stood in the well of the room, walking his overweight frame up and down in front of the blackboard, sweating profusely and smoking a cigarette, which he sucked deeply for dramatic effect, exhaling as he talked; his words became visible in the smoke that curled and drifted around him in little clouds under the classroom lights.

"Ladies and gentlemen, tell me, what is this play about?"

None of the cast members wanted to be singled out for being stupid by such an intimidating figure on the first day of rehearsals. None except Michael Shea, of course, who relished an opportunity to have some attention at a moment like this.

"It's about sex," he said.

Titters all around, but Finnegan had too much experience to be an easy mark for a wiseass like Mickey.

"Obviously Mr. Shea has been reading the play with a part of his anatomy substantially south of his brain. Too bad that part can't talk for itself. Or maybe it just did?"

Laughter all around.

"But let's give Mr. Shea's reading some credit. It *is* about sex. And Mr. Shea has the courage to say so."

Finnegan deftly ridiculed Mickey and praised him at the same moment. It was a peace offering, a gesture of respect, and also the first time anyone at Xavier had referred to Mickey as having courage. Confused about it, Mickey remained quiet.

"But is it only about sex?" continued Finnegan.

"It's about love," said Terri Rafter.

Astonished to see Terri pipe up like this, Helen glared at such an effort to upstage her. Terri did not even have a speaking role.

"Yes," said Finnegan. "It is one of the greatest works in the Western canon on the subject of love. Possibly the definitive work on romantic love. Obviously we see the play centered on the romance between Romeo and Juliet. What other forms of love does Shakespeare explore?"

It was Helen's turn. "We see love in families, the way the Capulets and the Montagues love the members of their own families."

"Quite right," said Finnegan, "and that's a deep and very important love. It creates the context for the play's action doesn't it? Romeo and Juliet are each the only child of their parents, and deeply cherished by them."

Nods all around.

"And what other kinds of love do we see?"

"The love between friends," said Nando.

"Very good. Can you give me an example?"

"Mercutio and Romeo are like brothers, but not related," he replied.

"Just so." said Finnegan, "This love is one of the keys to the whole play. What makes Romeo kill Tybalt is not his love for his own family: no, it is love for his friend Mercutio. Romeo's passion to avenge the death of Mercutio—who is not his own blood—starts the cycle of tragic violence. So the triggers for the whole tragedy are passions outside the familial context: Romeo's love for his friend, and Romeo and Juliet's love for each other."

A long pause.

"Now, what about the Friar and the Nurse?"

Helen jumped in, "They're like family friends. And they want to help but they end up hurting. They love Romeo and Juliet but their love is not always wise."

"Well said," mused Finnegan as he threw his cigarette butt on the floor and stepped on it. "Very well said indeed. They offer examples of a kind of love that dotes and coddles and spoils. What would this play have looked like if the Nurse had said to Juliet, 'Sorry Juliet, you're going to have to forget about Romeo, once and for all.' But that doesn't happen, does it? Instead the Nurse is drawn into the passion herself. The same with the Friar, who agrees to marry them as a kind of favor to Romeo and also as a scheme to mend the friction between their families. Love that exalts passion over reason is a theme in the play." He paused, lit another cigarette, and dragged deeply.

"So what else is this play about? It's about so much, isn't it?"

"Hatred," said Terri.

"Prejudice," said a boy in the chorus.

"Misunderstanding," said one of the girls.

"Ah yes," said Finnegan, "sex, love, hate, prejudice, misunderstanding, the play is about humanity, hmmm? Yes, as is all of Shakespeare." He paused again. Then he quoted, not with great drama, but as if he were just sharing a thought that had popped into his mind:

> What a piece of work is man... How noble in reason, how infinite in faculties, in form and moving, how express and admirable, in action how like an angel, in apprehension, how like a god, the beauty of the world, the paragon of animals—And yet, to me, what is this quintessence of dust?

They were spellbound at a man who could say such things off the top of his head.

"And who said that?" asked Finnegan.

"Shakespeare?" replied a voice in the crowd.

"Hamlet," said Nando with certainty.

"Shakespeare, yes, Hamlet, yes," said Finnegan, as he looked at Nando with admiration. *What a bright boy.*

"Alright then." Ian Finnegan prepared to change the subject.

"It's also about truth," Nando interjected.

Finnegan stopped, paused and decided to pursue the conversation a little further.

"The play is about truth? Share your thoughts, Ferdinand. How is it about truth?"

"It's about what people really are. What they are made of. Juliet says Romeo is not his name. Montague is not his hand, his foot, his arm, or his face or any other part of him. Juliet sees beyond his name to what he is because of love. Love sees beyond names to the truth of what a person is. The play is about the power of love to see truth beyond words."

Finnegan let a long pause sit in the air. He blew smoke contemplatively.

"Think about what Ferdinand has said, all of you. Think long and hard about it."

Then Finnegan said:

Love never fails. But where there are prophecies, they will fail; where there are tongues, they will cease; where there is knowledge, it will vanish away. For we know in part and we prophesy in part. But when that which is perfect has come, then that which is in part will be done away. When I was a child, I spoke as a child, I understood as a child, I thought as a child; but when I became a man, I put away childish things. For now we see in a mirror, dimly, but then face to face. Now I know in part, but then I shall know just as I also am known. And now abide faith, hope, love, these three; but the greatest of these is love.

He paused to let the words sink in. "And who said that?"

"Was it Shakespeare?" asked Mickey.

"No," said Terri, "it was God. God said it."

"That's right. Teresa Rafter, isn't it? Yes, Teresa, God said it, using Saint Paul as his main character."

Finnegan made it a practice to have the cast read the play through three or four times before beginning to work on staging. "A play is like a song," Finnegan would pontificate at The Plum, after rehearsals. "You have to hear it as one unified whole before you begin to sing it."

Before they began the first read-through, he took the principals, Romeo, Juliet, Mercutio, Friar Lawrence, the Nurse, Tybalt and Benvolio, to one side.

"Please, as you prepare, as you read, do not try to memorize lines, or words or phrases, or even whole speeches. You must understand your part as a whole. In your memory, it will become one item, like a place you know well. To you, it is not a part, but a whole world just the same as your real life is a whole world. Do not worry about how you sound, how you will hold yourself. Do not act. The most important thing for you to do now is simply to understand what you are saying. Understand the meaning of your own words. Understand what is happening in the scene. Let me reassure you: If you understand what is happening in the scene and if you understand what you are saying, then you will know exactly how to act, because your words will make sense and everything you see and hear will tell you just what you should think, feel and express. You will not need cues from me because you will give cues to one another. And when this is accomplished, your parts will combine into a seamless whole.

"Today the most important thing is to think about what you are saying—think— and ask yourself: 'Do I get it?' If you don't know what your words mean, no one else will. Do you understand me?"

Everyone nodded.

The first reading brought nothing unusual: an unbelievably painful mixture of dramatic maladies. The spectrum of ill favors ranged from incredible overacting and emoting (including badly feigned British accents) to bizarre and nervous failure to give sense to words.

That first read-through, Finnegan made what seemed to the cast like a strange choice. He skipped all the Romeo and Juliet dialogues. He made no explanation, just directing the group to move ahead in their scripts to the point where these exchanges finished.

Then, after the cast had read through Acts I and II, he dismissed them all, except for Nando and Helen.

"I'll wait for you, Helen," said Terri, as she walked out of the hall.

Helen glared at her.

"I'll wait for you at McDonald's, OK? I'm just going to get a soda."

Helen could see Mickey waiting for Terri in the hallway behind her. Had Mickey been a wolf, he would have howled and licked his chops.

Finnegan ushered the minor cast members out of the room, closed the classroom door and lumbered to the desk where he had been sitting. Then the 10th cigarette of the afternoon.

"Let me begin by saying… I know that you two are going to be the best Romeo and Juliet I have ever directed." Finnegan was given to this kind of flattery and hyperbole, especially around a boy he found attractive.

Helen's faced flushed, her practical, eldest-girl-in-the-large-Irish-Catholic-family persona unpracticed at receiving such praise.

Nando studied Finnegan intently, not yet sure what to make of him. His spider-sense tingled. He felt something strange going on, but not dangerous. At the same time, he found himself more than distracted to be almost alone with Helen. He turned his penetrating attention to her. She seemed to be in a state of high anticipation and also on guard. She would not look at his eyes. *How can we play a scene together if she won't look at me?*

"Have either of you ever been in love before?"

Finnegan paused and observed, enjoying the moment. Helen's blush went a deeper shade of pink. Nando smiled and looked at Finnegan with a confident but curious expression, as if to say, "What are you up to?"

"It's all right," said Finnegan, "I don't expect you to answer, but it's something I want you either to imagine or to remember."

"You see," he continued, "Romeo and Juliet have an instant attraction—an overwhelming attraction—to one another. For the play to work, the audience must believe this attraction. Now I don't expect you to be instantly attracted to one another."

He closed his eyes, took a drag on his cigarette and just felt the erotic tension in the room. Yes, it went beyond the radar screen—very, very good.

"No, I don't expect that." he repeated. "But what I would like as you read together is to try remembering, or imagining, what it felt like, or would feel like. What is it to see someone and feel an immediate, total, passionate attachment to this person?"

Finnegan opened his eyes and closely observed Nando, who gazed intently at Helen. His expression, though hard to read, was certainly not impartial. Helen, well, she seemed so troubled that she could not look at Nando at all. She had buried her face in her script. *I'm not surprised,* thought Finnegan, *I can barely look at him myself.*

"OK," said Finnegan, "let's start with your first exchange in Act I, Scene V."

They sat across from one another in chairs pulled up before Finnegan's desk. Nando carefully studied his Juliet. She had long, silky brown hair. Her eyes were deep bluish-green, not pale blue and shimmering like Mariel's. Her lips were full if delicate, her face, oval and crimson with health. She was not a skinny girl, not a slight girl. Nearly as tall as Nando, she was a voluptuous woman emerging inside the body of a girl. What was it about her? Something seemed inchoate and brooding in the way she held herself, as if a terrific storm were locked inside her, waiting to be released.

Nando began,

If I profane with my unworthiest hand
This holy shrine, the gentle sin is this:
My lips, two blushing pilgrims, ready stand
To smooth that rough touch with a tender kiss.

He stopped.

"May I touch your hand when I say that last line?" asked Nando.

Helen glanced at Finnegan, attempting to redirect the question to him, but he ignored it. He sat with his eyes closed, apparently listening to them. She did not know what to do. She could barely engage Nando's eyes; she felt afraid. Sitting quietly, Finnegan seemed to be meditating.

She finally stretched out her hand, without looking at him.

Nando inched his chair closer to hers.

He reached over and gently grasped her hand before repeating the lines. He had put his script aside so that he could focus his attention on her.

If I profane with my unworthiest hand
This holy shrine, the gentle sin is this:
My lips, two blushing pilgrims, ready stand
To smooth that rough touch with a tender kiss.

As he said "This holy shrine," he squeezed her hand.

His hand felt large and warm and she felt a little dizzy as an unfamiliar emptiness, a hint of longing, emerged deep inside. Afraid to look at him, her eyes pinned to the script, she replied:

Good pilgrim, you do wrong your hand too much,
Which mannerly devotion shows in this;
For saints have hands that pilgrims' hands do touch,
And palm to palm is holy palmers' kiss.

At this, she withdrew her hand. Her reading had been nervous and unsteady. They continued the exchange, with Nando leading:

Have not saints lips, and holy palmers too?

Helen responded in kind:

Ay, pilgrim, lips that they must use in prayer.
Their exchange continued.

Ferdinand:

O, then, dear saint, let lips do what hands do!
They pray, grant thou, lest faith turn to despair.

And Helen:

Saints do not move, though grant for prayers' sake.

At this, she looked at him. Would he try to kiss her? He sat up straight in his chair and looked directly into her eyes, just as he had that day in the hallway after he had knocked out Charlie's tooth. Then he said:

Then move not while my prayer's effect I take.
Thus from my lips, by yours, my sin is purged.

Juliet:

Then have my lips the sin that they have took.

Romeo:

Sin from thy lips? O trespass sweetly urged!
Give me my sin again.

Juliet:

You kiss by the book.

They both paused, sitting in silence for a minute, maybe two. Nando looked at Helen, who looked at her script.

Finnegan sat with his eyes closed, thoroughly enjoying himself. By hiding his work on the scenes between Romeo and Juliet, he achieved two objectives at once. First, he protected his leads from the tittering and ribbing that would come from reading the famous lines. Finnegan knew that even the most serious of teenage casts could not contain themselves about such matters. Second, he allowed the anticipation for these scenes to build. They would be hidden from the cast like a delicate treasure and not revealed until the very end, when they could be executed with such precision and freshness that they would be protected from childish mockery.

He had also organized the rehearsals so as to thoroughly enjoy himself. He wanted to maximize his time in the small-group work with his prized principals, and especially with his dashing Romeo.

He finally opened his eyes and looked about the room. He felt the energy between them.

"Right, very good. That's all for today. Good work, good work indeed. We're not going to overdo these scenes. We're just going to get a feel for them. I'm going to let you work on them in private a little. To do this right, we need to give these scenes a spontaneous feeling. If we over-rehearse them, they will lose their magical quality. Do you see? Very good. Helen, very good. Ferdinand, very good. Ferdinand already doesn't need his script. Don't let him intimidate you, Helen, all right? When you are ready to put down the script, you will. It's like taking training wheels off your bike. When an actor stops reading, he's ready to start living his role. But wait until it feels like the script is getting in the way, all right? You're a very bright girl."

"We've got to keep an eye out for James," whispered Terri as she and Mickey walked down the hall from the classroom.

"Don't worry, he's at drill practice," said Mickey.

James belonged to X-Squad, the precision drill team at Xavier that performed acrobatics with their bayoneted rifles. One trick involved two squad members pacing away from each other, throwing their rifles backward in the air and each catching the other's without suffering lost fingers or accidentally spearing someone. Terri thought it was a miracle that the X-Squad members had never killed each other. Every year some boy had to be rushed to the emergency room to get his hand stitched up.

"Oh," said Terri, "that's good."

"We have at least a half hour, follow me."

As the bulk of the cast proceeded down the stairs to the ground floor, Mickey broke off on the second floor and Terri followed him into a hallway. They walked out of sight of the staircase. He reached out and grabbed her hand and they broke into a run.

They had not been alone together since those few minutes on the fire escape. It was the first time in months that Terri had been out of school, out of home and out of the company of Helen.

They turned the corner of the hallway to find themselves in a poorly lit, empty corridor lined with lockers on both sides. They looked around. Seeing no one, Terri flung herself at Mickey, pushing him back against the locker, wrapping her arms and legs around him and planting a deep open-mouthed kiss on his lips.

Mickey reciprocated, lifting her off the ground, catching her slender ass in his two large hands and squeezing her to him. She tasted of Wrigley's spearmint. No perfume, but she had a delicious, girlish scent about her. He wanted to tear her clothes off and have her right there in the hallway.

They remained tied in their tangle of tongues for several minutes, then she relaxed a little and he set her down on her feet. They looked around again, finding the hallway still deserted. They had moved past the point of needing to make conversation or feeling awkward about silence. Mickey slid down the locker onto the floor of the hallway, leaning against it. Terri sat down next to him, and they just stared at each other, holding hands, smiling and giggling.

"Oh baby," said Mickey, "every day. We can do this every day!"

"Yeah, but we have to be a little careful, Mick. We have to watch Helen and James."

"James'll be easy, he'll be other places. What about Helen though?"

"Well, she'll have a lot of work to do and she doesn't have a single scene with you. So when she's tied up, you'll be free."

"Yeah, that's great," said Mickey. What an enormous stroke of luck to be cast in a role having nothing to do with Helen.

"How's Charlie? Is he still seeing her?"

"I don't know," said Terri. "I don't think she's really heard from him. It could just be he's busy. It's hard the first year at West Point. They have hazing and everything. James was telling us. And it's co-ed now, did you know? Helen thinks maybe Charlie's found a new girl."

"West Point is co-ed? Holy crap! Well, she shouldn't have to worry about West Point girls. Imagine what kind of chicks go to West Point! Tough broads, I bet."

"Yeah, that's what I told her," said Terri.

"She doesn't like Nando much."

"She's mad at him for knocking the shit out of James and Charlie. I guess it was you who got Uncle Sean?"

"I can't even fucking remember what happened, to tell you the truth."

"She's mad and she doesn't forget easily, believe me. She's madder than hell at you. She thinks you're the cause of every bad thing."

"Well I am, aren't I?" acknowledged Mickey, grinning.

"No, you have some help," she said, as she leaned in and stuck her tongue back in his mouth.

Terri felt like she was half a soul and Mickey was the other half, and if she could cling to him in just the right way, together they could be whole. This painful feeling at the same time seemed the most joyous that she had ever had—like it just did not matter what happened. The whole world could explode and as long as she had Mickey, everything would be fine. Even dying did not matter as long as they could do it together.

Mickey was not exactly thinking. Entirely in the moment, he actively anticipated—not his mind, but his body—what he would do to Terri when he could maneuver the two of them to a private, safe place. Mickey had been with girls before, but he had never been with a girl like this one. So much fun. It seemed like Terri could be his friend, like she really cared about him, and that was all new. Along with his explosive lust and bottomless desire, he had a feeling of wanting to make sure she stayed safe, of wanting to protect her. He wanted to kill a wild animal stalking her and show her how he had done it. Then he wanted to cut the skin off the animal and wrap her naked body in it, with the carcass still dripping blood. She would think this was gross but it would make his point: 'I will kill things for you and then decorate you with them.'

This unthinking—just being—part of Mickey was what drew Terri to him. She could sense a wildness inside him and in her heart she felt this making a giant fortress all around them. His wildness had included her somehow; she stood inside it now, looking out. But she knew they had to be careful, like there were forces—powerful evil forces—trying to rip them apart, to keep them from their happiness. And she had decided to take a stand against these forces.

"Mickey, we better go, come on, let's go to McDonald's. I want to be there when Helen gets out." She pulled him by the hand and he stood up reluctantly.

Helen and Nando had left Finnegan in the rehearsal room. Nando followed her down the stairs; she had moved a little ahead of him and seemed distracted, as if wanting to be alone.

"Are you going to meet Terri?" he asked.

"Yeah."

"I bet she's with Mick. I'll come with you— he and I go home together."

She did not respond, although she did glance at him.

"Are they not supposed to be together? Mickey told me there are still a lot of bad feelings?"

"Yup."

"Wait," he said, trying to get her to turn around and talk to him.

"I can't, I have to go." She picked up her pace.

"Please, wait."

She paused for a moment and turned around.

"Look, I'm, I'm sorry about what happened," Nando stammered.

"It's OK." She started walking again. "I don't want to talk about it. How is your girlfriend, what's her name again?"

"Mariel, she's… great. How about Charlie, how is he?"

"Fine since he got his tooth fixed."

Nando winced inside. No point in apologizing again. Better just to let it go.

He sensed her speeding up again and decided to let her go. But surprisingly, she slowed a little so he could walk alongside her.

He could not find her rhythm, could not think of what to say. She seemed different now, unlike how she had been in the rehearsal. Now she was all business and off to find her sister. But she let him walk next to her and he did not know how to read her expression, acknowledging him and moving away at the same time.

"They better be at McDonald's," she half muttered.

"I've never been in a play before," said Nando trying to expand the subject. "Have you?"

She shook her head.

"Are you nervous? I am, a little."

She shook her head again.

As they approached the corner of 16th Street and Sixth Avenue, a yell came from behind them.

"Helen!"

Terri and Mickey were walking toward them.

Nando and Helen stood on the corner as they caught up.

"Hi, we were, we were just, we were finishing some reading in the library, and…"

Terri's record of bad lying remained unblemished.

Helen grabbed her arm and tugged her off down the street.

"Goodbye," said Helen. "See you." With this, she shot Nando a sharp look that said simply: *Don't follow.*

"What a bitch," said Mickey, when the girls were out of earshot.

Nando stared in silence after the two of them.

Mickey and Nando stood on the filthy subway platform at West 4th Street, waiting for the A train.

"So listen, man, are you in this Saturday or what?"

"In where?"

"I got to make a delivery."

"Fuck, Mick, I thought we were done with that."

"I got one more I gotta unload. That'll be it."

"Mick, you said that last time."

"Are you in or what?"

"I don't know. I'm supposed to see Mar."

"You're fuckin' pussy-whipped. You're gonna leave me hangin'?"

"*I'm* fuckin' pussy-whipped? Man, then they're going to have to invent a word for what Terri has done to you. You're living in a fucking pussy dictatorship. Look at you man, all reading Shakespeare and shit, and you've got me all wimped out in it now too. I'm only going to the dojo on Fridays for the next two months. Me pussy-whipped? Let me tell you something. Now I'm not sayin' she ain't cute, but she's got your nuts in her little hand, and all she has to do is give them a little squeeze."

"I wish she would. Now get the fuck outta here. The play was my idea, shithead. How am I gonna see her otherwise? That Helen, it's like having a fuckin' nun as your permanent babysitter. Listen asshole, thanks to me you're a fuckin' star now."

"Well your bright idea backfired, man, cause Helen's gonna be there every day, right on your ass. And I don't wanna be a star. Thanks for nothin', man. I'm seeing Mar on Saturday because I missed her all week."

"Look, are you comin' or what? Bring Mar along if you want to. She's more fun than you." Mickey grinned.

"Ah shit, Mick, I really want to stop this, you're gonna get yourself fuckin' killed and me too. Mick, you gotta stop this, you gotta stop."

"I'll make it worth your while. Come on, I want some company. Bring Mar, it's good to have a chick along, keeps things light. She's come before, she can handle herself."

Nando had a sick feeling in his stomach.

"Mick, even if I did come, I don't want anything. Nothin'. You got me? I don't want any shit and I don't want the cash. I got paid over the summer. You know what? I'm done with it, I don't want to do it, you understand me? I'm out of this. I'm not coming."

"Fuckin' pussy-whipped."

CHAPTER 6

In Bedrooms

Septermber 28th. Nando lay awake in his room below Henry Street. The small apartment where he lived with his mother and father was buried a full story below the pavement. Dim on even the sunniest day, his "room," fashioned from a walk-in closet, lacked windows and much ventilation. His mind raced around Helen, Mickey, Terri. The play. Saturday night.

The last time they made a delivery, he had almost gotten badly hurt. The buyers— a 12-member black gang in Williamsburg called the Dirty Ones—had tried to change the price at the drop and Mickey wanted to pull out of the deal. The gang had then tried to steal the drugs, resulting in a brawl at the deal spot, a one-bedroom apartment in a rundown project covered with graffiti and barred windows. Nando thought the place was a shithole. Nothing like making a drop on the Upper East Side. Mickey ended up stabbing a man in the shoulder while Nando fought off two of the gang members, one swinging a baseball bat at his head. Mickey finally pulled out his .38 and finished the deal by threatening to kill the gang leader if they did not pay the up for about 50 bags of heroin. The gang chased them halfway back to the Heights. Nando did not know the details of prices and amounts. He counted the drops in his head. Five. They had made five over the past year.

How had it started? Mickey's family had a summer place in Maine—Boothbay Harbor. It began the summer of their sophomore year, when a lobsterman whom Mickey knew from Boothbay, Ricky Porter, had him over for beers in Wiscasset, and asked if he wanted to resell some imported stuff in New York City. It turned out to be marijuana, cocaine and heroin coming to the Maine coastline. It started small, a couple of pounds of pot, but slowly escalated over the next five deals. Mickey had paid Nando a total of $1,000 over four deals, $400 for the last, just to come along to the drop. After the last one, Nando had refused the cash, saying he was out. This was the first deal involving heroin. Mickey had accumulated wads of cash, thousands it seemed. Nando thought Mickey was now dealing directly with the suppliers, no longer operating on consignment from Ricky. Or maybe they had gone into business together. Something like this could fuck up their whole future, and he just wanted to get away from it before they got killed or sent to jail.

He knew drugs were wrong.

He knew how betrayed his dad would feel if he ever found out that his son experimented with—let alone sold—them. His parents did not have a lot of money and Xavier's tuition stretched their meager budget. They never discussed it with him, but he knew by the way they lived and how they winced when he asked for a few bucks. They were counting on him; drugs could ruin his life. "Your mind is the temple of God," his father had said through his gray whiskers, peering out over turtle-framed reading glasses, while behind him stood the rows of classics he had started reading to Nando as a toddler. Mr. Valdez valued reason, learning, artistic expression and faith. He had filled his little son's imagination with poetry and plays and romantic novels like *Don Quixote, Ivanhoe* and *The Deerslayer.* "Do not find your friends on the street, Nando, find them here," said his father, pointing to the bookshelf. Drugs were stupid, wrong, a sign of disrespect and worse, indicative of weakness and moral frailty.

But Mickey, not Cervantes, had become his best friend, and Nando did not want to leave him up to his ass in drugs. He loved Mickey like a brother. Mickey taught him what he could not learn in books, what he needed to know about the street to survive. He loved Mickey for teaching him, and cared about him. He wanted Mickey to get out. But like a great hunter who did not see the lion stalking him, Mickey was going deeper into the wild. Not just dealing, but using. Mickey always drank beer; he had started before turning 10. They had a running line about how his mother put beer in his baby bottle. By 14, he had started with a joint here and there. His older brothers had turned him on to pot. Then Mickey shared it with Nando, who did not mind getting high once in a while. But then Mickey progressed to coke, speed, LSD and Quaaludes depending on his mood, and Nando would not go with him. A painful rift developed in their friendship.

He remembered Mickey tempting him with coke one night during their sophomore year. They were in the brownstone on Montague Place, in the Shea kitchen, a huge room with 14-foot ceilings and giant windows overlooking the large unkempt garden. Mickey's parents were at a dinner party. Hunched over, he snorted two thin lines off the kitchen table using a rolled-up 20 for a straw.

"Come on man, this is good stuff," said Mickey.

"What does it do?" asked Nando.

"It makes you feel like your dick is two feet long," said Mickey.

"What good is a two-foot-long dick?"

"Why don't you check it out? You'll see. It makes you feel like Peter Frampton. *'Doooo... you... feeeeeel... like I do?'* It makes you feel like David Bowie. You're a fuckin' rock star."

"Yeah, but what about after? I bet you feel like shit, like your dick is missing."

"Naaa, you don't come down too hard. Nothin' like a hangover. You want more though. I like to smoke a joint when I'm comin' down. It stops the binge."

Nando thought about his father and his Sensei at the dojo.

"No thanks, I'm cool, my dick is big enough already."

"OK," said Mickey. "More for me."

Mickey had sucked in Mariel. She and other girls from the neighborhood would snort on Saturday nights and act like they were all in on a joke with Nando left out. Pot mellowed everyone, but the coke made them frantic; they wanted to stay up all night, drink a lot and do crazy things, like go out on the roof and sit on the ledge, or listen to the same song 20 times in a row. Then they were gone the whole next day. Mariel could not do anything on Sundays anymore. She could not even get out of bed until dinnertime. Sometimes she looked a little bad, all pale with gray circles under her eyes, like she had a cut that would not stop bleeding and heal. It made Nando feel sad to think of her like this, and stupid that he did not know what to do to stop it. He thought the scar on her face made her do it. He would watch her standing in her bathroom, staring in the mirror, tracing her finger along the line running down her temple. The scar seemed like the visible part of a crack in her soul, like it led down to the place where she had started to come apart inside.

Mickey seemed to tolerate it all much better. He could still play ball and sprint. In fact, he looked healthy. He did not smoke a lot. Never had. Mickey had a sense of how far to push things, he would go to the red zone, to make you nervous, but never completely overboard. Nando did not think Mickey would ever OD because beneath it all, he had street smarts. He had a way with people, always had them in the sights of his wrist-rocket.

But the drugs were changing things. Like Mickey had never carried a gun before. Sure, a stiletto, brass knuckles, a billy club, a buck knife, even a sling shot, sure, but a gun? Mickey had never carried one until they started making these deliveries. It scared Nando.

"What the fuck is that?" demanded Nando when he saw it on Mickey's bed when they were getting ready to make a drop. He wished it was a BB gun but knew otherwise.

"It's a .38. Don't worry, it ain't loaded yet."

Nando had fired a .38 once on the military firing range, when they learned to shoot handguns.

"Why do you need that?"

"What am I, a smacked ass? I'm going to carry around an inch-thick wad of cash and a bag full of coke and protect it all with nunchucks? Think about it, dumbass: They've got one, so we have to have one too. It's just like nukes. If everybody has one then nobody uses 'em."

"Maybe we shouldn't be doing business with people who have them."

"Everybody who does business has them."

Nando wanted no part of it. But how to get Mickey out? Terri—she was the best thing that could have happened. Mickey's attention had turned to her, to pretty little Terri and the play.

For what seemed like the first time, Mickey wanted to do something even though it presented no danger and involved nothing illegal. Not even mischief. No one could get hurt or even embarrassed. And they did not have to run away in the middle of it because people were chasing them.

Nando wished that he could have taken credit for it. He wanted to save Mickey the way Mickey had saved him. But Terri had made it happen. The play simply gave Mickey a way to see her. And it was cool how he, Nando, had gotten the play's lead. Really cool. He had something else to put on his college applications. Extracurricular stuff mattered. His dad had told him so, as well as his college counselor. He had already made up his mind to talk about it at his interviews for Yale, Columbia and Harvard. His college boards were good enough—720 verbal, 740 math. For a Cuban kid, the scores were fantastic. "You will be the first Valdez from Cienfuegos in the Ivy League," his father said, clapping him on the shoulder. Nobody asked him about his Canadian mother. As far as the teachers were concerned, his family had floated over from a sugar plantation in a refugee boat. He remembered once at St. Bart's when a girl had asked him if Cubans were cannibals. Never mind that his Cuban family actually had more money than his poor Canadian family. His father really did have a degree from the University of Virginia. Nobody knew. They assumed that his dad did hard labor, or worked construction or food prep. Whatever. If it gave him an edge, so be it. This was New York City; he had to fight for every little thing. In the morning, he had to jostle for a place to stand on the subway platform. He realized what an oddity he was: a poor street spic, yet smart and well read. He saw the puzzled looks on the faces of his teachers, like they had found a gold coin in the middle of roll of nickels.

Oh Romeo, Romeo! Wherefore art thou Romeo? Deny thy father and refuse thy name....

Fuck that. Embrace thy father and celebrate thy name. He thought about his part. He did not feel really like Romeo at all. Impulsive Romeo, all passion and no forethought. Nando wrapped his passion like a dagger sheathed in reason and careful observation. He always saw the danger approaching. He had seen people stabbed and shot and beaten, knew what blood looked like when streamed or spurt from an open wound. He didn't read about street violence in the paper or watch it in a movie. He saw it happen. He saw how it could and did happen when you least expected it. *You have to be cool and detached to survive in this mess called Brooklyn.* Mickey had taught him well and now he knew better than Mickey himself. *If you want to live and stay in one piece, you have to learn to look. Look into the shadows... see when you are followed... run or strike before the attack.* Those who failed to anticipate became victims.

He would never have let *Romeo and Juliet* turn out as it had. He would have been smarter and quicker and more vigilant and somehow stopped it. He would have cut the tragic logic before it could take hold. He would never have let Tybalt kill Mercutio. *One roundhouse kick to the head and Tybalt is unconscious.*

But what if he failed? Would he, Nando, kill someone who killed Mickey, if he saw it happen right in front of him? Nando knew that he would. In such a moment, he would, he felt certain. Mickey was somehow even closer than his own blood. But then, would he, Nando, kill himself, if his girlfriend died? Would he kill himself for Mariel? Probably not. Definitely not. He would be sad, but not sad enough to kill himself. Did that mean he did not love Mariel? Maybe not. Did real love mean wanting to kill yourself? He thought of that soppy *Love Story* movie and its tagline: "Love means never having to say you're sorry." The tagline for *Romeo and Juliet* should be "Love means death."

He did not feel impulsive like Romeo, who would not sit and think about it at all. He would just do it—just do what popped into his mind. Romeo seemed more like Mickey. Romeo was an ass. Mickey and Terri should be Romeo and Juliet, he thought, not him and Helen.

What did the play mean? *Yeah, it sounded good what I said at rehearsal about love seeing the truth and all. But what did it mean?* And those lines from the Bible that Finnegan had quoted, about faith, hope and love, and being a man, and putting away childish things. *What did it all mean?*

He thought of the play's message: Hate leads to bad things. Big insight, he scoffed. And you should not judge people by their names. Maybe the whole thing was overrated. Still, he saw something in those scenes with Juliet. They seemed to capture the power of the attraction between people and how it could make you do things you never would otherwise, and how it could surprise you and change you. He thought about Mickey and Terri. She had changed Mickey, or started to change him, anyway. And the scenes with Mercutio, like in the Queen Mab speech, where he gets himself all worked up in a big fantasy and then Romeo says to him, "Shut up man, you're talking about nothing." He and Mickey had shared dozens of such moments. It seemed that Shakespeare wanted to show how people's dreams could take them off a cliff. And about fate too. About how a little detail can change everything. You make a little mistake, a message gets somewhere too late, and everything gets fucked to hell.

Tossing on his pillow, he hoped that he would not dream again about PS 13. Dread. That same moment replayed in his head, that moment of dread, right before the razor cut Mariel's beautiful, innocent face. How long had it taken to scar her for life? One second, not more. What if he had come down from the roof before, instead of after? What if he had mustered just a little more courage to come sooner? What had been the cost of his cowardly hesitation? What had been gained? His life? He hated his moment of hesitation, and his dream—as if his dream knew about his weakness in that moment—returned him there to relive it. How would the world be different now if that single second could be erased? Would he and Mariel even be together now? In his stomach he felt something had gone terribly wrong in that moment, something still playing itself out.

He felt the sick feeling again, thinking about Mariel and Saturday night. One mistake—just one—and everything could be gone. He could end up missing his whole life, sitting in a cold tomb somewhere on Staten Island. *That was tragedy, to show you how flimsy existence was, how fragile like the patch of skin stretched over your heart. Like a flower you put on your windowsill, and the next day it's covered in soot from the foul New York City air. You're walking home minding your own business and some asshole blows up a pile of dog shit all over you.*

His mind came at last to focus on Helen. It seemed that he had been saving all day to think about her. Why? She did not much care for him. Or did she? Maybe she did like him but did not want to admit it even to herself, as though he were a magazine

71

she kept at the bottom of a stack, and she only read it alone in her room because she felt embarrassed to be seen reading that particular one.

He lingered on her, imagining her oval face. Her hair. Her body. He imagined her frowning at him as they walked on the street outside Xavier. He remembered the way she had looked at him when she grabbed Terri and dragged her away: her terse goodbye and fierce scowl that whispered, *Leave me alone.* It pleased him to think about her scowl. *How strange to be pleased by that.* He drifted off into an uneasy and fitful sleep.

Helen had resolved to be free of her script within two weeks. She felt irritated at having to read her part while Ferdinand could sit there staring at her. She thought she was every bit as smart and good an actor. Once she knew the play better, she would be able to answer Finnegan's questions, just like he did, with deep, philosophical answers worthy of Finnegan's praise.

They skipped rehearsing on Fridays for the first month. So Thursday night of the first rehearsal week, Helen pressed Terri into service as her coach. Helen had determined that they would work together on Thursday, Friday and Saturday, with the goal of getting her off the script for at least some of her scenes by the following week.

Terri would play all the other roles so Helen could just focus on her own lines. Terri as Romeo, Terri as the Nurse, Terri as the Friar, Terri as Lady Capulet. It was a workout of Terri's fledgling thespian abilities, but she did not mind, because the more excited Helen became about the play, the easier it would be on her and Mickey.

They commandeered their little bedroom for rehearsals, forcing everyone else out into the kitchen and living room—Colleen, Stevie, James and Mrs. Rafter, who took this earnest investment in reading Shakespeare as a sign that she had made the right decision in twisting Mr. Rafter's arm to allow their participation in the play, despite the bizarre presence of the juvenile delinquents who had beaten up Charlie and James and compromised Terri in some way best not to think about.

Uncle Sean had held a private conversation with Terri, and having convinced himself that her chastity was uncompromised, he decided to leave the lurid details of the evening to James. He in turn had decided to withhold those selfsame details until some future date, like a box of gourmet candies from Europe to be presented on a special occasion. Since he had incurred a broken rib defending his sister's honor, the family respected his silence for the time being. Helen had lied and said that she did not see exactly what happened. Terri had pleaded alcohol-induced amnesia regarding the entire incident except for the preservation of her chastity, of which she pled the certainty of Saint Thomas. In Mrs. Rafter's view, the sorry state of Terri's dress showed that a terrific crime had been committed, but all the sordid details were better left obscure. To be locked in a diminutive bedroom with your angry and bitter older sister rehearsing Shakespeare for hours seemed to Mrs. Rafter like a penance almost equivalent to saying the rosary for an equal amount of time. Perhaps worse.

Mrs. Rafter had also taken it upon herself to write a note to Mr. Finnegan, inquiring about the rehearsals and whether her daughters would be adequately supervised.

In response to her note, she received the following handwritten reply:

> *Dear Mrs. Margaret Rafter:*
>
> *I am very pleased that you and your husband have decided to permit your daughters, Helen and Teresa, to participate this year in Xavier's production of William Shakespeare's classic, Romeo and Juliet. I was very impressed with Helen's reading of Juliet. I feel that the rehearsing and presenting of the play will be one of her most enriching high school experiences.*
>
> *Not only will she have the opportunity to immerse herself in one of the greatest works of literature in the Western canon, she will also gain the confidence that comes from shining in the dramatic and artistic spotlight. Success is not just about good grades, it also springs forth, like Athena from the head of Zeus, from artistic cultivation and the development of interpersonal skills and confidence. Teresa will have the chance to observe her sister as a role model, and may well be inspired in the future to pursue leading roles in dramatics as an extracurricular activity.*
>
> *Of course, we are very proud that you have also entrusted your son James to us at Xavier. I know James well. He is a serious student and a real credit to the Rafter household. Let me assure you that Xavier, the finest Jesuit Military Academy in New York City, has the highest standards of professionalism and competence in the administration of after-school activities for youth. At no time will your children be unsupervised. I can say with confidence that their participation in Xavier Dramatics will provide a safe as well as culturally and educationally enriching environment for them to spend their afternoons.*
>
> *With highest regards,*

Ian Finnegan

Mrs. Rafter had been extremely impressed. And thus, the closeted evening rehearsals in the Rafter apartment were understood to be an important extension of the cultural enrichment activities for Teresa and Helen orchestrated under Mr. Finnegan's excellent and gracious leadership.

Inside the room, a strange thing began to happen, even during that first night. Helen Rafter began having fun. Sometime during the first hour of reading with Terri, it dawned on her. Helen entertained the notion that Juliet could be someone that she, herself, was not. In this way, the character became a permission slip to explore feelings, attitudes and beliefs that she, Helen, had forbidden to herself.

She was forbidden to be attracted to Ferdinand. But Juliet was allowed—nay, encouraged—to be. Helen was *forbidden* to be madly, instantaneously in love. Juliet was allowed. Helen was *forbidden* to crave the sexual expression of her passion. Juliet was allowed. Helen was *forbidden* to be impulsive. Juliet was impossibly, romantically impulsive. It was as if the volcano inside her had discovered a weakness in its outer crust, a way to release its pent-up pressure and heat—and look out, an eruption was impending.

Helen was looking at Act I, Scene 3, her first scene.

"This will be easy," she said. "I barely have any lines at all."

"That's true," replied Terri, "but it won't be easy."

Helen frowned.

"The audience will be looking at you. They'll be watching how you react to what the Nurse and Lady Capulet are saying."

"How I react?"

"Of course, you're not acting only when *you* talk. It's like Mr. Finnegan said, you're responding to what's happening in the scene."

"What is happening?"

"Read the scene, Helen."

"You tell me." Helen became impatient. "You're the one who got me into this."

"I'll tell you," said Terri. "Imagine if Mom came in here and said, 'Helen, we're having a party and I've invited the boy you're going to marry,' and you were my age?"

"Is that what's happening?"

"Read it, Helen, *read it!*" insisted Terri. Helen had been just reading her lines without any sense of how they related to what the Nurse and Lady Capulet were saying to her. *How lazy.*

"Well, how should I react?"

"How do I know? I'm not playing Juliet, you are."

They were silent for several minutes while Helen read the scene to herself. Then she looked up.

"But I'm not sure," she said. "It's not clear."

"It's not?"

"No, look here, her mother says, 'Speak briefly, can you like of Paris' love?' and then Juliet says, 'But no more deep will I endart mine eye, then your consent gives strength to make it fly.' It's not clear whether she likes Paris or not."

Terri paused for a moment. "But Lady Capulet is raving about Paris. It's clear that she wants Juliet to love him."

Another long pause.

Then Terri said, "Helen, it makes perfect sense."

"It does?"

"Yes, I mean, if Mom said, I've got someone I want you to marry, and I didn't know him at all, I'd want to hedge my bets. I mean, if she said, do you love him? I'd say, 'Are you kidding, I don't even know him.'"

"But Juliet doesn't say that."

"Well, she did, she just said it politely. In those days you couldn't just tell your mother to piss off."

"Oh," said Helen.

"So maybe you should think 'piss off' inside your head when you say that."

Helen paused. "So you mean I should think one thing in my head and say something else?"

Terri nodded.

"But how does the audience know what I'm thinking?"

"By the look on your face! Jesus, Mary and Joseph, Hel, use your brain."

Helen blushed.

"Look," said Terri, "you're the queen of this. You could let someone know what you're thinking a mile away if you wanted to. You do it to me all the time. You have looks that might as well be flames from a flame-thrower."

"Oh," said Helen pensively.

"It's called *acting*?" pushed Terri, burying her face in hand.

They read the scene again and again. Helen practiced reacting to Terri, who watched her and started to worry, because Helen's facial expressions were getting more extreme with each reading.

"Helen, you've got to tone it down. It's like we're playing charades and I'm cueing you. You can't do it like that. It looks comical, Helen."

"This is all your fault," said Helen. "I can't act at all."

Terri felt a sense of panic coming over her sister.

"You *can so*, Hel. Look, it's like Mr. Finnegan said. Remember: Don't act, just understand what's happening in the scene."

"But how will the audience know what I'm feeling?"

"Helen, you can't hide your feelings. If you had a pain in your little toe it would read on your face like a billboard in Times Square."

"*No....*" Helen was horrified at the thought that her internal emotional life was so transparent to the entire world.

Terri nodded emphatically. "Just feel it inside and don't worry about your face."

They tried again and this time it was far better.

"That's good, Hel," said Terri. "So tell me, what does Juliet feel?"

Helen paused.

"I think... I think she's never been with a boy. I think it's all new to her and she's very worried. She's uncertain. She's scared. But she also wants to seem grown up, and she feels a lot of pressure that way. And she's afraid she won't like Paris at all. But she's thinking, *What if I do like him?* So she wants to be careful to leave herself an escape hatch?"

"I think you've got it," announced Terri.

A smile dawned on Helen's face that rose from deep inside; she was thrilled and relieved with her progress. She sat on the bed next to Terri and hugged her.

"Thank you."

"Don't thank me. It's fun," said Terri.

They sat quietly for a while. Helen was looking ahead to Juliet's next scene.

"Hel?" said Terri, almost in a whisper. "Can you tell me, what's it like to, to be with, to be with a boy? I mean, you know. Do you know?"

Helen looked at her sympathetically if cautiously.

"Why do you want to know that?" asked Helen, with a big-sister inflection.

"Oh, oh, forget it," said Terri with an edge in her voice.

Helen put her arm around Terri's shoulders.

"Do you mean, what's it like to have sex?"

Terri looked up into her eyes and nodded.

"Well," said Helen, "I don't know for sure."

"You and Charlie?"

Helen shook her head.

"Oh."

Helen could see that Terri had not been able to get access to *The Joy of Sex* and so it was all a horrible mystery.

"I know a little. I mean, I know from reading and talking about it. Um, I know a little from Charlie. Well, nothing much really. Not much from talking, either. Mostly from reading."

"You didn't talk to Mom about it?"

"Oh yeah, I did, and then Father McLaughlin did a slide show for me."

They both burst out laughing. It did seem ridiculous to think they could talk about sex with Mother Rafter.

"What do you know from reading, then?" asked Terri.

"You're not planning anything with him are you?"

"Of course not," said Terri, as if Helen had asked her if she was plotting to burn their apartment building to the ground.

"Well, it's mostly a question of what you let them do to you. I'm sure you figured that out already."

Terri sat quietly. She wanted to go beyond the obvious.

"Well," Helen continued, "you know they want to squeeze you and touch you everywhere, first on top and then in your panties."

Terri's eyes were wide.

"And of course you have to slow that, slow that down as much as you can."

"You do? Is it hard? I mean, is it hard to slow them down?"

"Yes."

"Why?"

"Well for one thing, you feel sorry for them. Especially if you love them. They have a look in their eyes. It says, 'If you don't let me touch you, I think I'm going to die right now.'"

Helen paused, reflecting on her altogether limited sexual experience.

"And another problem is, the more you let them touch you, the more excited they get. They get all red-faced and bothered, like they're going to explode or have a stroke."

"Yep," Terri nodded. She had seen this in Mickey.

"But if you love them—this is the hard part—then you get feelings, too. You *want* them to touch you. It, it, um, it feels good. You know about that, don't you? So you have to fight your own feelings as well as theirs."

Terri nodded again, very knowingly, looking into Helen's eyes with a gaze that said, *Now you are getting somewhere.* She knew that Helen wanted to say something more.

Helen searched for words.

"And they also want *you* to touch *them*. They want you to touch them *there*. They want to, to … they want to just, um, have you, completely have you, wherever you might be at that moment. On the stairs, in a bus, it doesn't matter to them. It's like they have a fever that's driven them mad."

"Oh my God," said Terri, "and so I guess you have to let them?"

"Let them? Jesus, Mary, Mother of God, no, no, no you don't let them!"

"No, of course not," admitted Terri, as if she had missed an elementary math problem.

Now they had disrobed the thorny problem, at least in Terri's mind.

"But if you don't let them, then what do they do? How do you help calm down their, um, their fever?" asked Terri.

"Well," replied Helen, who had now exceeded her personal knowledge and was mentally turning the pages of the Playboy and Penthouse magazines she had seen at Professor Howard's apartment. "They, they, um, can rub themselves on you. They want to do that. It's sort of the way a dog behaves."

Terri looked at Helen incredulously and they both erupted into fits of laughter.

"And you can help them by letting them do it, and patting them on the head," said Helen.

More laughter.

Helen thought that maybe she would leave it there. They sat for a moment but Terri wanted more.

"Is that all?" she asked, with a tone of disappointment.

"Well." Helen gave Terri a look that said *You're an evil girl,* and then said, "You can really touch them back, of course, with your hand, or your knee, or, or with your mouth."

Her face was red; she put her hand over her eyes and squelched a laugh. In her own mind she could not believe what she had said.

"With your mouth?" asked Terri incredulously.

"If you do that, you might as well let them fuck you in the church sanctuary," Helen whispered, "because you're going straight to hell anyway."

They shared a long silence.

"But some people do it," Helen finished, imagining that particular page from *The Joy of Sex*, which had made a substantial impression on her consciousness.

"Imagine," said Terri with great wonder. "Why would you go straight to hell?"

Helen gave her a look that drilled into her soul.

"Let's see. Because you've given in completely to the lusts of the flesh outside of wedlock and behaved like a monkey?"

CHAPTER 7

Into Manhattan

September 30th. "Come on, Nando...."

"Mariel, let's go catch a movie instead. There's a good one I want to see, *Days of Heaven*. It's playing at the Heights Cinema."

"Come on, Mickey says it'll be fun. He's gonna pay me $100 just to stand there. But he wants you to come too."

"It's dangerous Mar."

"Mick says it's cool, at a place in the Village, Quimica on Queen Street. Latin music, it'll be fun, we can disco."

"Mar, it's bad, we could get hurt."

"Mick's got some business, big deal. Come on, please? I really wanna go."

Nando was silent on the other end of the phone.

"Nando?"

"Yeah."

"Are you gonna come?"

"What time?"

Twenty minutes later, on his way over to meet her, he felt stupid. *What's the matter with me? But what choice do I have? Stay up and watch Saturday Night Live alone in my closet?* Maybe it would be OK. Maybe it would be over quickly, and then they could go somewhere to drink a few beers and relax.

If it was no big deal, why had he felt compelled to strap on his bowie knife under his right jeans leg and tuck nunchucks under his belt in the small of his back under his jacket? *Just a precaution,* he lied to himself.

When Mariel opened the door, anger began to creep like a spider out of his gut and up the back of his throat. She was high already. Her eyes glistened red and shiny and she kept sniffing. Her enlarged pupils made her look like a cheap plastic doll. Normally cool and quiet, tonight she chattered in a disjointed stream.

"Nando, hi, alright, Nando, wait, be right back …. *Hey Dad! I'm going,* OK, where are we goin'? To the city, right?—*Dad we're goin' to the city, OK* —Let's go, OK? *Mickey's driving over! Dad, don't worry I'll call.* Let's go. Shit, wait, I forgot, be right back, OK— *Dad wait, Dad, do you have some money?*"

She carried on a conversation with Nando and her father simultaneously. Her father was somewhere upstairs at the back of their brownstone on Cranberry Street, so she yelled up to him while collecting her things, running up and down the staircase to her bedroom on the second floor. Her mother had died of cancer right after her 10th birthday, leaving her father alone with her older sister, brother and herself, the baby of the family. The kids all worked in their grocery store a block away on the corner of Hicks and Middaugh. In the afternoons, they would stay alongside their father and uncle making sandwiches and selling cold cuts, cheese, milk, OJ, cereal, crackers, candy bars and just about anything one could imagine. In the evenings, dad would drink Dewars and did not pay much attention to what Mariel did or where she went.

Finally stepping out onto the front stoop, she pecked Nando on the cheek and grabbed his hand. They started to walk down Hicks Street to the Shea house on Montague. She wore fringed bell-bottom jeans, a tight purple T-shirt, and a light blue cotton jacket embroidered with peace signs. She kept looking over her shoulder and wiping her nose with the back of her hand.

"Stop staring at me," she said.

"I'm just looking at you," said Nando.

"You're not looking, you're staring."

"You're, you… you look… . Did you do something already?"

"Just a little Saturday-night blow to pick up my head, just a couple lines. You want some?"

"Where did you get it?" Nando already knew the answer.

"Mick gave it to me this morning."

That fucking Mick.

"They had a little party at their house Friday night Eugene had some, and I crashed there and he gave me a little this morning their mom and dad are away in Paris again I think and we were listening to Mickey's Yes albums and then they started doing lines off a big mirror they took from the wall it was radical and they brought the speakers down to the living room and turned off all the lights and Eugene had a strobe light and they started throwing the Frisbee around and one of the windows got broken."

Mariel sniffed and rubbed her eyes.

"And then Jennifer came late and she and Eugene were in up in the waterbed and somebody was smoking a cigarette and put it out on the waterbed mattress, which split and the water was dripping through the ceiling and they had to patch it with bicycle patch and Mick said his mom is gonna be pissed but they're not gettin' back for another week so there's plenty of time to fix it but Mick said he can just buy a whole new bed if he needs to 'cause they know someone who sells waterbeds from a head shop in the Village and he's gonna invite him to come over on Monday but he might not be able to 'cause he's, he's got to go visit his aunt, he knows Mick's aunt and she lives somewhere else in Manhattan they have a big pad somewhere in midtown...."

She gasped for breath.

"And it's suppose' to be amazing like it's like a mansion near the park and they're gonna have a big party there and Mick's invited and he said we should go too 'cause it'll be wild and they'll have some weed they got from Maui, where's Maui? Near Jamaica? 'Cause the Jamaican shit was really good...."

As Mariel rattled on like a subway train in her coke-induced stream of consciousness, Nando decided that he would not take anything—not even drink a beer—until they had done whatever business Mickey had planned, because if he had been snorting, the night could turn out even more fucked up than he feared.

When they got to Montague Terrace, Mickey was already in the cockpit of his dad's Lincoln with Led Zeppelin blasting so loud from the car stereo that Nando could feel the vibrations in his chest.

"Get in," Mickey yelled over the tunes, motioning for Nando to get in up front and Mariel in the back.

Nando climbed in and over to the back seat. On the red-carpet floor, a black duffel bag lay next to two six-packs of Molson Golden Ale. Mariel had already opened one and taken a swig. "Dry mouth," she said, gurgling through a beer gulp.

Nando surveyed Mickey. He looked very focused, but this did not mean that he was sober. Mickey liked to get high, then do something that required a lot of focus, like climbing a tree or riding a moped or shooting something. When completely shitfaced, he loved to shoot squirrels out of trees with his wrist-rocket. He did it well, knocking them out of the highest branches.

Mickey's eyes were bloodshot and he said nothing, listening to the tunes, locked in his own head. He held out his hand to Nando in a gimme-five gesture, which Nando slapped in return.

Mickey leaned over and under his breath whispered in Nando's ear, "What have you got?"

"My bowie and nunchaku," replied Nando into Mickey's ear, under the pounding music. "You?"

"Knuckles, buck and the .38," said Mick. 'Buck' meant the buck knife, his giant folding pocketknife with an enormous blade, sharp as a diamond laser. He was all business, no grin.

Nando nodded. *What a fucking nightmare. God, please let me get through this again.*

As they cruised over the buzzing metallic lanes of the Brooklyn Bridge into lower Manhattan, Nando tried to calm himself. *These people don't know how little protection we have. For all they know, we could be part of some enormous organized Brooklyn operation. We can bluff our way through this.* Mickey could bluff the devil himself. Maybe everyone who did this just bluffed their way through.

A voice in the back of his head asked, *Why wouldn't they just steal these drugs and try to kill us, like last time?* He thought about it. *They're businesspeople, that's why. They don't want to do just one deal, they wanted to keep doing deals. If Mickey can provide good stuff, they'll want to keep working with us. You can't work with someone if you kill him. For all they know, if they kill us, our people might come back and kill them.* They didn't know that "our people" did not exist except for a drunken lobsterman in Maine and Mickey's brothers, and Nando with his nunchucks tucked in his butt crack. All *we have to do was pretend.*

He looked at Mickey, who wore blue jeans, a black leather jacket and white turtleneck. He did not look much like a big-time drug dealer with his square Irish face framed by curly vanilla hair. Nando looked over his shoulder at Mariel, grooving to Led Zeppelin and doing another line off her pocket mirror. Where was the Mariel he thought he knew? What had become of the sweet, sunny Mariel who liked to walk with him to Baskin-Robbins for an ice-cream cone, the Mariel who told him that she loved him while resting her head on his lap in the afternoon as they listened to a James Taylor album? Instead of those Mariels, he saw a vacant, babbling girl whose thoughts seemed to rattle around in her head like an empty soda can rolling down the street in a winter wind.

"Stop staring!" she yelled at him from the back of the car.

All that and paranoid, too.

In the snaking lanes into Lower Manhattan, Nando had lost track of where they were. They finally arrived in a deserted business area filled with old warehouses, some abandoned. They rolled to a stop on a corner, about half a block away from the club, which sat in a large middle-of-the- block warehouse. A small crowd dressed in disco clothes moved back and forth between the entrance and a cluster of cars parked in front. When Mickey turned off the engine and killed the car stereo, they could hear and feel the music pounding from the open loading dock that served as the club's portal.

Mickey turned to him. "Listen man, you stay here with the bag, OK? I'm gonna check out the scene. If it looks good, I'll send Mar to get you."

"No, if it looks good, you come get me," said Nando. *What am I, fucking stupid? I'm going to carry the drugs into the club alone?*

Mickey paused.

"Mick," said Nando, "if you send Mariel out, I'll take the fucking bag out and hoof it back to the Heights."

Mickey gave him a hard look.

"Listen dickhead," Nando whispered in his ear. "If they have a fuckin' gun to your head inside, Mariel will be so freaked out she'll say anything to me. Look at her, man, she's whacked. I need to see your ass out here so I know everything's OK."

This logic penetrated Mickey's buzzed but nevertheless intensely focused psyche.

"OK," he said. "I'll come out." He tossed the Lincoln's keys on Nando's lap.

"If I'm not back in half hour, go get Eugene."

A lot of fucking good that'll do. Nando imagined the older Shea brothers trying to extract Mickey from the club with baseball bats and M-80s. *What a fucking joke.*

Nando sat on the Lincoln's warm hood and waited for what seemed like an hour but was only 15 minutes.

Mickey jogged up to him, opened the back door and grabbed the duffel bag. "It's cool," he said.

Nando followed. They passed through the loading area, moving toward two muscle-bound bouncers decked out in polyester leisure suits and platform shoes. They looked like Conan the Barbarian comic-book characters dressed in Saturday Night Fever outfits.

Mickey nodded at the bouncers, who let them pass through. Inside, in the darkness, Donna Summer's orgasmic "I Love to Love You Baby" blared from a massive sound system. The large dance floor, dimly lit overhead by a gigantic disco mirror ball, was still pretty empty. *It's early*, thought Nando, *I bet they want to sell some of this shit tonight.* At the far end of the cavernous room patrons clamored at a bar and behind it he could see a hallway. Skirting the dance floor, Mickey entered the hallway with Nando close behind; they went up a narrow staircase to an interior suite of offices.

Mickey opened one of the doors to reveal a large round coffee table with a glass top surrounded by a larger oval sofa covered with crushed red velvet. The room felt tight, poorly lit with lava lamps and a dim bulb underneath the table, keeping everyone in shadows. Nando surveyed the setting. Mariel, wide-eyed and spaced, sat on the sofa in front of lines of coke and a vodka tonic. On the table, a briefcase lay open containing bundles of $20 bills, stacked as if they had been counted. Seated an arm's length from Mariel on either side of her were two black men wearing silky disco shirts with paisley prints seeming to glow in the dim light. A third man—Italian, Nando guessed—stood in the back corner of the room toward a narrow shoulder-high strip of window looking out onto the dance floor below. Built like a fullback, he looked stocky and muscular, mid-30s with a full beard, smoking a cigarette, wearing jeans and a polo shirt.

Mickey closed the door and put his duffel bag on the table. The thick man sat across from him. Mickey removed two large and full plastic bags, one clear the other opaque, and put them on the table.

"The clear bag is the blow," he said. "The other one is H. We've got 10 bags of each, like I said. If you like the price and quality, I can get more."

Mick has balls, thought Nando. *I bet they'll like the price. A promise to deliver more could get us out of here in one piece.*

"We gotta check it," said the Italian guy.

"No problemo," replied Mickey.

He reached for the bag, but Mickey grabbed it first. "I'll come, where are the scales?"

"OK," said the Italian guy. "Walt," he said to one of the black men, "take him to the kitchen and weigh this shit."

"Stay here, I'll be back in a minute," said Mickey to Nando.

Then he turned to the Italian guy. "Sammy, this is Nando, he's cool."

Sammy stood up and held out his hand; Nando shook it.

Nando could feel Sammy measuring his potential for menace as Mickey left the room. Nando worked to calm himself. He had to project confidence without signaling an overt threat.

After the door had closed, Sammy said, "Where you from, Nando?"

"The Island," Nando lied. He had planned to imply that they were associated with a mob family on Staten Island. Several of the major Italian crime families had their sons enrolled in Xavier and Nando knew some of the names. He had to keep it vague because he did not know exactly who Sammy was or what Mickey had said. He felt sure that Mickey had not revealed much about them.

"Really?" said Sammy.

"Yeah, we live in Brooklyn but our people are from the Island." *Our people! Fuck! How ridiculous.*

Sammy nodded. "You want a drink?"

"Nah," said Nando.

They sat uncomfortably for moment.

"Relax Nando, have somethin'," said Mariel.

"Nah, I'm cool."

He realized that refusing to drink showed his nerves. *But I'd rather be alert. Sometimes my nerves are my best friends.*

"So where did a coupl'a kids come across a buncha shit like this?" wondered Sammy aloud.

Nando knew that Sammy had decided to probe now, trying to figure them out.

"The shit blows where it likes. You can hear the sound of it but you have no idea where it comes from or where it goes," said Nando. *I will surely go to hell paraphrasing Jesus in the middle of a drug deal.*

Sammy smiled at the poetic response. It seemed to calm him. His face registered approval at an answer revealing nothing. "Ain't that the truth, kid? Ain't that the fuckin' truth."

Nando relaxed a little, looking around. His eyes were adjusting to the darkness. It did not look like Sammy had a weapon, at least not a gun. A wooden desk stood against one wall and Nando wondered if there could be weapons in there. The other black guy was not visibly armed. Of course, either of them could have had an ankle holster or a gun in the small of their back, like where Nando had his nunchucks.

Nando did not think so, though. Apparently they were put at ease by Mariel and the youthfulness of the delivery squad. *Mick had been right to bring Mariel. A chick did lighten things up.*

Sammy turned his attention to her. "How 'bout you, jailbait? You from the Island, too?"

"I'm with Nando," said Mariel a little nervously. "He's my boyfriend." Sammy walked behind her and started to massage her shoulders. His hands were big, with thick, short fingers.

"If you and Nando wanna party with us tonight at Quimica, please, yous be my guest."

Mariel smiled nervously.

"Thanks man, we'll talk with Mick when he gets back," Nando said.

He walked over and stared out the interior window at the dance floor below. The crowd had thickened, like a human stew simmering over a low flame.

He moved around and sat across from Mariel. Leaning over, he whispered in her ear, "Don't do any more blow, OK? Your nose is gonna bleed."

She laughed but narrowed her eyes in a way that said, *Mind your own business.*

A few more minutes of uncomfortable silence passed and then Mickey burst back into the room. The anticipation of finishing the deal had animated his face.

Walt, who entered behind him, said, "It's cool boss, it's like he said."

Sammy walked around the table, threw the cash into the briefcase and handed it to Mickey, who looked at Nando as if to say, *Let's go,* but before they could move to the door, Sammy put his hand on Mickey's arm.

"Listen," he said, "a favor. I got somebody I want you to meet. He's downstairs. Here's the deal. He's a distributor, already has his own territory. Not a retail operation like this. We're buying this shit to sell to our customers, you got me? I ain't a drug dealer, I'm in the club business. My problem is, if I don't have this shit, I don't have any business, 'cause the chuckleheads downstairs will go someplace else where they can get it."

Mickey nodded.

"This dude has a street business across the river but needs a bigger supply. He can't move enough of this shit and he's paying more than he wants. I ain't gonna lie, he's paying me a tip if I bring him good shit. But like I said, I ain't a drug dealer, so I ain't gettin' in the middle. I'll take a one-time fee for making the intro—from you, not him—but after that, yous are on your own. You move some shit with this dude, you up the price on the first load, I get 10 percent for the intro. You got me? Now I know this dude and he'll tell me if you sell him, so don't think you can go around me. He'll buy a big load the first time, 'cause he's gonna trust me that the shit is good and he's gonna like the price. I want 10 percent of the first deal and that's it. I'll even take that as a rebate on our next, if you want. After that, it's back to just you and me. What you do with him after? That's your business."

Mickey thought a moment. "What the fuck," he said. "No harm meeting the guy."

"One other thing," said Sammy. "He's a real motherfucker. Don't fuck with him, 'cause he'll cut your balls off and make your mother eat 'em, you got me?"

He turned to Walt. "Get Dingo."

Walt disappeared through the door, and the three of them sat down again.

Sammy turned to the other man. "Sterling, get a round and bring 'em up. Mickey, what are you drinking? Nando, my man, what about you? And your little lady, Sterling, bring her another vodka tonic."

"I'm cool," said Nando. He had a bad feeling.

"I'll have a Heineken," said Mickey.

"Can I have a daiquiri?" asked Mariel.

"Get her a daiquiri. Strawberry?"

Mariel nodded as Sterling left to get the drinks.

They sat for about 10 minutes, with Mickey and Sammy making small talk, Mariel in a stupor, and Nando sitting quietly, the tension building up in his gut.

The door finally opened and Sterling entered, followed by a barmaid with a tray of drinks. Behind the barmaid came two others, one obviously a bodyguard, another black man dressed completely in black: leather boots, jeans, T-shirt, leather jacket cut like a blazer.

Nando felt sure that the guard had a gun under his jacket.

The man who walked in behind the guard wore a jumpsuit open to the waist with a leather dress coat draped over his shoulders. He looked Puerto Rican, with a large gold chain around his chest, a dark hat over greasy hair, and silver aviator glasses.

He tossed his coat on the sofa and sat down next to Mariel, across from Mickey and Sammy.

"Dingo, meet Mickey," said Sammy. "He just brought me some very nice shit, very good price, and I wanted to introduce yous to each other. And this over here is Nando and his girl Mariel."

Dingo looked out over the top of his glasses at Mickey and shot quick glances at Mariel and Nando, then he pushed his glasses back up to his brow and snorted.

"Sam, ma man," he asked in high whining voice. "Where do your friends come from? I never seen them before. They're babies."

"These babies brought me some good shit. I'm just making an intro, Dingo, business is up to you."

Mickey said nothing, taking in the scene.

"Let's do some, let's see what they bring you, Sammy," he said, continuing to talk to Sammy as if the others were not in the room.

Sammy nodded at Walt and produced a small yellow envelope, tapping some coke out on the table in front of them. *That was quick,* thought Nando. *They must have processed a bag in the kitchen so they could sell some right away.*

Dingo put his finger in the pile and then licked it. Then he dipped it again, put it up his right nostril and snorted.

"You can get me this, amiga?" he said to Mickey. Nando noted that Dingo had used the feminine in addressing Mickey, which had gone right over his head.

Mickey nodded.

"How much can you get?"

"As much as you want," said Mickey.

"What price?"

"The price ain't always the same," said Mickey. "Depends how much you want."

"Where you get it, amiga?"

Nando read Mickey's face. He knew that Mickey's instinct had kicked him, told him to end this conversation and get the fuck out of there. It was their old telepathy, developed over years of roaming the streets together. Nando felt a sense of panic rising. He took a deep breath and calmed himself, reached down and stealthily slid his hand under his right pants leg, unfastening his bowie knife so it lay loose in its sheath. He noted the position of the bodyguard, who stood nearby holding a small plate of cashews in his left hand, eating them with his right. *He carries the gun on his left side,* thought Nando.

"Tell me how much you want, I'll get back to you with a price," said Mickey.

Dingo turned to his left and looked again at Mariel, then across at Nando.

"This your bitch, huh? How much does she cost?"

The word 'bitch' registered in Nando's ear and set off a chain reaction in his head, breaking like a cluster of eight-ball billiards. He absorbed Dingo's face and body, posture and voice, the scar under his left eye, the faint tattoo of a five-pointed star on his neck half concealed by his collar. Within seconds he knew. A wave of liquid energy surged through his spine into his arms and legs, flooding the small of his back with a nearly overwhelming sensation of fear and power combined. This was the motherfucker from the schoolyard who had cut him and Mariel three years ago. He checked and double-checked his observation. His eyes darted from Mariel to Mickey and back to Mariel. They did not recognize Dingo; nor he likewise. Mariel was whacked on coke, and in the shadows, not staring him full in the face, it would have been difficult for her to identify Dingo. Mickey had not really even seen him that day as he cycled out of the schoolyard. Nando's formerly fleshy face had matured and changed between ages 14 and 17, and in the dim light Dingo did not recognize him.

Three scenarios flashed through Nando's mind in parallel. First, he could attack Dingo right now. This would draw in the bodyguard and probably Sammy, as well as his backup. A violent melee would ensue with no certain conclusion and Mariel caught in the middle. In the alternative, he could submit to the insult or attempt to deflect it in some way by joining in the put down, to say something like, "Yeah, this my bitch." Nando predicted, however, that this would to lead to a series of escalating challenges from Dingo, setting the stage for an argument. By challenging his opponent, Dingo could learn about his strengths and weaknesses before fighting. Dingo was throwing a jab at him, exploring his defenses, planning an attack, toying with him like a feral cat with his paw on a cornered field mouse. In the third scenario, he could just walk: get up, take Mariel and leave. This would force Dingo's hand, calling his bluff before he could properly assess what they had. Dingo would either have to let them go or stop them. A fight might break out, but on the other hand, Sammy probably would not assist in an attack launched by Dingo. Nando instantly decided to go with option three.

Ignoring Dingo's insult, he stood up, held out his right hand to Mariel and said, "We gotta split, come on Mariel."

The move took Dingo by surprise. He looked at Sammy, who also looked surprised but made no move to stop them. Nando glanced at Mickey, already on his feet. Seeing Mickey and Nando rise cued Mariel; she too stood up.

Dingo immediately said, "Excuse me, motherfuckas, sit the fuck down. You ain't leavin'." He looked straight into Nando's face.

Nando leapt in the air and whirled against the bodyguard, taking him completely by surprise and delivering a knife-hand strike into the man's right clavicle, which he felt to his satisfaction crack like a wooden stick under the force of the blow. The guard's right arm now hung like a broken tree branch. Nando followed with another strike directly into the bodyguard's testicles, which he drove up into his scrotum and hammered against the man's pelvis. Finally, he fired a stabbing, left-hand punch to the bodyguard's Adam's apple, sending him sprawling backward over the sofa, choking.

As Nando delivered his strike to the bodyguard's throat, he reached under his pants leg and grabbed the bowie knife's handle with his right. As the bodyguard reeled back over the sofa, Nando slipped the knife loose and threw himself straight into Dingo, who had stood up during the seconds required to eliminate the bodyguard. The dive knocked Dingo over the back of the sofa and onto the floor.

Behind the sofa, Nando maneuvered the bowie knife so the sharp edge of the blade dug in beneath Dingo's chin, against his neck. Then with his left hand, he grabbed the gold chain around Dingo's neck, hoisted him up on his feet, and thrust him back against the wall. Dingo's glasses had been knocked off and Nando glared straight into his face.

Dingo looked back at him through a killer's eyes, purposefully drained of feeling and life so as to convey a fearless menace. "Do it motherfucka."

Nando pictured his knife slitting Dingo's throat, blood pouring over the star tattoo. Then he felt metal against the back of his head. Sammy stood behind him.

"Kid, put that fuckin' knife down," warned Sammy. Nando could feel the gun barrel but he could not see it. He stood motionless, staring into Dingo's eyes, remembering the scar on his chin and the long one that ran down the right side of Mariel's face.

Sammy continued in a calm voice, "I don't wanna clean your brains off my carpet. I'm a fuckin' club manager, not a hit man. Now put down the knife."

Then Nando heard Mickey cock his .38.

A pause.

"God fuckin' dammit," said Sammy glancing at Mickey. "You little bastard."

Nando heard another click and, in his peripheral vision, saw Walt point a gun at Mickey.

Mickey broke in, keeping his gun trained on Sammy's head. "Listen… here's what we're gonna do. Nando's gonna check Mr. Mouth to see if he has a gun."

Keeping the edge of the bowie against Dingo's throat, Nando groped Dingo for pistol.

"Nothing."

"Good," said Mickey. "Now Nando's gonna walk Mariel out of here, and he's gonna take the cash with him."

Another pause. No one moved.

"Nando, get the cash and go," said Mickey with his gravelly voice, forcefully.

Mickey looked at Sammy, who nodded.

"No," said Nando, "we're leaving together."

Another pause.

"Just get the fuck outta here and don't come back," said Sammy, talking this time to Nando.

Nando felt a sinking, unnatural sensation. His gut told him to cut Dingo's throat, but his brain interfered, warning him that the results might be even worse than living with this menace. Nando finally gave in to his brain, lowering the knife slowly and backing up, not looking at Sammy, keeping his gaze focused on Dingo, who looked back at him with intentionally dead, lifeless eyes. Nando knew the look well, the look

91

of death that one street hoodlum gives another to indicate his comfort with killing. Dingo was an animal. He grabbed Mariel by the hand, picked up the briefcase and backed slowly toward the door.

The bodyguard groaned, rolling over on the floor.

Mickey started to back up, too, pointing his revolver in succession from Sammy, to Walt, to Dingo and back to Sammy, who had turned and pointed his gun at Mickey. Then Nando moved into the hallway with Mariel. Mickey followed, closing the office door behind him, and they half ran, half fell down the stairs to the dance floor below.

They stumbled through an emergency exit into a dark, empty alley running alongside the dance floor. Mickey still gripped his gun as they ran in the shadows toward the corner where they had left the car. As they approached the light from the main street, Nando squatted and stuffed his bowie knife back in its leg sheath. On the way to the Lincoln, they repeatedly looked back in panic.

Mickey made a U-turn to avoid driving by the club. Then he turned and stared at Nando.

"Oh my fucking Christ! What the fuck, man? Would you fuckin' calm down? What'd you do that for?"

"That was the guy from PS 13."

"What?"

"Yeah, the animal who cut Mar and gave me this," said Nando urgently, pointing to the scar on his chin.

"You're fuckin' whacked. That was him?" Mickey looked disturbed.

Nando turned and glanced at Mariel. "Mar, you didn't recognize him, did you?" She had a faraway look on her face, like someone waking from a nightmare.

"Oh my God," she murmured, "Oh my God…. Was that him?"

"I should have killed him," replied Nando, his voice soaking with pent-up violence.

They shared a long silence.

"It's a good thing you didn't," said Mickey, "or I'd be driving your dead ass back to Brooklyn in the trunk."

"Yeah, or we'd be dead together in a fucking pile," said Nando. "Are you ready to give this shit up yet? Are you ready? Jesus Christ, for what Mick? For what?" He glanced toward the back seat. Mariel stared out the window, touching the place on her right temple where the scar ran. Tears streamed down her face.

"You were right," she said to Nando softly. *Right about what*, he thought, *about Dingo? About how going along for the delivery was a bad idea?*

He clambered into the back seat and encircled her in his arms. Wiping her slick cheeks with the palm of his hand, he gently ran his finger down her scar. He was the only one she would let do this. Mickey watched them intently in the rearview mirror and smiled grimly.

For the first time since he had left to pick up Mariel, Nando dropped his guard and relaxed, just a little. She lay curled under his arm as he opened a Molson, draining a third of the bottle. Unscathed and alive, he promised himself that there would be no more of Mickey's drug deliveries. *If he wants to get himself killed or fucked with the law, it's all on him.*

As the Lincoln sped back over the East River, gliding through the narrow, luminous lanes of the Brooklyn Bridge, Mariel gently touched her scarred temple to Nando's chin. His memory circled the moment like a looped movie clip; he saw his blade, longing for blood, drawn across Dingo's star tattoo.

CHAPTER 8

Going to Church

October 8th. Terri Rafter started her Sunday by faking a stomachache, an ingenious strategy to earn four hours of relative solitude. She enjoyed her first two from 10 to noon while almost all the Rafters went to the mid-morning Mass at Queen of Angels on Skillman Avenue. She snoozed in her bunk bed for 45 minutes, and then lounged in the bathroom for a full hour, quietly in order not to wake her dad, who slept in after his night shift.

She spent the remaining 15 minutes preparing to look sick again when the family returned—sick, but clean-smelling.

At one o'clock she feigned a partial recovery, helping her mother with Stevie in spite of her phony illness. By 2:30 she staged a miraculously complete recovery, followed by some scrambled eggs and toast and a heart-to-heart talk with mother about, well, nothing.

At 4:30, on schedule, Mrs. Rafter suggested that since Terri felt better now, she should go to 5:30 Mass, even though she would have to go alone. Terri protested just enough to make her mother insist.

"But Mom, I'm not sure I feel well enough and I'll have to go alone."

"Young lady, if you're well enough to be up and about and eat eggs and chatter with your old mother, you're well enough to pay your respects to our Lord Jesus."

"OK, Mom."

And thus Terri earned her second two hours of solitude, a precious gift in a family of seven living in a two-bedroom apartment. She left early to meander through the streets of Sunnyside on her way there, and think.

Mickey had asked her to go to a party planned at his aunt's big fancy apartment in Manhattan, another party with no parents, just like the one after the Military Ball. Terri felt all twisted inside about it.

94

Spending time after school with Mickey made her happier than she had ever been. She would not tell anyone how much she felt for him, not even Helen. She had confided in her how she *might* love Mickey, but the truth was, she had fallen completely in love with him. She thought about him all day and at night before she went to sleep and—she giggled to herself—even on the way to church. It seemed to her like something just good and healthy and right.

But she also wanted to have Helen nearby, and felt relieved that she and Mickey could meet only at Xavier or maybe at McDonald's. Helen provided a little protection from what she had come to think of as Mickey's wildness. The problem was not only the way he was crazy and strong and wanted to have her; his wildness infected her like a virus and made her throw away all caution.

Mickey was an ocean; you could not dip your toe without getting your whole foot wet. And then you wanted to go in further, because it seemed like so much fun and felt so good. The next thing you knew, you were swimming and rolling in the waves. But how long before being carried out with the tide and soon drowning? Here was the problem… How to spend time with Mickey without going under?

Terri thought that she could solve the problem by getting Helen to the party as well, who could then offer a life vest in the Mickey Shea storm. He would be more careful seeing Helen there. Of course, Helen's presence did not merely provide protection, it was essential; Terri could not go anywhere without Helen to chaperone. Terri could try to convince her to cover and say they were together when they were not, but Terri did not want to tell lies and Helen absolutely would not.

Lying opened one of the infinite roads that led a girl straight to hell. Terri was perfectly willing, however, to avoid telling the whole truth about everything. In the Catholic moral code, a misleading silence was just fine. If people got the wrong impression when you left out some details, you did not have to straighten them out. The Ten Commandments did not say, "Thou shalt explain thyself fully." They simply said, *Don't tell lies*. In fact, the pertinent commandment was more specific: It said not to bear "false witness" against your neighbor. This meant do not say bad, untrue things about people close to you. Morality certainly did not require telling all your personal business in all its terrible detail. Jesus did not seem to have much to say about filling in the details. He asked questions and told ambiguous stories to make people think and then let them figure it all out for themselves.

All of this meant that it would be fine for Helen and Terri to leave out some details of the evening in question, as long as none of the separate facts they chose to provide proved false. They would have to present their selected details very carefully, so they could handle any questions by a thorough vetting of their entirely truthful responses. For Catholic children, talking to your parents was an art form that could lead to a successful career in the law.

Terri approached the question of sex with Mickey with equal subtlety. During Mass, she thought of it while going through the rituals of crossing herself, kneeling, standing and responding to the liturgy. Terri did not think one should look at things like this in a black-and-white, all-or-nothing way.

The extremes presented themselves clearly. Of course she could not just blatantly have sex with Mickey like husband and wife. That would be a mortal sin and the only thing worse would be to do it using birth control. A double mortal sin! On the other hand, in Terri's view, nothing in the Old or New Testaments forbade her and Mickey from holding hands or kissing, or even tongue kissing, although she did not feel a hundred percent sure about the tongue part. Anyway, the Bible said nothing crystal clear about that, so it could not be a mortal sin.

The gray zone involved Terri and Mickey touching and feeling one another. Saint Paul said a lot of nagging things that jumbled up lust and sin. And Jesus said that if you lusted, you committed adultery in your heart. And all of the priests and nuns whom Terri had ever known had done the same thing: put an equals sign between lust and evil. And her mother definitely thought lust was evil. With all of this in mind, she zeroed in on the problem. Touching and feeling definitely got straight to lust.

Terri thought about this for a long time before having a breakthrough. Mickey already had lust for her and so did she for him. So they had actually accomplished the sin of lust and could not do anything about it now. *I just have to keep on confessing it and saying my penance. Once you have a case of lust in your heart, you can't have more or less of it. Isn't that the very point Jesus made about lusting in your heart?*

To test this theory, she imagined confessing her lust to Father Quinn and asking him whether the total amount mattered or whether the mere presence of a lust smidgeon did her in. She felt sure that Father Quinn would have remembered the sermon he gave explaining carefully how when Jesus talked about a case of lust in your heart he had made a really important point: The mere fact of the lust, not the total degree of lustfulness, was all that really mattered. Otherwise, you could say, well, I'm only lusting a little, so it's nothing. *The whole point of what Jesus said was if you lusted even a little, you've already sinned as far as lust is concerned.* So in her own mind, by lusting after Mickey, Terri had already bonked him in her 14-year-old heart.

But this insight yielded a surprising consequence: A little touching and feeling on top of the desiring really did not matter that much. After all, you were already sinning.

Going a little deeper into the same level of sin did not make any difference because, as Jesus pointed out, you were already over your head in it. The important challenge, as Terri saw it, was clinging to the same level of sin that she had already fallen to, but not going even deeper to achieve a new level involving actual full-on sex as opposed to heart-and-mind sex.

Terri tried this out a few times in her mind just to test her theory. It seemed to work beautifully. It was just like being pregnant. *You can't be a little bit pregnant, that's what everyone says. You either are or you aren't.* And once you are, you just have to keep going. Going backwards by having an abortion just compounded your sin. You had to just carry on through and let the sin play its way out.

Same way with lust. I can't just unlust myself. The moral challenge was to avoid compounding lust with out-of-wedlock sex, like speeding without having a fatal car accident. Looked at this way, touching and feeling surely increased your risk, because they could lead to a greater sin, but they were not more sinful than only *thinking* about touching and feeling, even if transitioning from thought to action did increase your overall lust level. And maybe, just maybe, touching and feeling could eliminate lust completely for a short while.

For example, when Terri could not be with Mickey, she felt lust for him. But sometimes after tongue kissing him for a long time—more than a half hour—her tongue got very tired and she felt ready to *not* think about him for a while. It felt then that her lust had been relieved. And if you had no lust at all in your mind, then at least for a little while you had relieved your sinful state. Just as when you found yourself drowning, coming up for air could give you a little more life, and as long as you could breathe again, then by definition you were not drowning.

Terri wondered if it would be like this for Mick. *Well, it didn't matter anyway. Mick doesn't care a whit about his sinful state. Mick has boarded a missile pointed straight for hell.*

This thought disturbed her, but as she sat in her pew at the back of Queen of Angels, she had another revelation. She could bring Mickey to Jesus. *Wasn't this God's way, to convert the darkest, evilest lust into something blessed?*

She imagined herself and Mickey Shea sitting in the pew together. She sensed her power over him. She could make him follow her like a wild animal follows prey, and she could tame him before he devoured her. It would be very dangerous, like cuddling with a bloodthirsty wolf. *It would be like Beauty and the Beast.* But Jesus had more power than any wild animal, including Mickey. Jesus could tame his wildness through Terri. A little feeling and touching might be required, but it could all be part of God's plan, could it not?

She picked up her New Testament and read the words of St. Paul in Corinthians from before where Mr. Finnegan had quoted during rehearsal:

> If I speak in human and angelic tongues but do not have love, I am a resounding gong or a clashing cymbal. And if I have the gift of prophecy and comprehend all mysteries and all knowledge; if I have all faith so as to move mountains but do not have love, I am nothing. If I give away everything I own, and if I hand my body over so that I may boast but do not have love, I gain nothing. Love is patient, love is kind. It is not jealous, is not pompous, it is not inflated, it is not rude, it does not seek its own interests, it is not quick-tempered, it does not brood over injury, it does not rejoice over wrongdoing but rejoices with the truth. It bears all things, believes all things, hopes all things, endures all things. Love never fails.

She closed her eyes and savored these words, feeling sweetness and lightness in her heart that she knew was the Holy Spirit. She felt the power of her love for Mickey beating like her own heart, and she knew in her soul that no matter how sinful Mickey was, her love for him was good. It had an overwhelming healing goodness to it. She knew this as certainly as she knew her own flesh and blood and breath. She knew it as certainly as she herself would die one day. She felt the Holy Spirit whispering to her, right there in church, saying: *Don't worry, don't fret, everything will be fine.* It said her plan to go to the party—be with Mickey, even to touch him and let him touch her— was good.

CHAPTER 9

Paraphrasing

October 24th. Finnegan sat behind his desk in the large third-floor classroom at Xavier, looking at Helen and Nando. He had released the other cast members and decided to spend 45 minutes with his principals. He had also decided that it was time to read through the balcony scene. His Romeo and Juliet sat across from one another, each in classroom chairs—Nando in his blue blazer and tie, and Helen in her plaid Sacred Heart jumper.

They were making progress. Helen had almost learned her part and nearly felt ready to put down her script. Nando obviously understood all his lines and had been experimenting with his reading. Yet something seemed wrong to Finnegan. The chemistry had gone awry, and he could not put his finger on why. They had ceased to engage one another—almost as if they were each playing to imaginary counterparts. He knew the time had come to let them work alone. But before he released them, he wanted to try putting back the spark. There was no need to light a fire; he just wanted to make sure the pilot light was still on.

Almost to amuse himself, he conducted an exercise that he felt sure would stir them up.

"Very good… but," he said as they finished reading through the scene for the second time. "Very good… but."

He paused and paced around the room.

"Here's the 'but': I'd like you to think about, to really be sure, that you feel what these words mean. You understand them, but can you feel them inside? This is the most famous scene in the play. Many people have heard and read these lines before and they will know them. What they may never have heard is two people truly feeling these words when they speak them. To play the scene is to feel these lines in the moment when you say them."

Another reflective pause.

"I'd like you… you can keep your scripts with you… I'd like you to try paraphrasing your lines in this scene into your own words. Say them while looking at each other. Now, you needn't obsess about each word of the play; if you can simplify and summarize, go ahead. I'd like you to express to each other the feeling, the emotion between and beneath the lines. Take a moment, Nando. When you're ready, begin. If you have to pause and think in the middle, take your time."

Nando felt excited by the challenge. It required more than knowing the words; it called for a deep understanding of the scene. He, too, felt something had gone wrong and this might put it all back on track. He studied his opening speech for almost a minute, then began:

"He scorns heartache whose heart has never ached.

Shhhh, there's a light, and there's Juliet.

I wish she knew how much I love her.

I wonder what she's thinking?

She is so beautiful that, um, er, she makes everything around her look… ordinary.

I wish I could get closer to her, I'd give anything for it."

He stared into her eyes when he said this; she absorbed it, saying nothing.

Nando continued, "I wish more than anything she would just, um, just speak to me."

It was Helen's turn.

"Why do you have your name, Romeo? Give up your name, walk away from your life. Or if you can't, if you'll say you love me, then I'll walk away from my life, just, just to be with you."

Nando interjected, "Should I let her know I'm here, or should I listen quietly to what she's really thinking and feeling inside?"

Helen paused a moment, then continued. "You're not my enemy, it's only your history and your name, because of what it means about your family and the company you keep. But I see this isn't who you really are—your name and your family are not who you really are. You are just you, that's all, and what people are in themselves is all that matters, not the labels we put on them. Romeo, give away your labels and I'll give you my whole heart."

"All right, if you can love me, I'll be whatever you want, I don't care, I'll give up my name and be called whatever you want."

"I thought I was alone, who are you?"

"I don't know how to tell you who I am, I hate what I'm called, because… because it's your enemy. If I could tear it off me, if I could tear it up, I would."

"I know who you are, you are Romeo Montague."

"Not if you don't want me to be."

"How did you get here? It's dangerous and my family will kill you if they find you here."

"I love you and I am not afraid."

"They may kill you."

"If you love me, I am protected."

"I don't want you to be hurt."

"I am more afraid of not loving you than I am of death."

They paused and stared into one another's eyes. His reading had caught Helen off guard. He had said it with drama and intense finality, forcing her to pay attention to him. It seemed that Nando had actually said this to her, Helen, and not to the character, Juliet. She looked at him strangely, wondering, *Was this just good acting?*

She had made a pact with herself to love Romeo, and to forget about Nando, to pretend he did not exist. But Ferdinand stood before her. Romeo.

She continued, "How did you find me? How did you get in here?"

It seemed to Nando that they were no longer talking about the characters. They were now speaking in code to one another.

"My love for you has guided me," he replied.

"Do you really love me? I know you'll say yes, and I'll believe you, but if you swear your love, you might be lying. If you love me, um... say so, and if you think I'm too easy, I'll say I don't love you, so you'll... you'll... um, court me."

She paused before continuing, "I do love you Romeo, and I'm afraid you won't take me seriously, but I promise you I'll be more true to you than a girl who would pretend not to like you so you'd pay attention to her—I would have played hard to get, but you overheard my private thoughts, you overheard my heart, so please don't think I don't really love you because I've been so honest about it."

Nando thought this was an impressive rendering. He continued, "I swear I love you by the moon."

"Not by the moon, it changes all the time, I want your love to be more solid."

"What shall I swear by?"

"Don't swear, or if you're going to swear, swear by yourself, swear by the you who I love so dearly, and I'll believe you."

"I swear..."

"Don't swear, you're making me so, so happy, but I'm, I'm so worried, this is all, it all seems too fast, it's like a flash of lightning, and it's gone before you can see it."

She stared at him quietly for a moment.

"Good night my love," she continued. "Our love is, it's, um, our love is just beginning, it's going to grow like a flower, and it's going to blossom, and you'll see next time we meet, I, um, hope you'll sleep as sweetly as the sweetness deep in my heart... because of how you make me feel in my heart."

"I want something more from you, right now, I want... something more."

"What can you have from me tonight?"

"Promise me you love me, as I've promised you."

"I gave you my promise before you asked for it, but I wish I could go back now."

"Would you take back your promise? Why?"

"So I could tell you for the first time that I love you, all over again, but I can tell you again and again and it always seems like the first time. I have everything I want now, and the more love I give to you, the more I have, and my love for you has no end. It's like, it's like the ocean. Someone's calling, don't go yet, I'll come back."

"I'm afraid this is all a dream."

"Romeo, if you are serious about me, and you want to marry me, tell me tomorrow, I'll send someone to find you. You tell that person where we should meet to get married, and I'll, I'll give you my whole future— *Hold on, I'm coming*—But if you're just playing with me, then leave me to my, um, leave me to my despair, and um, sadness."

"I don't want to leave you, even for a moment."

"Oh, no, has Romeo gone? I'd give anything to bring him back."

"You are my own soul calling me back."

"Romeo?"

"Yes?"

"What time shall I call you?"

"At 9"

"It'll be 20 years till then."

They both paused for a good while, staring at one another.

Then Helen said, "I can't remember why I called you back."

"Let me stay here until you remember."

"And I'll forget so you'll just stay here. I want to be with you."

"And I'll stay so you can keep forgetting, and this will become my home."

"It's almost morning, you have to go, but I wish you were my bird, so you could go just a little away and I could pull you back whenever I wanted."

"I would want to be your bird."

"I'm afraid I would kill you with loving you. Leaving you with this feeling I have inside, it hurts, but it, it feels so good at the same time, that I, I, um, I just want to make this pain, and this sweetness, last forever."

"I wish you sweet and peaceful dreams, and I wish I could be your dreams, um, ahh, I wish I could be inside your dreams, so I could stay tangled up with you forever."

They all paused in silence for nearly a minute. Nando looked at Helen and she looked back at him, holding his gaze. Then something crucial happened. She smiled at him: not a passionate smile, but much simpler and less intense that seemed to form a foundation between them. The smile, open and warm for the first time, said, *I want to trust you.* It was the first time she had ever really smiled at him. Helen the real person, smiling at Nando the real person. He smiled back.

Finnegan watched them carefully through the clouds of cigarette smoke from the corner of his eye, and inside he smiled too.

"Well," he said, "very impressive. Beautiful. Really beautiful."

He paused. "I don't have to tell you that there's something special happening here, and…" He paused again.

"I think we'll just leave it there. Next week, I want you two to begin rehearsing on your own while I work on some of the other scenes. You can use my classroom on the second floor. Then I'll see what you've accomplished before you leave each day. You might want to use this exercise at home and also with each other as you work. Very good progress. Our master Shakespeare is smiling down on all of us from his spot in heaven."

Helen walked into the hallway in front of Nando. But instead of rushing off to find Terri, she waited for him. He was surprised but pleased, and walked alongside her down the stairway, trying to think of what to say.

"That was interesting," he said. "You did a really good job with it."

"You too," she replied self-consciously. "I feel like I learned something."

"So, are you looking for Terri again?"

"Yeah, unfortunately," she said, with another smile.

"Hey, did you hear about the party Mick is having in Manhattan?"

"No, in Manhattan? He didn't invite me… not surprised about that!"

"Well, he definitely invited Terri… I mean, he's hoping she'll come."

"She probably can't, 'cause she's really not supposed to see him."

"Yeah, well," said Nando, "could she come if you do?"

He had caught her off guard.

"I'm, I'm um, I'm not sure. I mean, I'm not sure I can come myself, and he didn't invite me, like I said."

They had reached the first floor as Nando slowed to a stop, to make her turn around.

He continued, "'Cause I was, um, I was really hoping you would come, 'cause I'm going… and I was thinking, maybe we could hang out. I was thinking maybe, if you wanted to, we could rehearse a little here at the school and then go… together."

"You mean as, as, you mean we could go as friends?"

He paused. This wasn't the clarification he wanted.

"Well sure," he said, "as, as friends… because, I'm sure Mick is going to ask Terri. I mean, I know he asked her already."

Helen looked a little tense. Nando sensed this and started walking toward the lobby with her.

"I might have to babysit my little brother Stevie," said Helen, pulling out her tried and true excuse to avoid any engagement about which she felt unsure.

"Sure, well, it's OK, I mean, I was just suggesting it, no big deal. I thought it might be, um, the place is supposed to be really cool."

"Will Mariel be there?"

Now Nando felt off balance.

"Mariel? Mariel? I'm, um, I don't think so," he faltered. "I don't know. I mean, I was thinking about us—you and me—going."

"Yeah. Like friends? OK," she said uncertainly. "I don't know yet. But thanks. And I hope I can. Bye now. OK? Thanks." She smiled at him again, but this time the smile looked fake and she seemed to hide behind it.

She left him standing in the Xavier lobby. He felt unsure of himself and frustrated. *What am I doing?' I have a girlfriend who loves me and I—I love her, right?* But he was nonetheless filled with doubt.

It didn't make sense for him to try to be with Helen, he puzzled. How weird would it be, to actually date her and then play opposite her in this famous love story? It would almost feel like incest. *What would happen next, would they have to kill themselves?* He laughed silently. *It doesn't make sense. Maybe I could date her after it's over. That could make sense.*

But he had to admit, at least to himself, that he had started to think of her more and more. He had not planned to ask her to go to Mickey's party. It had just blurted out. Mickey would be surprised. The way she had behaved in rehearsal, he expected her to say yes. *But was she just acting? Maybe she has only stopped hating me. That's great it's progress, it's really great that Juliet doesn't hate my guts....*

By the time Helen found Terri, Mickey had left, and Terri was sitting alone in the McDonald's in the block north of 14th Street on Sixth Avenue. She was daydreaming, nursing French fries and a vanilla milkshake, which tasted like plastic but comforting all the same.

"Hi Hel!" she said brightly.

Helen slipped into the chair beside her and started to nibble on her fries.

"Terri, are you planning to go somewhere with Mickey, like out somewhere on Saturday night?"

"Not planning. I want to, but I'm not planning to, not yet."

"And when were you gonna tell me about this?"

"When I figured out how to get you to come too."

"He hasn't even invited me."

"I told him not to mention it until I talked to you about it. It's not like you would actually talk to him...."

"So, Teresa, tell me, why would I want to go? I know why you want to, but why would I? Plus, do you expect me to lie to Mom and Dad about it? Hmm?" She smiled in a teasing way.

"Well, Romeo, Romeo, wherefore art thou Romeo?" Terri did a good imitation of Helen. "He'll be there."

"I know," said Helen. "He asked me to go with him today."

"*He did?*" asked Terri.

Helen nodded with a satisfied expression on her face.

"What did you say?" Terri's eyes lit up like street lamps. She had been hoping that Helen and Nando would have a real romance to underlie their stage one, but she had never breathed a word of this to Helen, because she had been so hostile to him.

"I don't know, Terri. I mean, yeah, he's handsome and all, but he's *so* serious. And I don't know I should date him while we're doing the play. I mean, wouldn't it be confusing to play being involved with someone you were *really* involved with? And then... what about Charlie?"

"What about Charlie? You haven't heard from him in weeks. Or is it months?"

"That doesn't mean anything. He's in his first year at West Point."

"He's too busy to send a postcard?"

Terri felt a little guilty about saying this because she and Charlie had been good friends. He had been sweet and friendly, like a big brother who would always look out for her.

Helen was silent. She thought about Charlie and remembered the last time they had been together. They had seen each other for one final date on a Friday night in June. He had been planning to leave the next day. They had gone out to dinner at Angelo's in Little Italy and she could tell how much he thought he wanted her, but she just felt so squashed inside. She had taken all of her feelings and put them in a smasher, like the kind they used to compress abandoned cars. She had squeezed her emotions into the tightest possible container and then put it at the bottom of a cold pit in her innermost soul.

How could you give your heart to somebody leaving you by choice? After all, Charlie had not been drafted to fight in World War II. He could have gone anywhere. He had been accepted at Columbia University! Why not go there? The whole military career he wanted had placed him beyond reach. He had left her, and made it quite clear there would be no commitment between them. She could date whomever she wanted and so could he. No guilt. No problems. No expectations. She had not shared their conversation with anyone, not even Terri. It left her with a brittle, bitter feeling inside, a feeling impervious to his niceness and overtures. Now everyone kept asking, just assuming they still had contact. How's Charlie? Helen, have you heard from Charlie? How does he like West Point? She wanted to scream at them.

She had tucked a card in Charlie's pocket that night in June as he left for the subway, and said, "Don't open it until you're on the train." It was a thank-you card, inside of which she wrote:

> *Dear Charlie:*
>
> *I'll always remember being your girlfriend and the fun we had, especially going with you to the Military Ball. I'm sorry that evening turned out the way it did. We had fun and I've been very proud to know you. Just remember, you had a Queens girl who really liked you. I'm sure you'll go very far, Charlie, and I wish you the very best of luck.*
>
> *Love,*
> *Helen*

She had cried and cried when she wrote this. Not because she was sure that she really loved him, but just because it seemed like there could have been so much more to their relationship. She had thought about writing on the bottom of the note another line to say, 'Write me' or 'I'll see you in the fall' or even 'I'll miss you,' but she did not want to promise herself there would be any future to their relationship. She wanted to assume there just would not be.

She paused and thought for a moment about Nando, and how he had not mentioned Charlie that afternoon. He could have asked 'How's Charlie?' when she had questioned him about Mariel, but he had not. This pleased her and she smiled again to think of it.

She broke her train of thought, returning to Terri sitting across from her at McDonald's. "Anyway, Nando's still with Mariel, so what's he doing asking me to go somewhere with him?"

"How do you know he's still with Mariel? Maybe he's not."

"I asked him if he was bringing Mariel to the party."

"Hel, are you daft? He asks you to go with him and you ask him if he's bringing Mariel?"

"It wasn't like that, 'cause I said, well, I wanted to make it clear he only meant as friends."

"Did he mention Mariel first?"

Silence from Helen.

"He didn't, did he?"

"No, he said… he said he didn't think she would be there and… he wanted to go with me."

"And that confirmed he's still with Mariel?" Terri gave her a withering stare imitating the look she received from Helen three times a day.

"Well he could have said, 'I'm not going out with Mariel anymore,' but he didn't, did he?"

"So he's supposed to break off with Mariel on the possible chance you'll think about having a date with him, maybe, someday?'

"Oh look, I don't want to talk about it. I don't think I even like him. I'm so sick of boys anyway."

"Now there's a good mood to be in when you're playing Juliet."

"It's all your stupid idea anyway."

Helen went to the counter to order a Coke and Terri sat mulling it all. It was like trying to thread a microscopic needle. You couldn't get the thread through the little needle eye. You knew it was possible, even though it seemed like a ridiculous task, because people threaded needles every day. Helen was the thread, and the eye of the needle was getting her to go to the party. And the hole had become impossibly small because her mother and father and James, and Helen herself, were defending it. This is why it seemed so impossible, like threading a needle with itself. There had to be a solution.

Nando asking Helen to the party had been a stroke of luck. Terri could tell that Helen felt really excited that he seemed to like her. But that did not mean Helen liked him back. *It always feels flattering when a boy likes you, even if you don't like him at all.*

Still, she sensed something more in Helen, like a smell that only she could detect in her sister. She knew that Helen felt a physical attraction to Nando. *You'd have to be a lump of concrete not to be physically attracted to Nando.* But something was happening in Helen's heart as well.

Strangely, Terri saw it in the way that Helen claimed not to like Nando, not the normal kind of dislike where you thought somebody was awful or gross in some way. Helen's dislike was an upside-down like; she took the things she really liked and told herself instead that she didn't like them.

She thought about Helen's comments the evening before:

"That Ferdinand is too smart for his own good. He knows all about Shakespeare, he knows the plot for a dozen of the plays. He was talking about it with Mr. Finnegan, comparing one to the other. How does he know so much? And do you know James said he's in AP calc, a year ahead of himself in math. How does he know so much?"

"I think James said his dad is a teacher. Teaches high school," said Terri.

"How did his father get to be a teacher? Don't all those people work in restaurants and construction sites?"

"Like the Irish are all cops and bartenders?"

Then in the morning on the way to school Helen had asked, "Do you think I look pretty enough standing next to him? Is it believable he'd fall for me?"

"What do you mean?" asked Terri.

"He's such a prettyboy. He's prettier than I am," she complained. "With his red lips and long eyelashes and high cheekbones, he makes me look like a nun." As she said this, Terri caught Helen picturing Nando's face and enjoying the thought of him, the way one would admire a movie star. What Helen felt inside did not fit with the tone in her words; what she said masked her real feelings, like a metal crate with a velvet lining inside. And now she was coming back to Terri complaining that Nando had asked her out, while secretly enjoying it.

The conversation continued along the same track all the way back to Sunnyside, with Terri wheedling Helen and searching for some clear path to the party. Upon their arrival at the apartment, Mrs. Rafter complicated matters further.

"Helen, I've had a call from Charlie Cunningham." She sounded somber.

Helen felt a sense of urgency flood her stomach. "What, Mom?"

"His father's had a heart attack."

Helen frowned and braced herself for bad news.

"He's stabilized, and Charlie has a special leave from West Point to come home for the weekend."

"Oh thank goodness," said Helen. "Thank goodness his dad is alive."

She had only met Charlie's father once. A tall, imposing man, he had served as an officer in the Korean War and now worked as a business executive for IBM. Charlie was his only child, and they were close.

"Well, Charlie said they don't know what will happen, but he's wondering if you would see him on Saturday. Maybe you could go to the hospital with him, Helen," suggested Mrs. Rafter. "It would be a very kind gesture." She seemed to understand that the relationship between Helen and Charlie was not quite what it had been.

Terri's mind raced. She felt evil and selfish but couldn't help it, because she saw the needle bending and threading itself. She only had to give it a little push.

"Where is he, Mom, what hospital?" inquired Terri in the most innocent voice she could muster.

"Mount Sinai."

Terri knew that Mount Sinai was on the Upper East Side, within walking distance to the party. A plan emerged in her mind. She would go with Helen and Charlie to the hospital on Saturday night to provide 'moral support,' but then would let them have some private time. 'I'll just go to the cafeteria to get some tea,' she would say. Then she would get lost for about three hours. 'I couldn't find the room, Helen.' It seemed like just the kind of stupid thing that might really happen to her. During this time, she would be with Mickey at his party.

Then she could go home and just explain how she had gotten completely lost in the hospital maze and finally abandoned all hope of finding them. As long as she returned to Sunnyside clean and sober, the plan would work perfectly. She had to really get lost in the hospital to make it convincing, but that would be a cinch. She would just walk around for 10 minutes in a muddle-headed fog.

Then she could leave out the part about going to Mickey's party and still not have to tell a lie. No one would ask her: 'Did you stay at the hospital all the time you were lost?' Because that question would be ridiculous. But even if—by some incredible happenstance of total mistrust—this question presented itself, she could answer sarcastically and still be technically truthful. She could say something sarcastic but true like, 'No, I left the hospital and went to a party!' It was brilliant. No one would ask about Mickey because they didn't even know that he had planned the party.

"I'll go with you, Helen, just to pay my respects."

"You don't have to pay your respects because Mr. Cunningham isn't dead yet," said Helen with a glare so hot that it seemed to Terri that she could feel it on her own nose.

"Helen!" chided Mrs. Rafter curtly. "What's gotten into you? Of course Terri can go. It's a nice idea. Terri can represent the family."

This suggestion made perfect sense to Mrs. Rafter because in Irish-Catholic culture, a grave illness, impending demise and death itself were generally understood to be a series of escalating social occasions, each providing a wonderful justification to the adults enabling the practice of drinking to excess and telling desperately sad or howlingly funny stories. Over a period of weeks—the longer the better—all of this would culminate in a three-day wake, after which it seemed a real blessing not to think about the dearly departed for a very long time.

As soon as they were alone in their bedroom, Helen cornered Terri.

"Do you think I'm stupid?"

"What?" asked Terri innocently.

"You're trying to use this tragedy as an excuse to get yourself a night with Mick. You're the most evil girl in the entire borough of Queens. You'll be French-kissing Mick while I'm holding Charlie's hand at the bedside of his dying father? That's just great. Lucky me."

"I would never do that," insisted Terri, trying desperately to erase from her brain the bizarre scheme that she had hatched only moments earlier.

Helen scowled at her.

"Hel?"

More scowling. Helen fumed because she suspected that Terri had cooked up some foolproof plan.

"Listen," said Terri. "Maybe Charlie would want to come to Mick's party. He's been stuck at West Point since July. He'll need a pick-me-up, especially with his dad being sick and all. You can't stay at the hospital all night." She paused to let the idea sink in.

Helen was silent, then dismissive.

"Right, he's going to go to a party while his father's dying of a heart attack."

"Hel, why do you think he called? You are so stupid sometimes. The day you were born, the Lord shorted you on common sense. Charlie wants to see *you*. He wants to spend time with *you*. He doesn't need you at his father's bedside. He needs you in his arms. The party will be a perfect place for you and Charlie to talk and be together. He wants some comfort, and not the hand-holding kind."

Helen felt terribly conflicted.

On the one hand, if she went to the party, she wanted to go with Nando more than Charlie. On the other, she felt worried that Terri was right; what if Charlie really wanted to see her?

But the circumstances could not be worse, could they? She did feel sorry for Charlie. But was that a reason to act like his girlfriend?

But would it not be cold and cruel beyond measure to refuse to see him when he needed her so?

Still, it would be painfully awkward to see him in a hospital with his sick dad. Terri was right about this too: They would not be able to do anything together at the hospital except maybe hold hands. And it would feel strange to be with Charlie's other family members. The most awful way to spend a Saturday night.

And why see Charlie at all when he planned to turn right around and go back to West Point? Might as well date someone in the seminary. Good-bye, see you again never! And if Charlie did go to the party, the whole relationship, or its lack, would be put on display for Nando, who would probably be there alone. He would either see them get along or watch them be cold to one another.

She did not want him to see either picture. She wanted to leave Nando right where he was, suspended in a state of confusion about how she felt.

And no matter what Helen did, Terri would find a way to turn it into a romantic adventure with that gorilla, Mickey Shea.

An unbelievable nightmare.

"I don't know what I'm going to do, Teresa Rafter, but I do know one thing," said Helen with finality. "I'm not going to let you conjure up another mad brawl."

But Terri could almost feel fortune's wheel spinning and rearranging the future in her favor. When the moment came to advance her cause, she would pounce.

CHAPTER 10

Before Mayhem, Mischief

October 26th. Mickey was sitting in his bedroom in Brooklyn with the door locked. He reached under his bed and pulled out the small package Dingo had delivered to him that night. The courier had been a 9-year-old black boy on a beat-up, chopper-style street bike. He opened the package, a shoebox emblazoned with a five-pointed star. It had been sealed with several rubber bands. Inside, he found a plastic bag full of white powder—heroin.

Nando would not have believed that Mickey had the balls to go back the same night that Nando had attacked Dingo. *I am a crazy motherfucker*, thought Mickey to himself. But he could sense a good deal when he saw one, and he would not leave this one behind. What better way to get even with Dingo than to do business with him? Mickey felt that the moment to get revenge would come eventually. Nando kept trying to plan out the whole future, whereas Mickey just thought about right now.

You couldn't plan out the future, he thought. *Just had to live it*. Right then, there in front of him, stood a man—Dingo—who could move enough shit that he might never have to work again. He could buy a fleet of lobster boats and sit on his ass drinking beer on a pier in Maine while his lobstermen did all the work. He had cooked up this plan with his lobsterman partner Ricky Porter. "You move this shit for me," said Ricky, "and I'll set you up in the lobster business." After all, the business gave them a perfect cover. Nobody knew how many lobsters they caught. *It was a perfect way to move shit. You collected it from Canadians out in the middle of the ocean on a clear day. Who could hide and snoop on you? You'd need a fuckin' submarine. Who knew those lobster guys toted so much shit? Nobody.*

They had all drawn on him that night in the club—Sammy, Walt and Dingo. *As soon as I opened the office door, three guns were pointing right at my fuckin' head,* he remembered. "Listen man, I'm here to do business," he had said. "You want shit and I can get shit and the rest of this is just bullshit." That had grabbed their attention.

When Dingo started whining about how he would kill the "little baby and his bitch," Mickey interrupted and said, "Listen man, you don't remember this, but you cut him and his girl three years ago in a schoolyard in Brooklyn. And me and my brother, we threw M-80s at you and beat your asses with baseball bats."

This earned the respect of Sammy, who, being Italian, understood how matters were settled on the streets of Brooklyn.

Then Dingo remembered how he had left Nando and Mariel bleeding at PS 13. Who could forget having M-80s thrown at them? He still looked pissed, but now he had a grudging respect for the retributive beating inflicted on himself and his bodyguard.

After the conversation that followed, Mickey more fully understood why the purity mattered as much as it did. The purer the shit, the more he could cut it. So people were willing to pay a lot more for purity because it would spread the shit further. Plus, he could put the dope out at multiple quality levels—cheap for the homeless addicts; good quality for the lawyers and businessmen. Purity gave flexibility.

Plus, purity reduced risk. The more pure you got the shit, the closer you were to the source, which meant less of a chance that people upstream would rat on your ass. He could control downstream because he could manage what buyers knew about him and whom he chose for clients. But he could not control upstream.

One other factor: Masses of pure dope reduced the number of big buys he had to make. The risk got bigger with every one. He risked getting screwed by anyone— his partners, clients or the fuzz. His stuff had been midlevel. To deal with Dingo, he would have to go for better purity. The shoebox in Mickey's lap held the sample that Dingo had sent to show him how pure he had to go. If he could source that level of purity from Ricky Porter, he would sell to Dingo and make a fortune.

Mickey thought about the weekend. Ricky was coming down from Boothbay, Maine. Perfect timing. His Aunt Sheila and Uncle Robert were in London for two weeks, and he and his brothers were taking care of their dogs, two gigantic if friendly German shepherds. They were watching their dogs and also their sprawling, six-bedroom apartment at 93rd Street and Fifth Avenue overlooking Central Park. An impressive place with a formal dining room, game room and multiple bedroom suites, the apartment had expansive views of trees and grass from the living room and master bedroom. In midtown, the majesty of the place and great view—a rarity in Manhattan—said one word to Mickey Shea: party.

It would be a real blowout because they had a massive sound system and his cousin Kate had the best record collection he had ever seen. The pad had a room that was just walls of albums. Kate had gone away to Harvard College and she would not need them. She liked Mickey—had he asked, she would have said 'just don't break anything.'

Mickey had decided to blow some bucks on the bash. Three objectives in mind.

First, impress the shit out of Ricky Porter. He worked as a fisherman, most of the time drunk, and did not know the ways of the big city nor anything about Mickey's family. The Central Park pad and the rest of New York … it would blow his sunburned mind.

Second, impress the shit out of all Mickey's and his brothers' friends. He wanted an open bar, kegs, coke room and some rooms set aside for couples. This party would make him famous and expand his burgeoning drug-dealing business. And, well, it was just good to be famous, just for the hell of it.

Third, he would nail Terri Rafter. As soon as this thought passed through his mind, he massaged it. He could admit to himself a soft spot for that little piece of ass. He did not really want to 'nail' her. Well, he wanted to, but he would not go any further than she wanted to go. Damn, he was pussy-whipped just like Nando had said. *How pathetic*, he thought, *buying her a dress and climbing up her fire escape, and spending every afternoon in rehearsal, reading Shakespeare, just so I could spend half an hour tongue-kissing her.* He had to laugh; tongue-kissing Terri seemed like the most important thing he had ever done.

He could not help himself, he loved her. What a thought! Michael Shea in love. He would never admit it to anyone. They would laugh and make fun of him. But he could not care less—he wanted to impress Terri Rafter. He wanted to take her to a special place, a place where she would feel completely safe, out of the grasp of all her stupid uptight family members. Then he wanted to go as far as she would, all 14-years of her.

For this he had a plan. Sheila's apartment had a back bedroom and bathroom suite that was off the master bedroom. So he could lock the master bedroom, and then also the back bedroom suite. This would give them the feeling of being in an inner sanctum, locked away in total privacy even in the middle of a wild party. He even had a good excuse to lock all this up, because it definitely would not be cool to let kids party in Aunt Sheila's private chambers. Mickey knew that Sheila would find out about the party, but as long as her personal shit remained untouched, she would not be too pissed off. Uncle Robert would just say to her, 'Sheila, you left our apartment in the hands of Michael Shea. What did you expect?'

So he planned to use the inner bedroom as a personal suite just for him and Terri to be alone. The rooms were full of antiques and marble and oil paintings of the seaside and mountains—it beat the best hotel room he could buy. Kate had decorated the back room and it was so cool, all 60s and mod. Plus he that knew that he could get Terri in there. He would open the door and say, 'Let me show you something really cool.' And Helen would not be able to follow them, even if she were there. She would be dumbfounded. Like Terri would actually disappear right out from under her nose. He had needed to invite Helen but hoped that she would not come. *What a pain in the ass*, he thought, *always dragging Terri away and giving me that cold-bitch expression. Thank God I don't have any scenes with her in the play.*

When he got Terri into the back bedroom, he would give her something special. He had been working on it all week, remembering how she had responded when he gave her the dress on her fire escape. He wanted to do that again, to see that look on her face. He wanted to give her a piece of jewelry that would take her breath away. He had imagined giving her something that she could wear when they were naked together. A ring? Or even better, a pendant. His mom had a beautiful diamond pendant that dad had given her. She wore it on special occasions, like to go to a wedding or formal dinner. He wanted to give Terri one like that, but even with all the money he had earned dealing drugs, he could not afford it, especially with the party expenses. "Diamonds are fuckin' expensive," he said under his breath as he walked out of the jewelry store on Madison Avenue near his aunt's apartment.

So in his inimitable way, he had improvised. His Aunt Sheila had a big chest of family jewelry that he had discovered in her bedroom, one of those he planned to show Terri. Inside the chest lay an elegant pendant with a diamond about the exact size that he could not afford. It would cost as much as a nice car; the jeweler had told him so. He could afford to get a new setting, just not the diamond part.

So he decided to "borrow" the diamond part from his aunt and replace the real diamond with a fake one that he could afford, made of something called cubic whatever. He sure could not tell the difference. *You'd have to be a diamond man.* His aunt probably would never know. She would never know because she was one of those '60s people who never wore any jewelry or makeup. She also would not know because he promised himself that he would replace the fake diamond with a real one as soon as he had enough money, sometime after he supplied Dingo with all the shit in the universe. Meanwhile, he put the real diamond into a new setting that he had bought so he could give it to Terri.

Presto magico! Terri would be amazed. He imagined himself screwing her while her cute little body wore nothing but that diamond pendant. It gave him a hard-on, until he again thought of Helen. Terri would have to hide it from her and from everyone else, too. He knew that he could trust Terri.

He thought about their conversation after rehearsal that day.

"Are you gonna come and boogie with me baby? On Saturday night?"

"I'm gonna get there somehow, with or without Helen" she had said.

He knew that she would make it. *What a girl!* Like they could know what each other thought and wanted through some kind of weird telepathy. And there was a strange trust between them, as though they had known each other in another life or something. And when Helen dragged Terri away, he felt like a little part of her was left behind, sitting there inside his stomach all the way back to Brooklyn. *Who could explain it?* He wanted to mull it over while sitting on the roof of his house, leaning against the chimney, smoking a joint.

In rehearsal they had been working on one of his big scenes. He had done well and almost had the whole Mab speech committed to memory. *It sure has some whacky shit in it.* Mab was queen of the fairies, and Shakespeare had written about how she rode in this miniature coach over people's faces when they were sleeping. *Shakespeare must have had some serious dope to dream this shit up.*

He had impressed Finnegan, who quizzed him and would not let Nando or anyone else answer the questions. Mickey liked Finnegan, who saw that he was not a dumbass after all. The adults in Mickey's universe took turns yelling at him, threatening him and giving him guilt. And they always had that stupid look on their faces, the one that Mickey translated as, "Shea, you fucking little asshole." Finnegan was different, offering a friendly invitation and trusting that Mickey could rise to meet it.

"Mr. Shea, who is Queen Mab?" Finnegan had asked.

"Queen Mab is, um, she's, uh, she's like a fairy godmother."

"A fairy godmother?"

"Yeah, 'cause it says she's the fairies' midwife, so she helps them get born, the fairies, they're kind of like little magic angels, and she watches over them."

"And what does Mab do?"

"She kind of gives head-trips to people while they're asleep, makes them dream things they want."

"Very good Mr. Shea. Can you give me some examples?"

"Well, she makes lawyers dream about bucks, and she makes guys think about their girls, and girls think about guys, too."

"Very good. What else?"

"And she makes the priests dream about a full collection basket in church, and she makes soldiers dream of cutting their enemies' throats, and, and, she makes women dream about, uh, sex."

"Good, " observed Finnegan. "Now tell me, why do think Shakespeare has Mercutio talking about dreams at this point?"

"The whole scene is about dreams."

"Can you elaborate, Mr. Shea?"

"Uh, when the scene starts, Romeo is all pissed off 'cause he can't have this girl. See, he's dreaming of her, but he can't have his dream and that gets him all depressed."

"Yes. And?"

"And his friends are trying to get him to forget his dreams and go have some fun. They're sayin', 'Lighten up, Romeo, forget about that chick you're dreamin' about.' What's her name, Rosalita?"

"Rosaline."

"Yeah, Rosaline, her. See, here's what I think. I think Romeo's head is all full of crap 'cause he thinks he's in love. And to him, it's like his dreams are feelin' more real than what's *really* real. And Mercutio says to him, 'Listen man, your head's in the clouds, you're trippin'. Queen Mab's playin' with your mind.' He's sayin', 'Wake up, Romeo, look at what's happenin' right here, we're goin' to a party. Live your life, man, don't live in your head.' And Romeo says, 'Shut up, man, you're talkin' a lotta nothin'. And Mercutio says, 'Yeah, that's right, it's alotta of nothin'.' But see, he's makin' a point that alotta nothin'—dreams—that's what makes the whole world go 'round. The whole world is goin' nuts from all the dreams that are all nuts."

Finnegan paused for a good long while, considering.

Finally, he chuckled and said, "Well, Mr. Shea, well, very good. It's not how Shakespeare would have said it, but it's about right."

After rehearsal, on the way home, Nando complimented him.

"Hey man, you did great today. Finnegan thinks you're a fuckin' genius now."

Mickey punched him hard on the shoulder.

"What, man, what's up?" asked Nando

"Get outta here, man, that's what."

"Nah, I'm serious, you're acting, man. It's good. You're getting it."

"Yeah, sure," said Mickey. "So que pasa, man, are you comin' Saturday or what?"

"I don't know, Mick. All Mar wants to do is snort her brains out. I'm getting tired of it. I, uh, I, I asked Helen."

"What the fuck? To come with you instead of Mar? She's such a fuckin' bitch."

"She's a fuckin' bitch to you. To me she's all right."

"All right?"

"Yeah, she's warming up."

"I should fuckin' hope so. How is she going to look otherwise? Juliet the fuckin' ice queen."

"Shut up, man."

"I don't care. I told Terri that Helen could come, 'cause Terri, well you know, she's got to be everywhere with her. You and Mar, you've been goin' a long time. You done with her now?"

"I didn't say that."

"You said you're askin' Helen to go with you."

"It's not like that."

"Well what's it like?"

"I don't know what it's like."

Mickey was silent.

Nando continued. "I mean, she said that she, she maybe, she just wanted to go as friends."

"Well if it's only as friends then why can't you bring Mar?" Mickey liked Mariel a lot. They had known each other for years.

"Cause I'm gettin' sick of Mar, that's why. I'm gettin' sick of carrying her up her fuckin' stairs unconscious. She's a pothead, she's a cokehead, she drinks too much. Am I a fuckin' drug counselor?"

Mickey paused, unhappy with the apparent outcome. "So Helen is definitely comin'?"

"She, uh, she didn't say for sure."

"But you're not bringin' Mar."

"No."

"It'll be lonely without her. You and your friend Helen, *if* she comes, great company," said Mickey with a smirk. "Sounds like fun, Romeo. Maybe you guys can kill yourselves. If she does come, will you take her somewhere and keep her busy?"

"'If' is a mighty word," said Nando.

"What?"

"Nothing—I speak of nothing!" Nando responded in a mock Shakespearean tone.

Mickey lay back on his bunk bed, the shoebox on his chest, turning the situation over in his mind. Nando would deal with Helen… sure he would. Terri had said that she would find a way to get there. What else mattered? The day slowly fell away, and he drifted into a dreamful sleep, imagining what might happen when he and Terri could lie alone.

CHAPTER 11

Sheela na Gig

That night of October 26th, Terri had a vivid, disturbing dream. Her mother, father and Helen were holding her hostage on the grounds of a remote stone castle in Ireland, in the mountains. Mr. Finnegan was there too as some kind of high priest. He wore an old dress and a big pointy hat on his head like a witch.

She saw herself standing outside the castle walls while a cold wind whipped her cheeks and snow fell all about her. Then her father and mother went out into a field covered white with snow. Her father had James' bayonet in his hand, and he used it to kill a calf. Terri's heart filled with terror as the calf screamed and cried and took a long time dying.

When the killing was done, Terri went out and stood next to her mother. They watched the bright red blood pool around the calf like a great pond of red paint in the snow. A jet-black hawk flew down, landed in the puddle and began to drink the blood, leading Terri to see the image of a boy's face painted in blood. Michael Shea's face. She knew in her mind that this boy would be her lover.

Mr. Finnegan then turned to her and said, "His name is Shea."

"I want to meet him," said Terri.

Mickey and his two brothers arrived in his dad's long black Lincoln, which seemed to be out of place outside the castle. Mick's brothers sat in the back seat dressed in dark formal suits, with baseball bats curled over their shoulders in a menacing way, like they wanted to club someone.

Mickey got out of the car and strolled over to Terri, then the two of them went for a walk among some nearby trees. He wore torn jeans and his mouth had trickles of blood running in the corners, like the hawk's beak. His Steppenwolf T-shirt fit tightly across his chest and looked good on him. He held her hand. She felt happy walking beside him, watching his breath steaming in the freezing air.

"My brothers and I," said Mickey, "we're gonna take you away from this place. You're gonna live with us."

She stayed next to him in silence for a while. His hand felt large and warm around hers.

She stopped as they turned to face each other.

"I'd like to come and be with you and your brothers," she said. She put her palm under his shirt the way she had on the fire escape. She could feel blood coursing beneath his skin and the thump of his heart, strong and steady.

She then heard Mickey's brothers blasting the Bruce Springsteen song, *Thunder Road*, from the Lincoln's stereo system.

You can hide 'neath your covers

And study your pain

Make crosses from your lovers

Throw roses in the rain

Waste your summer praying in vain

For a savior to rise from these streets

Well now I'm no hero

That's understood

All the redemption I can offer girl

Is beneath this dirty hood

With a chance to make it good somehow

Hey what else can we do now?

Except roll down the window

And let the wind blow back your hair

Well the night's busting open

These two lanes will take us anywhere

We got one last chance to make it real

To trade in these wings on some wheels

Climb in back

Heaven's waiting on down the tracks.

Mickey picked up Terri like a bride in his arms the same way he had the night of the Military Ball and, as then, howled like a hound dog. He took her back to the huge black car and placed her gently in the passenger seat. She looked out the window as the car pulled away. Her mother and Helen were crying, her father had a strange, dead look in his eyes and Mr. Finnegan waved good-bye to them in his witch costume. As the car pulled away, she noticed on Mr. Finnegan's robe a bizarre, highly stylized image of a woman squatting with her hands under her legs, pulling open her vagina from behind.

She woke with a start and sat up in her bunk above Helen's, her heart racing and forehead moist with sweat. She peered in the shadows at the fire-escape window, left open a crack. She listened quietly, wondering if Mickey had climbed up again. Listening to the sounds of the street for a long time, and hearing nothing, she finally laid back and sighed deeply, trying to get her heartbeat to slow. She picked through the fragments of dream that lingered in her consciousness, fading rapidly from memory. *I won't remember most of this tomorrow morning.*

She could remember the red of the blood and the red in Mickey's cheeks. The black of the hawk and the shiny black of the Lincoln. The white of the snow and of Mickey's teeth, and her own white skin in the cold. She remembered the warmth of his hand and chest, and how she could feel his heart beating. She sensed that the dream meant she wanted to be with Mickey, to be away from Helen and her mother and father, who seemed to be in the way, between her and Mickey. But she could not see why her dream had dressed Mr. Finnegan like a witch, except that maybe she saw the play as a magic spell she and Mickey had cast to spend time together. And the awful symbol on Finnegan's robe? She shuddered to think of it. And her father's dead eyes... terrifying.

After a long while, a fog of drowsiness seemed to rise up from her pillow and immerse her again in sleep. She floated away, wanting to remember what it felt like to have Mickey's strong arms lift her off the ground and carry her into the air like a bride.

Saturday, October 28th. Terri walked a step behind Helen up the subway stairs from the Lexington Avenue stop at 96th Street. The Saturday-evening streets teemed with people returning from afternoon shopping in midtown, along with others heading out for the night. The air felt cool and a little damp. Terri wore a form-fitting cream-colored sweater dress over white tights and earth shoes and a blue jeans jacket, with a tin of brownies under her left arm that her mother had given her to leave with Charlie. Terri thought brownies sent a better message than flowers. Giving food seemed to suggest that people would be eating. Flowers suggested that you expected a funeral. In her gray suede bag she had makeup, 10 dollars, a hairbrush and an extra pair of panties that she had rolled up in a tight ball bound with two rubber bands.

Helen had worked herself into a state, like a toddler who had been deprived of a nap and then had her bag of candies taken away. Her stomach churned with anger and bitterness. She felt mad about getting to see Charlie only under such unpleasant circumstances, and upset that he had not called or written her for months. To be stuck with Terri again, like a ball and chain at her heel, produced a spiky, tense feeling in her core.

She would not admit it, but she felt frustrated at the way events had overtaken the possibility that she could see Nando. She had basically refused to say clearly whether she would or would not come to Mickey's party, deciding to hedge her bets, thereby ruining the evening for as many people as possible. She had refused to indicate that she would cover for Terri in any way. Her unspoken message said: 'If you have a trick up your sleeve, it's your responsibility, not mine.' Terri had decided not to discuss anything and let the evening go where it would; she was prepared to exit and flee as soon as the opportunity presented itself.

They entered the hospital on Madison Avenue, and just as Terri hoped, immediately became tangled in a confusing knot of hallways and departments and floors leading to other hallways, departments and floors, so one quickly lost all sense of place. Terri made a point of saying, "This hospital is huge," several times on the way to Mr. Cunningham's room, as well as "Now where exactly are we?" and also, "How do people find their way around here?"

Extremely preoccupied, Helen basically ignored everything that Terri said. Her distraction pleased Terri because it meant that Helen would have a foggy recollection that the hospital had confused Terri. This would make the whole episode more believable.

Finally they arrived at the hallway leading to the cardiac intensive-care unit. At the end of the hallway, they could see Charlie slumped in an armchair in the waiting area—asleep, alone, dressed in a black peacoat, jeans and a plaid lumberjack shirt.

"Helen, you take these," said Terri, thrusting the tin of brownies into her hands.

The reality of Charlie caught Helen off guard, flooding her with a confusing mix of warmth, anger, sympathy and anxiety.

"Where are you going?" she asked Terri.

"To find the cafeteria and have some tea. I'll just give you two a chance to catch up and say hello."

Helen started to protest, but Terri stopped her.

"Look Hel, it's bad enough. You don't want me here right now, do you?"

Helen sighed. "What do I say to him, Terri?"

"Don't say anything to him. Listen to what *he* has to say. Then you'll know, OK? Just hold his hand, OK? He probably feels scared."

Helen nodded as Terri retreated into the hospital maze.

Helen approached Charlie quietly and sat down on the sofa next to his chair, reaching out to touch his right hand. He stirred and opened his eyes, coming up from a light sleep, and focused on her.

"Helen," he smiled at her.

She leaned in and kissed him on the cheek, then sat back and looked at him. He looked good. He had lost about 15 pounds and she could see his broad chest and flat stomach beneath his shirt. His face had a ruddy, healthy glow, with cheekbones and chin that now stood out now, giving him a chiseled look more handsome than she remembered. He appeared physically bigger, although it could just have been how he sat in the chair. It seemed to Helen that he was a man breaking out of a boy's shell.

"How's your dad?"

A cloud passed over his sunny smile, his eyes narrowing with worry.

"I'm not sure. I haven't been able to talk with him at all. He's been unconscious, some kind of new treatment. And he's all tubes." His throat tightened and he looked at his feet, reining in his feelings.

"The doctors are keeping him knocked out. They can't say what'll happen, but he does have a chance." He looked up at Helen and smiled again.

"Should we…" Helen paused. "Are we supposed to check on him? Is your mom here?"

"No. We can't do anything. I got here this morning. They only let me come because Mom begged. Because when it all happened on Tuesday, they, uh, they thought he was gonna, um, not gonna make it. And I didn't want Mom to be alone."

"Does your mom have any other family here?"

"Yeah, my aunt came up from Virginia. So that's real good. She's with Mom now. They went home."

"Good, Charlie, that's good. I bet that's a real relief for you."

"Yeah, she's really freaking out, my mom. I mean, she's keeping it together on the surface, but, well, you know."

Helen nodded. They sat quietly for minutes, like two puzzle pieces that looked right but did not quite fit together.

Then Helen asked, "When are you going back?"

"I'm leaving tomorrow. Got to be back in school Monday, 'cause, well, unless he doesn't pull through. Then I'll come back right away."

"He'll pull through Charlie. He's a strong man."

Charlie nodded, uncertainty in his eyes.

"Mom made these for your family," said Helen, passing him the tin. "They're brownies."

"Thanks." He smiled again.

She reached out and held his hand. Her small gesture obviously meant a lot to him. It felt to Helen like Charlie had been starved for tenderness.

"They're good," she said. "Your dad can have one when he wakes up." As soon as she said this, she knew it was a mistake.

Charlie's eyes slowly filled with tears and one ran down his cheek. Helen felt really awful for him and so selfish for having thought only about herself all the way to the hospital. She moved over into his chair and put her arm around his neck.

He put his thumb and forefinger to the bridge of his nose as if to pinch the tears away. He blushed, embarrassed to cry in front of her.

"Thanks," he said again, pausing, trying to control himself. "Look at me. I'm a tough guy."

"Charlie, he's your dad," Helen whispered. "Of course you're worried about him. You wouldn't be human if you didn't feel this way."

"Yeah, ah, that's right," he said under his breath, having trouble speaking through the grief that had become clogged in his throat.

She gently folded his head into her neck, feeling tears running down his cheeks, like a soft rain against a windowpane, and held him this way for minutes. She kept holding his hand like Terri had said to do, really glad that she had come. She wanted to do something right by him, to make him feel better. She understood that he had made himself vulnerable, and his openness made her relax, drawing them closer than she could ever remember, giving her a fluttering warm feeling, as though she had wrapped him with her under a tartan blanket.

Finally he sighed and pulled away, straightening up.

He moved deliberately to kiss her on the lips but she stopped him before he could. She could feel his confusion. In her mind, though, he had crossed a line that he should have respected. It was not right. There was kissing him as a friend, on his cheek—she felt comfortable with that. Then there was kissing him as his girlfriend, and she did not feel ready for it. She had not come on to him. She saw nothing sexy

125

in her behavior. Now he was trying to convert friendship—close friendship—back into *girl* friendship, but he had not treated her like his girlfriend for months.

"Not yet," she said, haltingly. "I'm, I…" she paused again.

He stared at her blankly.

She looked at him squarely in the eye. "Charlie. I haven't heard from you since the summer. I know you said that we're free to see other people, but I'm not sure what that means for *us*." She paused again, allowing confusion and upset to sweep across her face.

She felt drawn to him, yet did not even want to be his girlfriend anymore. He had been right, after all, to break it off. *How can I maintain a relationship with someone off somewhere else, far away,* she thought. *He doesn't communicate, has no definite plans about when or whether we would ever see each other. Will I only see him at his family emergencies? What if my dad got sick, would he come to visit me? Of course not. But we can't sort all this out now, can we? And he has already made the decision to be done with me, hasn't he?*

"I know this is the worst time to talk about it," she said.

"I'm sorry, Helen," he said, looking down again. "You just don't know. It's been hard."

"How do I know… if you don't tell me?"

He paused, searching for words.

"It's been night and day and I barely have time to, to do anything. I'm doing well Helen. I mean, I'm going to make it. I know I can pass. I mean, more than pass, I can be at the top. But it's just, it's even harder than I thought…. I think about you all the time, Helen, all the time. I wish, I wish we could have had the summer. I miss you… so much. You don't know how much."

It felt to Charlie like he had been marching through an infinite desert, and Helen was a cool pool into which he wanted to dip his burning face. But when he tried, she turned out to be a mirage. Instead of cool blue water, his parched face found hot sand. Yet he could still sense her out there somewhere, cool and refreshing. And he knew that if he did not find her right now, there would be just thousands more miles of empty, dry sand before him.

If I could just find the right words to say, the cool pool would open up before me, he thought. He did not care what the right words were to access this refreshing flesh—she had never seemed more inviting. He would have said literally anything, a bunch of curse words or even "I love Satan"—whatever it took.

Eighteen years old, he had not touched a girl since June when Helen had kissed him good-bye and given him that depressing note. Now she was the only girl he could remember, the only one he had the slightest possibility of touching or talking to for the foreseeable future.

Helen had become more than herself. To Charlie, she had become the personification of all the femaleness in the universe. He recognized how his longing for *any* girl had totally distorted his view of Helen. He did not care. It was not that he lacked real feelings for Helen the real person, or that he did not really miss her. He did. But the infinite emotional and sexual desert surrounding him had obscured whatever he felt.

Getting through basic training had required him to double- and triple- and quadruple-fold all of his emotions—all except aggression—and stuff them carefully into the bottom of his trunk, forgetting them. Aggression was the one emotion he allowed himself, the one feeling he could channel into everything. He had committed to himself to fight, fight, fight, to be the best, the strongest, the proudest, the most competitive.

He did feel an emotional bond with classmates, but it came from shared aggression. He submerged himself into the group, feeling solidarity, not affection, for his classmates. He had expanded his definition of himself to include them, and they, him. Affection and love and warmth seemed completely different to him, because these feelings entailed preserving and enjoying the identity of the person he loved, not just her treating her like an extension of his own ego. Love and tenderness emerged from difference rather than sameness. He wanted desperately to treat Helen as unique, not as part of himself. He wanted to kiss her and experience her intense otherness, her femaleness, not slap her on the back.

It had been months since Charlie had allowed raw feelings to travel from his heart into his mind. He wondered if he could ever explain it to Helen in a way she could understand. He could not call or write her because it took all of his focused rage just to stay competitive, just to stay in the game. To let himself feel a full spectrum of emotions at school would swallow him alive. He was on a practice battlefield; he had to rule himself completely.

But his father's being deathly ill had unleashed all of these distracting, volatile emotions from their chains, up from the bottom of his trunk. He felt so unpracticed at them and totally unprepared to control them. When he had unlocked his sadness and anxiety and genuine love for his father, he had also unintentionally released his surging sexual desire and unfulfilled longing for contact with a woman, any woman.

To Charlie, Helen now seemed to radiate sex. She felt so immediate, her thighs against his, holding his hand, her breasts, her softness, her lustrous brown hair inches from him, with her deep, sea-green eyes staring into his. He had a dim, instinctual sense that the only way to find the cool pool was to tell the absolute truth. He seemed to speak not from his brain but from a more primitive part of himself.

"You don't know how much I've been thinking about you, you don't know, I keep seeing your face, and remembering what it felt like to kiss you. I don't know why I didn't call or write you, I don't know why, I don't know why, I don't know why. I just want to kiss you, Helen, right now."

He moved to kiss her again and this time she let him. Something in his directness, in his unabashed statement of need, moved her. While she did not reciprocate, nor did she resist. He read her passivity as an invitation, pressing his mouth against hers harder and pushing his tongue between her lips.

She felt cool against his skin, against his lips, like drinking a glass of ice water on the hottest day in hell. He could tell that he had connected someplace inside her that did not think; he had reached a part of her able to just respond. The animal part.

She moaned a little and pushed her tongue back into his mouth, then around his lips. In a first for all of the times they had been together, he did not feel her stiffen up. Her body responded to him instead of her mind. She threw her leg over his and rubbed her calf on his knee.

She pulled back and looked at him. Her face glowed red. "Charlie, we can't do this here," she whispered.

"Why not?" he said.

"Because it's too… it's too public."

"Where can we go?"

"I know a place." she said, "It'll be a little wild, but we'll be OK."

CHAPTER 12

Queen Mab's Party

October 28th. Mickey tapped the keg at 5:30 that afternoon; 15 minutes later, he and Ricky Porter were already substantially buzzed. The keg sat in a large trashcan full of ice in the fancy kitchen, surrounded by glass-fronted cabinets rising almost all the way up to the 14-foot ceilings. The giant kitchen windows looked out on the building's interior courtyard, complete with planters and quaint little park benches—the quad remained from an earlier era in which such interior spaces allowed for ventilation.

"No sah," said Ricky in his thick Maine accent. "I never seen so many cars in all my life, and not a single fuckin' place to park. You'd fit a whole town of Mainerts right in one of these here buildings."

"A lobstah-man in New York!" said Mickey, imitating his accent, slapping him on the back.

"I'm tellin' ya, I know they can all see I'm from away, yessah, they saw me squinting out my window all the way down every tiny fuckin' street. I'm wearin' a 'Where the fuck am I?' shirt."

They were standing in a large circle with Mickey's brothers telling stories about life in Maine and life in New York City. Mickey had spent summers in Maine since age 3 and had known Ricky almost his whole life.

About 10 years older than Mickey, he had the weathered look that comes from working in the sea. His handsome face and torso were deeply bronzed, his brown wavy hair bleached from the sun. His limbs had grown gnarly and as tough as goat leather from years of hauling lobster traps.

Ricky had always refused to work for anyone else, starting his lobster business at 17 with his own small boat. A clever businessman, he had saved his profits for many years and then gone into the drug-dealing business, for which the lobsters provided a perfect cover.

Ricky knew every inch of his boats and lobster traps, and cops had no place to hide on the open water. When he made a connection, he knew exactly with whom he dealt and whether anyone was watching. There never was.

Even in the dark, he could maneuver through each little inlet and cove of the Maine coast around Boothbay Harbor. There were houses and docks built everywhere into the shoreline. His boats could go any one of a thousand places and who could say he was not just selling some fresh lobstahs? He would not retail the drugs locally. He would work only with trusted middlemen, the type who would go to the gas chamber before they would give him up.

The business could not be audited. Who knew how many lobsters you caught? Nobody except you and "the bugs" as Ricky referred to them.

"I never seen a bugged bug," he would say, laughing deep in his throat, "and I never seen a bug questioned by a lawyer."

His lobster business had become substantial because he had reinvested the proceeds of his drug-dealing, as well as using it to launder money. Of course, the bigger the business grew, the easier it became to hide money in it. "Lobstah and reefa, perfect together!" he would say.

Smart enough not to attract too much attention, Ricky lived in a modest house, ate most of his meals at home, and drove a restored '67 Chevy Impala with a muscle engine. He dressed humbly, like a Maine fisherman. Well-liked by his fishing and drinking and hunting buddies, he drank heavily, smoked like an old diesel engine, and had girls in places up and down the coastline, mostly bartenders in local taverns. Except for pot, he did not touch drugs himself, just the way he did not eat lobstahs. "Me eat a bug? I'd rather have a spidah burger!"

No one would have believed the amount of cash he had tucked away. Ricky did not believe in banks. He put some of his money in Camden Bank in Wiscasset to pay bills, but kept the rest either tied up in his business or buried, literally. Ricky spent a huge amount of time digging holes around a cabin he kept in the woods and depositing suitcases full of cash. He also had a number of chests anchored to the sea-floor and marked with buoys that he would eyeball once a week when out in one of his boats. As a result of this avoidance of the financial system, the abundant spoils of his crimes remained invisible.

His partnership with Mickey came about because he had basically tapped out what he could do in Boothbay. His suppliers wanted to move some larger quantities.

Ricky saw Mickey as a trusted window to one of the largest retail markets for illegal drugs in the United States.

In his spare time, Ricky loved to hunt, especially with his bow. He and Mickey had hunted deer and moose together a few times and, as a present, he had bought Mickey his own hunting bow, a thank you for all of his hard work moving a massive quantity of product over the prior three months.

"So when are ya comin' back to the cabin with me, Mick? There's a moose waitin' for ya. I'll draw a bullseye on his forehead for ya. Mick can't hit the side of a barn with his bow, ya know. Ya couldn't hit a deer if she planted a kiss on ya cheek."

"You expect me to run around the woods with a fuckin' bow?" asked Mickey. "Am I fuckin' Robin Hood?"

"I don't know, are ya fuckin' Robin Hood, Mick? Is Robin's ass sweet enough for ya?"

They howled with laughter, draining their beer mugs.

"Look at this dumbass," said Mickey to his brothers, pointing to Ricky. "He thinks he's fightin' fair 'cause he uses a bow instead of a rifle. You think a moose gives a shit whether you shoot him with a bullet or an arrow? I can hear the fuckin' moose now. 'Thank you, Mr. Ricky, thanks for shooting my ass with an arrow, now I can die real slow. God bless you, Mr. Porter, you're such a fair and honest man.'"

"Am I tryin' to be fair to a moose? Ya think I give a rat's ass about a moose? A moose is just a giant rat with antlers. It's about the chase, Mick. Any asswipe can shoot moose with a rifle, they're fuckin' huge, any asswipe but Mick that is," he chuckled. "Now usin' a bow, that takes a hunter."

"Well why don't you strangle the moose with your bare hands? Now that's what a real man would do. Or beat the antlers off his head with a stone. Now there would be a good challenge for you."

Ricky thought about this as if he were considering it seriously.

"'Cause I'm a fuckin' Indian, not a fuckin' caveman. Lobstahmen have standaahds, Mick."

"Glad to know it, 'cause you're lookin' more like a fuckin' caveman everyday."

More laughter.

"I ain't the one that beats critters to death with boulders. That would be you, Mick."

"Ah shit, not this story again."

"It's fuckin' true though. When we was kids my old man had a nasty old hound he kept to guard the chickens. And one day little Mick comes runnin' up the yard, couldn'ta been more than four years old. He's cryin', 'Ya pooch bit my ass, ya pooch bit my ass.'—It was a fuckin' hoot, I'm telling ya. My old man says, 'Ya should keep your fuckin' ass outta his mouth then, Mick.' Well, little Mick is pissed and stomps off down the yard, picks up a brick in his little hand and hammers that ugly old bitch right on her noggin. Kills the old bitch dead as a fuckin' stone. And I says to myself, 'That little Mick, he's got some balls, he's got some brass.'"

The conversation continued in this vein, reliving all manner of their ridiculous exploits over the years, complete with pantomime where required, so that each absurdity could be remembered and embellished for full comic effect: the time they had capsized Mr. Shea Sr.'s fishing boat, the time they had gotten so drunk they drove a truck off a pier, the time they simultaneously vomited their breakfast all over the Wiscasset Diner because they were so hung over, the time they had both fallen asleep on their girlfriends at the drive-in. There was no end to their love of drinking beer and retelling these stories. Meanwhile, more and more people arrived at the party. Music and dancing were underway in the large living room they had emptied of furniture.

At about 7:15, Mickey, now fairly drunk, started to suspect that Terri would not make it to the party. This depressed him. He wanted to see her so badly, and to introduce her to Ricky. He thought of the diamond pendant in his pocket. *A big fuckin' party, a big diamond and no Terri. How fucked is that?*

He went into his aunt's room where he had stashed his bag with a lot of cash and drugs and the sample from Dingo. Ricky had agreed to take some of that so he could source the right quality. Mickey pulled out a sheet of acid tabs from the bag. He had been planning to sell some but no one had asked him for any.

Neat rows of little pictures dotted the acid blotter like postage stamps. *Lick one and mail yourself out of the universe.* Each little picture showed four salmon fish interleaved to form the shape of a cross. He imagined the tripping Canadian who must have imprinted the page while sitting wasted in a basement somewhere north of the Maine border. *This ought to make things interesting, taking three tabs.* Mickey only had a few experiences with acid, but never at a dose this high. 'I'm a fuckin' space cowboy,' he said to himself. He felt a sense of excitement, as if boarding an expedition boat headed for uncharted waters.

People were arriving in bursts of five or six. Many had come from Brooklyn, friends of Mickey and his brothers, as well as other Xavier friends and people in the school play. The place had filled up; the living room dance floor was packed like a subway car. Mickey had decided to let the partiers pour the hard liquor, having made an inventory of the booze on hand before the party started so he could replace whatever they poured down their throats. Pot was not a big deal because Mickey's aunt, a '60s radical, smoked it, and his cousin Kate and their friends smoked in the house all the time. People were toking everywhere; Mickey thought that kids could probably get buzzed just breathing. The walls vibrated from the music but it was still early and Mickey thought they probably would not draw any complaints for a few hours.

Nando had arrived alone. He stood by the keg nursing a beer, talking with some of their mutual friends including Ricky. Mickey walked up to him.

"Hey shithead, you finally made it." For Mickey, names like shithead, asshole, asswipe and dickhead served as terms of endearment.

"Yeah," said Nando. "No sign of the Rafter girls, huh?"

"Nah, they're probably in church praying," said Mickey, rolling his eyes. "Did you hear Charlie's in town?"

"No."

"Yeah, his dad had a fuckin' heart attack on Tuesday."

"Who told you?"

"I heard it from Iamele."

Tony Iamele was the new colonel of the regiment. At the party on invitation from one of Mickey's brothers, Iamele was worse than Charlie. Nando though he was a real prig.

"That sucks," said Nando. "Is his dad OK?"

Mickey shook his head and shrugged. "Fuck if I know."

"I wonder if Helen is with him."

"Who gives a shit?"

They stood surveying the crowd, drinking. Mickey began to feel sparks of electricity in his head, like someone had turned up the voltage in his brain. He felt several flashes of alertness, as if plugged into a wall socket with the hue control in his brain turned up so everything now looked brilliant and saturated. The acid had started to kick in and Mickey knew the ride was going to be outstanding.

"Put on your seatbelt," said Mickey to Nando. "We have liftoff."

"What?" asked Nando.

"Just took three tabs of acid."

"Three tabs? Holy shit, Mick, you're gonna blow your brains out."

"What brains?" asked Mickey, laughing.

At that moment, he felt two soft hands sneak around his head and cover his eyes.

"Michael Shea, have you been drinking again?" Terri whispered in his ear, from behind.

Mickey laughed and swung around, picking her up in his beefy arms and twirling her around. "*Yee-haa!*" he bellowed in a sandy, rumbling roar. He put her down on the kitchen counter and kissed her. She opened her mouth and they French-kissed to the kitchen audience in an embrace of tongues lasting a full minute.

He released her and pulled back, before reciting Mercutio's celebrated Queen Mab speech:

> O, then, I see Queen Mab hath been with you.
> She is the fairies' midwife, and she comes
> In shape no bigger than an agate-stone
> On the fore-finger of an alderman,
> Drawn with a team of little atomies
> Athwart men's noses as they lie asleep;
> Her wagon-spokes made of long spiders' legs,
> The cover of the wings of grasshoppers,
> The traces of the smallest spider's web,
> The collars of the moonshine's watery beams,
> Her whip of cricket's bone, the lash of film,
> Her wagoner a small grey-coated gnat,
> Not so big as a round little worm
> Prick'd from the lazy finger of a maid;
> Her chariot is an empty hazel-nut
> Made by the joiner squirrel or old grub,
> Time out o' mind the fairies' coachmakers.
> And in this state she gallops night by night
> Through lovers' brains, and then they dream of love;
> O'er courtiers' knees, that dream on court'sies straight,
> O'er lawyers' fingers, who straight dream on fees,
> O'er ladies ' lips, who straight on kisses dream,
> Which oft the angry Mab with blisters plagues,
> Because their breaths with sweetmeats tainted are:
> Sometime she gallops o'er a courtier's nose,
> And then dreams he of smelling out a suit;
> And sometime comes she with a tithe-pig's tail

Tickling a parson's nose as a' lies asleep,
Then dreams, he of another benefice:
Sometime she driveth o'er a soldier's neck,
And then dreams he of cutting foreign throats,
Of breaches, ambuscadoes, Spanish blades,
Of healths five-fathom deep; and then anon
Drums in his ear, at which he starts and wakes,
And being thus frighted swears a prayer or two
And sleeps again. This is that very Mab
That plats the manes of horses in the night,
And bakes the elflocks in foul sluttish hairs,
Which once untangled, much misfortune bodes:
This is the hag, when maids lie on their backs,
That presses them and learns them first to bear,
Making them women of good carriage:
This is she....

The speech stunned them. Impressive, well acted, passionate, flawless. As Mickey said his lines, his brain—filled with lightning flashes—conjured a shockingly vivid picture of Queen Mab. He saw her first as a powerful and fearsome queen of a huge Irish kingdom, commanding armies of warriors of the dark ages, armed with buck knives, brass knuckles and nunchucks. He saw her on a white horse herding cattle, which surrounded a white bull, with a bullseye on his head, only the bull had moose antlers instead of horns and, in the middle of the bullseye, a phrase with his name emerged written in blood: "Mickey's Bull Moose." His mental image of Mab then morphed. She became an insect-sized fairy with the wings of a dragonfly, buzzing madly around the party like a miniature fighter pilot, casting spells on the revelers and giving them mad and undeniable passions.

When Mickey reached the end of his speech, Nando obliged him with Romeo's line:

"Peace, Mickey Shea, thou talk'st of nothing."

To Mickey's reply:

True, I talk of dreams,
Which are the children of an idle brain,
Begot of nothing but vain fantasy.

Terri applauded. "Mickrutio," she exclaimed, "that was great!"

135

Mickey stared at her as if he were seeing her for the first time. He pulled her close and whispered in her ear, "I have spread my dreams under your feet, tread softly, because you tread upon my dreams." He saw that his dreams had unfolded on the floor in front of Terri. Everywhere she stepped, his dreams would undulate and swim beneath her feet. His dreams were a swirling, pulsating fabric, a red liquid that somehow became a flimsy, billowing silk rug with an evolving geometric pattern. He looked closely at the pattern and saw that it was made of the salmon from the acid blotter, only the fish were dancing in a complex and coordinated thatch and cross-thatch motion, spilling down the living carpet of his dreams. These liquid images, which were also now releasing a red mist near the floor, spread before Terri in a ribbon and led down the hallway to his Aunt Sheila's chambers.

"What?" she asked, curiously. "Mick, are you OK?"

He laughed and took her by the hand.

"I have something to give you," he said. "It's wicked cool. You won't believe it."

Terri's eyes grew wide as she followed him down the hallway.

Upon reaching his aunt's bedroom, they stopped. His hand on the door handle, he waited for the hall to clear of people, then opened the door and quickly pulled in Terri behind him, so no one saw them enter. The main room lay in shadows and he lit a candle on his aunt's bureau, on the left side of a large window facing the park trees. The walls were covered with rich, reddish-pink paisley wallpaper that seemed to Mickey to be alive and breathing. They stood for a moment before a large four-poster canopy bed covered with a sheer white curtain. Beyond and behind this master bedroom, his cousin Kate's room was visible through a large bathroom connecting the two rooms. He locked the door.

"We're safe here," he said. "I've got the only key."

Terri smiled at him, holding his arm. "What are you up to, Mick?"

He led her through the bathroom to Kate's bedroom. As they walked, it seemed to Mickey that the bathroom floor had become the size of a basketball court. The old black-and-white tiles covering the ground and spreading halfway up the walls seemed to swim and extend in multiple directions so it looked to him like the tub and toilet and sink were hundreds of feet apart, and the door to the back bedroom had become a miniature portal they would have to crawl through.

"Check it out," he directed as they finally entered the back bedroom.

"Wow!" exclaimed Terri.

Kate had decorated the large room in a mod '60s style, with a wall-to-wall white shag rug and massive circular bed in the middle. There were multicolored beanbag chairs tossed casually in each corner of the room along with two sleek electric-blue egg chairs and a double-egg love seat. A delicious omelet. When one sat in the loveseat, it felt like the inside of a space capsule.

The walls had oversized, framed psychedelic posters, including a Salvador Dali print of a luxuriating naked woman being stung by a bayonet and attacked by tigers, who in turn were being eaten by a giant fish. There were also some wild Grateful Dead and Who posters from album covers, along with three art deco-style frames of goddesses including one called Aine. Mickey looked at her poster and it seemed like the goddess had Terri's face. Aine appeared as a sexy bare-breasted teen surrounded by Celtic crosses. When Mickey looked closely at them, he could see that the salmon fish were moving again. They were drawing the crosses by swimming in that coordinated thatching pattern. It seemed to him that the posters had become three-dimensional, spilling their words and pictures out into the room. He started laughing.

"What's so funny?" asked Terri.

"This room is so cool, huh?"

Terri felt happy that Mickey had her alone already because she knew that she did not have much time. No one would believe that she could wander aimlessly around a hospital for three hours. It was already 8, and she wanted to try to leave by 9 or 9:30 at the latest. *Now is a good time,* she thought.

"I know what you want to give me," she said, her eyes twinkling coyly, arms around his neck.

"What?"

"Another kiss and a cuddle," she said giggling, pulling him onto the circular bed.

Mickey fell on the bed next to her, staring into her eyes. Her soft brown hair spilled around her face and began to shimmer. Her eyes and lips were floating and bobbing, like the reflection of the moon in a gentle ocean ripple.

As they kissed, he began to run his hand along the outside of her slender thigh. Her sweater dress had ridden up her waist, exposing her white tights. He continued to run his hand up over her hip and then further, up her flank and to her left breast. He started first just to run his hand along the outside of her breast, unthinkingly, as if he meant to touch her side and had strayed over her breast by accident.

She made no move to stop him, focusing on how good his hand felt and how excited she had become. She felt a tingle and warmth, wanting him to touch her right there but she did not dare move his hand. Instead she lay still and let his hand go where it would. She dimly remembered Helen saying how boys wanted to touch you everywhere and you had to try to slow them down. But the advice seemed to be so useless now, like advice to someone who had jumped off a bridge about the best way to hit the water.

Mickey then began to run his hand over her chest in a bolder and more direct way than he had ever done before. *It is intentional,* she thought, *nothing accidental about it.* His hand, firm but gentle, felt like a soft breeze caressing her and, as he lightly touched her, the tingling and pleasing and slightly aching feeling intensified. She moaned softly, "Oh, Mick."

To him, it seemed that her body had become luminescent. The greater her excitement, the more brightly she burned. He wanted to get the light inside her to build slowly in intensity, then explode. He sensed that the physical feeling and form of her body was an illusion; she was pure liquid energy, which had taken on this form—the real Terri. But she did not have to stay like this and in fact could become anything in the universe. He felt that the increasing intensity of light coming from her, spilling out from her eyes and mouth and breasts and from between her legs, flowed from a source deep within another world. He was connecting her to the source and filling her with energy by touching and kissing her with tenderness and feeling. He was planning a pilgrimage to the very center of the energy source now flooding her with light.

He could also feel himself. In the middle of his acid trip, he felt massive and throbbing. As he focused on his own excitement, it became clear to him that he had not one brain, but two. There was one in his head and another between his legs. He understood that he was not only a man with a hard-on attached but a hard-on with a man attached. Mickey then felt the center of his consciousness actually relocate, as if the command post of his nervous system had traveled south. It seemed to him that his ability to talk and think was actually moving from his head to—his dick! And he believed that this part of him had now acquired the ability to communicate telepathically with the rest of him, perhaps also with Terri. In the middle of his psychedelic trip, he realized that this second consciousness, the one between his legs, was called 'McMick.' He did not know why, nor who had named it. But that was its name, he was sure. When Terri moaned, "Oh Mick," he understood she was actually talking to McMick, the dick with the man attached, and not Mickey, the man with the dick attached. And McMick was more than tired of not being able to clearly see what was happening and not able to talk to Terri directly.

McMick got up off the bed and told the rest of Mickey that it was time to get undressed. The rest of him obeyed as he stood and stripped off his T-shirt and jeans.

"What are you doing?" asked Terri, with surprise.

"I'm hot," answered McMick, "I'm just trying to get cooled off a little." Mickey was astonished that McMick could speak so plainly and clearly, and apparently with such complete independence.

Terri's eyes traveled down Mick's muscular chest and flat stomach to the astonishing arrival in his jockey shorts. She had seen the outline of Mickey's flaccid, vomit-drenched equipment before, but what faced her now was something beyond her imagination.

"I'm gonna take these off, too," said McMick.

Terri nodded with terrible fascination, as McMick removed his jockeys.

"My god, Mick," she said, staring at him in wonder.

McMick lay down on the bed next to her, and sighed with enormous relief at finally being able to breathe properly and talk to Terri directly.

Terri now felt confused. It did not seem right for Mickey to be lying stark naked next to her while she kept all of her clothes on. She wanted to hold his naked body and kiss him again freely, but not through her sweater dress. *But wouldn't getting undressed be like bathing myself in blood before swimming with a shark?* But she felt somehow responsible for Mickey's condition and that she should definitely do something to bring him relief. She also had a wonderful tingling, turned-on sensation; her panties were moist and she felt hot as well. *But wouldn't it be terribly forward to take off my own clothes, willy-nilly? Isn't he supposed to pressure me to undress?*

Meanwhile, McMick waited patiently, sensing that his unexpected and glorious arrival was working some mysterious transformation and that he should just see what would happen next.

"Should I—um—do you want me—uh—Mick?"

She paused and looked at him.

"Mick, do you think I should take these off? Should I get undressed, like you?"

McMick directed Mickey's head to nod emphatically.

"But we won't, Mick, we can't, OK? I mean, I'm not ready. I just want to touch a little, OK? Just touching? Is that OK, Mick?"

McMick now had full command of Mickey's mouth, and said "OK."

Terri got up off the bed and pulled her sweater dress over her head, unclasped her bra and pulled it off. Facing away from him, she hesitated for a moment at her white tights. It just did not seem right to keep them on. She shimmied them over her slender ass and thighs and pulled them off her feet. The air did feel wonderfully cool and pleasing against her bare skin. Her nipples were hard; an absolute sexual energy ran through her, a hunger she had never experienced before. It was hard to feel embarrassed at all because he was lying there completely naked and he looked, well, he looked so exposed and red, and seemed to be in some pain. She could see that her panties were damp but kept them on and crawled back onto the bed next to him.

At this point, the brain between Mickey's ears completely disappeared and he fully became McMick.

Mickey had not been with many girls, but during the winter when he turned 12 and his cousin Kate was 15, he had stayed with his Aunt Sheila and Uncle Robert for a week. A very free spirit, Sheila thought nothing of letting Mickey and Kate play games behind closed doors or leaving them alone in the apartment for hours while she shopped or walked in Central Park. Sheila, who had been to India in the '60s and studied Tantra, had provided Kate with the Planned Parenthood book, *Our Bodies, Ourselves*, as soon as she had had her first period. Sheila had also talked openly with Kate about sex between consenting adults.

Kate happily shared all she had learned with Mickey in the very same bedroom he was now occupying with Terri, including very explicit and detailed anatomy lessons in which she used her own body as a textbook model in exchange for the opportunity to study and handle Mickey in similar detail. They had not had sex—Kate felt that was not something she should do with her cousin—but they had looked at one another and touched and explored each other's bodies completely, if without any romantic element to the interaction. As a result, McMick knew exactly what to do for Terri.

McMick was plotting carefully. First he had to get her to take off those panties. Then, when she was completely naked, he would give her the diamond pendant to serve as a sort of magic charm that would transport McMick to the energy source, a kind of Valhalla where he would reside for all eternity.

He ran his right hand slowly and gently along the inside of her thighs and up over her slender belly, feeling her shudder slightly before running his fingers back down, slightly catching the waistband of her panties. Every third or fourth time he repeated this, he would run his forefinger horizontally across the top of the waistband, then back below its line, but still on top of her panties. Each time, he would move slightly closer to the V at the very center, sometimes letting the palm of his hand brush gently against its center. They were not kissing anymore. She lay next to him with her eyes closed, and with his left arm he had propped up his face, which had become a mere lookout for McMick; Mickey had vanished.

He observed her intently. Her face and neck were flushed red, with eyes closed. She had lain back passively and relaxed. Her panties felt soaked and clung to her.

Terri had never felt anything like this in her young life. How gentle and strong he seemed, and how totally energized. It felt to her like Mickey had become a bow pulled so taut that it could shoot an arrow to the moon. She felt herself slipping completely into his power, hearing herself moaning with pleasure. It seemed that she was becoming someone else entirely. She again remembered—if so far away—Helen telling her about how boys wanted to put their hands everywhere, and how you had to slow them down, and how it was hard because you wanted them to touch you, and how boys wanted to rub themselves on you. She realized then that something had gone wrong, because Mickey's body had not touched her at all and she had not touched it at all. Mickey was not playing by the rules—he had focused all his attention on her, ignoring himself, and driven her mad with desire. She had to get control somehow, but also wanted him to continue.

She opened her eyes. Her gaze traveled down his torso with fascination. The sight was horrifying and also strangely intriguing. She reached down and put her hand around him and squeezed. He moaned with pleasure. Holding him in her little palm, she felt an incredible rush of power, as if he were the A-train and she the conductor with her hand on the controls.

If Mickey had not been in the middle of an acid trip, he would gladly have let her finish him off right there. But he was not in charge. Inside his acid trip, Mickey's entire ego had taken up residence in an alternative consciousness between his legs. It was McMick directing traffic, and so he moved back a little, and whispered in low voice, "Wait, not yet."

She felt surprised and unsure; what should she do? *He said 'not yet,' so does he want me to touch him there later?* She surveyed Mickey's muscular body, his curly hair, his beautiful hazel eyes. He looked gorgeous and she wanted just to trust him. For the first time, he ran his finger up the middle of her V and let it linger for just a moment right on the most sensitive spot. She shuddered and moaned again, "Oh, Mick."

"I want to give you something," he said.

"What?" she said, breathing hard, her forehead moist with sweat.

"But first," he said, "I want you to take these off too."

He let his forefinger wander beneath the waistband of her panties and tugged them just a little.

"You do?"

He nodded.

"Why?"

"Because I want you completely naked when I give this to you."

"You do?" she repeated, looking into his eyes searchingly.

"Yes," he said.

She reached down and tugged off her panties, kicking them off the bottom of the bed. She had two conflicting feelings: one of final arrival at the place she was most supposed to be in the universe and, at the same time, a feeling of grave concern about what would happen next.

He leaned over the edge of the bed, reached into the pocket of his jeans, and grabbed the small gray felt bag containing the pendant. He lay down next to her again and said, "Close your eyes."

She slid next to him so that her body lay against his, all the while looking into his eyes. When right up against him, she closed her eyes as he had requested.

With his right hand, he stroked up the inside of her thigh again and rested his finger just there, just above the center of the center, and she shifted to allow him, causing a shudder of pleasure to course through her. With his left hand, he placed the bag below her navel.

Her hands were free, and without moving his hand from that place, she reached down and grabbed the bag.

"What is it Mick?"

"Look inside."

She pulled the diamond pendant out of the bag and held it up to the light. The diamond seemed enormous to her, sparkling magnificently in the light from the street.

"It's a real diamond," he said.

McMick realized that he now understood the secret of the entire universe. It all came down to this. Terri was not just the most beautiful girl who had ever walked the earth, she was actually the portal to another universe, another world. The gateway was through her beautiful body. Terri was an ancient goddess, her body the magical barrier between the two worlds. The other world was an infinite paradise kingdom of pleasure and fulfillment and total bliss. It seemed that he had been on this quest for ten thousand years, maybe for an entire eternity, and now he stood at the brink of fulfilling the purpose not only of his present life, but of all the lives he had lived throughout all of time. McMick saw that the diamond pendant had talismanic power. It had magic that would allow him to reach the other realm. But it also required some secret incantation to go with it, and some other magical rite: There was still a part to the quest he had not solved.

Terri was enraptured. The pendant was by far the most beautiful gift anyone had ever given her. It could only mean one thing: Mickey loved her. Truly. What 17-year-old-boy would give a massive diamond to a girl that he did not love? Only one other gesture of love could be greater: *for him to kill himself.* It was, beyond doubt, the most impressive display of true love she could imagine, next to the dress he had bought her—the most thoughtful gift, under the circumstances, that she had ever heard of a boy giving a girl.

"Michael Shea, it's the most, most beautiful thing I've ever seen save for your own lovely face."

McMick smiled deeply, feeling like an arrow shot from a gigantic crossbow toward the other world.

Terri sat up and turned to face Mickey. She pushed him onto his back, putting the pendant over her head so it hung sparkling between her budding breasts. His painful excitement no longer seemed a distraction. It was simply a fact, a symbol of Mickey's enormous pulsating love for her.

She straddled him, grabbing his face between her small, soft hands, pouring kisses onto his lips. "Michael Shea," she said, "you don't know how much you mean to me."

She showered him with kisses, all over his face and chest and stomach and arms and hands. She came finally to his navel, and Helen's voice echoed in the back of her brain, *If you do that, you might as well let them fuck you in the church sanctuary.* She thought better of taking him in her mouth, and began to stroke him with her hand.

Under normal circumstances, a straight Mickey would have come quickly, but acid-infused McMick had other plans; he had asserted extraordinary control. A prolific masturbator, sometimes twice a day, Mickey loved to practice taking himself to the brink and then stopping, the way one might practice doing a bicycle trick. As a result, his self-control was already quite impressive for a boy of his age. At that moment, through some bizarre mind-body connection related to the fantasy of traveling to the other world through the gates of Terri, he had complete mastery over his orgasm. McMick would see Valhalla, no matter what it took.

Terri stroked and stroked, to no avail. She needed more lubrication. The whole experience—the way Mickey had touched her, their nakedness, his arousal, his extraordinary gift to her—had made her tingling, wet and wanting deep within. Dripping all over Mick's thighs, she felt about to go over a cliff. Did it not make sense to rub him there, right there where she wanted him to touch her most? But would that not lead exactly where she said they were not going? Helen was right: *This is so difficult.*

She studied Mickey from head to toe; he seemed to be in another world, in a frightening state. He now appeared to her as a monumental problem, a ticking time bomb, a puzzle that had to be solved right then or something just awful would happen, like maybe he would explode or something. She had to solve the riddle right now, defuse the bomb, return the world to normalcy, and turn Mickey back into a person with whom she could talk and cuddle. This realization—that relieving him was the only kind thing to do, the only responsible thing to do—combined with her own now rushing sexual excitement, amounted to an inescapable conclusion: She would have to have him there and then.

Yet the thorny problem had disrobed itself completely: Her conclusion, that sex had become inevitable, meant she was going to graduate to a new level of sin. Everything up until this moment had just been the sin of lust—yes, they had been descending deeper and deeper and deeper (they had traveled as deep into lust as they could go, discovering its true outer limit, total lust immersion)—but they had still only committed the sin of lust. As Jesus said, if you look at someone lustfully, you've already done lust, so taking off all your clothes and stroking them, well, it's just more lust, that's all. Now they were going to graduate to fornication, out-of-wedlock sex, and this was a more advanced level of mortal sin. Professional almost. They were inching closer and closer to eternal damnation.

Another serious problem came to mind. If she was going to have sex with Mickey, she needed him to confirm his love for her verbally. *You never should have sex with a boy who doesn't say he loves you out loud and with clear diction.* She felt sure of that; it was like elementary arithmetic or learning to spell three-letter words like 'cat.' Even if the boy had proved it other ways, he still had to say it clearly, to make it legal, like a sort of pre-marriage. She felt sure that if the boy professed his love, less sin would come from having sex with him because it opened a possible road to marriage, even if the whole map was not yet clear. Plus, if the boy said he loved her, then it was not *only* about the lusts of the flesh, which she could see now were completely and hopelessly overwhelming. Professing love would make the sex be a simple expression of that love, the kind of that love that Jesus said one should feel for everybody, even enemies. So the love part could mix with the lust part and reduce the overall sin level resulting from the sex, like drinking liquor with something healthy. *Like fruit juice.*

Deep within his acid trip, McMick could sense Terri's internal confusion and struggle. He realized that he was confronting the crisis of his quest. The goddess Terri planned to ask him a question, a puzzle question, like how many hairs are on the head of bald man, or what kind of shoes does a man with no feet buy? If he answered the question correctly, McMick would march triumphantly through the pleasure gates of Terri into paradise. If not, he would wither at the inter-world portal, his quest doomed for all eternity.

"Mick, is there something that you…"

Her own desire overwhelmed her, making it difficult for her to think or talk.

"Mick, you're so quiet, can you talk to me? Can you say… something?"

McMick was stymied. What could it be that he was supposed to say? Was it 'Rumpelstiltskin' or 'Eeny meenie chillie beenee'?

"Mickey, I want to give you something very special, just like you gave me this," said Terri, fingering the pendant, "but I need to, to, know whether you… I just want to hear you, Mickey… talk to me, I feel like you're… somewhere else."

McMick was having a serious mental block. What magic incantation was he supposed to utter? McMick now felt a sense of panic; the whole mission was in jeopardy!

McMick now saw that he had no choice: He had to wake up the brain between Mickey's ears to get some help. His other brain had been locked in a dank jail cell behind McMick, near—if not actually inside—Mickey's butt. That brain felt very glad to see his McMick toss the keys to the cell through the bars. Within a few seconds, his main brain lurched out of confinement and staggered up through his body toward his head. When that main brain reached the eyeballs, it struck up a bargain with McMick. They had to work as a team now. It was possible, after all, for a man to think with both his real brain and his… other brain… simultaneously, and then they could pass through the pleasure gates of Terri into nirvana together. McMick agreed. He had done an excellent job of getting them this far, and now this band of brothers— the two of them—had to put aside their differences and work together.

Terri looked at Mickey, who had been lying back with his eyes closed in an erotic trance. His eyelids fluttered. He looked at her.

"Mick?" she said softly, still holding him in her little hands.

"Oh, oh Terri," he said, moaning. Hearing the sound of his own voice further awoke the Brain Between My Ears. This usual brain had now asserted its dominance and told McMick to stand back and watch, which McMick did with grudging admiration and wonder about the feat that Mickey's Brain Between My Ears was about to perform by solving the devious non-riddle of the Terri-pleasure-portal goddess.

"Teresa I love you. I love you. I've never felt this way before in my life, you're so beautiful, but it's not just that."

He paused.

"I love… I even loved it when you puked on me, Terri. It's one of my favorite memories. And when you drooled on me and vomited on me again."

He paused yet again, thinking, searching for words.

"And I'd take a hundred beatings from every member of your family just to hold your hand. I'd love you even if they ripped the skin off my body."

That felt very true to both Mickey and McMick.

"You're everything to me. You're the stars in the sky, you're the waves in the ocean, you're the mountains, and the trees… you're my dreams, Teresa. It's like I said before… I've laid… I've laid my dreams at your feet."

McMick was thunderstruck. Clearly these were the exact special magic words that the epic moment required and only the everyday brain could possibly have come up with them. McMick had been right to trust his other brain after all. Now they watched together as the mountains moved before them. They felt the earth tremble, the walls of something came tumbling down around them, the clouds parted and the sun—warm and brilliant—burst through. Mickey did not know Beethoven's Ninth Symphony by name, but this very music, the tenor's Turkish March from the fourth movement—a piece he had heard his father play dozens of times during their oft-repeated seven-hour drive from Brooklyn to Boothbay, Maine—now played in his head as his two brains danced together somewhere between his eyes and his McMick.

> Froh, wie seine Sonnen fliegen
> Durch des Himmels Pra'cht'gen Plan,
> Laufet, Bru"der, eure Bahn,
> Freudig, wie ein Held zum Siegen.

Terri was overwhelmed with what he said to her. It started with calling her Teresa instead of Terri. And how he had said he would love her even if her whole family beat him again and again and actually flayed him alive. Well, it was pure poetry. She needed no further encouragement and responded not with words, but by gently placing him into what felt like her very soul. She felt completely charged, liquid, buzzing and humming in the most intoxicating and gratifying way.

She felt him meet her barrier, and now, in addition to overwhelming physical and emotional arousal, she felt pressure and pain. A moment of ultimate truth. She knew this was something profound that she had to pass through, like being born, giving birth and, eventually, death. She was determined to face this, confront it head on, just the way she could meet the devil himself head-on if she knew she had Jesus by her side. Still sitting on top of Mickey, she put her right hand behind his head and pulled him up to change the angle of his entrance into her. She put her forehead right on his and looked straight into his face. His eyes were closed.

"Mick, look at me, look at me now," she whispered with intensity. "Look at me, my love." She said this the way a quarterback might talk to his receiver in the huddle before a big play.

Mickey opened his eyes as she started to push him against her.

He felt her soul entering him through her eyes in exactly the way he was physically entering her. She was breaking through some bloody barrier between their souls just as he was physically breaking through the portal into the infinite space that was Teresa. And he knew it would be painful in an overwhelmingly meaningful and eternally satisfying way.

"Mick," she cried. "Mick, it hurts, Mick."

It struck him the way she said his name, just like when she felt sick, the first time her bare ass had straddled him, months ago—like he was her best friend in the world. She was not asking him to stop; she was not even asking for his help—she was just sharing the pain with him because she knew how much he cared. In whimpering "Mick, it hurts" while she looked right into his eyes, he thought she had wrapped those words around his heart in the most loving way one person could wrap something painful around another person.

He saw tears form in her eyes and suddenly felt a powerful surge of unexpected emotion and tenderness rush up from within, seemingly flowing from his soul's origin, as if he had accidentally tapped into the purest reservoir of love in his spirit. His throat tightened and tears welled up in his own eyes and one rolled down his cheek. He... loved her. He loved her more than life itself.

Keeping her forehead pressed tightly against his, she put her right hand over his heart, so she could feel it beat, and she moved her left hand down around his hip, pulling him toward her in one final, intense, steadily increasing thrust that broke through. As he entered her, she cried out in pain, a primal cry combining the most human, paradoxical and ironic mixture of pain and pleasure, of fear and desire, and also of innocent love. Her cry at the moment of this break was the dearest sound that he had ever heard in his life.

And they held a moment, right as she pushed him through her, in which he observed a single tear fall from her eye, and saw the whole world psychedelically reflected in that tear, and especially, the two of them locked in the most passionate embrace he imagined that the world could have ever known. This image of her tear, as it appeared in Mickey's acid-inflamed mind—of her total beauty reflected in it as well as the image of his entering her—and the feeling of her breaking through at the same moment into his innermost being, was something he would never forget in his entire life and something he would think about at the very moment he died.

Mickey felt his two brains combine in a healing and strengthening way, as if some fundamental fracture in his soul had been restored permanently. Entering her, he felt a sense of arriving at the true meaning and significance of life and death. Through her, he was encountering the mystery of the other world. Teresa was a goddess, but she was also just the girl Terri he knew, both the infinite and the finite, wrapped into one being.

Terri noticed that she had bled on Mickey, but the pain receded, pleasure slowly transcending it. As he moved beneath her, she knew that she was about to fly burning over the cliff and fall. He was leading her to the jumping-off place with confidence. But she had one task left to accomplish before she threw herself into oblivion: to bring Mickey to Jesus. She knew this was the only way to save her mortal soul and his, to somehow make faith rise from the ashes of this incredible fiery freefall of fornication.

She pressed her forehead to his again, opening her eyes.

"Oh Mick… Mick," she said, calling to him. "Look at me," she whispered, as if she were going to perform a magic spell on him.

He opened his eyes again. This time he knew that she was already deep inside his head. She seemed to be talking to him not from her mouth but through her body, via the portal connecting the two of them.

He looked into her but had the strange impression that he was only looking backward into his own being.

"Mick, I need you to know that Jesus loves you and he wants you to be with him in paradise," she whispered to him breathlessly.

When she said this, for the first time Mickey saw Jesus in his role as the one true God of all creation. He saw Jesus waiting for him in the other world, the one on the other side of the portal. He knew that in Valhalla, Terri served as Jesus' goddess. Now she would lead him to this paradise and they would be together with Jesus forever.

"Teresa," he said in a hoarse whisper as he thrust again and again inside her, "Teresa," he gasped, "I believe you."

He looked at the diamond pendant bouncing between her girlish breasts and erect nipples, watching it sparkle in the street light's reflection.

Within the twinkles of the gem he saw an image of Jesus on the cross unlike any crucifix he had seen in his more than a decade of Catholic education. Completely naked, this Jesus had battle scars—deep wounds and cuts on his arms and legs. Bound to a stone cross with ropes, rather than nailed to a wooden one, this Jesus had a spear wound like the Jesus he knew. But unlike any Jesus he had ever seen, this one held a bloody sword in his right hand and a raven sat on his shoulder. Jesus awoke, fully coming back to life after being dead, and began to pull against the ropes binding him to the stone. The raven flew off him; he snapped the cords holding his muscular arms and then kicked off the ropes binding his legs. He had arisen and, separating himself from the stone, walking out of the diamond pendant and into the air between Mickey and Terri as Mickey thrust and thrust.

About the size of Queen Mab when she had flown around the party, the little spirit Jesus stretched and looked out of the bedroom window at the bright moon. He howled like a wolf—a long, impassioned and soulful howl that said to Mickey, 'I'm alive!'

The miniature Jesus then looked him dead in the eye and spoke in a deep and commanding voice, thick with an Irish brogue:

"Michael Shea! The way? Ay am da way! The trut? Ay am dat. And da life too, dat am ay! Now me boy, can ya come on your own? Yah can't! No, not a single solitary soul, and most especially not your sorry Irish arse, can come to me fadder. Yah can't come but troo me."

Building toward a cosmic orgasm, Mickey responded, gasping, to the floating image of Jesus by saying, "Jesus Christ, Jesus, oh Je-sus." Terri took Mickey's words not as a taking of the Lord's name in vain by one approaching an epic climax, but rather as a follow-on ratification to Mickey's profession of faith, almost as a prayer. She responded in turn, "Oh yes, oh yes, Mick, Jesus, Jesus."

As Mickey launched himself from the summit, he saw Queen Mab herself deep inside him, delivering an impassioned speech to the army of millions and millions of sperm about to cannon into the other world. He saw that each sperm was a fairy—but not just any fairy. Each was a fiery little angel armed to the teeth for battle with buck knives and .38s and wrist-rockets and nunchucks, and they were not just warriors, they were also poets and scientists and priests as well as warriors. He saw that Queen Mab—the Queen of Angels—acting on behalf of Jesus, had given to each angel his own personal, unique dream. He saw that the millions and millions of dreams were the animating, quickening power in the universe, and that the universe without these dreams would be like a creature without blood beating in its veins, without a life force. Mab had worked each of these angels into an orgasmic battle frenzy, so each one violently burned with life, ready to blaze forth like a billion fighter pilots, like a billion rockets, like a billion ignited M-80s with barely a fuse left on any one.

Terri heard Mickey gasp, saw him shudder deeply, saw him extend his hands and grab both of hers, felt him pull her to the edge of the precipice, and she flung herself by his side with utter abandon, with unrestricted, uncompromising and all-forgiving love, the love that hopes all things, bears all things, endures all things—the love that never fails—as oceans surged through them both and through every inch of her legs, up through her hard nipples, and up through her tongue into her throat, ears, eyes, nose and mouth.

As he felt Terri follow him, at the peak of his acid trip, Mickey saw a nuclear flash of light emanate from the place where they were joined, a wave engulfing them both; he knew in the blinding heat that Terri's soul had been blasted and infused into his own, so now they would forever be one and the same, no matter how far apart they might be. And he knew, from this moment on, that his mind and heart were completely and forever hers.

CHAPTER 13

Mab's Moose

A t the very moment Terri collapsed onto Mickey in a warm puddle of blood, sweat, arousal and semen, Helen tugged on Nando's sleeve as he stood in the kitchen, drawing himself another beer from the keg.

"Nando?"

He spun around. "Helen, you made it!" he said, beaming.

"Yeah, I, um, can you come with me a second?"

"Sure," he said, following her out of the kitchen and into the hallway. They headed into the small vestibule where the elevator came up. There were only two apartments on the floor, one where the party was blaring facing the park, and the back one belonging to someone else. They stood in the empty vestibule as Helen pulled the door to Aunt Sheila's apartment closed behind them.

"Hey," said Nando, "it's really noisy in there, huh? I'm really glad you came."

Helen had a worried expression on her face.

"I've, I've got a problem. I… I've got a question for you."

"What?"

"Well, um—Terri isn't here, is she?"

Nando did not know what to say. He had seen Terri, but only for a minute; he suspected that she was not supposed to be there without Helen. He did not want to get her and Mickey in trouble. He had not seen either of them for 45 minutes.

"I… just got here a while ago," he said. "I'm not sure. I don't know where Mick is right now, maybe you should go ask him."

"I would, but I've, um, I couldn't see him, no one can find him," said Helen.

"Well, just come in and have a beer," said Nando. "If Terri's here, I'm sure you'll see her soon." He smiled at her again, feeling a little buzzed.

"Is Mariel here?"

"Mariel? No, no she's not." He tried to read her expression.

"Oh," said Helen. She seemed disappointed and happy at the same time.

"Oh, damn," she said.

"What is it? What's up?"

"I don't know how to say this, so I just will: I have Charlie down in the lobby, and I want to make sure, and he does too, that it's OK to come in."

Nando frowned.

"His… um… ah… whew," said Helen, trying to explain. "His dad had a heart attack on Tuesday, and he's only here today, and he asked me to visit his dad with him at the hospital, and Terri was with us, and…."

She paused, looking at Nando. He looked irritated and slightly injured, like someone had just stepped on one of his toes.

"I'm sorry," she whispered. "Charlie's really depressed, and I just couldn't say no, and we're trying to work out some stuff…. I couldn't think of anywhere else to come, and Mickey did invite me and Terri, and we lost Terri at the hospital, and I thought, maybe, I thought Terri might be here. But I don't want, I mean, I don't, we, uh, we can't have another fight, can we?"

They stared at each other in silence for a few moments.

"Nando, will you help me? I can't leave him down there. He's really sorry about what happened just like you and Mick are."

Nando grunted. "I heard his dad was in the hospital. Mick told me."

Helen nodded.

"Is he really sick?"

Helen nodded again. "He might die."

"Ah, fuck."

Helen stared at him expectantly.

152

"Wait here," said Nando. He went back into the apartment and returned five minutes later with Mickey's brother Eugene, all 250 pounds of him in a very good mood.

"So Charlie's downstairs?"

Helen nodded.

But not your Uncle Sean?" Eugene gave a big belly laugh.

Helen smiled and shook her head.

"Well, I don't know where Mick is right now, but I know he's forgotten all about it. He doesn't want to fight Charlie—Mick's in love with your little sister, but don't tell him I said so!" He laughed again.

"If Charlie'll behave himself and not cause any trouble, he's welcome. No need to say anything."

"He's forgotten about it too," said Helen, "and he's going to apologize to Nando."

Nando glared. "That's OK. I mean, I'm the one who knocked out his tooth. But I'm not apologizing for that, OK? 'Cause he was beatin' the shit out of Mick."

"Never mess with Nando, that's what I say!" laughed Eugene. "Not unless you want to be eating his foot and rolling on the floor in agony!" He laughed again and pounded Nando on the back.

"Thanks," said Helen.

Eugene grabbed her arm. "And you tell Charlie that the Shea family wishes the best to him and his dad and the rest of his clan."

"Thanks," repeated Helen to Eugene.

He went back into the party, leaving Helen and Nando alone.

"Thanks Nando." She took his hand, just the way he had taken hers that night in Long Beach. She caught his eyes. "I really mean it. Thank you."

Then she let him go, looked at the ground feeling terribly awkward and pressed the button for the elevator.

Pissed off, Nando spun around and walked back into the apartment. He felt like leaving the party right away. On the other hand, the way she had grabbed his hand, and the way she had apologized… he wanted to see what was going on between her and Charlie. Seeing them would provide important information. It might be painful but he would be able to see what was really happening between them. He felt so angry, as though he wanted to break something valuable, or fight someone dangerous and powerful, where he might get really hurt in the battle. A ragged agitation raked through the nerves in his gut, seeming to pump anger down his arms to his fists, which he clenched and relaxed, trying to reassert emotional control. He felt alert and violent.

He knew that he had to calm himself down somehow. He had no right to be angry with her, he rationalized. There was nothing, absolutely nothing between them. They were in a play together—nothing more. The time had come to separate fantasy from reality. He found an empty, dimly lit seat in the corner of the main party room, away from where the throng was rocking to Meatloaf's *Bat Out of Hell.* Unnoticed amid the noisy revelry, he sat quietly thinking, quietly watching, quietly waiting.

Back in cousin Kate's bedroom, Terri had used her moist panties to clean the blood and semen and other bodily fluids from herself and Mickey. Then she had rinsed and wrung them out in the bathroom. She felt so glad to have packed some fresh ones in her bag. She surveyed Mickey and smiled. He looked normal again, much more like Michelangelo's David statue. Mickey in a state of arousal… she giggled to herself remembering the unbelievable transformation; it was scary to think of it.

Mickey seemed to be in a stupor. She had lain on top of him, he still inside of her, for about 10 minutes. She almost fell asleep. She felt so close to him now.

She put on her clean panties and wriggled back into her tights.

"Mick, I've got to go."

"Go where?"

"I've got to go home. I'm not even supposed to be here, remember?"

He looked confused.

"I left Helen at the hospital with Charlie, remember? I told you about his dad."

"Oh yeah," murmured Mickey, a thousand miles away.

He pulled on his socks and went over to the window, looking out at the park. The moon beamed brightly in the night sky.

She came up behind him and put her arms around his waist. Standing on her tiptoes, she whispered in his ear, "You've got a cute ass, Michael Shea, but you need to put your clothes back on. Will you walk me to the subway?"

Mickey stared deeply into the middle of Central Park, looking for something.

"Mick, are you OK?"

She had fixed her dress and checked her makeup in the bedroom mirror. She was ready to go.

She could see Mickey putting on his sneakers, but he had not put on his underwear or jeans yet.

"Mick?" She started to giggle. "Mick, how 'bout your pants?"

Mickey had found a pink sweatband that belonged to Kate, put it on, and now wore nothing but his sweatband and running shoes.

"I've got to go hunting," he said.

"Did you say hunting?"

"Yeah, hunting, we're going to shoot a moose with a bow and arrow, me and Ricky."

Terri giggled uncontrollably.

"Mick, you're such a hoot. What're you doing? You're mad."

He had wandered into the other bedroom, coming back with a roll of cash and the hunting bow Ricky had given him.

"Terri, you'll need this to get back to your castle."

"My castle?"

"You know where it is, don't you?"

He stuffed the cash into her bag.

"Mick, what are you doing? I have money for the subway, I don't need any— Mick, what is that?!"

She stared at the hunting bow he had hung over his shoulder so the string fell at an angle across his broad chest, along with a sack of arrows.

"It's my bow," he said, "what I'm going to shoot the moose with. Rick put a bullseye on his head for me."

"Mick, have you lost your mind?"

He hoisted her into the air, his left hand behind her back, his right under her knees, like a fireman carrying a child out of a burning building.

"Mick, you don't have your pants on."

"I don't wear pants when I hunt," he said, looking at her seriously.

"What? Mick wait, Mick, what are you doing, Mick? … Put me down Mick, OK?"

She continued to try talking to him as he opened the doorway to the hall and carried her out to the vestibule, and called the elevator. By a miracle they did not see anyone until they were on the street. He carried her to the corner and stood out on Fifth Avenue. People started staring at them and pointing. Terri told herself that Mickey had decided to play some kind of funny joke. He walked over to an empty cab stopped at the corner of 93rd and Fifth, placed her gingerly in the passenger seat and kissed her again on the lips.

"Mick," she whispered, giggling but now also worried. "Mick, would you go back inside and put your clothes on? You're going to get arrested!" She paused and stared at him, taking note of the intense, wild expression in his eyes, like he was running to catch a football. She grabbed him by the hair and pressed her forehead to his one more time, with her eyes closed so she could listen intently. "Mick, tell me again."

At that moment in Mickey's acid brain, it seemed that he had placed her into a flaming chariot. He believed that Terri was a minor but influential goddess of the other world beyond the pleasure portal, as well as just being herself, and he had a hunting quest now to perform, which had to do with capturing a moose with a bullseye on his head in order either to fulfill or avoid some ancient prophesy—he was not sure which. The moose had gigantic antlers and needed to be added to Queen Mab's herd. He did not know why, but believed that fate and continued good fortune required it, that he should do this task alone if necessary. Immediately.

"I love you," he whispered to her in his sandpaper voice. "I love you more than anything or anyone." He paused. "I'd die for you, Teresa." His eyes were red and far off.

"Don't die for me, Mick, just, please, go and put your pants on!" She searched his face. "And meet me tomorrow for church, OK Mick? Come to Queen of Angels at 5:30? On Skillman Avenue. Promise?"

"Angel of Queens," he said, "you're the Angel of Queens. I'll be there," and slammed the car door.

The cab driver shook his head in disbelief. *Naked kid wearing a pink sweatband, carrying a bow and arrow.* Not the craziest thing he had ever seen, but certainly high up the list. *New York, wacko town.*

"Where to?"

"Hold on," said Terri, as she opened her bag and looked at the roll of 20s that Mickey had stuffed in, at least $500, the most cash she had ever seen in her life. Where did he get it from? She looked out the cab window, but he was gone.

"Sunnyside," she said. "Take me to the subway at 46th and Queens Boulevard."

Terri had decided to wait for a train to arrive at the Sunnyside station near home and then walk back from the subway stop. No one should see her get out of a cab. She took off the diamond pendant and put it in her bag under the cash.

She leaned back in her seat and sighed. And smiled.

Nando watched Helen sitting next to Charlie, who had his arm around her. Nando's mood grew blacker as each minute passed. Helen had kissed Charlie three times. Three times! In public! Knowing Nando was sitting out there in the party! Knowing that he had been waiting for her. He felt like a gigantic fool.

And where had Mickey gone? He had been right. Why had he bothered with Helen and why had he left Mariel in Brooklyn? Nando stewed. *Fuck, in this mood I'd rather be alone than with Mariel.* Having her there would just have distracted him from his misery. And what if she had been there? She would be all coked up, stoned and drunk and, like Mickey, probably on an acid trip. Where had they gotten to, Mickey and Terri?

It was good that Mickey was not there, anyway, he thought. Mickey on acid could be such a pain in the ass. The last time he had dropped acid... holy shit, thought Nando, remembering. He had run down the subway tracks at Washington Square and almost got flattened. He had carried on and on about the treasure on the tracks, how a suitcase sat out in the tunnel full of cash and drugs and dynamite. Mickey on acid was a fucking nightmare that went on for hours and hours with his overactive imagination. If he turned up in the middle of a trip, Nando would just leave. Anything would be better than watching Charlie talking to Helen and kissing her.

Fuck his apology, too, thought Nando.

"Hi Ferdinand," he had said. "I just wanted to say I've got no hard feelings about what happened, you know, last spring, at Mick's place in Long Beach. I mean, I know you were just trying to break up the fight, and things got out of hand. I'm sorry 'cause we never should have let it go like that." Charlie kept glancing at Helen, who had obviously put him up to it.

"Nothin' to be sorry about," said Nando. "Mick's my friend and I never let anybody kick his ass without kicking theirs."

"Yeah, um, well, I just wanted to make sure we're cool now, you know, you and I."

"Yeah, don't give it a thought. Don't fuck with Mick, I won't fuck with you, OK? Then we're cool," said Nando, giving Charlie a hard stare and wishing for conflict. Nando just ignored Helen completely, like she was invisible.

Charlie had held out his hand and, after a moment, Nando shook it reluctantly.

He felt thoroughly disgusted with the whole situation. Nothing burned him more than phony manners. Better if Charlie had just spat at his feet and said, "Stay away from Helen." At least that would have been honest.

Or would it? Maybe Charlie did not even sense anything between them. *And maybe there isn't anything. I'm gonna get the fuck outta here.*

Ziggy Stardust boomed from the living-room stereo, the place now loaded with drunk and stoned teenagers. Mickey was missing. It was definitely time to go, concluded Nando for the 10th time in half an hour.

Then he heard someone yelling over the sound of the music. It sounded like Eugene saying, "Turn it down, turn it the fuck down!"

Someone cut the stereo, and then he heard some confused muttering and saw Ricky moving to the gigantic windows in the living room facing the park.

"Look there, oh my Christ…. Gene, is that Mick?"

Eugene stood next to him, peering out the window into Central Park. Ricky pointed to a group of trees just inside the park wall.

A long silence took hold of the group as they stared.

"What the fuck!" grunted Eugene. "That fuckin' chucklehead. Now I've seen every fuckin' thing. Every single fuckin' thing! What in the name of fuck is he doing up there?"

"Oh my Jesus," said Ricky, "he's got the bow. Look, Gene, he's got the bow."

"Nah… Nah… It can't be."

"Yes it fuckin' can. Right there, look, it's over his shoulder."

"Jesus Christ."

"And he's all bare-assed."

"Jesus fuckin' Christ."

They continued staring and now a group had gathered at the window, including Charlie and Helen.

Eugene opened the window on the side of the room and leaned out.

"Mick, what the fuck are you doing?"

Nando's curiosity overcame his jealousy; he walked over and peered out the window next to Eugene.

Mickey sat high inside a tree with the hunting bow, naked except for his running shoes and a pink sweatband. Nando had to laugh. This was a surprising level of insanity—even for Mickey.

"Mick, come back here!" yelled Eugene.

The rest of the crowd watched with a mixture of confusion and amusement.

Nando leaned over to Eugene and whispered in his ear, "Three tabs of acid."

Eugene shot him a look.

"Oh fuck," he said.

Eugene called Ricky over.

"He's trippin', Rick, on acid. Did *you* bring it?"

Ricky shook his head. "Never touch the shit."

They formed a plan to get him, gathering up the least drunken of them. Eugene included Charlie because he was cold sober, the only completely straight one in the group.

"We might have to catch him if he falls," said Eugene, "and he's big and solid, it'll be like catchin' a fuckin' sack of hammers."

By the time they got downstairs and crossed the street to the park, Mickey had vanished from the tree. They jogged toward the reservoir, scanning the park for any sign of him. When they reached the water, Nando took charge.

"I think he's going around the reservoir—I'll follow the path downtown. Ricky—you and Eugene go uptown and we'll meet on the other side. One of us will find him."

Nando had intentionally left Charlie out of the plan. Sensing that Nando did not want company, Charlie followed Eugene and Ricky as they started to jog slowly around the reservoir, heading north.

Running downtown at a good clip along the reservoir path, Mickey had enjoyed only about a three-minute lead. The moonlight and cool air made his naked body feel alive. He imagined himself to be a primitive hunter running through a wild forest on a nighttime hunt.

To his right, the reservoir looked like a black mirror reflecting a glittering necklace of city lights. The lights reflected in the water seem to swirl and swim, like an animated van Gogh painting. He felt that the ground and reservoir and glow of the city and rustling trees were all parts of a massive living being guiding him toward his prey—the moose with the giant antlers. He had the bow in one hand and the sack of arrows in the other.

He passed a few vagrants and several brave (or stupid) evening joggers, but he ignored them completely, focusing on his quest. Before long he peeled off along a path leading to open grounds behind the Metropolitan Museum of Art. The grass had worn away in spots and he could smell dust rising into his nostrils. He felt the need to kick off his sneakers and did. He tore off the pink sweatband to stand completely naked, carrying only the bow and arrows. He continued out into the empty field, where he could see by the distant glow from the far-off streets and moonlight.

At first he could see nothing, but then it became visible in the shadows. He sensed a guardian to yet another world, one that lay beyond the pleasure world that he had entered through the portal that Terri had opened for him.

Large and white as bones, its skin formed a stark contrast with the blackness, as if it had broken into the night from a place beyond it. It was the most fantastic moose he had ever seen, at least 10 feet high at the shoulders, with massive strange antlers—also 10 feet wide—that seemed like a gigantic pair of crossed and upturned hands with sharp claws pointing up and menacing the heavens. Between the antlers, which seemed to Mickey like the wings of a dragon, it had a bleached skull rather than a face. Painted on the forehead of the skull a kind of bull's eye appeared—not exactly a bull's eye, but a circle with a five-pointed star in the middle.

He knew that he was reaching the highest point of his acid trip, but did not feel like he had conjured the creature in his imagination. He felt rather that the acid had allowed him to see the world in a different way—more clearly—than he could have with his straight brain. The acid had revealed something there all along behind reality.

They stood for a long while, in a mind lock, Mickey and the moose.

The beast communicated with him using telepathy, thinking in iambic pentameter, with one point of the star on the skull's forehead lighting up on each iamb.

> From where you come, or go to, no one knows,
> Though come you have, and go you will, and soon,
> The sun, arisen joyful, falls in woes,
> Your soul toward midnight flies from morn and noon;
>
> Your fuse is lit; your timer's ticking down,
> The final couplet rhymed before the start,
> The bull's eye's shot before the arrow's flown,
> And numbered are the beatings of your heart;
>
> You dream beyond this wound-up, wounded world,
> Of worlds from which this world can be erased,
> You dream of times before the fates unfurled,
> Of roads down which your steps can be retraced.
>
> I guard the path to fantasies from facts,

All those who pass must cross through bloody acts.

In response to Moosian poetry, Mickey felt that he should shoot an arrow into the middle of the skull star, and so he loaded an arrow into the bow and drew back the bowstring. As he took aim, the moose spoke telepathically again, this time with a Maine accent.

"A great huntah, I see."

Mickey responded out loud.

"I'm gonna put this arrow right through your fuckin' skull."

"Look before you shoot, or you might hit yourself in your own ass!"

Mickey paused, squinting into the void.

Sure enough, there in the middle of the pentagram on the skull head, words had appeared: "Mick's Ass."

"That isn't funny," said Mickey. "I don't give a shit, I'm gonna put this arrow through your pixie moose brain, right now. Then you can read me some more moose poetry with an arrow stickin' out of your fuckin' skull."

He let the first arrow fly and it missed the moose entirely.

"Nice shot, Mick, can't even hit your own ass. Come over and kiss me. Never French-kissed a moose before, have you?" asked the creature.

Mickey felt frustrated. He took a few steps toward the moose and reloaded his bow.

The moose's skull eyes began to glow red as Mickey felt the hair on his ass stand up.

"Better not miss this time, Mick, let me tell you, you're not the only one with a bow now, are ya?" said the moose in a threatening tone.

"Shut the fuck up, will you?" insisted Mick. "You're disturbing my concentration."

Mickey drew the bow again, trying to point the arrow carefully, but his arm started to shake and he lowered it. The tension on the bow was set too high to hold and aim for even a short while.

"Somethin' wrong with your *concentration,* Mick? Relax, I'm not in a hurry." said the moose.

In response to this, he drew the bow quickly and shot again. This time his arrow hit the moose in the shoulder.

The moose's skull eyes continued to pulse red and a glow also showed from the place where the arrow stuck out of its chest.

"Nice job, Mick. Quite a shot. You're a fuckin' huntah after all, Mick. It should take me less than nine months to bleed to death."

Mickey felt a hand on his shoulder. His skin crawled, his heart skipped a beat and he whirled around. Nando stood there, breathing hard.

"Mick, you're stark naked man—Mick, you're gonna get gangbanged out here, man, come on. Jesus, we'll try to stay in the shadows till we get back to 93rd Street. Come on."

"You scared the shit out of me. Shhh," said Mick, pointing to the moose.

Nando looked where Mickey pointed, toward a large bush.

"I don't see anything," said Nando.

"You're fuckin' blind, it's a moose."

"Mick, there's nothing, come on man, this is so fucked up Mick, you're trippin' your brains out man. You've got to go home."

Nando grabbed him by the arm, but Mickey shook him off.

"It's the fuckin' moose of death. It's the fuckin' devil moose. I'm gonna kill that fucker before he kills me."

"Mick, relax man, relax, take it easy, OK? There's nothin' there. It's all in your head."

"He's guardin' the entrance to the dreamworld man, and he has this world all wound up and it's fucked—it's a fuckin' time bomb. I've got to get into the dream world so I can straighten this shit out. I'm takin' his dead moose devil carcass back to Queen Mab. It's him or me, Nando. You got it? It's him or me. Now are you with me?"

Nando looked at Mickey in the moonlight; his eyes were absolutely wild, darting all over the place, his forehead and chest liquid sweat.

"I'm with you, Mick, I'm your friend, OK? Now listen." He paused for emphasis. "Mick, there's nothin' there. You're shootin' arrows at the empty nothin', OK?"

Mickey grabbed Nando around the neck, pulled his face close and put his sweaty forehead on Nando's.

"Listen man, this is fuckin' life and death, you got it? Life and death, life and death, I need to know, if this fuckin' moose bastard kills me, will you do him for me, man—you have to kill him. Have you got your bowie? If he kills me, I want you to rip out his fuckin' throat. It's him or me man, him or me, have you got my ass, are you backin' me man? Don't leave me in my hour of need, don't leave me, don't leave me here. Look at those fuckin' dragon horns man, holy shit."

Nando grabbed Mickey's hand, stared into his wild eyes and said, "I've got your ass, man, if the moose comes and kills you, he's mine."

"Swear?"

"I swear it. Now come on now, let's go."

Mickey pushed Nando away and loaded another arrow in the bow.

"My demons are coming for you," said the moose, in telepathy.

Behind the moose, Mickey could see a figure running toward them in the shadows. He drew the bowstring as far as he could, aimed and shot again.

CHAPTER 14

Upon Waking

Terri sat at the kitchen table drinking warm milk with honey and McCormick vanilla extract. The deeply comforting warmth and taste were not enough to overcome the concern building just below her navel. The little hand approached midnight and her mother had been pacing between the small living room and kitchen for the last hour.

"Where do you suppose they got to? This isn't like Charlie and Helen at all. Why haven't they called? Well, I imagine he's very distracted with his father. I just hope it's not that Mr. Cunningham's taken a turn for the worse. Teresa, you are such a stupid girl, I can't believe you lost them in that hospital. Your head is empty as a beggar's belly. You could have had them paged, couldn't you?"

"I didn't think of it, Mom, I didn't want to bother them, they seemed to need to talk in private."

"Well, I imagine so, they haven't had much time over the last few months. I was beginning to think we'd seen the last of Charlie. He's such a smart boy. He has a straight back, like James does. Did he look well?"

"He looked tired."

"Well of course he did."

At 10 after midnight, the phone rang.

Mrs. Rafter darted into the kitchen and answered.

Terri heard Helen yammering through the phone line in a long stream.

"No, no," said Mrs. Rafter, "Teresa's here, she's been here since 10, she couldn't find you in the hospital. Yes, yes, she's a stupid girl."

More yammering from Helen.

"Oh my goodness! No!"

Another long pause.

"What is this world coming to? I'd never believe it! Did they catch him?"

Yammer yammer.

"Mother of Mercy, that's the most horrible thing I've heard. Have they released him? Is he going to be alright?"

Terri wondered what in God's name had happened.

"How are you coming home, Helen? … Be careful, my pet. Be careful."

Mrs. Rafter hung up the phone and sat down in a heap of exhaustion at the kitchen table across from Terri.

"What a world it is! With an arrow, can you believe it? In the middle of Manhattan! Have you ever heard of such a thing? Savages! They're just savages!"

"With an arrow?" asked Terri, horrified. "What happened?"

"Charlie Cunningham. He and Helen were walking down Fifth Avenue from the hospital, nice as can be, and *thwack*! Shot with an arrow! Isn't that just strangest thing a body ever heard? What do you s'pose is next, scalping?"

"Oh my God," said Terri. "Um… where did it hit him? Is he all right?"

"Well, he's alive at least. He was hit somewhere in his leg I think. They went back to the hospital and the doctors took it out and gave him shots and Helen said he has a great big bandage now. He's all wrapped up and his mother and aunt came to get him. How awful! They're driving Helen home in a few minutes. As if they didn't have enough problems. First a heart attack, then shot with an arrow. Isn't that enough for one family, don't you think?"

Mrs. Rafter went on and on and on like this until finally James woke up, only to repeat the story again and again and again until Terri felt like screaming. Her mother sounded like a radio news announcer. James absorbed the story with great fascination and Terri imagined that he would be telling it for the rest of his life as his special most shocking and appalling tale: "The day Charlie Cunningham was shot with an arrow on Fifth Avenue."

"Mom, this is so *shocking*, I feel I just have to go to bed right away," said Terri.

"I understand, dear. I'll tell Helen not to wake you when she comes in."

Fat chance, thought Terri.

She could not sleep at all, wondering what had happened and unable to rid her mind of naked Mickey with a pink sweatband and his bow and arrow.

Helen came into their room after 1.

"I know you're awake," she whispered fiercely, standing at eye level next to Terri's bunk.

Terri opened her eyes and looked at Helen. She looked just awful: pale, tired and scowling.

"Well I hope you'll be all finished with him now," said Helen.

"With who?"

"I'll tell you with who: with that, that, oh, I just want to scream, Terri, I want to scream. Do you know what he did?"

"Helen, calm down, what who did?"

"What who did? What who did? Who do you think? Do you think I'm talking about Saint Patrick? Do you think I'm talking about Saint Francis of Assisi? Who do you think I'm talking about?"

"Mickey?" said Terri meekly.

"Michael Shea, your pet baboon, the wild animal, the rabid dog, the bloodthirsty wolf. Honestly, Terri, how can you let him kiss and paw you? He's, he's disgusting."

"What did he do, Helen?"

"He, he, he shot Charlie with an arrow."

Terri sat up, feigning bafflement.

"Why would he do that?"

"I don't know why! Am I a criminal psychologist? He took some drugs and it made him think Charlie was attacking him? But Charlie wasn't attacking him, was he? He was trying to help him. I don't know why! Why do morons do stupid things?"

"Why did Mickey need help?"

"Because he was running around all naked in Central Park, climbing trees and showing off his bare ass to everyone who was there to see it."

"Oh," said Terri. She did not know what to say.

"Well why did Charlie have to get involved?"

"How dare you! Why did he get involved? Because Eugene asked Charlie to get involved, and Charlie helped because he's a decent person and he didn't want Mickey to embarrass Xavier, or, or you! Because he knows you're—he knows that you and that beast were going together."

"How did Eugene come to see Charlie?"

Helen fumed inside. She had not been able to establish that Terri had been at the party at all. By now, Terri knew that Helen did not know she had been there, because if Helen knew, it would have been the very first thing out of her mouth.

Helen glared at her.

"So you went to Mick's party and left me wandering the hospital?" asked Terri.

Helen reasoned that there was no way Terri could have been at the party when she herself had been there for so long and not seen her. She also reasoned that Terri would not have let Mickey run naked through Central Park.

"I thought you were *there*," insisted Helen, drilling into Terri's face by the light from the street.

"But I wasn't," said Terri in a calculated half-truth. To her knowledge, they had not been at the party at the same time.

"No, you weren't," acknowledged Helen.

"Of all the places, I thought you were against taking Charlie there. Did you see Nando?"

"I did see him, and thank God Ferdinand was there to carry Charlie out of the park."

"Out of the park? I thought you were on Fifth Avenue."

"No, no, no. Oh my Jesus, what a night. They all chased Mickey into the park. He was having an LSD trip, climbing trees, running down paths, all naked and talking to himself. And the next thing I knew, Nando's carrying Charlie out of the park with an arrow stuck in his thigh. And he said Mickey shot him."

"What happened to Mickey? He's not in jail is he?" asked Terri, sounding alarmed.

"Who cares about Mickey? Did you even think to ask how Charlie is?"

"Mom already told me that Charlie's OK."

"Sure, if you call having a big unnecessary hole in your leg being OK," said Helen, sarcasm dribbling from her face.

"Helen, is Mick in jail?"

"I don't know where he is. He's probably in the zoo now. That's where he belongs. The others chased him after he shot Charlie."

"What's an LSD trip?" asked Terri.

"It's an evil drug that makes you see illusions and twists your brain all up like a cat's cradle. It gives you permanent brain damage and lowers your IQ in half so you become an idiot."

"It does not."

"Wait and see. Your boyfriend was already a half-wit, now he's less. He'll probably be tossed out of the play because he can't remember his lines."

"I don't see why you're angry with me, Helen. It's not my fault."

"It's your fault I got invited to the stupid party in the first place."

"It's not my fault you invited Charlie to come."

"Charlie and I were just starting to get along again. Now it's all ruined. He must think I'm cursed. Every time we're together he's struck by a tragedy—the Tragedy of Mickey Shea. First Nando knocks out his tooth and now this. How embarrassing for him… carried to the hospital by the boy who knocked his tooth out! It's all your fault for getting involved with that, that awful, awful, awful boy. He's a waking nightmare, Terri, I'm telling you. I hope you'll see now that you should never talk to him again."

"Isn't that a bit extreme, Helen?"

"Extreme? Oh yes, it's very extreme, let's wait till Mickey chops off somebody's head."

Terri turned quiet.

"That party, Terri, drugs everywhere. He's a drug dealer, Terri, do you know what that is?"

"Of course I do."

"Well, there it is. He's a criminal. He's an evil boy, Terri, evil as Satan himself."

"Helen, don't say that. Don't please."

"You can see the horns coming out of his head. He's got fangs."

"Helen, stop."

"He's probably sitting naked somewhere in the park now drinking the blood of a rotting dead animal."

"*Helen, stop it right now.*" Terri angrily spat the words at her.

Helen looked at her in amazement. "You're defending him? You're far gone, far, far gone, girl. He's got you all in his clutches. Look at yourself. What has he done to you? He's got inside that silly girl brain of yours and he's turning you mad like he is."

"Shut up, shut up, shut up, shut up."

Terri wanted to show her the gift that Mickey had given her, wanted to tell her all that had happened, that he had committed himself to Jesus now, but she dared not, knowing that it would come out terribly wrong. She felt completely alone.

"I will not shut up," said Helen. "I'm trying to protect you from a danger you're too stupid to see for yourself."

"I don't care what he did, Helen, I don't care at all."

"I can see that."

Terri did care, but she wanted Helen to stop more than anything. It seemed as though every condemnation of Mickey damned her as well. And she did not know what to think about the drugs. Mickey's behavior had been very strange. She thought he was being funny. But what if he had been on drugs the whole time? Would that mean that he did not really love her as he had said? Had she given her heart and her body to a fiend on a drug trip? *Would he even remember to come to church?*

She wanted to just throw herself into a dark pit and be buried alive.

The next afternoon, Terri asked her mother if she could go to the 5:30 Mass at Queen of Angels to say special prayers for the Cunningham family. She had whispered the request in her mother's ear when they were alone in the kitchen. How could Mrs. Rafter refuse such a modest and selfless request? She granted Terri permission, and also gave some errands to run on the way home.

She left early so she could walk slowly and think on the way. It had been a more than difficult day. Helen had given her the silent treatment, sitting all day doing her homework, with her nose stuck in her social-studies book preparing for a test on Monday.

During the Mass that morning, sitting with Stevie on her lap, the full gravity of what Terri had done began to weigh upon her. Like a rocket without fuel, she now spiraled in a free fall back to earth.

She had committed a mortal sin—she knew that—and she had also exposed herself to pregnancy; God forbid, she could not even imagine the possibility. How stupid could she have been, to think she could avoid sex with Mickey by lying naked with him and letting him touch her all over? She had been taken in by his gifts and seductive ways and by her own immature passions. She had given up her virginity to him while he had probably been zooming through a mental stratosphere somewhere. And where did he get all that money to give her five hundred dollars and a diamond? He did not have a regular job like pizza delivery or any other kind of work that Terri knew about.

And what about Mickey saying he believed in Jesus now? And that he loved her? *A boy would say anything to get sex, especially when you were sitting on top of him naked, holding his erection in your hand, wouldn't he? Of course he would. To trust what a boy said under those circumstances was ridiculous, wasn't it?*

She almost started to cry there in the middle of the street. Helen was right. She was a stupid, stupid girl. She wondered if Mickey would even come to the church. *Of course he won't.* Maybe he was in jail now? Maybe he was still on his trip? How long did a trip like that last? Hours? Days? She remembered one of her friends had a brother who got into a 'bad trip' from some drugs, then sat locked in his room for days before getting mental counseling. What if Mickey was all different now? What if he had landed in a hospital? What if he had hurt himself in the park, or if someone else had hurt him? What if he had become an imbecile, as Helen had said?

Helen was right about everything. Mickey was the kind of boy who her mother and father would not approve of. Did not approve of. If her father knew what she had done…. At the thought of his searing, explosive temper, she felt cold and small and shaky inside her belly. She remembered how once he had thrown James down the stone stairs outside their apartment for talking back to him. And after the Block X Ball…. She cringed as the moment flashed before her. He had slapped her so hard that it seemed her jaw could have flown right off her face.

There must be a way to crawl out of this black pit of sin. She planned how she would go to confession and do her penance—it would probably be a thousand Hail Marys. She wondered whether some sins were so great that the priest could not forgive them. *What if you were an apostate of Satan and you came into the confession booth and said you were murdering people in evil ritual? Could the priest forgive that? Could everything and anything be forgiven?*

How could she confess what she had done? There would have to be a euphemism. She imagined herself confessing:

'Bless me father for I have sinned. It's been three months since my last confession. I've gone too far with my boyfriend, and we've engaged in… things we shouldn't have.'

What if the priest said, 'Can you be more specific?' Terri guessed that she would have to tell the whole truth, otherwise she would fall into an infinite regress of sin from lying during confession. In that case, the confession itself would add to her sins rather than taking them away. But if the priest did not ask her to be specific, then could she get the whole sin forgiven, even though she never clearly stated and described it? *Why confess at all if you weren't sure your soul would be all wiped off? You had to expose all the smudges clearly, didn't you?*

But she had a deeper problem with her confession plan. *You really were not supposed to confess a sin unless you were truly sorry for it, right?* She had to be sorry in her heart and, deep within, she did not feel sorry at all. She had wanted to be with Mickey; it had felt so good and so right. If their having sex were not a terrible sin, her mind would have lingered on it and lovingly replayed it all day. It made her feel wet again just to let her mind wander through the memories of the way he had touched her. She loved Mickey more than ever. If he really loved her—if she could trust him—it would make her the happiest girl in New York. *How could you confess if you weren't really sorry?* This thought sat in her mind like a misshapen puzzle piece, throwing all the others out of joint, so they could not form a proper picture.

Helen had been right about Mickey. He had changed Terri. He had gotten inside of her heart and mind and body. Was he driving a wedge between her and Jesus? And what if she liked that wedge? Then was Mickey not just as evil as Helen had said?

That morning, when she had taken communion, she felt like an imposter. She knew that having sex with Mickey had injured her soul. This injury had to heal before she could be right with God. But she could not confess a sin that she wanted to commit all over again. So now she would be estranged from God. She could not have a proper confession unless she made herself truly sorry. Now it was God versus Mickey, and how could that ever be right? If God did not win, Terri would go to hell.

Was there not some way for God and Terri and Mickey to come to a truce? *But you don't make deals with God—that's what Father McLaughlin had said to the congregation. God has all the cards, and he knows all the ones you think you have but really don't.* When Terri read the Old Testament, though, it seemed like the Jews were making deals with God in every chapter. And what about the thief who stole heaven, didn't he make a deal for himself? Maybe not, because the thief had only asked Jesus to remember him when he got to heaven. Maybe she could make deals with Jesus, but not with God the Father? Surely she had to have a pure heart to make a deal and did not have that any more. Her heart had been mistakenly dropped into a sewer and now it had to be fished out and rinsed off.

As she walked up the stone steps into the church, she bit her lower lip, which had started to tremble as her eyes welled up. It was all so confusing. She kneeled in the last pew and buried her face in her hands and wept.

'Just pray,' she told herself, 'just tell God you're confused and he'll help you. You're not the first sinner he ever met.' She remembered Jesus' words in Luke. *And I say unto you, Ask, and it shall be given you; seek, and ye shall find; knock, and it shall be opened unto you.*

She prayed and cried and asked God to please help her feel real remorse, to be sorry in her heart as well as her head. She thought about how Jesus forgave adulterers and prostitutes and thieves, and she knew that she could be forgiven too, even though she loved Mickey and loved having sex with him more than anything she had ever done before.

As often happened when she prayed fervently, she felt the sweet breath of the Holy Spirit descend upon her, quieting her aching heart and troubled conscience. She felt the Holy Spirit telling her to trust God and put her life and future and soul into his hands. She could trust that, in her faith, God would make it work somehow, in some way beyond her limited capacity to know and understand.

171

She stayed like this for a long while, her face buried in her hands praying, lost in her private reverie, the Mass going on around her. She felt someone sit next to her and then kneel beside her. She looked up, and there was Mickey—he had come to be with her at Mass. More than surprised, she felt giddy and unsure. Her heart seemed to open and flutter inside her chest like a sparrow. She had never been so glad to see him. She felt that God must be talking to her in sending Mickey there by her side. *How else could I explain Mick's arrival, in the middle of my prayers?* It seemed as though God was saying to her, "Don't worry, Terri, don't cry, I can create love and goodness and joy from despair and hopelessness." God was telling her that he could transform Mickey's misguided heart.

She smiled at him. He put his hand down beside her and grinned. She let her hand fall by her side; he grabbed it, rubbing his thumb over her knuckles affectionately. She leaned over to him and whispered in his ear, "I love you, Mick." He drew her hand toward his mouth. Lowering his head, he kissed it.

Tears ran down her cheeks, and he gently wiped them away.

"What's wrong?" he whispered, looking worried.

"I thought you wouldn't come," she whispered back.

He nodded in understanding and squeezed her hand in a reassuring way.

They sat together quietly, listening to the service. Terri thought she could just sit there forever next to him. It made her feel still and calm and safe to be by his side, even though she felt all of his frightening wildness seething beneath his skin. He seemed like a huge guard dog, tame to her but a dreadful danger to everyone else. She let herself enjoy the moment with him, without thought or wonder or doubt about what would become of them next.

After Mass, they walked out into the street, into the fall evening light, ambling slowly toward Queens Boulevard. They felt a breeze that rustled the trees and blew dead leaves into the air. She could feel winter approaching like a plane flying in the distance.

"Are you OK, Mick?" she asked. "What happened last night?"

"Oh, aahh, I, ah, I fucked everything up," answered Mickey. "Took some drugs I shouldn't have. Took too much acid and it, uh, it whacked me."

His face turned red.

"I heard from Helen."

"Yeah," said Mickey with a combination of guilt and resignation.

"When did you take it?"

"Ah, shit.... Before you got there." He stared at the ground.

"Oh."

She looked at him, seeing that he felt stupid.

"When did it start to, to, to.... When did you start to feel it?"

"It got me while we were together, it was, uh, aaah, I started.... I was fuckin' flyin', Terri. I think I remember what happened, but I'm not sure if my mind is leaving out some stuff, you know?"

"Why, Mick? Why did you do that?"

"I uh, uh, aahh, I just... felt like taking a risk, like doing something crazy. I just wanted to take a big risk."

"Do you remember us being together?"

"Yeah," he stopped and squeezed her hand and pulled her toward him. He kissed her on the lips and put his arms around her and squeezed her to him. "I remember us. I remember us together. I remember everything."

They walked a little farther.

"Mick, you gave me all this money, and a diamond. I have to give them back to you."

"No."

"I don't want them. It's too, it's too much, Mick. Where did you get so much?"

"I won't take them back. I won't. I gave them to you for a reason. The drugs didn't make me. I was planning it."

"Why?"

"Because I.... You know why."

"No I don't. Mick?"

He pulled her close to him and whispered in her ear, "Because your heart is in my heart now. You're, you're, part of me now. I...."

She could feel his awkwardness and clumsy words stumbling out of his mind like a gang of school children out of a classroom door.

"I... love you... Terri."

"Do you?"

He nodded seriously. She threw her arms around his neck and squeezed him tight to her, feeling that he was all she had in this world.

She grabbed his face and forced his eyes to look at hers.

"Mick, why did you shoot Charlie with that arrow? And why were you running around naked like that?"

"I thought, I think, I thought, Charlie, uh, I didn't know it was Charlie, I thought it, he was something else. I don't fuckin' know, Terri. I'm an idiot. And I had this idea about, about hunting, about hunting a beast. And I didn't need clothes to do that."

"Is Charlie, um, is he going to get you in trouble?"

"Nando said he just wants to forget about it—never wants to see me again. Big surprise! I'm gonna write him an apology. Nando said I should."

Terri nodded and they walked two blocks further in silence.

"I can do better, Terri." He paused. "I'm sorry."

She kept silent, finding his eyes.

"Terri," he said, "I know I can do better. I want to. For… for you."

They reached the subway. The time came to part, but she could not. Instead she turned to face him in the dying October light, grasping his rough hand, holding his gaze in hers. They remained, standing together, feeling unfastened from time. Reaching up, she brushed the curly hair from his brow, touched his cheek, tenderly, smiling, staring into his eyes, two hazel orbs gently sparkling in the descending dusk.

CHAPTER 15

Kissing

November 8th. Helen sat in a study carrel at Sacred Heart, with two free periods back to back, usually enough time to get ahead on her homework. But instead of working, she decided to indulge herself in a long daydream about Nando and Charlie.

She knew how much Nando liked her. He had almost pouted when she showed up with Charlie to Mickey's party—and no Mariel in sight. This thought excited her. To be pursued by such a smart, good-looking boy was a high compliment. And it seemed terribly romantic to play Juliet to his magnetically natural Romeo, suffused with unaffected intelligence and passion. She could easily picture falling in love with him. She loved to imagine it, to pretend. She could have a fantasy relationship with him that remained entirely safe.

She replayed in her mind how he had rescued Charlie from the park. Nando was so strong. Charlie was a big guy, and Nando had carried him blocks, like a fallen comrade. She had seen them coming up Fifth Avenue from where she waited outside the apartment at 93rd Street. They looked like two soldiers coming together from a battlefield, Nando's shirt soaked in blood from Charlie's wound. He had wanted to pull the arrow out of his thigh, but Nando said no, because they might not be able to control the bleeding. Later the nurse said that Nando was right—Charlie might have passed out, maybe even died from the blood loss, had they tried to take it out.

After the ambulance took Charlie to the hospital, Helen had gone upstairs with Nando to get her bag and watched him strip off his bloody shirt. He looked so lithe and muscular. She had never seen anyone like him before. He did not have big muscles like a weightlifter or football player. His body looked like a dancer's, sinewy and rippling, like Mikhail Baryshnikov or Bruce Lee, she thought.

And his eyes… they seemed to look inside her. She could barely hold his gaze when they rehearsed because his eyes were so intense. What was it… that look? It was the intelligence behind them. She knew that he was just a person, with feelings and desires like anyone else, but he somehow could look right into the core of her psyche in a way that frightened her. He was nothing like Charlie, so lovable and easy and somehow always focused somewhere else. She could not remember Charlie even trying to stare into her eyes.

Charlie. So strong and brave and morally straight. Any girl would be proud to have him. He looked handsome in a traditional way, like a JC Penney catalogue model. Before Helen had met Nando, if Charlie had asked her to wait for him, to be with him when he graduated from West Point, she would have said yes. Now she felt ambivalent. Now something made Charlie seem too safe, almost tame, next to Nando.

Charlie focused on being *Charlie* and on grasping for something out there, away from Helen. Nando did not think about being anything or anyone: he just was. He directed himself to her, not to some far-off, faraway mission or cause. He centered on matters right before him at that moment. He saw what he wanted and reached for it. Nando wanted Helen, nothing more.

Charlie had drifted far away. The question returned to her. How could she be the girlfriend of a boy who was not there, physically or mentally? Nando was fully present to her. She found herself looking forward to their daily rehearsals and enjoyed just practicing with him. He was a good coach in their private sessions. She most anticipated this time of day, when they could sit together and read their lines and practice their staging. Nando listened and hung on every word she said. He seemed to really care how she sounded and stood and inflected her lines. When she got close to him, it seemed that she was standing in a riveting spotlight, one that thrillingly threatened to reveal her, strangely and pleasingly, to herself and, at the same time, to him.

She tried to think about what made Nando so different. *He completely ignores how smart and handsome he is. He either doesn't know or care.* A lesser person would have been vain and selfish. He made Helen feel aware of her own vanity. She honestly believed that Nando had no idea how magnetic he was, how a girl could be drawn to him. This was part of his charm… so unselfconscious.

She imagined what it would be like to be his girlfriend, to date him, walking down the street with him, holding his hand, kissing him, sitting next to him in a movie. Where would they go? What would they talk about?

He seemed so easy with Mariel, like they shared something that no one else understood. *What about Mariel? Was he still with her? Had he stopped seeing her?* Nando had not said anything clear about it. He had just seemed evasive and uncomfortable whenever Helen mentioned her name. *Could he really be stringing Mariel along? Did Mariel know that he was pursuing Helen?*

Helen knew that Nando wanted her, but did she want him? Did she want the real him, not the fantasy? She felt unsure. She would not let herself see Charlie and Nando at the same time. Helen and Charlie had agreed not to be exclusive. But she still had to tell Charlie and, once she told him, their relationship would be finished; she felt sure of that. Here was the whole conundrum: Even though Charlie had clearly said they would see other people, he had also made it clear he still wanted her.

So if she went with Nando now, she would be rejecting Charlie, who would never come back again. Nando was such a powerful rival; Charlie's ego would not accept it. Nando had knocked out Charlie's tooth; he had carried him like a baby out of the park. It would be an insult of the highest order for Helen to choose Nando in Charlie's absence.

She did not yet feel ready to let Charlie go, nor ready to say yes to Nando. She wanted to leave it all ambiguous as long as possible. She wanted to make Nando be completely in love with her, but not to commit herself to him, so there would be nothing to say to Charlie, nothing to disturb their potential relationship. It was really a perfect situation, Helen concluded, because she could act the part of being in love with Nando, and let him see what it would be like if she were in love with him, but still hold their relationship as an illusion.

To walk this fine line made Helen feel completely in control of herself and her universe. She had these two boys exactly where she wanted them. She pictured the two of them on each end of a seesaw, her in the middle, keeping them hanging in the air, uncertain of when they might plunge. That she could capture their competing desires, holding them in perfect equipoise, gave her an unfamiliar but exhilarating feeling of power. It seemed to radiate from a secret, unfamiliar place, residing just below her belly button.

Watching Nando and Helen in rehearsals, Ian Finnegan could see the dynamic unfolding between them. He applauded it, understanding that Shakespeare had captured the essence of Romeo and Juliet in the image of a lightning flash, "which ceases to be ere one can say 'it lightens.'" To have your Romeo and Juliet played by actual lovers could not work. What *would* work is to have your Romeo and Juliet played by two who denied their mutual love for each other. It was a form of physics—the romantic, erotic charge between them would be exactly equal to its *un*fulfillment. For Nando to grow more in love with Helen every day, and for her to fall ever more deeply in love with him, while neither could admit it to one another in person, put them exactly where they needed to be. Their dramatic roles had become the only channel through which they could express their hidden longing. The theatrical tragedy would perfectly reflect the actual tragedy of unvoiced, unlived passion. *What brilliant casting.*

He had seen Irish teen girls like Helen before. She sported the kind of fierce, untamable beauty that gave rise to what Finnegan called 'Irish suicide,' a slow, untimely death begotten of fighting, drinking and smoking, fueled by years of heartbreak. She was the kind who could not love the boy she did love, only the boy she thought she should love, but did not. It would haunt her for the rest of her life, just like Finnegan's own repressed gay lust. This girl had the beauty and psychology required to push Ferdinand over a cliff. The challenge was to let him get to the edge, but not over it.

One of Finnegan's techniques was to let them rehearse alone, but not really. He would spend about 10 minutes with them in the beginning, then disappear, leaving them in a classroom to practice while he worked with other principals. Then he would arrive unexpectedly, unpredictably. This prevented them from getting too comfortable or letting their passions run away with them. He would watch what they had done, comment, correct, and then either leave again or bring them together with the cast to run through a piece of the play together. In the urgency of early November, Finnegan had been thinking deeply about Act Three, Scene Five, the last scene Romeo and Juliet play together before their deaths.

Finnegan knew the play stood on three scenes: the balcony—Act Two, Scene Two; the death —Act Five, Scene Three; and between them, Act Three, Scene Five. He felt that, if played right, the audience would have the impression of courtship, followed by consummation off stage. Then in 3/5 the audience should have the impression of the lovers being torn apart and with their hearts likewise. In this way, in 5/3 the audience saw the reverse: the lovers re-united through their deaths. If the audience saw Romeo and Juliet braving death in order to come together, the emotional wallop of the play would leave everyone in tears. If 5/3 was misplayed, the audience would see the lovers die from the sorrow of this life without each other—missing the point entirely. The scene involved confronting the fear of death, feeling the loss of this life, but looking forward to the release of death and uniting with the beloved in death. That had to be conveyed.

To do it right, 3/5 had to set up the transcendent reversal that would take place in 5/3. This would require the finest, heartfelt acting. It would call upon Romeo and Juliet to convince the audience that this departure from one another was the hardest, most painful step they had ever taken.

Finnegan launched his usual effort at Socratic directing.

"I want you to work today on 3/5. This is a very short scene really—Romeo's part with Juliet. Short, but can't be rushed. It has to be felt. You're both doing very well with the lines. I like the readings. Now we have to take it a little further, a little deeper. I need you both to really project yourselves into this moment. I want you to do some more interior work. What would these characters be thinking and feeling at a moment such as this? I want to talk it over with you, and then I'll leave you alone to work on it."

He smiled his best grandfatherly smile.

"I know you've given it quite some good thought, both of you. This is a moment of high drama in the play. Done right, it can be the second most heartbreaking moment—the most, of course, being the finale. Why would I say that? What is heartbreaking? Can either of you tell me, speaking from the perspective of the characters, why is your heart is breaking at this moment?"

"It's a lot about time," answered Nando. "They're sleeping together, I think, and Romeo hears something. He knows it's the lark—the herald of the morning. The lark represents time, the sun rising in the east is time, time is change, change is driving them apart."

"Good Nando, good thinking. But what about feeling? What is Romeo feeling?"

Nando took a moment.

"He feels torn in two. He wants to stay with her. He wants to lie with her forever. But if he doesn't leave, he knows he'll die. So he'll endure the pain of leaving now so he can see her again later. But they both know that they probably will never see each other again. And they don't ever see each other again alive. So this is really goodbye forever. But they want to pretend that it isn't."

"Good."

Finnegan paused and drew on his cigarette, pacing, before exhaling the smoke thoughtfully in a great cloud.

"Helen? Is it the same for Juliet?"

"No. I think at first she really believes it's not the morning yet. So she tells him it's not. She can't believe that it could be the morning because it feels to her like they've barely been together. She feels that it's been the sweetest moment of her life and how could it already be gone? So she's almost begging him to see that it can't be gone yet."

"Yes. Very good." He paused. "Have you ever heard of 'denial'?"

"It's a word used in psychology," said Nando.

"Yes. What does it mean?"

"It's when you pretend that something is there, when you know underneath that it isn't. Or the opposite—pretending it's not there when deep in your heart you know it is."

"Very good, Nando. How did you come to know this?"

"My dad. He likes to teach me about things."

"He's doing a good job."

Nando fell silent.

Finnegan continued, "Do we see denial here?"

"Yes," said Helen. "Juliet is denying it's morning. She knows it is underneath, but her mind tells her it isn't because she can't bear the pain of morning arriving."

"Excellent," said Finnegan. "Juliet can't bear the pain of morning arriving. This is the most painful morning of her life. If you can play that pain underneath—not on top, but underneath, this scene is going to work. What happens next? What is Romeo feeling?"

"Romeo's love for Juliet overwhelms his fear of death," Nando responded. "He says, let me die, I'd rather die than leave you, because being with you is the purpose of my life."

"Exactly," said Finnegan. "The challenge is this: Can you play that moment in which his love overwhelms his fear of death? Can you let the audience see you struggle with it and then let them see you give in, to abandon yourself to Juliet? If you can, it will be an unforgettable moment. Because it captures something profound, when Romeo's love of Juliet exceeds his care for himself."

Helen, looking at her script, piped in again.

"And it's that change that drives Juliet, because when she sees that Romeo is willing to die for her, she remembers how precious his love is and how she wants to keep him safe more than anything."

"And how does she feel?"

"Scared, and… and she feels like it's all happening so fast, too fast… and then when they part, she feels like her heart is being torn to pieces."

"Can you show beneath the surface how your heart is torn to pieces?" Finnegan paused again and continued pacing. "This is a very challenging scene. The language matters, of course. The language in Shakespeare always matters. But what matters more now is the feeling, the emotional undercurrent of the action. The audience has to feel you being torn from one another and torn apart inside. Not overplayed, but underplayed. Understated. I want to see you fight to contain these feelings, not to put them on display. Let them be something we see in your eyes, feel in the way you stand, in the way you hold yourself, something we sense in your voice, but deep, not on the surface. I don't want you to worry how it looks right now. I just want you to discover the emotional content of the scene. Talk it through some more if you need to. I'll be back in a bit."

He left the classroom and closed the door.

"He's so intense," said Helen. "He's so brilliant."

Nando nodded. Finnegan had definitely helped him think more clearly about the underlying feeling of the scene. How it developed. Now, to feel it… *I have to feel this,* he thought. *I have to feel my fear of death overwhelmed with a feeling of love.*

"What do you think happened right before this scene. Where are they coming from?"

"Don't say 'they'," directed Helen. "Say 'we'."

He looked at her questioningly.

"Let's be the characters from now on. You and me. When we're rehearsing, let's not think about them as other people, but as us. So the question is, 'What were we doing before this scene?'"

Nando smiled. He liked this idea.

"OK, what were we doing?"

"I think we were sleeping together, holding each other."

"Yes, and, and did we make love?"

"Yes, I mean, it's our wedding night, so of course we did, for the first time."

"So before this scene we were lying together, sleeping, after having made love for the first time."

"Yes."

"It's hard for me to feel that," he said honestly.

Helen nodded.

181

"Well, let's start by just feeling closer to each other. Come closer to me," she beckoned.

He walked over, standing right in front of her.

She moved right next to him and slowly put her head on his chest, just below his chin.

"Imagine we're asleep, like this," she said quietly.

He put his arms around her waist and they stood like that in middle of the classroom together for a minute, two minutes.

Then she picked up her head and pulled back a little. "How did that feel?"

He looked into her eyes and she looked back into his. There was no playfulness, no coyness. She was open; she was there.

"It felt good."

She nodded.

"Now imagine you've woken up and you know you have to leave me and I know it," she continued. "But neither of us wants that moment we just had to be over."

"Neither of us wants it," he said, stepping away.

She nodded and spoke:

Wilt thou be gone? it is not yet near day:
It was the nightingale, and not the lark,
That pierced the fearful hollow of thine ear;
Nightly she sings on yon pomegranate-tree:
Believe me, love, it was the nightingale.

He replied:

It was the lark, the herald of the morn,
No nightingale:

"It feels like I would come back to say this to you."

"Well come back then," she smiled.

He put his arms around her and repeated the line, looking into her eyes.

It was the lark, the herald of the morn,
No nightingale:

"It feels like I would kiss you now."

"As Romeo?"

"Yes, as Romeo, not, not as myself."

"OK, then kiss me."

She closed her eyes and held her face up toward his lips. He moved in to kiss her slowly, tenderly. She did not purse her lips at all. Instead she left them relaxed, so they received his kiss, and gave way beneath his lips like a pair of soft pillows would have received his head. She put her hand up to his face, and held him there for a long moment. Then he pulled away. It was the most incredible single kiss he had ever experienced.

He looked at her and said his lines:

Look, love, what envious streaks
Do lace the severing clouds in yonder east:
Night's candles are burnt out, and jocund day
Stands tiptoe on the misty mountain tops.
I must be gone and live, or stay and die.

Now she approached and put her arms around him, again putting her head against his chest.

Yon light is not day-light, I know it, I:
It is some meteor that the sun exhales,
To be to thee this night a torch-bearer,
And light thee on thy way to Mantua:
Therefore stay yet; thou need'st not to be gone.

He kissed her again, this time not seeking permission, and again she received his kiss with complete passivity. To him, her yielding transformed into the highest sense of erotic action. He felt like she had thrown her mouth open to his in a way that was intoxicating and beguiling. *My god, she wants me.*

He pulled away and looked at her again in the eyes.

Let me be ta'en, let me be put to death;
I am content, so thou wilt have it so.
I'll say yon grey is not the morning's eye,

'Tis but the pale reflex of Cynthia's brow;
Nor that is not the lark, whose notes do beat
The vaulty heaven so high above our heads:
I have more care to stay than will to go:
Come, death, and welcome! Juliet wills it so.
How is't, my soul? Let's talk; it is not day.

As he said these lines, he meant them. His look bore into hers and he could see that she knew he meant every word.

He felt a shock as she grabbed his shirt with her hands and pushed him away, still holding him, but separating.

It is, it is: hie hence, be gone, away!
It is the lark that sings so out of tune,
Straining harsh discords and unpleasing sharps.
Some say the lark makes sweet division;
This doth not so, for she divideth us:
Some say the lark and loathed toad change eyes,
O, now I would they had changed voices too!
Since arm from arm that voice doth us affray,
Hunting thee hence with hunt's-up to the day,
O, now be gone; more light and light it grows.

He pulled away and stepped back, pausing, staring at her. He felt like they were one person now.

More light and light; more dark and dark our woes!

They stood together in silence.

"That felt amazing," said Helen. "I could really believe it."

"And me. Too. It was a good idea to try to imagine what we were feeling before the scene started. It set up the rest for us."

She approached and put her hand on his arm.

"I trust you," she said.

He fervently wanted to hold her, vividly imagining how her soft, slender hips would feel in his palms and forearms, drawn urgently against him. He tried to understand. He knew that she felt the same connection, but she was pretending that it was not there—that it was all for the play: a way to deny how they really felt about each other. They could kiss and he could put his arms around her and act like he loved her, because it was not real; she could respond because it was only acting. And somehow, if they acknowledged it to be real, it would—or could—evaporate. So they could pretend and have their love within the bounds of the play, or acknowledge its reality and destroy it. What did she mean when she said she trusted him? Did she mean that she trusted him to understand this boundary?

"I trust you, too," he replied, thinking he would do anything to kiss her again like that—believe anything, say anything, pretend anything. Things had been changing during the three weeks since the party and the "kill-Charlie" incident, which was how he thought and referred to it when alone with Mickey. Helen had been relaxing more and more in rehearsals. Before, she had completely ruled out any relationship with him. Now it was open for consideration. More than that, she had started treating him like a friend. He felt that when she said, "I trust you," she affirmed that they were friends but not more.

After rehearsal, they walked out of the school together. Mickey and Terri had gone ahead to McDonald's, their usual after-rehearsal hangout. Up the block from there was a pizza place.

"Helen, let's not meet them yet. Let's stop here for a few minutes."

She looked at her watch.

"OK."

He ordered two Cokes and they sat at a small table away from the entrance.

"How's Charlie?"

"He wrote me to say his leg is feeling a lot better. He got to spend a lot of time on homework because he was on crutches and couldn't drill or train properly. He wanted me to thank you again for helping him that night."

"How about you and Charlie? Are you going out?" He knew that he was prying but did not care.

"Well, sort of. We're… uh… he said that we… What about you and Mariel, how are you guys?"

"I'm going to break up with her." He was surprised to hear himself say this; it was the first time that he had articulated the thought out loud.

"But, why? … You seem so good together."

He wanted to study her eyes, but as he tried to catch them, she looked away evasively.

"Did I ever tell you how Mariel and I got involved?"

She perked up and looked straight at him, curious.

"We had a real bad experience together. We got attacked by a gang in a schoolyard in Brooklyn. Three of my ribs got broken, stitches inside my mouth and everything. That's how she got that scar on her face. One of them cut her with a razor blade. And that's where I got this." He fingered the scar on his chin.

"Oh that's awful," she said, her expression darkening with concern.

"I tried to fight them off as… as best I could, but they were bigger than me and I was outnumbered 10 to one. Mick rescued us."

"Oh… oh…." Helen looked as if she were finally understanding something about Nando's relationship with Mickey.

"He and Eugene. I'd probably be dead now if it wasn't for him. One of them was gonna…. I think he was gonna cut my throat."

Helen's eyes widened, "Wow. I never knew, I mean, how could I have?" she said, almost talking to herself.

"And Mar, we were friends then, and she was a wreck. Because she thought no one would ever date her because of that scar, like she was ruined for life or something. And I told her, 'Mar, you're so beautiful, a guy isn't gonna care about your scar.' It was hard to convince her. I told her, 'Mar, you're beautiful outside and inside, too, and that's what a guy is going to care about.' And I said to her, 'Look, I think you're beautiful, I want to date you.' And that's how it started. We had this bad experience in common and we both had our scars. We've been dating for three years."

"So what happened?"

"Nothing happened. I just… I don't feel the same way. Um, no, that's wrong."

He paused. "I realized something, being in this play, hanging out with you."

"What?"

"That I'm not in love with her and I never have been. I mean, I'm just doing it 'cause it's easy, because it's there. I realized I can feel something more. A shared bad memory doesn't make two people in love with each other. It might make them close, but that's not being in love. I want to feel the way I do about you—the way Romeo feels about Juliet."

He did not blush. It wasn't a mistake.

"Do you know what I mean?" he pressed.

She did not want to look him in the eyes. She nodded, staring at the table in thought.

"Tell me about you and Charlie," he said, feeling that his display of intimacy deserved something in return.

"Charlie, ah, Charlie." She glanced up at him, smiling wryly. "Charlie isn't here, is he? He's at West Point. Kind of like having Romeo in Mantua?"

Nando smiled and nodded. *She's being honest.*

"But you guys were pretty serious. I mean, at the ball, and at the party he came with you."

"I guess so. I always felt he wanted something more than I could give him."

Nando liked the way she used the past tense.

"So what's happening now?"

"I don't know. That's the truth. I just don't know."

"Because you haven't decided?"

"And neither has he. We're in limbo."

She paused and looked up at Nando.

"So," she said. An awkward moment. "So… let's pretend."

"Pretend what?"

"I'll pretend there's no Charlie and you pretend there's no Mariel," said Helen. "We'll just be ourselves and see what happens."

"Ourselves Helen and Nando or ourselves Romeo and Juliet?"

"Both."

"What does that mean?"

"I don't know either," said Helen. She sighed and smiled at him.

Nando understood. *How can I know what someone thinks or feels when they don't know themselves?*

CHAPTER 16

The Cliffs of Moher

November 10th. Nando went over to visit Mariel at the brownstone on Cranberry Street. Their typical Friday-night activity involved spending a few hours listening to music in her bedroom, maybe fooling around a little, then hanging out somewhere in the surrounding streets.

She was glad to see him.

"Hi Romeo! With that stupid play I don't get to see you anymore."

"It's only a few more weeks."

She took him by the hand and led him up to her bedroom on the third floor. A white terry bathrobe clung to her slender frame. Her hair still wet from the shower, she had makeup on and her eyes looked pretty. She enjoyed this activity—greeting him in her bathrobe, and then letting him watch her get dressed, helping her pick out clothes to wear. She knew that it turned him on and it sometimes meant they did not get out of her bedroom for a while.

She looked sober, a first on a Friday night in months. Usually, by the time he got there, she had already started on something—weed or coke—or a few mixed drinks with her sister Carmella.

"There's nobody home," sang her voice in a way meant to tell him that she wanted to have some fun.

"Where is everybody?"

"Dad's with Uncle Frank, Eric and Carmella are out at a party. We can go later if we want. It's all the way down on Atlantic Avenue."

"That sounds good," said Nando. "Whose party?"

"Marisol Irrigary, a friend of Steve's—he and Deb are going to be there."

Steve and Deb were also neighborhood sweethearts. She went to Brooklyn Friends with Mariel.

Nando sat on her bed and leaned back against her pillows.

She loosened her robe to start getting dressed and peered at him to see if he was watching. *Yes.*

She turned to face him and he could see that under the robe she wore nothing but her pale blue panties.

She walked over to him and sat on the bed, a four-poster with lace canopy top, resting on white wall-to-wall carpet that looked a little worn and stained in spots. It was a girl's room, with lots of artsy tables and clothes everywhere and copies of *17* magazine and makeup and Pink Floyd and Yes albums and cassette tapes in piles.

On her bureau she had a big picture with Nando taken on her front stoop last summer. He had his arms around her; they both smiled. She also had last year's Valentine's Day card from him right next to it.

She moved closer and reached inside his fitted rayon shirt, open at the neck, and rubbed her hand on his chest before leaning in to kiss him warmly on the lips.

"I missed you."

"Yeah," said Nando, an edge in his voice. "I've been really busy."

She gave him a sexy look and let her robe open a little more to reveal her small, shapely breasts. Then she reached over and grabbed his belt buckle to loosen it.

Nando wanted her terribly, but he knew that it was not her that he wanted, just sex. He fought with himself to reassert control over his lust, putting his hand on her arm and stopping her, then leaning over to kiss her lips and brushing the wet hair away from her eyes.

"I've been wanting to talk with you, Mariel."

She looked at him with doubt and concern as if she sensed something unexpected. He tried to read her expression; he knew this would be very hard and felt unsure whether to go on. She was sober: a good start. But now she was moving on him. If he let that go on, he could not tell her. He still cared about her. He still loved her. He could not use her like that. He wanted to be honest but did not want to hurt her. Hurting her felt like the very last thing in the whole universe he wanted to do.

She seemed to read his confusion and anxiety.

"What, Nando? What's wrong?" He could hear a tinge of panic in her voice.

Nando felt as though he had led her from a sunny street into a dark, dangerous alley; now she wanted him to hold her and whisper that they would be fine. But there was no way through, only a dead end... and no way to turn back.

Before he could say anything, she continued. "I know we haven't seen each other a lot. I feel like I'm, like I'm losing you. You feel, it feels like, you're far away. It's ever since you started in that play. I... I wish Mick had never gotten you into it."

He nodded.

"I'm... I still love you so much, Nando. I just want everything to be good between us, you know? You, you're, you know how special you are to me, don't you?"

She ran her fingers up through his wavy hair.

"I love you too, Mariel," he said hesitatingly, watching her eyes. *My god this is getting worse.* As he said this, she seemed to relax a little. He did not want her to relax, though; he had to tell her what he had come to say. He had to deliver the message.

"I love you and I think we should, we should just be friends for a while. I think we should be friends."

He hated himself for being so oblique. It was unfair to her. He owed her more than that. He had to just tell her what he wanted in a straightforward way.

"Mariel, I want us just to be friends. I don't want you to be my girlfriend anymore."

He felt like he had given her poison to drink. It felt so bad, the most awful feeling he ever had being with a girl. It felt all wrong. 'Why did it have to be so cruel?' he asked himself.

She seemed shocked at first. He watched her lost expression, as though she were trying on different emotions to find the right one for how she felt. Like someone had hit her with something and startled her, and now she was trying to decide whether to fight or flee or cry. She tried on anger and it did not fit. She did not want to run away, to leave him. She felt too stunned to cry yet.

"What... what do you mean? I don't understand," she said plaintively.

"I feel like we need to be only friends, not going together," he said, this time trying to find more confidence.

"Why Nando, why? I thought you loved me."

It was the most obvious question and the way she put it to him—not her words but her voice and the way she looked at him—made him almost want to say, 'Forget it, I made a mistake, of course I love you.' But he was caught up in something beyond himself. It no longer mattered to him whether he would be alone or not. He had decided that he would rather pine for Helen than distract himself with Mariel. He did not want to tell her that he had fallen in love with Helen because it was completely unclear to him whether he would ever have any real relationship with her. He was breaking up with Mariel without certainty of anyone else.

"I do love you," he said. "I'll always love you." He got down on his knees in front of her and grabbed both of her hands.

"Mariel," he said, "there's something between us, there always has been. I don't know what's going to happen with it. All I know is that it's changing, turning into something different. I feel like we're growing up, growing out of it, or like it's moving on into something else. I'm changing and I need to just be, to just be your friend now. I want you to be free to go with someone else. I want to be free also. I want to know I can, without feeling like I'm betraying you. I care about you too much to betray you."

He felt stronger, that he would get through it, even though she would be angry with him, maybe even hate him. But she did not get angry. Instead, she looked at him with her beautiful pale eyes, soft blue like the August sky over the promenade. They filled with tears as she started to weep. It was not a little-girl sob, but a frank, mature weeping that showed how deep her soul ran and how much she really cared about him. The pain of what he had said was bringing out everything he had ever loved about her and driving it to the surface, as if to say, 'This is what you are leaving behind.'

"Why Nando, why?"

He felt like she was saying to him, 'Don't lie to me, don't give me a bunch of shit. Tell me the truth. I need to know the truth.' He kissed her on the lips.

"Mariel, I love you and I want you to be with someone who is *in* love with you, and that's not me. We have… we're too comfortable with each other. It's too safe. It's too predictable. There's a whole world out there waiting for us. We have to get on to it. You deserve more than you're going to get from me. I know that now. It's the same for you. Mariel. You want to be with me because I'm here and you still think no one else will ever love you. I'm telling you, it's not true. You are so beautiful; everyone is going to want you. I think that's why you're doing so much stuff, because you're bored and you think this is it."

She looked at him in a surprised way. "Is that it, Nando, is it the stuff? 'Cause I can stop. I swear I can."

"No, I want you to stop, but that's not it."

There was a long silence between them as they looked at each other.

"Then why don't you want me? If everyone knows I'm beautiful, what about you?"

"I'm going through something. I don't want to talk about it. I can't talk about it."

She stood up and walked over to her bureau, picking up the picture of Nando and her. She looked at it and sat down on the floor next to him with the picture in her lap, before turning to look at him, tears running down her face.

"This is my whole life. You. You're the only one who knew me before this. She ran her fingers down the scar on her face. You remember me before. That's why you can love me now."

"No, that's not true," he said, kneeling beside her. "I'm not the only one who can love you, Mariel, I'm not. You are so beautiful, that scar, that scar makes you more beautiful. It shows you're real. You're unique. There are a million pretty girls out there, but there's only one beautiful girl with a scar. You're gonna say I'm nuts, Mariel, but that scar, it's part of you, it belongs to you now, you own it, and anything that's part of you has to be beautiful because that's how you are, inside and outside. Mar, please believe me, there's not a guy on earth who's going to care about that. Guys aren't made that way. Guys meant to be with you won't be like that, anyway. That scar makes you special. And you know what? The way you don't hide it, the way you don't put makeup on it, that just makes you, it makes you rock."

She smiled through her tears and reached for his hand. "No one else will ever say things like that to me, things like you just said. No one. 'Cause you're special too, Nando. You're special to me. And I'm not giving you up. I'm not letting you go. You're in my heart all the time, you're… I carry you around right here, she said, holding her hand to her chest. 'Cause I'll never forget how you risked your life that day to help me. Never. I'll never forget as long as I live. I know you love me… even if you say you don't anymore… because no one ever did anything like that for me, what you did that day, facing them all when you could have hid or run and just let them have me. I know you love me. Look at me, Nando."

He stared into her eyes.

"I know you love me, Nando. I know it."

Nando felt like his own heart would break. He felt so confused and overwrought. He kissed her and held her in his arms and rocked her and felt like he was actually in love with her and was making a profound mistake.

"Do you understand?" he said finally.

"I understand you're going to go away for a while. Not forever."

"Not forever, not forever," he repeated.

"It's OK… it's OK," she said. "I'll wait for you. Do what you have to do."

"It's not OK, I know that you, you have to know that it's OK for you, Mar, you have to do what's right for you. Love who you want to love, OK?"

"I love you. I don't want to love anyone else."

She seemed so clear now.

"But you might. You might if you let yourself."

She looked down, holding one of his hands, her face wet, contorted in pain.

"He jests at scars who never felt a wound. We don't jest at scars, do we?"

Facing him, she touched the scar on his chin, and put her hand on his cheek, composing herself.

"Can I call you?"

"Of course you can."

"Will you come if I really need you?"

"Of course I will. You know I will."

She stood up, as did he. She leaned in, kissing him openly, vulnerably on the lips, and looked hard into his eyes again. He felt her looking to find his soul. He knew that her heart had broken in pieces and she was trying to keep herself together.

She put her hands on his chest and gently pushed him away, as if sending away someone she wanted desperately to hold on to, as if sending him out into a storm.

"Go on now," she whispered. "*Go.*"

That same night, Helen dreamed of him. In her mind, she had stopped calling him Nando, because Ferdinand seemed so much stronger and more beautiful, as beautiful as he was in face, body and spirit. Smart and strong, loving and brave, gentle and noble. What he had told her about Mariel—how he had built her up and told her she was pretty in spite of her disfiguring scar, how he had fought to protect her—had just made him seem even more than she already knew.

In her dream, she saw them standing on the Cliffs of Moher, on the western seaboard of Ireland in County Clare. She had been there once as a little girl and it made a terrific impression with miles of tall cliffs rising sharply and dramatically from the Atlantic Ocean. They looked like something out of Arthurian legend. On the clifftop stood Ferdinand to one side, and a bit farther stood Mickey, with Terri and Mariel on either side of him. Helen had come to the cliffs from the sea in a crystalline canoe.

She did not scale up the cliffs like a rock climber, but instead floated up as if she were a seagull rising above a balmy ocean breeze. Far off, she could see Ferdinand, looking gaunt and sullen, while Mariel and Terri and Mickey laughed and played, with healthy red glows. But as she approached, their colors changed and Ferdinand began to smile and blush while the other three grew pale with heavy circles under their eyes. She somehow silently called to Ferdinand, asking him to go with her; he wanted to, but the others were calling him back, arguing with him.

Finally she stood on the clifftop with them. Ferdinand and Mickey and Terri were dressed in the Elizabethan costumes that Finnegan had selected for the play. Helen noticed that she herself wore the silky white nightgown she planned as her costume for the balcony scene. Mariel had on the same strapless cream-colored gown that she had worn to the Military Ball. As she grew closer, their lips—Terri's and Mickey's and Mariel's—grew white, while Ferdinand's went red as blood and his eyes glowed the same color. But his red eyes did not scare her; she knew somehow that they would return to normal once she led him away.

She ran to Ferdinand and grabbed him by the hand. They raced together toward the cliff ledge and jumped. She lifted him into the air and they gently floated down toward the rocky sea below. As they slowly sailed down, she looked around and saw the menacing storm that had gathered over the other three. Then she called to Terri to come as well, but Terri was with Mickey, and simply smiled at Helen brightly. Although her lips were white as chalk, she waved as if to say farewell.

Then Helen and Ferdinand reached the crystalline canoe. The hull seemed wider than she remembered, and the ocean had become smooth as a dark pane of glass; she could see their reflections in it. The sun descended in the west, lighting the sky with streaks of pink and red and gold. Inside the canoe she saw a luxurious bed with embroidered pillows and colored sheets and heavy woven blankets. She dived right into it.

Then she realized her naked skin beneath the bedcovers, and called to Ferdinand to join her. He stripped off his shirt just the way he had the night of Mickey's party and she eyed his flat stomach and rippled arms, slender and powerful. He finally stood stark naked before her, and she looked over his body from head to toe. She wanted to hold him. He crawled into the canoe with her and it began to move—by dream energy alone—away from the Cliffs of Moher toward the open ocean.

They left their costumes behind as he said to her, "We don't need those anymore. We can just be as we really are."

She said, "Yes, I don't want to be covered in your sight." She tugged off the blankets so he could see her naked. Even though they were out on the open ocean, the breeze felt warm in the sunset's golden red light. He leaned over and kissed her, running his hand across her breasts and feeling her stomach. Then she let him put his hand between her legs and touch her there. She felt aroused and abundantly wet as she kissed him and opened her mouth to his tongue. She looked over. The cliffs had been encircled in a mist and she could no longer see the others at all. She looked off toward the horizon and knew they were headed toward some other land of joy and happiness. She felt the intense crest of an orgasm spread though her, a surge and pulse… before awakening in her bunk beneath Terri, drenched in sweat and arousal, her hand between her thighs. It was a dream that she did not care to unravel, just to remember and replay as she drifted back to sleep.

CHAPTER 17

Playing at Death

The week of November 19th. With the play less than three weeks away, Finnegan had moved into high gear. He felt this production might be the best staging of a Shakespeare play in his entire high-school directing career. The principals, with one exception, were outstanding. Ferdinand, Helen and Michael were the troika he thought they could be. *Romeo and Juliet* was a perfect play for the setting, because, unlike other plays that one could do in high school, his dramatic leads were the approximate real ages of the characters. Ferdinand and Helen, if they could stay the course, were going to deliver the most passionate rendition of the play any school kids ever had. Why? They were really in love with each other, that's why—as well as being intelligent and beautiful, physically and in their souls. *Ah, the magic of theater all comes down to casting!*

Michael Shea had blossomed just as Finnegan had predicted. Beneath all of his bluster and rebellion, an extremely intelligent boy with real potential as a human being had begun to emerge. His father would be proud of him, as proud as a surgeon could be of a C-average son. Finnegan suspected, though, that this experience could mark a turning point for Mickey Shea, the incorrigible rake. He could take the boy out of Brooklyn, and he could take Brooklyn out of the boy as well, if the boy consumed a diet of Shakespeare's greatest love story.

Finnegan, in his psychic role as Prospero, now had to complete the high conjuring required for his final work of magic: the grand orchestration of music, scenery, costumes, lighting and final polishing of the acting.

For music, he borrowed the soundtrack from Franco Zeffirelli's 1968 version. This was an unoriginal and shameless theft of artistic expression, but it did not matter to Finnegan a whit, because the soundtrack—well, he felt it was perfect. He had also borrowed liberally from the movie's staging and interpretation of the underlying

196

drama. This also did not bother him in the slightest because perhaps one percent of the audience would have seen the movie, and those who had would deeply appreciate his tilting his hat at the Italian's definitive presentation of the play, Franco's deep cuts in the script notwithstanding.

For the set, Xavier had a simply fantastic stage crew, thought Finnegan, under the direction of the fine-arts teacher, Gail Clark, an excellent albeit unknown painter. She had wanted to do a set design for *Romeo and Juliet* for more than 10 years and now lived out her deepest fantasy of recreating the streets and orchards and rooms and tombs of renaissance Verona. In Finnegan's view, the set would have been worthy of Broadway.

Gail had also worked closely with him on costumes. He decided to go straight classic, like the Zeffirelli production, with brocade jackets, tights, satin blouses, velvet gowns and realistic weapons—including period rapiers, swords, daggers and proper scabbards.

To stage the fight scenes, Finnegan had even hired a fencing consultant with knowledge of the history of sword combat. He wanted special care and attention paid to the fights between Tybalt and Mercutio and then between Tybalt and Romeo.

This massive three-dimensional living installation that he carefully pared and rendered in fine detail was taking shape. There was one exception. One amorphous lump of this sculpture tenaciously resisted his artistry: Carmine Castellano in the form of Benvolio.

Carmine would have been a good Bottom in a production of *A Midsummer Night's Dream*. A big, dumb, beefy Italian kid, a lineman on the football team, Carmine believed that being Italian made him an expert in all things to do with *Romeo and Juliet*. Finnegan knew that problems were entering stage left when he overheard Carmine explaining to Ferdinand that the play, originally written in Italian, was much better in that version, which Shakespeare had, according to Carmine, stolen and translated into English.

"You got to hear it in the Italian language, it's like poetry."

"It's not *like* poetry, Carmine, it *is* poetry," said Ferdinand.

"Yeah, but in Italian, it's, uh, our people call it, *poesia*."

"Carmine, that's Italian for poetry."

"Yeah."

This was how conversations went with Carmine.

In his mind, he had elevated the character of Benvolio to the play's lead so, in his view, the play's title was actually a mistake. Shakespeare should have called it *Benvolio*, because he was the major tragic figure.

"If youse t'ink about it," said Carmine, "Benlovio [he had an attack of misplaced consonants] is the one who's in the most pain, 'cause it's like all his friends get bumped off, Mercutio and Romeo, and then he has to hang without them, just like Horace has to go on living without Helmet at the end of that play."

"You mean Horatio and Hamlet?" said Nando.

"Naah, its Horace and Helmet—you better read your Shakespeare, buddy."

Having been cast in the most important role, being Italian and therefore having a deep understanding of the full spectrum of human passions, Carmine liked to help Finnegan coach the other actors.

"The way youse do it is like this. T'ink of somethin' real bad that happened to youse. Then transfer the bad memory onto the scene that youse are playin', see? Like I remember when I was a kid my great grandfather—in our culture we called him gramps—he choked to death on a piece of sausage that got stuck in his throat. And my mother—in our culture we call her ma—she tried to beat it out of him, even stuck her fingers down his throat. But then he had a big fuckin' heart attack in the middle of the chokin' and he was only 91 years old! I mean, he woulda lived to be 100 at least. Anyway, I t'ink about him lyin' there chokin' to death, youse know? I then transfer that remembrance to the other situation here in the play. See Mick, so when you're dyin' in the streets of Verona I'm t'inkin' about my grampa dyin' at our dinin' room table, and that's what makes my actin' seem so real. It's called methodical actin'. I learned it from watchin' the Brando movies, see? You see? Youse have any remembrances like that? 'Cause youse can use yours too, see?"

Carmine understood that his big scene was the fight in which Tybalt kills Mercutio and then is killed by Romeo. Benvolio then has to explain this tragic fight to the Prince.

The problems had started early in rehearsal, when Carmine started to experiment with his lines.

"I just wanna experiment, Mr. Finnegan. An actor has to try t'ings out to see what's workin', you know?"

After Mercutio is struck by Tybalt, he goes off stage with Benvolio to die. Then Benvolio reappears to announce Mercutio's death.

Carmine had run onto the stage, dropped to his knees in the exact middle of the stage, pushing Ferdinand out of the way, and screaming at the top of his lungs:

"Romeo! Rommmeeeooo!"

This he did as if he were Marlon Brando screaming *"Stella, Stelllaaa!"* in *A Streetcar Named Desire.* He had forgotten that Romeo was standing right there.

He sobbed for a full 30 seconds before screaming again and tearing out wisps of his own hair as if he were being tortured or had gone completely insane.

Then, through sobbing cries, he wailed,

"Brave Mercutio's deeeaaaddd!"

More screaming and wailing and rolling on the floor. Then he stood up, walked to the front of the stage, pointed to heaven and declaimed:

That gallant spirit hath aspired the clouds,

Which too untimely here did scorn the earth

Upon the word 'aspired,' he jumped into the air for emphasis. Before he said 'scorn' he cleared a mouthful of phlegm from his lungs and spit on the stage.

Then he stopped and broke out of the scene to get some immediate feedback from Finnegan.

"Whaddaya t'ink, Mr. Finnegan, my Uncle Sal helped me widdat. See, I had to get myself psyched. 'Cause I don't t'ink anyone else ever really did it dat way. It's real original, see? I was imaginin' every dead person I ever knew, 'cause it really hurts Benlovio, 'cause Mercutio is his best friend."

It took Finnegan nearly a full minute to stop laughing.

"Ah yes, Mr. Castellano, that's what I call acting. Real acting!"

Ferdinand and Mickey felt bad for Carmine, but it was funny, and pretty soon they were laughing as Carmine started laughing too.

"I guess I overdid it a little, huh, Mr. Finnegan, like a little too much garlic? Huh, that's what our people like to say, too much garlic. When youse overdo it, in our culture, we say stop, that's too much!"

"Yes, Mr. Castellano, too much. Here's what I'd like you to try out: Don't act. Don't act at all. Just say your lines as simply and plainly as you can, and let's try to let all this pain show in your face, just in your face, not in your gestures or voice, OK?"

This resulted in wild grimacing as Carmine attempted to steal the scene by using only his eyebrows and forehead and his ability to make his face red and eyes bulge.

"Mr. Castellano? Mr. Castellano, what are you doing? It looks like you are in need of the toilet!"

"I was doin' what you said, lettin' my facial expressions show all those emotions that can't come out anywhere else, like pushin' pasta through a sieve."

"Mr. Castellano, you're going to give yourself a stroke! Just say the lines for me, and don't act at all, OK? We need this performance to be subtle, very subtle—the audience will know from the situation how you must feel. You don't have to beat them over the head with it."

"Yeah, of course, I knew dat. OK, I got you, Mr. Finnegan."

The most unforgettable exhibition of Carmine's acting ability had come when he experimented with Benvolio's long speech explaining to the Prince the melee involving Tybalt, Mercutio and Romeo.

Instead of merely saying his lines clearly and with appropriate emotion, he took it upon himself to re-enact the fights fully, using his best pantomime, like a hulking, teenage, voice-enabled Marcel Marceau.

Tybalt, here slain, whom Romeo's hand did slay;

[He mimed one of his hands jamming a sword into himself.]

Romeo that spoke him fair, bade him bethink

How nice the quarrel was, and urged withal

Your high displeasure: all this uttered

With gentle breath, calm look, knees humbly bow'd,

[He dropped to his knees and held his hands up in the manner of one praying.]

Could not take truce with the unruly spleen

Of Tybalt deaf to peace,

[He stuck a middle finger in each ear.]

But that he tilts

With piercing steel at bold Mercutio's breast

[He ran across the stage, pretending to be Tybalt, thrusting his rapier.]

Who all as hot, turns deadly point to point,

And, with a martial scorn, with one hand beats

Cold death aside, and with the other sends

It back to Tybalt, whose dexterity,

Retorts it:

[He ran back the other way, pretending to be Mercutio.]

　　　—Romeo he cries aloud,

　　　—'Hold, friends! friends, part!' and, swifter than

　　　his tongue,

[For some reason, he gave Romeo a girlish voice with a lisp, and actually grabbed his own tongue between his thumb and forefinger.]

　　　His agile arm beats down their fatal points,

And 'twixt them rushes; underneath whose arm

[He grabbed a rapier and rushed to the middle of the stage, pretended to separate two fighters— then thrust the rapier underneath his own arm.]

An envious thrust from Tybalt hit the life

Of stout Mercutio, and then Tybalt fled;

[He ran back across the stage, this time Tybalt running away.]

But by and by comes back to Romeo,

Who had but newly entertain'd revenge,

And to 't they go like lightning, for, ere I

Could draw to part them, was stout Tybalt slain.

[He grabbed his own chest, crumpling to the floor reenacting agony and then death, and lay there still for 15 seconds.]

And, as he fell, did Romeo turn and fly.

[He ran back across the stage, this time as Romeo, then back to stage center, dropping to his knees in front of the Prince, ripping his shirt open to expose his chest.]

This is the truth, or let Benvolio die.

The other players stood speechless, as did Finnegan.

After a moment, Finnegan said, "Carmine, that was"—he chuckled under his breath—"that was very... expressive. It feels like we're doing the ballet of Romeo and Juliet! Here's what I think, Carmine. I'd like you to do exactly what you just did, except this time, stand in one place, don't move. Put your hands behind your back, and don't move them, all right? Mr. Castellano? Do you understand?"

"OK, OK, I was just, I thought that...."

"Don't think, don't think anymore, Mr. Castellano. You are officially relieved from thinking for the rest of the week!"

Next to Carmine, Mickey seemed like Sir Lawrence Olivier. His performance was calibrated. He had gotten deep inside Mercutio's character—not a stretch as it was so much like his own. He understood his lines, all the double entendres, the poetry, conveyed it all. Relaxed, comic and natural, Mickey provided a perfect counterpoint to the passionate and brooding Ferdinand.

In Finnegan's view, Mickey's choices in the death scene played in exactly the right way. Mickey understood it as the death scene of a real man, a man who faced death with a joke, a man who went to heaven cursing and fighting. There was no wailing or sobbing or crying to be had for Mercutio—that was for the audience.

"Mr. Shea, come over here," said Finnegan.

201

Mickey thought he was going to get a reprimand.

"Mr. Shea," Finnegan said to him under his breath, "how do you think you're doing? Do you think you're performing well?"

"I, um, I don't know, I guess so."

"Let me tell you what I think, Mr. Shea. Let me tell you."

Finnegan paused for dramatic effect.

"I think you're one of the best actors this stage has ever seen. And do you know how long I've been directing students here?"

Mickey shook his head.

"Longer than you've been alive, son. I'm very proud of you, Mr. Shea. You're not going to hide anymore, are you? Not going to pretend you're an idiot?"

Mickey shook his head again.

"You've got brains and talent, and it's time you put them to use on a consistent basis, isn't it? Let me tell you, we're doing another play in the spring, and I already know that I want you for a lead."

Mickey nodded.

"That's good son, very good. Keep up the good work."

He slapped Mickey firmly on the back, who in turn smiled and actually blushed. It was the nicest thing any teacher had ever said to him at any school he had ever been to. It made him want to apply himself.

As Mickey walked back to the stage, Finnegan chuckled. Moments like that made his life worth living.

Helen's silent treatment of Terri had lasted a week. Then Helen replaced the silence with icy, terse phrases.

"Good morning, Helen. How *are* you this morning?"

"Just fine."

"Are you still mad?"

"See if you can tell."

After another week, Helen finally abandoned this as well, mostly because she needed Terri's help to rehearse.

Not only did she want to go over her lines, she needed to talk and think them through. For some reason that Helen could not understand, Terri seemed to know things about Juliet that Helen could not see. Helen would ask a question, and offer her theory. Terri would then give her ideas in response, and Terri's always seemed better. Even worse, Terri's interpretations would make more sense when Helen tried to apply them on stage.

One night she was working on her opening speech in Act Three, Scene Two, in which Juliet is waiting to spend her wedding night with Romeo.

"Will you listen to this, Terri, and tell me what you think?"

"Sure."

Come, night; come, Romeo; come, thou day in night;

For thou wilt lie upon the wings of night

Whiter than new snow on a raven's back.

Come, gentle night, come, loving, black-brow'd night,

Give me my Romeo

"Terri?"

"Yes?"

"I've been thinking about this image, where I say Romeo will lie on the wings of night, whiter than new snow on a raven's back."

"Uh-huh."

"And... well... I think Juliet must think Romeo is really pure. I mean, I think she loves his purity, because that's what I think of, um, when I think of snow on a raven. Ravens are black and snow is white."

They sat quietly for a moment thinking about this.

"I don't know, Helen. I'm, I'm not sure that's what she's thinking."

"I think she's saying the night is dark and a little scary and Romeo is pure and white like starlight—that's why she wants to cut him and put him in the night sky, to light up the darkness—do you think that's right?"

"Well," said Terri, "I've been listening and listening to you in rehearsal, to those lines, and I, uh, I think it means something a little different."

Helen read the passage again, puzzling. "What do you think it means?"

"Think about it, Helen, at this moment in the play, it's before everything has gone bad. Before she knows about Romeo killing Tybalt."

"Yes."

"And now Romeo is your husband."

"OK..."

"And, well, imagine... imagine if you and Nando had just gotten married and now you were going to have your wedding night. What would you be thinking about?"

"Oh... yes.... I see."

"Look Helen, read it again, and think about it."

Come, night; come, Romeo; come, thou day in night;

For thou wilt lie upon the wings of night

Whiter than new snow on a raven's back.

Come, gentle night, come, loving, black-brow'd night,

Give me my Romeo; and, when he shall die,

Take him and cut him out in little stars,

And he will make the face of heaven so fine

That all the world will be in love with night

And pay no worship to the garish sun.

"What do you think it's saying Terri? Don't beat around the bush."

Terri sighed. "I think she's saying that she can't wait to have sex with Romeo. She wants him in her bed, in her arms."

"Well what about the raven and the snow?"

"Imagine you were a dark beauty, Helen, as you are," said Terri, giggling. "Imagine what part of you might look like a raven's back. Imagine what might look like snow on the back of a raven? What do you think she's saying when she says, 'Come Romeo, come, come night, give me my Romeo, come, come, come. What do you think all that coming is about?"

"Terri! Do you think it says that?"

"It says that without saying it. That's the point."

"But why does she think about Romeo being dead then? Why talk about what will happen when he's dead?"

"Helen, the whole play is about love and death, isn't it? I think she also means the other meaning of die, you know, to have a... a climax?"

"Terri, you have a wicked imagination."

"It's not my imagination, it's Shakespeare's."

The next day in rehearsal she had tried the speech while thinking about making love with Ferdinand. Finnegan loved it.

"Helen, that was, well... it smoldered! Magnificent!"

A week later she had sought Terri's help with her death scene. Helen felt very worried about it. She had read it over and over, trying to imagine the scene's action, but they had barely rehearsed it at all. Finnegan kept saying that he wanted it to be "fresh." But how could it be fresh if she had not the foggiest idea what to do with it?

"Terri, it's so short, I barely have any lines at all there."

"It's not the lines that matter. It's your face, your expression, how you hold yourself."

"I know that, but it's the feelings I'm not sure of."

"What aren't you sure of?"

"I really don't understand why. Why does she want to kill herself? Killing herself won't bring back Romeo."

Terri sat up in her bunk.

"Helen, who is the dearest, most precious person in the world to you?"

"I don't know. I really don't know."

"Charlie?"

"Definitely not."

"Nando?"

"Terri, I barely know him. I mean, maybe, someday. I mean, I'm, oh, how did you get me talking about this?"

"I'm trying to help you with the scene."

Helen sat on the bunk next to her. "I've been thinking about Nando a lot. A lot. Here's the thing. I feel like I could be in love with him."

"Could be?"

"But I don't know, because I'm not sure if I'm in love with him or with Romeo."

"Well it's good that you could be. When will you know?"

"Probably not until the play is over."

Terri nodded.

"All right, well, besides him or Charlie, who is the dearest person to you in the whole world?"

Helen thought for a moment, then she smiled.

"It's you, Terri. It's you. You're the person who means the most to me in the whole world."

Terri looked surprised, then sat up and gave Helen a big hug. She hugged back, and they both cried a little.

"All right," said Terri. "Well, imagine I was all you had in this world, that's all, the only single person who you cared about and who cared about you, then I died. Suddenly I'm gone. Would you want to live without me?"

Helen stared into space, reflecting.

"I see... Romeo is all she has, so if there's no Romeo, no point going on."

Terri nodded, but then she grabbed Helen's arm. "There's something more."

"What?"

"It's not just that she doesn't want to go on in this life without Romeo. It's more than that."

"What else?"

"She wants to join him in death. It's like he's there already, he's gone before her, the door is closing, and she has to slip through it to be with him, forever, before the others come and drag her back to life."

Helen nodded, deep in thought. "You're right, Terri, you're right. That's why it's a 'happy dagger.' She wants to go to him. 'Happy dagger, this is thy sheath.' She wants to die because she sees death as a passage to Romeo."

CHAPTER 18

Do You Love Me?

November 30th. Terri sat with her panties down around her ankles in the toilet in the last stall of the large empty bathroom on the top floor of Sacred Heart next to the empty science lab, and prayed:

Sweet Jesus dear Jesus I have to tell the truth because Jesus you know my heart and it's no good lying and I know that one day you'll give me the grace to love you more than anyone and you know I love you more than anyone except Mick and I pray you will give me the faith to love you and make you the complete center of my life Jesus I know I asked you to help me feel sorry for what I did with Mick truly sorry and if this is how you think I can best feel sorry then of course I accept it dear Jesus but if there is any other way or if you can think of anything else I'd hope I could try that too or instead 'cause I don't know what I'll do with this Lord if it's as I fear and I know you have the power to change the future and change time and make everything be different than it is and that's why I'm beseeching you dear Jesus to let this cup pass from me but it's your will that matters not mine.

In her school bag she had the test tube to be prepared with her "first morning urine." She wondered why that urine was special as opposed to her noontime urine or her late-afternoon urine. If a brown ring had formed, she was pregnant. No ring, no pregnancy. It was that simple. She felt so afraid to look at the tube that she decided to say one more prayer before checking it.

She said the *Our Father* in the way she best could, reciting each phrase and then silently thinking through its specific meaning, rather than just rattling it off like a child saying the ABCs.

"Our Father," she said out loud.

Then, in her mind: *I come from you God you're our father the source of our life and being.*
"Who art in heaven…"

God, you're in heaven, not here on earth. You come here to earth when you want to show us your mercy. But you put the earth in our hands, gave us free will to take care of it. So I know the universe has two parts, God, your part and the rest. Your part is heaven and it's perfect there, not like the rest, the fallen world, earth, where your children live now because they screwed up in the Garden of Eden.

"Hallowed be thy name…"

God, you aren't flawed like us. You're perfectly holy and all sanctified in yourself. People are made like you, in your image, but they're flawed and sinful because they have free will and abuse it, like I did with Mick….

She winced inside, thinking of it.

I'm sorry for that God.

"Thy kingdom come, thy will be done, on earth as it is in heaven…"

God, please make earth be like heaven is. Heaven's perfect, just as you want it; earth's an awful mess and has to be straightened out because our stupid free will has wrecked it. Please God, help us straighten out the mess we've made. Help me straighten out this mess I've made of my life.

"Give us this day our daily bread…"

God, please help us survive… we're so fragile and weak, aren't we? Our pathetic, sinful life needs your blessing. God, you're holding all the cards… I'm nothing without you.

"And forgive us our trespasses…"

God, can you forgive our sins? I know what sin is. It's every way that the world's not like it should be in your will. I just need to compare heaven and earth, and all the ways that earth's different, that's sin. This earth, in the state it's in, it's just a great big trespass against you God, isn't it? 'Cause you want the world to be perfect, like heaven, but only your love and mercy can mend these trespasses and make us holy again. Please God, make me holy again. Mend me.

"As we forgive those who trespass against us…"

And I know I'll never have more mercy from you God than I give to others. And I do forgive others God, I do… and I'm kind and loving and forgiving like you said to be, so will you give me another chance?

"And lead us not into temptation, but deliver us from evil. Amen."

And God, if I can find the right path in your will, please help me stay on that path, not wander off, and please give me the grace to please you in all that I do, and keep everything that would distract me from you (all that's evil) away from me.

She said the prayer like this twice, thinking carefully through the meaning as she repeated each word and phrase in her mind.

Then she held up the tube in the dim light of the stall and inspected it. A brown ring had appeared. Her heart sank into her stomach, she felt nauseous and light-headed, her eyes filled with tears.

Terri wanted to be angry with God for not giving her a miracle, but then she saw that would be incredibly stupid. It was obviously not God's fault that she was pregnant. She had asked God to help her feel *really sorry* about her behavior and this was it. She knew that she could make a full and proper confession.

She felt herself descending into a spiral of uncontrolled despair as her mind began to play out the scenarios of pain, misery and punishment awaiting her. She imagined herself telling Helen, telling Mickey, telling her parents.... What torments would follow these? Having a baby at age 14? Putting it up for adoption? She imagined the condemnation of Helen and James and her mother and father, and even Colleen, and her shame, her humiliation, all the terrible choices and experiences waiting for her.

The specter of a secret abortion entered her mind but she banished it immediately. Such a horrific sin of murdering your baby was intolerable to consider. How long did she have? She knew the exact date of conception. She was a little over a month pregnant. She would be showing by February or March. She would have to leave Sacred Heart. Where would she go to school? Public school? A little white Irish Catholic pregnant girl in a wild Queens public school?

And what about Mickey? What would happen to the two of them? He loved her, but could his madness love a child, even if the child was his own?

She stuck her head between her legs, wanting to vomit, grimacing and sobbing. These were the wages of sin, of thinking you could lie naked with your boyfriend, and stroke his erection, and have sex with him, and lust after him.

She cried and cried, then prayed again, this time asking not Jesus but the Holy Spirit and God the Father. Holy Spirit, please, in my hour of despair, give me courage and strength for what I must endure and how I will now cause unbearable pain to my whole family. God the Father forgive me, please forgive me and give me the grace I need to endure all that is to come before me.

She thought about death and her soul, about sin, about Mickey, about the baby inside of her—*What exactly did it look like right now?*—as these thoughts went spinning around and around in her mind like a carousel.

After a while, she found herself thinking not about the physical baby, the little fetus that she imagined was still too small to see, but about the baby's soul. She imagined the soul was formed from three parts: a little of her soul, a little of Mickey's soul, and a little thread that came from God to make the baby original and not merely a combination of the two of them. Terri thought how lucky it had that thread from God, to give it a real chance. And as she thought about the little spirit inside her, she also felt a sense of peace and strength. And she thanked God, as the tears cooled her cheeks, because she felt that the Holy Spirit had whispered in her ear to say that in the middle of all the pain and trouble she now faced, there was one good thing: the little spirit inside her body now being nurtured—another little soul wrapped inside her own, like the soft center of a chocolate. God was also telling her that a little shard of Mickey's wild spirit was in her belly, and would be there to keep her company even if he was not. Not that God was saying that Mickey would not be there, but just that, whether he would be or not, inside her now were Mickey and God as well as her own soul. This thought offered her tremendous relief and solace, like finding a warm blanket and hot thermos in the middle of a blizzard.

She sighed deeply, composed herself and got up out of the stall. Washing her hands, she looked in the bathroom mirror. *Teresa Rafter, you're carrying life inside you.* She looked at the teen girl staring back at her in the glass, wondering whether her baby was a boy or girl.

That afternoon, in their private rehearsal session, Nando wanted to work on the death scene.

"This scene is so intense," he said. "Do you think that's why Finnegan won't touch it?"

"I don't know," said Helen. "I said the same thing to Terri. We've less than two weeks left, and it seems like the most important scene and we haven't done anything on it yet."

"Have you worked on your part?"

"Yeah, a bit, with Terri, just reading the lines."

"Everything makes sense to me, up until this scene. Even wanting to kill yourself makes sense, but to actually do it? I can't decide: Am I just carried away with it? Or do I push myself relentlessly to follow through on a commitment I made but now resist? It seems like I don't want to die. Like when I say, "eyes look your last, arms take your last embrace," it seems like I'm dragging myself to it. But maybe that's just me, Nando, thinking about it, not what Romeo would think. It feels like my suicide is totally planned out, and yours is in response to mine, like something you thought of on the spot."

"That's because you know I'm dead long before I know that you're dead. The knowledge gives you time to think. Look, the key is here," she said, "in these lines:"

Ah, dear Juliet,
Why art thou yet so fair? shall I believe
That unsubstantial death is amorous,
And that the lean abhorred monster keeps
Thee here in dark to be his paramour?
For fear of that, I still will stay with thee;
And never from this palace of dim night
Depart again: here, here will I remain
With worms that are thy chamber-maids; O, here
Will I set up my everlasting rest,
And shake the yoke of inauspicious stars
From this world-wearied flesh.

She continued, "I think you're saying you want to be with me forever. It's wanting to be with me, as well as feeling there's no life without me. That's what makes you do it."

Nando thought about it. "Yes, I see what you're saying, at least I think I do."

"It's a combination of things, see, I think you're planning to do it, obviously you are, because you've gone to get the poison. But also seeing me there dead and then remembering how much you love me, that pushes you over the cliff, and it's your overwhelming grief that gives you the courage."

"Help me feel it," implored Nando. "How?"

They sat quietly for a long while. She finally rested her hand on his arm, and they sat a little longer.

"I've broken up with Mariel."

Helen looked at him, surprised.

"Friday night," he said.

"Oh, I, um…. Was it… how was it?"

"Hard."

She stood up and walked across the room.

"What did you tell her? I mean… did you tell her why?"

"Yes."

He sat on the desk in the front of the classroom where they had been rehearsing for weeks. He gestured to her to come back and sit next to him. She slowly obliged. He put his arm around her shoulder and she did not move.

"Helen?"

"Don't say anything."

"Why not?"

"Just don't, please?"

"OK."

They sat together in thought.

He started to say something; she put her finger to his lips.

"Shhhh."

More time passed as she stared at the floor.

"I'm not ready, OK?"

He looked at her uncertainly. She looked back at him with her ocean-blue eyes. *Possibly, definitely, the most beautiful eyes any woman in the universe in all of time ever had.*

"I'm not saying I won't be ready, OK? I'm not promising either. I just saying not yet, OK?"

He nodded.

"Now listen to me. When you do this scene, I want you to imagine, pretend, that I am totally, completely in love with you. OK? And that I want you now, right now, more than I have ever wanted anything or anyone in all my life. Anything or anyone. So much so that I am dreaming about you in my bed at night. I want you to imagine that the way I feel is so intense that I can't... I can't handle it. Pretend all that, all right?"

His heart beat fast.

"And this too. I want you to imagine that I died, and we can never, ever be together in this life. But... but that I am right there, right there on the other side of death, waiting for you. I'm right there waiting for you to come, Romeo, come, come day in night, like snow on a Raven's back. I'm waiting for you to come to me, come to me, and possess me, *completely*. So when you say, 'eyes look your last' and 'arms take your last embrace' you're saying goodbye to this life—but you're also coming, coming into my arms, coming to me in death. And when you say, 'thus with a kiss I die,' that's *you*, falling into my arms, for all eternity."

She grabbed his hand in both of hers.

"I want you to trust me. Ferdinand, trust me. OK? I'm going to be there waiting for you after the death scene is over, after this play is over."

Her eyes were fierce. Serious.

At that moment, Finnegan walked into the classroom.

He lit a cigarette and took a deep drag, then blew the smoke into the air where it hung in a cloud of Finnesophical thought.

"I think it's time for us to approach the final scene."

While Helen and Nando were working with Finnegan, Mickey rehearsed with the fight-scene expert, staging his sword fight with Tybalt. He was having a hard time concentrating; he knew something was wrong with Terri.

She had not arrived with Helen as usual. Mickey asked Helen, who said that Terri would be late because she had to run an errand on the way to rehearsal. She came in half an hour later, looking bad. Her eyes red, she appeared worried and pensive. At the first break he had gone to find her.

"Hey baby."

She smiled at him weakly.

"Hey, how was school?"

"Good," she said, nodding.

"Missed you, baby."

She nodded at him and smiled again but her eyes were screaming at him that something had gone drastically wrong. The Rafter sisters wore their hearts on their eyebrows.

"Hey, what is it? You OK?"

"We'll talk when you're done, all right?" her voice felt brittle, like a dry leaf about to crumble in the wind.

"OK, I'll find you."

It was 5:30 by the time they had worked through the blocking for a 20-second fight scene. The staging ensured that they never got close enough to hit each other until the last, carefully scripted moment when Romeo would step between them, the death blow delivered to Mickey. Nothing dramatic, just a jab and gasp.

The fight director, Mr. Verde, a tall, broad-chested man with long hair and goatee—Mickey thought he looked like a musketeer—had delivered specific instructions.

"Some fights are dramatic. Not this one, OK? It's a skirmish with a surprise. What surprises the audience is the look on your face. You step back and pause, and there is absolute stillness on the stage as the audience reads your expression of surprise. Then, only then, after everyone has read your surprise, you say, 'I am hurt.' When you say that, I want you to think in your head, 'This motherfucker killed me, I'm a dead man.' Let this thought read across your face, OK?"

Mickey got it one hundred percent. Finnegan was right. He was a natural.

As soon they were done Mickey ran to find Terri.

Usually he would spot her chatting with the other crowd players, but today she sat by herself with her head on her knees.

Mickey came up behind and put his arms around her.

"Wanna get a soda?"

"Mick, let's go upstairs."

"Upstairs?" Going upstairs usually meant they were going to fool around, but it did not seem like she wanted this now.

"Find a quiet spot?" she said.

"OK, no problem, come on." He grabbed her by the hand.

They went up to the fourth floor, to the top back corner of the building, where there were a few empty, locked classrooms. It was perfect because the only way to get up there was the stairs, and they could hear someone coming up at least half a minute before reaching the corridor doorway.

Mickey sensed that they needed even more privacy. She watched him as he took the buck knife out of his back pocket and jimmied open the door to one of the reading resource rooms. Empty, with large round tables and bookshelves lining the walls, the room had high windows out of which they could not see, but that let in the evening light.

They sat on the floor in a corner. He put his arm around her as she rested her head on his chest.

"What is it, Terri? What's the matter?"

He pushed her away a little so he could look into her eyes.

"Hey baby, what it is it? Huh?"

She looked at the floor, then at him. She tried to bring herself to talk, but could not.

"Terri, you're scarin' me. What is it? Did somethin' happen at home? Did somebody die?"

She shook her head.

"Is somebody dyin'?"

She shook her head again, staring at a spot on the carpet, like her eyes were glued there.

"Terri, is it me? You're sick of me and you wanna break up?"

She looked up and leaned in and kissed him on the lips.

"No," she said.

"Hallelujah! It speaks!" He grinned at her.

Her lower lip started to tremble.

"Terri, Terri, Terri, baby… tell me," he now said with real worry. "How can I help if you don't tell me, baby?"

She put her face into her hands. He tried to lift up her chin, but she resisted like a toddler.

"Terri, you're freakin' me out, please, baby, please?"

Nothing.

They sat at an impasse.

Then he said, "Terri, baby, I love you so much, whatever it is, tell me, we'll deal with it. How bad could it be baby? You're not dyin', I'm not dyin', we can deal with it. OK? Please, come on, darlin'."

She dropped her hands, her face red, her eyes lost, a little wild.

"It's so bad, Mick. I'm afraid, I'm so afraid."

"What are you afraid of?"

"I'm afraid you won't love me anymore."

"Did you, uh, did you kiss somebody else… or, uh, sleep with somebody else?"

"No. Did you?"

"No fuckin' way." He smiled at her.

Still no smile from Terri.

He held her hands. "Terri, I promise you, whatever it is, I'm still gonna love you. I promise you baby."

"You can't promise that, you don't know what it is yet." She again looked at him searchingly. Her look scared the fucking hell out of him.

"Terri, please, tell me, you're freakin' me out totally."

"Oh Mick… oh." She stared at the carpet again.

He put his hand on her chin and pulled it up toward his face. He stared into her eyes and waited.

"I'm… I'm… Mick, I'm… pregnant."

He looked at her, the information registering inside his brain like a quarter working its way through a pinball machine.

"Fuckin A… wow… pregnant?"

"Yeah," said Terri. "Wow."

"From that one fuckin' time?"

"Yeah," said Terri.

"Holy fuckin' shit. That is fuckin' unbelievable."

"Yeah," said Terri, looking at the floor again, "fuckin' unbelievable."

"Beginner's luck, huh?"

"Yeah," said Terri, her eyes glued to the same spot on the carpet.

"Whew! Wow!"

She looked at him, his expression as though someone had smacked him on the head with a shovel.

She felt so painfully, overwhelmingly alone. A huge wave of sadness washed over her, like she was drowning in a black stormy swell of solitude.

"Mick?" her voice was trembling. "Mick?"

"What?"

"So I guess that's it, huh?"

"What?"

"We…" Her lower lip quivered and her face twisted. "We won't be able to see each other now, huh?"

"What?"

"We're done for now, aren't we?"

"Huh?"

"Mick? We're not going to see each other anymore?"

"Who said that?"

"I'm asking you."

"Asking me what?"

"Are you still going to see me?"

He remained in a fog.

She kneeled in front of him and grabbed him by his shirt. "Mick, what are we going to do? Are you going to leave me?"

"Leave you?"

"Mick, look at me, stop, listen to what I am saying. Do you still love me? Are you going to keep seeing me?"

He looked at her for a long time, finally focusing on her again.

"Seeing you? Of course I'm going to keep seeing you. You're pregnant, and it's mine, I mean, it's ours, isn't it, ours? Our baby?"

"Yes. I mean, it's ours, if… if… if you want it."

"If I want it…? Well is it ours?"

"Yes."

"Well then I fuckin' want it. If it's ours, I want it."

"You do?"

"You bet I fuckin' do. But Terri? I mean, shit, you're 14 years old. Shit. Wow! Unfuckinbelievable."

"Mick, do you love me?"

He swept her up into his arms and kissed all over her face and neck.

"I love you, I love you, of course I love you. I love you. I love you, OK? I love you. I love you. I love you."

She burst into sobs and her nose ran profusely, so that she covered him with a combination of hot tears and dripping snot, but he did not care. He just kept kissing her and she kissed him back, again and again, like they had been separated for 30 years and had just found each other on a stretch of forgotten desert. And she wanted to make love to him again right there on the carpet, and she knew he would have, but she stopped herself.

"I want the baby, Mick. I mean, I don't have a choice, but I do want it. I've been thinking about it all day, since I found out. And I was just so afraid… afraid that you'd, that you'd want to kill it, or that you wouldn't want to see me anymore."

"Well forget that, OK, forget that shit, 'cause I love you and I'm right here. Look at me, Terri, I'm right here and I'm not leaving you. And I'm gonna stay with you through this whole thing, Terri, and if we have to, we'll get married, OK? Shit, I already gave you a big fuckin' diamond, didn't I?"

"Mick, do you mean that?"

"Of course I mean it. I don't say things I don't fuckin' *mean*, do I?"

"Well of course not," said Terri.

"Listen, don't worry OK, don't worry, I can get money. I can get a lot of fuckin' money and I will. Whatever it takes—and if we have to get the fuck out of here, we will. I have a friend. I have a friend in Maine, and we can go, we can just get the fuck outta here whenever we need to. OK? And I'm not gonna leave you, never, ever, ever. You got that, Terri? You can take that to the fuckin' bank and deposit it."

She wrapped her arms and legs around him and stuck her tongue in his mouth and so far down his throat that he thought he was going to choke, but he did not care at all. She terribly wanted to make love with him, but she knew they could not. She wanted to take off her clothes, and feel him naked against her again. While they tongue kissed, she prayed again in her mind. *Thank you God, thank you Lord Jesus, thank you for sending Mick to take care of me, thank you, thank you… thank you.*

As he crushed her to him in his powerful arms, deep within her the words of St. Paul seemed to trickle from a little tear in her heart, floating up inside her, echoing softly in her consciousness: *And if I have the gift of prophecy and comprehend all mysteries and all knowledge; if I have all faith so as to move mountains but do not have love, I am nothing.*

CHAPTER 19

Dress Rehearsal

December 1st. With a week to go before the performance, in their bedrooms a mile apart in Brooklyn Heights, neither Nando nor Mickey could sleep.

Nando lay awake thinking about Helen, feeling that something extraordinary and unexpected had happened to him over the past few weeks of rehearsals. Ever since the day that Helen had suggested they stop thinking about the characters as different from themselves, he found himself fully able to become Romeo in the action of the play as if immersed in a dream. The play had become so real; the suicide scene deeply disturbed him. In his gut, he felt anguish and fear as he prepared to drink the poison, and overwhelming heartbreak upon seeing Juliet in the tomb. In the balcony scene, he felt himself to be madly in love with Juliet. In the scene where he killed Tybalt, he felt rage and overcome with desire for revenge in reaction to Mercutio's death.

His ability to shift from one psychological reality into another scared him, but his confidence increased with Finnegan's effusive praise, saying that he was the most

219

convincing Romeo he had ever seen. Finnegan did not seem to Nando like a bullshitter. If he thought you sucked, he told you. It had been painful to watch the criticism delivered to some of the other cast members. Not only that, everyone else also praised him—Mickey, Helen and the other leads. They could not all be flatterers, could they? He felt like perhaps he had discovered a talent for acting.

More confused than ever about Helen, he felt himself to be in a free fall for her. Or was he? Maybe he was plummeting for imaginary Juliet? He could not tell the difference anymore. He knew that he had never experienced anything like this before with a girl… as though she had purchased part of his soul. He seemed to swim in an endless, sweetly painful longing that nothing could soothe except closing the distance between them. But again, who did he love? Helen, or a creature of Shakespeare's imagination? Did she feel this desire and confusion too? She had seemed to say in code that she loved him. But was it possible that they were just playing out a fantasy with each other? This worry, which had simmered in his stomach for weeks, grew more intense. He wanted the play to be over, because he wanted to find out. On the other hand, he did not want it to be over, because he feared that the bubble would burst, that Helen and Nando, stripped of their Juliet and Romeo personae, would not care for each other in the same way.

In his mind, the play had become real life, and after the play, a form of afterlife. No one knew what would happen in the afterlife. Would she be there, waiting for him, as she had said? Or would there be no afterlife at all and, instead, just cold, empty death? They had never kissed out-of-character. All of his advances were met with evasion or requests to stop and wait, because she did not yet feel ready. After the play, those excuses would stop. Or would they? Would they be replaced with something else, some new reason to wait? Or would she simply say, 'I can't, I'm still dating Charlie.'? He had worked himself into such a frenzy that he almost wished, if they could not be together, that he would literally just die on stage. He knew this was insane. Somehow Romeo had started thinking and feeling through him. And he had become the character, had he not? There was no Romeo out there. Romeo was him—how he looked, felt, acted. Romeo's only real life was in him. Who was Romeo, after all? Black ink on a white page? If Romeo was an idea, then he was nothing. He was a dream, a fantasy, an idol. Romeo lived in Ferdinand or Romeo did not exist at all.

On Montague Street, Mickey had been wildly plotting. He felt responsible for now-pregnant Terri in a way that, had his father known about it, would have tempered his anger with pride. Mickey wished that he could pack her away in a car and drive her to the middle of the woods somewhere, but he knew this would not work, at least not right away. He could not turn her into a runaway because she was not ready to leave her family. He felt like they had been over it four times at least.

Terri was afraid to tell her parents, and rightly so. Her father would want to kill her and Mickey as well—so she said. Not to mention that idiot James, thought Mickey, who like any Irish teenager was capable of causing a catastrophe if his actions were fueled with a few shots. But at age 14 to leave the comfort of her mother and sisters, her home—that would be Terri's last resort. If he could take her somewhere, he could support her—maybe for as long as a year—but how would they get medical care? Would their families not come looking for them?

Mickey felt like he was preparing for war. To fight a war, he needed supplies. For supplies, he needed more cash. He called Ricky.

"Rick, remember that shit I showed you before I went hunting in Central Park— the pure 'H' that the gangland dickhead wants? The one I told you about that Nando almost killed?"

"Ah-yuh."

"Can you do it?"

"Already have, been waitin' for your call."

"Next weekend, Saturday, party at our place in Long Beach. Won't get started 'til about 11. Can you bring it there?"

"Early on Saturday bud, need to go straight back. I need 30 Gs for it."

"Within a week."

Rick knew that Mickey was good for it.

He then called Dingo.

"You remember what you asked me for?"

"You got that shit, muthafucka?"

"I got it."

"All?"

"I got it all."

"Price?"

"Forty."

"Good price muthafucka, you some shit. Some big shit, huh? Forty for the whole shit?"

"Forty."

"Where, when?"

Mickey gave him the details, then said, "Listen, Dingo, if you don't show, it'll be gone. Don't come Sunday, there won't be a Sunday. Are we clear?"

"Claro muthafucka."

Mickey had discounted the price substantially, but he would walk away with $10,000 in one deal. He would give up $5,000, but he felt desperate to close on it, even though he knew the street value could be up at 70 or 80 thousand. With 10 thousand, he could pay for Terri's medical care, if he had to, out of his own pocket.

He worked out the contingencies with her.

"OK, so you're gonna tell them on Saturday afternoon, before the play. Why then?"

"Dad, um, Dad won't hit me if he knows I'm to be on stage that night. I don't think he will. If I wait till Sunday, Mick, I'm afraid—the last time I had a bruise for a week. I need to tell him and then give him time to absorb it. If he can think about it, he'll calm himself down and come to terms with it. And if he comes to the play, then he'll see you, and you can... meet them, Mom and Dad, without it being dangerous. At least... they'll see you in a different light. He's never actually seen you, Mick. They'll see you're a smart boy, not how James talks about you."

"Won't this ruin everything for Helen?"

"I don't think so. I mean, I'm thinking it'll take their mind off it, much as it can be."

"What happens if they freak out?" asked Mickey.

"You tell me. I don't know, Mick, I don't." She was heading down the despair trail again, her voice breaking.

"OK, here's what happens. I'm having a cast party in Long Beach Saturday night. If they freak out, we're gonna split. We'll send them a postcard and tell them you're not comin' back unless they're cool with the whole thing—you, me, the baby. This way you'll be safe and the baby will be too. He can't beat you over a phone line."

"Mick, where will we live? How will we afford it?"

"We're gonna stay with a friend of mine. You met him. Ricky. He's worth over a million, OK? He's a lobsterman and I do some business with him on the side, and he'll let me into his business. I'm old enough, I done it before in the summers. I know it, know how it works. I can buy into it even, if I need to. He owes me, Terri. I've helped him a million times—we, uh, we grew up together. I've got a shitload of money, OK? Enough to last months."

"But what about school?"

"What about it? We're gonna have to deal with the baby first, then we'll worry about school. OK?"

She looked distressed and uncertain.

"Look Terri, hopefully it won't come to this. But we need a getaway plan, you know? What if they freak out? Shit, be real, OK? I mean, look, we gotta expect they'll be breathing fire on your ass, don't we? Imagine it: 'Hey Mom and Dad, guess what, good news, I'm pregnant from the asshole you told me I should never see again or you'd kill me.' Think about it, Terri: 'Good evening Mr. Rafter, I'm Michael Shea, the one who knocked up your 14-year-old daughter?' 'Oh yes, pleasure to meet you Mr. Shea, have a seat.' Shit Terri, you think it's gonna go down like that? It's gonna be: 'Where's my fuckin' gun? I'm gonna blow your fuckin' head off, you little bastard!'"

Mickey was well acquainted with the Irish love for immediate and overwhelming violence.

"Mick, don't say that."

"Terri, we gotta be real, OK, this ain't no dress rehearsal, baby, this is the real thing. Don't think they're gonna be all happy and shit, 'cause they're not. If you expect them to be happy you'll be drowning in a big puddle of tears."

"I know that, Mick."

"OK, so then if the shit hits the fan and it's all going to hell in a hand basket and we're fucked—you're gonna be ready—you're gonna come straight to Long Beach and we're gonna get right the fuck outta here. I'll steal my dad's car. I really don't give a shit. OK? I love you baby, I'm gonna protect you."

"OK, Mick, OK."

"You still got that money I gave you?"

"Yes."

"How much?"

"Four eighty."

"Good, so take that and you can get a cab. Shit, you can get a limo if you need to. If you call me in Long Beach, I'll come and get you myself. I don't hear, I'm gonna assume you're on your way. Terri, they might not let you go to the play."

She had not thought of that. "I think they will, 'cause they'll want to talk alone. They'll be in shock, just like we were."

"If you're not there, I'm gonna know somethin' is going wrong. I'll wait for you in Long Beach. You call me if you need me to get you. I gave you the number there."

"OK, Mick."

She hugged him so hard that he thought his neck would break.

To Mickey, it was like planning the escape from Mischief: without an exit, he could find himself in the back seat of a cop car.

223

Five miles away in Queens, Terri and Helen were faring no better.

Helen tossed and turned, she sat up, she went to the bathroom, she changed her nightgown, she could not stop her brain from humming along about every single concern of the past six months.

She felt highly confident in her performance, anticipating—actively imagining—a standing ovation. Finnegan had told her that after all the other players, she and Ferdinand would bow together, then Ferdinand alone and finally Helen by herself. She would stand last, as the most important player. She thought of her mother and father, her extended family, all her friends at Sacred Heart… even people they knew from Queen of Angels.

It would be the biggest accomplishment of her whole life. She had already written about it on her college applications. But more than that, into her mind and soul had been burned a series of fantastic memories. To be the lead in this play had given her more personal attention and praise than she had received since infancy. Everyone kept telling her how incredibly beautiful and talented she was, again and again, and it would just continue on and reach a crescendo in a standing ovation; all of these wonderful memories would be hers to keep and hold forever.

But the experience had done something more than inflate her ego. Her appreciation of Shakespeare had been transformed. To read and listen to this play 50 times had shown her his true genius. This play said more about life and truth in more beautiful ways than anything she had ever read. For the rest of her life, she would carry this moving body of poetry in her heart. There was no way to gain such an appreciation of the work other than being in a production. By far the best way to experience Shakespeare was as a performer. Through constant repetition and reflection, the poetry had been seared into her soul.

But something even more precious had happened as well. Ferdinand. This part seemed like magic to her. She had gone from hating and loathing him to believing he was possibly the most gorgeous and desirable creature on earth—he was handsome, noble, brave, deep… and in love with her.

She fantasized for hours about what might happen after the play. In one such fantasy—the primary one—they would walk off the stage and he would immediately grab her. They would lock in a passionate kiss that would be their first-ever kiss as Nando and Helen. In another fantasy, they would go to a cast party, and he would ask her to dance a slow dance, and then he would start kissing her in the middle of it.

In yet another, nothing would happen after the play, but on the Monday afterward, he would be waiting outside school for her, and then she would walk up to him and they would embrace and kiss in the middle of the street, like that famous picture of the sailor with his date in Times Square. Her mind invented 50 variations on this theme, all of which ended in romantic epiphanies, kissing and declarations of true love.

In the back of her mind, though, an intense worry had taken hold. She feared that somehow it would go all wrong—the play would be over and the spell would be savagely broken. She would look at him, or he would look at her, and one of them would just not feel anything anymore. It was possible, was it not? Worst of all, she knew that it might be her who would feel this way. Why had she put him off so many times? Why had she carried on this shameless flirtation with him in which she had channeled their whole relationship, including kissing, hugging, holding hands and longing, lustful looks, completely into these fantasy roles? She knew the answer: fear. She felt terribly afraid of him and of the power of her own feelings for him. What if all this delay somehow caused everything to be destroyed, ruined like a rare piece of crystal stowed away in a cupboard and, when finally removed, accidentally dropped and shattered?

Finally her mind turned to Terri. She knew something distressing had happened, or was happening, but Terri would not share it. Helen wheedled and pried but Terri had obviously made an unbreakable pact with herself and would not discuss it. Helen felt sure it had something to do with Mickey. Something had gone wrong in the Mickey-Terri relationship. What? They were still spending time together—a lot of time. Helen suspected that Terri was simply worried about what would happen after the play. How would she and Mickey keep seeing each other then? But if that was it, why did Terri not simply say so? It was such an obvious problem that Helen concluded that this could not be the trouble. There had to be something else. Terri had something buried inside her, like a nasty virus she had contracted but without symptoms yet.

In the bunk above her fidgeting sister, having walked the plank of her own sanity, Terri stared numbly into the roiling emptiness of the deep. She had shared her terrible situation with no one but Mickey. Beginning to feel early signs of pregnancy, she was sick to her stomach and overwrought emotionally, with sore and tender breasts. She felt so painfully alone, like a small creature lost in a dark wilderness. She felt herself to be on the verge of a complete emotional collapse all day long, the only exception being the few minutes she had with Mickey, when he would hold her in his arms.

Mickey's idea about running away to Maine seemed crazy. How could she leave her bunk bed, Sacred Heart, Helen, her mother and church, all at once, during this time of starkest vulnerability? What would happen at Christmas? Would she just miss it? Would she ever have another normal Christmas again? This intense fear of leaving meant that she had to find a way to explain it all. She had to say what had happened in a way that would be understandable, that would keep her father within the realm of reason.

Unfortunately, no such understandable, calming explanation could be found. The truth was that she and Mickey had engaged in flagrant unprotected sex while he zoomed through an acid trip, after which he had shot Charlie in the leg with an arrow while running naked through Central Park. Her mind projected scenario after scenario after scenario in which her father ended up screaming at her and violently beating her, with her mother looking on approvingly, angry condemnation in her eyes. She felt like she was about to strip naked before suffering medieval tortures.

Even if everyone could get over the fact of her being pregnant, she still had the problem of carrying the baby to term—something only she could do, her personal cross to bear. She felt totally overwhelmed with the thought. And then there would be another reality to confront: Once the baby came, it would still be there, and it would be hers and Mickey's to care for. Then what? Would they get married? When? How? Could a 14- and a 17-year-old even get married? She had never heard of any such thing.

She had promised herself that she would not share her calamity with Helen until after the play. There were three reasons. First, she could not bear the guilt of ruining Helen's performance. She knew that Helen would be terribly distracted and worried by the news. Second, she could not trust Helen to keep her confidence. She felt it would be like telling Helen that she, Terri, had caught on fire, and please do not tell anyone. Finally, she could not bear to receive the withering scorn and condemnation that would inevitably follow from her older sister, coupled with a sense that Helen would feel that she herself should somehow be held responsible. She had fallen into the most hopeless, deepest pit of despair, at the true gates of hell, and there was nowhere to go but down. In the end there was no solace, no sleep, no relief, except through prayer, and she lay on her bunk silently praying Our Father, and Hail Mary, in turn—again and again and again.

Finnegan sat in his corner at the San Francisco Plum. The hour had grown very late, after midnight, and he was in a strange mood. His masterpiece was nearly ready to be born. The week had been enormously satisfying as he focused on the details and put the finishing touches on each act and scene, on each word and gesture. His cast of teenagers, mostly age-appropriate for their roles, all dressed in their Elizabethan costumes, their lines memorized, against a magnificent set, with a little background music played at just the right moments, were ready to perform at a level far exceeding everyone's expectations, including his own. *Per ardua ad astra*—through adversity to the stars—they had lived the Xavier motto in their work.

He was no fool and could see this moment for what it was: nothing at all, nothing but high-school theater that would go poof the moment the final curtain descended, like the lightning that flashed and vanished *ere one could say it lightened*. After that it would reside only in memory. In all likelihood, 90 percent of the audience would not even remember his name on the Monday following the show. He was not famous, not even close.

He realized this performance could possibly be his greatest achievement in the medium; this thought troubled him with its intimations of mortality and finality. He doubted that he would ever again see three principals with as much talent and beauty and intelligence and sheer energy as his Romeo and Juliet and Mercutio. Theater was a collaborative art, after all. To achieve his potential as a director, the expression of his talent depended on finding those glittering diamonds on the rubble heap that represented the vast majority of high-school thespians. He directed at Xavier High School, not Juilliard. How often could he expect that to happen in quite this way? Most likely, never again.

He ordered a third Manhattan and savored the moment. To the more than a thousand children he had worked with in his career, he would add another 50. This meant something, because many of them would write and visit, often years later, to say what a difference he had made in their lives—how they treasured the experience he had provided. For some, it would be their only moment in the spotlight.

Slipping into intoxication, he permitted himself some immodest delusions of grandeur. To organize a theatrical performance, he mused, was a high ritual of Western culture, was it not? Through his art, he bound high-school students in New York in 1978 to Greeks who had presented tragedy more than 2,500 years ago. In this sense, he saw himself almost a kind of high priest. To present Romeo and Juliet was like saying the most elaborate Mass he could imagine. Yes indeed, tragedy was an ancient high Mass, a ritual complete with human sacrifice, or at least the gesture toward it. The death in tragedy echoed deep in the collective unconscious, and adolescents understood its meaning without attending graduate seminars. He imagined himself in a stylized tragedy mask, wearing a toga and performing some ancient rites of Greek drama. A tear welled up in his eye. Tragedy reminded the audience about the shortness of this life, the sanctity of it, and of the search for significance that was deeply primitive and also thoroughly contemporary. He felt that he should consider writing an article about this someday.

He would write about how *Romeo and Juliet* touched teens in a way that other works of Shakespeare could not and did not because it celebrated the ardent youthful passions to fight and to love, the passions of the burning sunlit day, and related them to the universal and terrifying reality of death—endless, dark, and solitary: the passions of the night and the moon. *When the cast heard the play through in its entirety 30 or 40 times in the course of a production, it penetrated their thick little skulls,* thought Finnegan, chucking to himself, *in a way that no English teacher would dream it ever could.* Even the densest and most distracted cast members would be quoting this poetry for the rest of their lives. Finnegan felt his achievement was not only as an artist, but as an educator, as a guardian of Western civilization.

He then looked down at his enormous belly and laughed out loud. He saw that he was full of horseshit.

Finnegan's increasingly inebriated mind finally settled on Ferdinand and Helen, and he felt a sharp pang of guilt. The experience of playing across from one another had, just as he expected it would, driven these two magnificent creatures mad with desire. This would make for two truly fantastic performances, but would it harm their little adolescent souls? Desperately lonely Finnegan, chain-smoking Finnegan, borderline-alcoholic Finnegan, who now, after Manhattan Number Three, would be on his way to an expensive evening of depravity with a male prostitute in the Village, knew better than most about the dangers of festering passion. Its denial could cause serious damage, no? He remembered the five-Manhattan midsummer night when he had encountered gentle Father O'Malley in that conceding position at the Anvil and Mineshaft. And now, when O'Malley led assembly prayers, Finnegan could not help but picture his kind face in that leather mask.... He shuddered.

If Ferdinand and Helen could not find a way to sort this out, might they both be scarred for life? He cared for them. This was beyond his power to control, but it could be influenced, could it not?

He thought of Friar Lawrence and the Nurse and Prospero and Pandarus and Puck and every other inspired and misguided character in Shakespeare's pantheon of matchmakers. He toasted them in his imagination and formed a plan—not too much, nothing deus ex machina—just a little stage direction, a little dramatic device to lead them toward their appropriate end. He smiled to think of it. *Perfect.*

CHAPTER 20

I'm No Poet

December 9th, 11 a.m., the Saturday of the big show. Terri dialed Mickey's number in Brooklyn from the payphone at the corner of 43rd and Queens Boulevard.

"Is Mick there…? Thanks… Mick?"

"Hey baby."

"Mick…. I'm so glad you're there."

"Have you told them?"

"No, no. Not yet. Didn't sleep at all last night. Nothing."

"When are you gonna tell them?"

"After Helen leaves. She has to be at Xavier by 3. You have to go early too, don't you?"

"Does Helen know yet?"

"No. No. I can't, she… she… I just don't want her to think about it. She has to focus on… on… on her part."

"Yeah."

"What do I say, Mick? What do I say?"

"Terri, we've been over this."

"I know, just, please, tell me, tell me again, OK?"

"Tell them about us first, then, you know, then tell them about it. Tell them you're sorry, tell them you're sorry we made a mistake."

"Then what?"

"I don't know, Terri, you have to see what they say. Maybe they won't say anything. Maybe they'll just need to think about it and want to talk later."

She sighed and hung quietly on the phone.

"Do you want me to come over there?"

"You can't Mick, you have to go to Xavier."

"Fuck Xavier, I can come over there if you want. I don't care, I'm not afraid."

"No Mick, no, it'll… it'll just… I'm afraid it'll just make things worse."

"I know you're scared, Terri, but look, whatever happens, you can come to Long Beach. If a nuclear war breaks out you just come to Long Beach, OK?"

"OK, Mick." Her voice cracked again. "I just wanted to hear you. I'm so lonely, Mick. I feel so… lonely."

"I'm with you, Terri. I'm with you."

"I know. Tell me again, Mick. Tell me."

He whispered, "I'm in the kitchen, Terri, wait…. I love you. I love you, I love you, I love you."

"Say it different. Say it a way you never did."

"I love you more than… more than… ahh, I'm no poet, Terri."

"Try."

"Ah… OK… um, if a genie popped out of a bottle and said Mick, you can have three wishes, anything you want, I'd just say Terri, cause you're… you're all I want… and, and if I had everything, all the stuff in the world, all the money, and boats and cars and gold and shit, and everything, everything, but I didn't have you, then… then I'd feel like I had nothin' at all, nothin'… and, and, um… uh… all I wanna do is sit somewhere with you, OK, right by your side, and just be with you, that's all I need… that's all I need to make me happy Terri that's all I need, and… and… if you told me that you didn't want me, I'd want to die… and I'm thinkin' about you all night long and all day 'til I see you and then when I see you I just… feel… I just feel happy. And if you disappeared, Terri, if you disappeared, I'd never stop looking for you, never ever, and if you went somewhere, I'd follow you, I'd follow you… Terri… Terri… I just love you, OK? You remember that. Remember that, Terri. Terri, I love you more than… more than my words can tell… and, I wish… shit… I wish I could say it… in… in… in a way you'd never forget."

"Good, Mick, that was real good," she sniffed. "Thank you. I won't forget." Her throat tightened. "Mick?"

"Yeah?"

"I love you too. So much."

"Long Beach."

"OK."

She walked back to the Rafter apartment with a foreboding festering in her stomach, like having swallowed a delayed poison. She had never felt so much dread in her life. A nasty stew simmered inside her combining fear of the unknown, wild fantasies about all that was to come, and black guilt sitting heavily on her head and chest like an awful flu.

Amid all the attention riveted upon Helen, Terri's distress went almost unnoticed. She felt nearly invisible and, had she not been suffering so intensely, she would have felt envy.

She sat on Helen's bunk watching as her sister buzzed around the room packing a canvas bag to take to the performance. Terri tried to remember what it was like to feel carefree.

"Isn't it exciting?" asked Helen, who had been so absorbed with herself over the past few days that she barely noticed Terri's pervasive tension and limitless unhappiness.

"Yes, it is," answered Terri as brightly as she could.

"Do you think this will look OK for going out?" asked Helen, holding up a soft, low-cut sweater that she could wear with her jeans.

Terri nodded.

"What about you?" continued Helen. "What are you going to wear?"

"I'll find something."

"Will you try to come a little early so you can check my makeup?"

"I'll try."

Helen sat on the bed next to her. "Terri, thank you, thank you for helping so much with my lines. I know I couldn't have… done all this… without you. You've given me just as many ideas as Mr. Finnegan, you know? And, you know what, I was thinking, if it wasn't for you, I never would have even tried out. It's turned out to be one of the best things I ever did."

Terri felt so emotionally overloaded that she began to cry.

Helen hugged her. "You silly bean," she said. "Are you all right?"

Terri nodded and wiped her eyes. "I'm just glad something good could come from all this."

"Me too."

"Helen?"

"Yes?"

Terri leaned over and whispered in her ear, "You're going to be great tonight, Helen... I love you... very much."

Helen smiled, looking surprised, before hugging again and whispering back, "I love you too, little T. We're going to have fun tonight, aren't we?"

Terri nodded and looked down at the floor to mask her eyes, leaning back on Helen's bunk. "I'm just going to rest a little, Hel. I didn't sleep much last night."

"Me neither. I feel just like a Super Ball."

Helen left Terri alone as she went out to the kitchen for lunch before leaving.

Terri tried to doze but the awful fear kept coming over her in waves. She imagined that she felt just a sliver of how Jesus must have felt in the Garden of Gethsemane, knowing that his torture, suffering and death were imminent. She wanted to pray but even that seemed impossible now. She felt that prayer might be possible after she had made a confession. Telling Mickey did not count because he was an accomplice, not someone who could grant her forgiveness. So this would be her first confession, to her parents.

Helen left. Terri could hear her mother and father talking and walking back and forth between their little kitchen and living room. Stevie was napping, Colleen was at a friend's house and James was out.

At 2:30 she sat up, stood and steadied herself in her bedroom. *Now or never, and it has to be now.* She reached under the bed and pulled out the pouch that held her diamond pendant and stuffed it in her jeans pocket. It seemed like tangible proof that Mickey loved her and she thought that she might need it. Like a zombie, she dragged herself from the bedroom and through the living room to the kitchen doorway.

Her parents were talking quietly over tea at the cramped kitchen table, pushed up against the wall so they could only sit on three sides of it. There was one empty seat and she squeezed herself into it, her mother on her right with her father across.

They continued to talk and finally she interrupted.

"Mom, Dad?"

"What is it, Terri?" asked her mother.

"I have something I want to tell you." Her voice broke just a little and she tried with all her strength to contain the fear and sadness exploding inside her heart.

"What is it, dear?"

It seemed impossible to contain her feelings for another moment. Her face twisted into an awful grimace and she started to cry. She put up her hands and covered her face.

"Mom, something… bad happened, something really bad," she said through her hands. She could look neither of them in the eyes.

They were quiet as she sat at the table crying.

"What, dear? What has gotten you so upset? Tell me."

She felt her mother's hand on her shoulder, large and warm.

"I don't know how." She could barely get out the words. "I don't know how to say it."

"Teresa, my girl, my girl," said her mother, seeing that something was desperately wrong. "Now take a deep breath and say what it is. Your father and I are both here with you."

"Oh God, oh God, I can't say it."

"Oh my dear, you can, you can tell me."

"Do you remember…?"

"What dear, what do I remember?"

"Do you remember Mickey Shea?"

Her mother pulled back her hand.

Terri now had the sensation that she had climbed to the very top of the universe's longest slide. Once she pushed off, it would be a winding, twisting free fall to the bottom, where she did not know what would happen.

Her mother and father sat in a darkening silence as she sobbed quietly with her hands over her face.

"Go on, Terri," insisted her father. "Go on."

"I, we, we've, we've been seeing each other… at the play, after rehearsals."

Her father grunted and she felt an icy wave come from her mother. She glanced up and saw on her face a look of absolute, withering condemnation.

"Teresa, I am so, so disappointed in you," said her mother. "We expressly, specifically told you not to see that boy again. Didn't we tell you that? Didn't we warn you? You promised us you wouldn't see him again and you broke your promise. Does Helen know about this?"

Lying, Terri shook her head and additional waves of guilt crashed over her beleaguered soul. She was afraid to look at her father.

"Is there more, Teresa?" he asked stiffly.

She continued sobbing quietly and after a moment he asked her again. "Is there more to this?"

"Oh God… I'm sorry, I'm sorry, I'm so sorry, I made… I made a terrible mistake," she said as the tears burned her cheeks. She felt like she had a terminal illness and now she would die in front of them.

Her father sensed something more awful lurking beneath the surface and he pressed her.

"Teresa Rafter, is there something more you have to say to me? If there is, then say it now. Please."

"Oh God, yes, there's more."

Her mother had folded her arms and sat back in her kitchen chair, bracing herself.

"We've… made love… once," Terri whispered it like a horrible, frightening truth.

"What?" asked her mother.

"Mickey and me, we've made love, to each other."

"You *made… love?*" asked her father incredulously with a tone of abject disgust. "What are you saying, girl?"

"Mickey loves me, and we, we made love, to each other, one day," said Terri over glistening cheeks.

"Oh my God, oh my goodness, God forgive you," said her mother as if to herself, while her father grunted again and shifted in his chair. Terri dared not look at him.

They sat quietly for a long time.

Her father stood up.

"I can't listen to this," he said. "I can't listen to this… *rot.*" His voice choked with anger and emotion. "You toil and sweat and you sacrifice to give your children a chance and this is how… this is how they… repay you."

"No, please please please don't go, don't go, please Dad, I'm… I'm not… finished."

Her mother and father sat in complete shock, dimly sensing what was coming next.

She lowered her hands from her face and composed herself. She felt completely exposed.

"And I'm… I'm… oh God … oh God… I'm… pregnant," she said, and in her mind it felt like she had said, *I'm dead*.

They stayed there, the three of them, Terri and her mother sitting, her father on his feet, in total silence for a long while.

She heard her father shift decisively and she looked up at him. His eyes were on fire with anger and he raised his hand to strike her, leaning forward before he froze in mid gesture. She could feel the venom strangling his love for her, strangling all the love in his heart until it was completely gone. His eyes went dead and he looked straight through her, as if she were a ghost.

"Margaret," said her father quietly, "will you tell me who this is? Who is this sitting at our kitchen table? We used to have a daughter; we used to have a little daughter that I loved. I think her name was Teresa, but she died. She killed herself. When did she die, Margaret? Do you remember? I don't know, how long ago was it? Her corpse is here in this house with us. I see her *corpse*."

He leaned over the table and put his face up close to Terri's and asked quietly and calmly, "What have you done with my sweet daughter Teresa? Can the dead talk?"

She looked into his eyes and what she saw terrified her. His eyes looked like those of the market's dead fish.

"Dad, please, oh please, it's me, it's me, I'm still here, I'm still here, I'm still myself, Dad, it's Terri, Dad," she cried.

"No it is not… no it is not… no it is not," he responded coldly. "I know my Terri in my heart; this is not my Terri. This thing here, this *thing*, is not my Terri. This… thing. No, no, no. This isn't my sweet little girl who sat on my knee and went to church with me on Easter Sunday. What are you? What in the name of God are you? What kind of creature are you? Some kind of creature who strangled my Terri and left her dead. My Terri's in here, she's in here, in here," he said with a bitter voice, while touching his heart.

"Dad, please, please, please, I'm begging you, I'm begging you, I'm sorry, I'm so sorry, I made a mistake, a mistake, it was a mistake." She reached out to touch him but he withdrew to the corner of the room, again staring right through her.

Terri looked at her mother, whose eyes were pinned to the floor, her cheeks red and slick. Her mother would not look up.

Terri stood and walked around the table, standing in front of her father before dropping to her knees.

"Please Dad, please, please… beat me if you want to. Please… beat me, beat me… beat me." She was crying and sobbing, knowing perversely that if he could beat her it would mean that there was some little shred of love left in him.

He stood over her and, under his breath, he said, "You… don't… exist."

Dazed and so hurt, she did not know where to turn or what to do.

Then she reached into her pocket and pulled out her little pouch.

"Look," she said. "Look, Dad," she sobbed. "I do exist, I do so exist… he gave me this, this diamond. He loves me. He loves me. He loves me, Dad, please." She pulled the diamond pendant out of its pouch and held it up to him.

He took the pendant from her hand and held it up in the dim afternoon light. He looked at the diamond, how it sparkled, and then he looked at her, down on her knees in a mess of tears and mucus. He walked over to the kitchen window and pulled it open. Then, staring at her, he blithely tossed her gem into the alley below.

They left her. Without saying goodbye, Mr. and Mrs. Rafter left her crumpled in a puddle of despair on their tiny kitchen floor.

CHAPTER 21

Showtime

At 6:20 in anticipation of a 7 p.m. curtain, Finnegan assembled his cast in the large amphitheater-style classroom on the fourth floor where they had begun their rehearsals 10 weeks earlier. They looked spectacular in their Elizabethan costumes and stage makeup. The room crackled with energy and excitement.

"All right, quiet down, quiet down, ladies and gentlemen, quiet down please."

In a few moments there was silence. Finnegan let it hang in the air as a final illustration, as he liked to say, that 'silence is often more powerful than speech.'

"Let us pray," he said, closing his eyes, "in the name of the Father, and the Son, and the Holy Spirit. Lord, we come to you this evening after spending many weeks working hard so that we could, each one of us, now put forward our best effort. Thank you for giving us our talents and thank you for helping us to improve and shape those talents toward your greater glory. Lord, we have learned from you how special and important this play is, what it has to teach us about love and hatred, about similarity and difference, about prejudice and violence, about sorrow and forgiveness, about hope and despair, about beauty, about loss, about death, about families, about friendships, about truth, and again about love, the extraordinary power of love, the love that comes ultimately from you and of which your love for us is the finest example, dear Lord. And we ask you tonight to help us share this inspired poetry, which you gave to the world through your servant William Shakespeare, and we ask that you help us to enrich and entertain all those who have come to support us this evening. And we ask you to help us support one another and we thank you for the love and support we have given to one another over the many weeks that we have been working together. And we ask for your blessings upon us, and our families, and upon this community of Xavier that is our home, that we may honor you in everything we do. Amen."

"Amen," said the collective cast.

"Very good, very good, very good. I am very proud of all of you. I know you are going to push the limits of our great tradition of excellence in Xavier dramatics tonight. Relax and enjoy this experience, have fun with it, treasure it always, and do your very, very best. All right, go on, and I'd like Mickey and Helen and Ferdinand to stay behind for a minute."

After a few moments the room emptied but for those three. He called them to the front.

"I couldn't be more proud of the three of you than I am. If I had my own children I would wish them to be you. None of you had any previous experience in drama, and yet, and yet, I believe you are about to give the finest performances the Xavier stage has ever seen. Now some might say that's a compliment to me, but I know otherwise. I know it comes from your faith and your hard work and your dedication over these weeks. Theater is a collaborative art. I can give direction, but if there is no one to receive it, there is nothing. You are stars, all of you, and tonight you will make the face of heaven so fine that all the world will be in love with night and pay no worship to the garish sun."

It was shamelessly over the top, but in the manner of adolescents hungry for praise, they devoured it and beamed with pride.

"Now Michael, you go on because I have something I need to say to Helen and Ferdinand in private."

He nodded and left. Finnegan had spent so much time one-on-one with Ferdinand and Helen that this seemed absolutely appropriate; after all, the play's title is *Romeo and Juliet.*

Finnegan went around the desk in front of the classroom, sat down and lit a cigarette.

After a moment, he blew smoke into the air over their heads. He said, "You are really, really special, the two of you. I hope you don't mind my saying what's in my heart at this moment. You have brought such passion and sensitivity and intelligence and real feeling to your roles. This audience is going to have an unforgettable experience. I have watched you over these weeks become Romeo and Juliet in a way I would never have imagined possible. I have the feeling that the two of you… I hope I'm not out of place, but if I am, let it go. I have the feeling that the two of you really feel something profound for each other."

Helen reached over and grabbed Ferdinand by the hand, as if to say, *It's true.*

"Anyway, I want to give you a gift, because it has been a real treasure for me to get to know and direct you. It's a sensitive gift, a secret gift, a gift that could be misinterpreted, if it were, um, if it were taken out of context."

They looked at him, puzzled.

"I know what happens after performances like these. You'll be surrounded by your families, and you'll be swept along into a bar somewhere, maybe to a cast party. And I just want you to have the chance, if you want it, to treasure this moment, just the two of you. So I've taken the liberty of renting a room at Hotel Curragh nearby. It's all paid for, room 353. Now it's completely up to you how you use it. If you'd like to go there with a few close friends, or with some family members, or if you just want to go, just the two of you, to have... a conversation... and be away from everyone else, even if it's only for a few minutes. It might be, well, it might give you some closure, or the opposite, if that's what you want. It's completely up to you, and the keys are in this desk drawer in front of me. Of course, I won't be there myself, but the room is at your disposal, at your sole discretion until noon tomorrow. So even if you just want to meet for breakfast, you can. And if you don't, that's fine too. It's just an opportunity, that's all, and I'm never going to ask you about it, or talk with you about it again, ever, and I would ask you to use your discretion. You're both very bright and I'm sure you realize how this could be... misunderstood."

Helen looked astonished, eyes wide.

"I don't want you to say anything, you don't have to answer, all right? I'm going to give you a few minutes by yourself. I'm going to the back of the theater. Come down when you're ready. I won't see you again until the performance is finished. As they say, break a leg!"

The door closed behind Finnegan as Nando and Helen stood there.

"Wow," said Nando, "that was weird, huh?"

"Yes. What do you think? What do you think about it?"

Nando walked around to the front of the desk and opened the top drawer. Two keys. He put one in his pocket and offered the other to Helen.

She hesitated, then took it willingly.

"If I come, I don't want to go there with anyone else," she said.

"Me neither."

"So, if we go, just the two of us then?"

He nodded.

"When?"

"After midnight. I'll be there between midnight and 1."

"I'll try to get there. I'll try."

He nodded again.

"All right, I'm not going to think about it now."

"That's right," he said.

"Romeo?"

"Yes?"

"Will you kiss me… for practice?"

He walked over, encircled her in his arms and kissed her. He released her slowly and gently. Her face was flushed and she sighed.

"Good ," she whispered, grabbing his hand as she led him through the door.

It was the largest audience in Xavier's history. One thousand two hundred. They had to bring in extra seating and let people sit on the floor in the aisles and at the foot of the stage. They were over capacity for the fire code but, at $4 per ticket, Finnegan decided that the fire code could be damned. Several local schools had sent their entire English classes to see the play because it was required reading that year.

Nando's father and mother, a few of their family friends from Brooklyn Heights and some of his father's fellow teachers occupied reserved seating on the right side of the audience. A little behind them was a substantial gang of Sheas, including Mickey's brothers, his mother and father, and his Aunt Sheila and her husband. On the left hand side sat the Rafter contingent, over 30 of them—aunts, uncles, cousins, friends and even church acquaintances. A few rows back on the left, Mariel had come with her sister Carmella. The entire faculty of Xavier and their spouses and family members had come out, along with a large number of people who lived on the block next to the school and the massive St. Francis Xavier Church on 16th Street. And so it went, on and on, row after row after row of spectators who had come to see what Xavier's legendary dramatics club could do with Shakespeare's classic under the tutelage of the great Professor Finnegan.

Nando and Helen peered through the curtains on the main stage.

"My God," said Nando. "I can't believe how many."

Helen nodded soberly. "Where is Terri?"

"Maybe she got sick?"

"She didn't look well this afternoon. Oh, goodness, I can't think about it now."

"I'm sure she's OK," said Nando.

Helen was an arrow to the bullseye. She had only one mission, which now informed the reason for her entire being: to be the best Juliet ever.

Finnegan paced at the back of the hall, in wonder. He could sense something extraordinary about to happen.

At the stroke of 7 p.m., the lights were turned down, the room went completely silent and Finnegan watched as his spellbinding masterpiece emerged at an unprecedented level of perfection.

To start, Finnegan had parceled the lines of the prologue out to six stunning 14-year-old girls from different girls' high schools—all Catholic—around the city. He had placed them not only on the stage but also around the audience; each one seemed to flash into being upon receiving the spotlight. It appeared that a series of fairies, adolescent angels—all proxies for Juliet—were serving as heralds for the play.

Center stage, a dark beauty...

> Two households, both alike in dignity,
> In fair Verona, where we lay our scene,

Stage right, a little blond...

> From ancient grudge break to new mutiny,
> Where civil blood makes civil hands unclean.

Stage left, a brunette, Italian-looking...

> From forth the fatal loins of these two foes
> A pair of star-cross'd lovers take their life;

Back of the audience, a Spanish girl...

> Whose misadventured piteous overthrows
> Do with their death bury their parents' strife.

Left side, an Irish girl...

> The fearful passage of their death-mark'd love,
> the continuance of their parents' rage,

Right side, an Asian girl...

> Which, but their children's end, nought could remove,
> Is now the two hours' traffic of our stage;

Center stage, the dark beauty again...

> The which if you with patient ears attend,
> What here shall miss, our toil shall strive to mend.

Instead of the Prince, these same girls would read the closing lines at the end of the play in the same way, lit by a spotlight that moved across the stage and around the audience.

Between the prologue and finale, Finnegan watched with satisfaction as his principals immersed themselves in the scenes with a natural credibility and depth that would have been the envy of Stanislavski himself. You could not teach children to do this, he thought; they either had it in them or did not. His leads embedded their psyches in every moment of every scene, living each phrase and word, imbuing them with the freshness and energy of spontaneous life. They were fully alive within their parts, discovering their characters moment to moment better than they had ever done in rehearsal, making small but authentic changes to his staging driven by the immediate reality of the action.

The audience responded to this total authenticity with an equal suspension of disbelief, which in turn reinforced the actors, who sensed that they had earned the audience's buy-in. It was a psychic bond forged between audience and players, thought Finnegan, because it relied on the symbiotic and spontaneous relationship between the players and those receiving their performance in one shared physical space.

When Romeo kissed Juliet the second time in their first scene, he wrapped his arms around her and lifted her off her feet. Ferdinand had never tried this in rehearsal. Had it been attempted, Finnegan would never have approved it; it would have seemed too much. Before an audience of 1,200, however, it played as being carried away by love. Such a gesture set the tone for all that was to follow.

In the balcony scene, Helen and Ferdinand added one dozen or more seemingly spontaneous kisses and entanglements that had never been blocked or scripted, not even in their private sessions. Finnegan had seen nothing like it in the entire week leading up to the performance. They interspersed the kisses with their lines, sometimes right in the middle of a line in a way that Finnegan could not have directed even had he done nothing but attend to the scene's nuances for two weeks. The effect imbued the action with an innocent eroticism that he never would have dared; at the end of the scene, as Romeo and Juliet parted, the audience audibly exhaled.

Mercutio's Mab speech arrested the crowd. They knew something vital to the meaning of the play inhabited the images that Mickey conveyed with perfectly calibrated emphasis and clarity. When he said that "dreams are the children of an idle brain, begot of nothing but vain fantasy," the audience knew vain fantasy as the most powerful force in the universe.

In their fight scene, Mercutio and Tybalt tangled like mountain lions. The most dashing Mercutio imaginable: Michael Shea. Funny and bawdy and brave. He played the death scene—his shocking realization of having received a fatal wound—with utter conviction and irony, so that when Carmine reappeared and, with great restraint—Finnegan thanked God—announced Mercutio's death, the audience, rather than Carmine, gasped. This set up Romeo's revenge in the most palpable way; when he slew Tybalt, the audience wanted to clap. But their glee at his demise was met with Romeo's cry that he was "fortune's fool." Ferdinand walked to the foot of the stage—something he had never done in rehearsal—and delivered the line directly to the audience, seeming to make them part of his very mind as if eavesdroppers upon his inner thoughts.

Juliet's soliloquy beckoning Romeo to come to her, come to her in the night, filled every adult heterosexual male in the audience with impure thoughts. It was almost shocking, done completely with her eyes and voice: her visceral ability to project innermost thoughts and feelings through Shakespeare's imagery of light and dark, filtered through his evocative poetic cadence.

Romeo and Juliet in 3/5, their final scene alive together, brought down the house. Finnegan would have preferred to put them on stage in bed naked, as in the 1968 Zeffirelli production filmed on location in Sienna and Tuscany, but impossible in a Catholic high school. He did the best he could, dressing Romeo in a pair of black tights stripped to the waist and Juliet in a flimsy nightgown. Helen appeared to wear nothing at all underneath that gown, of that Finnegan was sure.

The result was the most erotically charged scene ever presented on the Xavier stage. Lithe and muscular, Ferdinand moved with the grace of a ballet dancer yet conveyed something primal. Helen remained sensually soft and magnetically voluptuous, a fully mature woman inside the body of a 17-year-old girl. The addition of the poetry, the set and the powerful performances elevated erotic energy to high art.

Helen and Ferdinand continued to undertake an unscripted choreography that came just short of making love on stage. They spontaneously wove sex into their dialogue, touching and kissing and holding each other... in an unselfconscious way, completely convincing and appropriate to the scene's content. When Ferdinand said, "Let me be taken, let me be put to death," Finnegan felt he was saying, 'Let me have you one more time then kill me.' Helen proceeded to kiss his face and neck with an innocent urgency. One could have heard a feather floating. When Helen said, "Be gone, away" and "Let day in, and let life out," her voice cracked and her lip quivered in a way so real that it tightened the throats of women throughout the audience. When she said "O, thinkest thou we shall ever meet again?" before Ferdinand responded, the two of them clung to each other like shipwrecked lovers in a hurricane clinging to a raft for dear life. Finnegan was shocked to weep. In more than 20 years of directing he had never wept at a play. He knew well what moved him so. As in T.S. Eliot's poetics, Ferdinand and Helen had succeeded in becoming the objective correlative of impossible love. This manner of love was the only kind he knew. He was not the only one they reached; Finnegan reckoned that more than a third of the audience reached for handkerchiefs.

Finnegan felt like he had stumbled into the opposite of a nightmare. He wanted to pinch himself; how could every line in every scene be delivered with such craft? To his disbelief, the performance did not even slightly falter. He began to feel that either he had deluded himself through some temporary madness or else the play must now be building toward some spectacular final failure of execution, which would be required to bring the entire performance back to its correct, more modest level of excellence. He could imagine himself presiding over successes, but not over miracles. He felt like he was watching a lucky figure skater, albeit waiting for her to land on her ass. Instead of falling, though, she simply continued to execute one perfect triple axel after another. Finnegan felt that if something did not give out, God himself might need to balance the books elsewhere, and the level of failure required to normalize this level of success would be ruinous indeed.

They did not stumble. The miracle continued, through to the double suicide. Finnegan knew the performance had acquired an unstoppable momentum. He understood that, just like sex, the emotional purification of tragedy required foreplay. Shakespeare understood foreplay better than any other architect of drama. The emotional buildup, scene by scene, had prepared the audience for an inevitable final catharsis. The keen kisses and longing looks, the bloody battles and horrible homicides, the earnest embraces and forlorn farewells, had been leading all the while to this specific destination, to this terrible conclusion: *for never was a story of more woe, than this of Juliet and her Romeo.*

His leads had incited, inflamed and aroused the audience to a final tragic trigger point. Like lovers taking turns in circles stimulating one another in a steadily increasing erotic ritual, each scene had added rooms to the mansion of tension and sadness now about to implode in a final catharsis.

Finnegan observed a group dynamic similar to one that he had noticed in comedy. On many occasions, he remarked that there was a certain humor a large crowd would respond to that a small crowd would not—it all had to do with audience chain reactions. He now observed the analogue of this principle in tragedy. The large crowd had become capable of an emotional rawness and tenderness that a small one could not engender. One woman crying would set off three others, each of whom would set off an additional three and so on, in a reinforcing spiral.

Ferdinand and Helen had been nurturing and building toward this emotional climax, and as they took their lives achieved the highest level of dramatic intensity that Finnegan had ever seen and ever would see on a high-school stage. They led the audience to cliff's edge and, en masse, it jumped, following them into the abyss.

When Ferdinand said, "Eyes look your last," "arms take your last embrace" and 'thus with a kiss I die," Finnegan heard sobs erupt across the rows. Helen played death as a sexual invitation. She had kissed Ferdinand tenderly, lingeringly; she had actually licked the poison from his lips, running her tongue over and around and across them, and even into his mouth. When she followed this with her tragic cry, "Thy lips are warm," pain shot through the crowd, and he could not contain the cascade of tears. Her final line, "Happy dagger, this is thy sheath," unleashed a final surge of emotion that poured out and over the huge audience in throbbing waves.

His fairies and angels of tragedy, the 14-year-old Catholic beauties from all the boroughs of New York, each illuminated in turn, closed out the performance:

Dark beauty, center stage…

A glooming peace this morning with it brings;

Little blond, stage left…

The sun, for sorrow, will not show his head:

Spanish girl, stage right…

Go hence, to have more talk of these sad things;

Asian girl, back of the audience…

Some shall be pardon'd, and some punished:

Return to center stage…

For never was a story of more woe

Than this of Juliet and her Romeo.

The capacity audience spontaneously exploded, rising to their feet in a standing ovation, whistling and screaming, "Bravo! Brava!" It made Finnegan's heart race and filled his body with adrenaline; he felt he might have a heart attack and expire on the spot.

The applause grew ever louder, seeming to imitate the emotional roller coaster of the tragedy until the final bows from Mercutio, Romeo and Juliet together, Romeo alone, and finally Juliet, center stage.

As Helen curtsied and bowed, the stage crew dropped red and white rose petals from the ceiling; amid the howling and clapping and yelling, it appeared that a gentle rain of blood fell down upon her.

In a fashion befitting Shakespeare's thematic lightning flash—an image capturing the fleeting temporality of life that was the play's essence—it was done. The house lights came up, and in the tradition followed only in high-school theater, the cast walked off the front of the stage and out into the audience to find their family and friends.

Finnegan noticed an odd dynamic within minutes. The Rafter clan had formed a tight barrier around Helen. Finnegan watched her mother talking to her intently, and rather than the beaming smile he expected to see, the blood had drained from Helen's face; she was frowning and looking down. The group began to move deliberately toward the exit. Finnegan would have expected a visit from Mr. and Mrs. Rafter. He had planned to spend more than an hour talking to cast-member parents; Helen's would certainly have been at the top of his list.

Then he heard and saw a commotion from where the Shea family had been sitting. Parents and teens had formed a huddle apparently attempting to break up a fight. Finnegan lumbered toward the melee with a feeling of intense irritation. What miscreants would ruin such a beautiful event? At the bottom of the pile, Mickey Shea and James Rafter were being torn from one another. James frothed and spit and Mickey now had a forehead gash, his eyes poison and menacing.

"You won't see Monday morning after what you did, I promise you," James growled as members of his family hauled him off. Someone handed Mickey a towel and he wiped the blood. His brothers then descended around him and pulled him to the corner opposite from where the Rafter family was leaving the hall.

Xavier's rector, Father Reardon, approached Finnegan. "Nice work Ian, you've outdone yourself."

"Thank you," said Finnegan, looking across the room at Mickey, having a heated conversation with his brother Eugene, who pulled him toward the exit. Finnegan was again surprised; his leads were running from the theater. Why?

Reardon leaned in and whispered in his ear, "Do you know of some trouble with Helen Rafter's sister, Teresa?"

"Not until now. What have you heard, John?"

On the other side of the theater, Nando was receiving praise from his parents and their friends. His father put an arm around his shoulders and his mother kissed him on the cheek.

"Nando, you were terrific. Absolutely terrific. Not a dry eye in the house. You're a natural."

He smiled, "Thanks Dad."

"Do I get to meet your new girlfriend?" said his mother.

"Ah mom, she's not my girlfriend. We're… just friends."

"Anything you say, honey, can't I say hello to her though? Such a beautiful girl. I'd like to meet her parents. You two have been spending a lot of time together."

Nando looked around the room. Helen and the Rafters were gone, and for the first time in months, he felt lonely and somehow lost.

"They're gone I guess. I might meet her later. Mick's having a cast party in Long Beach."

"Don't stay out too late, son," said his father.

"You know what, Dad? I'll probably crash at Mick's place. I mean, we won't even get there till 10:30."

"OK son, now behave yourself, OK?"

"OK, Dad."

He hugged his mother, then his father, over whose shoulder he noticed Mariel. Blushing and looking terribly awkward, she approached him with her sister Carmella.

"Nando, I just wanted to say you were amazing. Every girl in here is in love with you."

"Ah, thanks Mar," he said. "You didn't have to come."

"I wanted to." She had a pained expression on her face. It looked like she was going to cry.

"Are you going out?" she asked, searching him for some sign of interest.

"I'm, uh, yeah, I'm not sure what I'm doing, OK, but maybe I'll see you somewhere, maybe."

She took his hint and looked down at her feet, crushed.

"OK, say hi to Helen, OK?"

"Helen's gone."

"Yeah, OK… OK. See you." She edged away with Carmella, staring at the floor.

He felt awful. She had made an overture and he had turned her down flatly. He looked around the room. Helen and Mickey were nowhere to be seen. An epic anticlimax.

He walked over to Finnegan.

"Mr. Finnegan, I just wanted to say thank you. For everything. For giving us this chance."

Finnegan patted him on the shoulder. "It's I who must thank you. It's rare for me to work with such gifted actors. You were... beyond belief."

Unpracticed at receiving such praise, Nando shifted awkwardly, distracted by Helen's abrupt absence.

"You come and find me on Monday, Ferdinand, all right? We'll talk it over and plan for the spring. I have an idea for you. Maybe another Shakespeare."

Nando shook his hand, turning toward the exit.

Finnegan could not resist, calling after him, "Go and find her. Find her my boy!"

Nando nodded with an uncertain smile, and ran.

CHAPTER 22

Five/Three

Mickey was frantic. He had dialed the Rafter number 15 times since reaching Long Beach, but could not get through.

"You killed my sister, you fucking bastard," James had said to him before the attack. He wanted to drive to Sunnyside to check on and possibly rescue her, but Eugene had talked him out of it.

"Mick, do you wanna spend the night in jail?"

"I gotta get her outta there."

"What are you gonna do, pal? Break down their door? She's 14 years old. You need to chill out, OK? You'll see her when everything calms down. Smoke a joint. Calm the fuck down."

Mickey had other plans. Dingo was sitting outside with his bodyguard and a hooker in a two-tone Cadillac. They had already completed the deal, leaving Mickey with forty thousand stuffed in a duffel bag in his bedroom. He wanted to pay Ricky, get Terri and go, planning to drive to Maine that night. First he had to find her.

He walked out on the front porch. *Why is Dingo sitting out there with all those fuckin' drugs in his trunk? Why doesn't he get the fuck outta here?* Mickey had made a point of leaving his .38 in plain view and introducing Eugene to Dingo, in case he had thoughts of coming back to get a rebate on the deal.

Mickey walked over to the car and tapped on the window.

The guard, a black guy in a leather cap, looked at him skeptically.

"Hey man," said Mickey. "I'm havin' a few people over and might need that spot you're in."

Dingo spoke from the back of the car. "I do some of your shit with my bitch back here man. I paid for my shit. I stay the whole fuckin' night muthafucka. Hey muthafucka look at this shit, man."

Mickey peered into the back of the car. Topless, the girl had her head in Dingo's lap.

"Shit," said Mickey. "Listen man, the cops come through here when we have parties. I don't think you wanna be sittin' here like that while a patrol car drives by."

"I'll worry for my dick," said Dingo. "You worry for yours."

The guard laughed.

"I send her to you when I'm done little Mick-man," continued Dingo. "She got a sweet mouth."

Fuckin' perfect. Mickey turned back to the house.

He saw Mariel sitting on the front porch by herself.

"Hey, it's cold out here," he said. "Come inside."

"Hi, Mick."

Her cheeks were slick with tears.

"Hey Mariel, what's happenin'?"

"You know."

"That dumb shit has his head all up Helen's ass right now."

She nodded.

"It won't last, she's a real fuckin' bitch."

"She is?"

"Yeah."

"But you're seein' her sister?"

"Yeah, that's the problem. She's s'pposed to be here right now—her name's Terri, you met her, remember? I might have to go and fuckin' get her."

"I miss him so much, Mick." She looked like a little lonely kitten.

"Me too. He's no fun anymore. Won't get high or nothin'. All he wants to do is sit and think about Helen. She's playin' with him."

"Mick, do you… do you have anything, any shit I could lighten up with?"

"Just a little weed, a little blow. Not much. I got some H, just a little. Ever done that?"

"Couple times. Carmella showed me how. I could use some. I just want to check out for a while, you know. Just float. It's a rush, you just totally chill. How 'bout you, ever done it, Mick?"

"Once or twice."

251

"You were so cool in the play Mick, really cool, how did you learn all that stuff?"

"It ain't hard. You say the lines a few times, then you just know 'em. The whole thing was a big accident, you know. I just did it 'cause I wanted a place to meet Terri. Her family is fuckin' nuts, they wouldn't let her even talk to me. I talked Nando into it, then he turns out to be Romeo. Fuckin' nuts, huh?"

"Yeah."

"Come on," he said. "I got some shit for you, Mar. Listen, you forget about Nando, OK? Don't think about him too much. He's just actin' like a dick right now. He'll come around, OK? He'll come back."

She followed him into the house, with still only a few people there. He figured the crowd would not arrive until after midnight.

"Wait a sec, OK? I'm gonna try to call her again. You know, Terri. She oughta be here by now."

He dialed again and then stuck his dial finger in his ear so he could hear over the music.

This time it rang instead of blaring a busy signal.

James Rafter Sr. answered.

"Is, ah, is Terri there?"

"Who's calling please?"

"It's Michael Shea."

"Oh it's Michael Shea, is it?"

"Yes sir, I was hopin' I could speak with your daughter."

"Well, you can't speak with her."

"Why not?"

"Because she's dead, that's why."

Mickey paused, trying to understand.

"What do you mean, dead?"

"You put a squirt of your poison into her, didn't you, and it's taken her life. Our Terri is dead and gone now, that's all. Dead and gone. You won't be seeing or talking to our Terri ever again. Never."

"Wait, I don't... I don't understand."

"Goodbye, Mr. Shea. Don't call again. We've enough sorrows without your adding to them."

Mr. Rafter hung up.

Mickey felt unsteady in his stomach, as though his guts had been replaced with an air pocket. He could not think, and felt numb in his hands and fingers. He put down the receiver and wandered into the living room without knowing what to do with himself now, what to think, how to feel. It seemed that his heart was gone, as if he were drowning in cold water at the bottom of a deep cave, drinking it in, filling his lungs with it.

"Mick, you OK?," asked Mariel. "Are we gonna get high?"

She grabbed him by the hand. Feeling lost, he followed her upstairs to the third-floor bedroom, which still had a massive dent in the wall where his head had slammed into it, and a huge chunk missing from the doorframe from when Charlie had rammed it open.

He sat on the bed and Mariel kneeled down in front of him.

"Mick, would you hold me, I just feel so… cold."

He put his arms around her and hugged her to him.

"Where's the shit, Mick?"

He pointed to a large green duffel bag in the closet. She pulled it out, quickly unzipping it.

"Mick, what's all this?"

She stared in disbelief at several hundred packets of $20 bills.

"I, uh… it's just some money, that's all." His head had started to spin and he rested his forehead in his hands to stop it.

"Is the H in here?"

"Yeah, it's at the bottom of the bag. There's a kit there, too, I think."

She rummaged in the bottom, pulling out the sample bag with the five-pointed star that had been delivered to Mickey weeks earlier. "OK, I remember how to do this. I just need a lighter and some water."

He pointed to the bedside table, on which rested the bong he had smashed against Uncle Sean's head, as well as his .38. Next to the gun lay a cup and Flick Your BIC lighter.

Mickey sat on the bed while she went to the bathroom. He kept thinking about what James had said: "You killed my sister you fuckin' bastard," and then Mr. Rafter's words, "You put a squirt of your poison in her." He tried to imagine Terri's face, her body, but could not. He felt so numb, like he was already stoned.

Mariel came back into the room and went to work with the spoon, the water, the lighter, the syringe.

"I'll do you first, OK?"

"OK," he said impassively.

"You're cool, Mick," she said, kissing him on the lips. "Give me your arm."

253

He held out his hand to her.

"Take this off," she said, pulling at his red turtleneck.

He pulled it over his head, sitting bare-chested in front of her, wearing only his jeans.

"You're beautiful, Mick," she said, kissing him again, rubbing her hands across his chest.

She tied the elastic around his upper arm, turning over his hand, smacking the soft part of his underarm above the wrist.

"There," she said, finding a vein. "This one will do."

She took the syringe, gently put the needle into his arm and squeezed.

"Get ready for the rush," she forewarned, removing the band from his arm.

In a few moments, Mickey felt like the sun had swooped down from outer space, entering him, exploding inside his soul, sending waves of warm, pure light through every molecule in every cell of his body.

The chilling void he had been feeling completely evaporated, replaced with wave after wave after wave of comforting nothingness, so Mickey felt that no matter what happened to him, he would be forever encased in an infinite state of meaningless contentment.

"Wow," he said clearly. "What a fuckin' rush…."

He stood up with an astonished look on his face, weak in the knees, a disturbing sensation.

"God," he said. "I'm hurt…. I am so fucked. I am so fucked, man. I'm nailed shut. Exit stage left. I'm goin' down man, all the fuckin' way down. I got to walk off… got to walk off this shit."

"Relax," said Mariel. "I'm gonna do some, too, then we can play. You and me. We can play here on this bed, if you want to? Mick?"

"Yeah," he said, feeling dizzy. "I got… let me… I'm gonna get some air, just go into the air."

He stumbled down the stairs, dizzy and weak, like he might walk right out of himself, yet still with an overwhelming sensation of protection, as if surrounded by an infinite cloud of sunless warmth left over from the initial flash.

He wandered out onto the front porch and down the street.

Eugene saw him go out and called after him.

"Mick, put your shirt on! I'm not chasing your naked ass around Long Beach."

Mickey could feel himself floating a thousand million miles away. It seemed to him that Eugene was a tiny, miniscule ant calling to him from the remotest edge of an impenetrable green forest, while he stood right in the middle of its densest part, warm and all complete in himself, needing nothing and no one, ever again.

He wandered up to the boardwalk; the cold ocean breeze on his bare chest did not even slightly bother him.

He walked about a hundred feet to the first lamp on the ocean side, then dropped to his knees underneath it.

He looked out at the clear moonlit night, listening to the waves curling on the beach, and thought of Terri. 'She's not your Terri,' he thought, remembering what Mr. Rafter had said, about 'our Terri' being 'dead and gone,' 'dead and gone.' She's not your Terri. *She's my Terri, my Terri… my Terri.*

He thought of his best memory of her, the moment that she had pushed him into her, how she had cried out gently, with her heartbreaking sob at that moment of crested passion, how he had seen the two of them reflected, contained, fused together in a single teardrop on her cheek, and the sweet melody of her voice, how she had penetrated his soul, how their two beings had become one as they came together, how much he loved her. Infinitely, that was how much. Infinitely.

At that moment, Terri sat in a coffee shop on West Park Avenue, a couple of blocks from the Shea house. She had been there for two hours, waiting for 11:30 to come. She felt sure that Mickey would be at the beach house by then. She could not bear the thought of talking to people if he had not yet arrived. She had ordered some scrambled eggs but could barely touch her plate. She still felt so ill, her head throbbing and buzzing like a broken neon lamp.

It had been the most heartbreaking day of her life. She felt as though someone had cut her heart out of her chest, then sliced and diced it into tinier and tinier pieces, so that nothing remained but mush. After her mother and father had left, she cried herself into a fitful sleep in the middle of the kitchen floor. She woke up with her consciousness feeling painfully dislocated from her head, waves of nausea rippling through her. She had diarrhea and tried to vomit as well, but there was nothing in her to come up. She dozed on the couch, then sipped a glass of milk, knowing there was no way she could go near the play.

She had not known what to do with herself. For a while, it seemed that she had really died, just as her father said. She felt that she really was a ghost, having leaked her soul. Could a ghost have a baby, she wondered? There would be nothing substantial to hold the little baby spirit inside—she needed a body for that. It felt like her father had cracked her open and now her inner stuff, her life essence, was running and draining out, slowly and steadily, leaving behind the corpse he had called her.

At about 5, she had gone into the filthy alleyway to find her pendant. She crawled on her hands and knees in the dusk, in the alley's muck, wondering where it could have gone. She gave up after an hour. Dragging herself back upstairs to the little Rafter apartment, she showered, washing the filth from her hands, arms and knees.

Having dressed, she walked numbly over to Queen of Angels, to the Saturday-evening Mass. She could not pray and that depressed her further. She wanted desperately to hear God's voice in her ear, but he was utterly silent. Tonight there was no Jesus, no Holy Spirit, no God the Father, no Virgin Mary.

She tried to cry, her face in her hands, but found herself all cried out, feeling cold and black inside. She wanted to try confessing her sins, but no one was hearing confessions.

After church, she wandered east on Queens Boulevard like a drunkard, weaving back and forth across the sidewalks and streets, walking for what seemed like miles and miles, past blocks and blocks of apartments, houses, cars, shops, restaurants, thinking maybe she could walk to Long Beach, if only she knew where it was.

As she walked, she thought with amazement about the people in all of those buildings, mothers and fathers and children with their own desperate individual lives and trials and heartaches and dreams and fears and sorrows. How could God keep track of it?

Finally, with $480 in her purse, she had hailed a cab to Long Beach, arriving at 9:30.

Sitting in the shabby diner, she tried to imagine what it would be like to be with Mickey and never leave him again. They would stay right next to each other, always within arm's reach, sleeping in the same bed together every night. She smiled at the thought.

She tried to picture Maine. Never having been there, she imagined that it might be some rustic place like Ireland with hills, moors, cows, sheep, farms, cliffs… and a seaside, with little fishing villages. Maybe it looked just like Ireland, she thought, except with the open sea on the other side.

She longed for him, to feel his beefy arms around her again, to make love with him again. She could not tonight though: too exhausted, but they would rest, sleep, then be proper lovers. She would learn to please him. They would not even have to worry about being pregnant because she already was.

She imagined that he would be a lobsterman with his friend, Ricky, and they would live together in a fishing village, in a little one-story cottage by the sea. He would come home after a day on the ocean his face brown and handsome with the sun and wind and they would kiss and cuddle by a fire and she would make him dinner and they would have children perhaps more than the one they would already have and she wondered again would it be a boy or a girl and what they might call it and if she had a girl she thought they might call it Hope because the world needed more hope in it and if she had a boy she hoped they would call him Colin because Colin sounded so strong and beautiful and she had always wished that James or Stevie had been called Colin instead.

She wondered whether her father would ever forgive her, guessing that he would not. She imagined that one day, years in the future, she would get a note from Helen saying that Dad had died and she would cry and remember how he once had loved her, long ago, when she was only a child, before she had become a monster, before she had died to him that day decades ago in that coffin-like kitchen in Sunnyside, Queens.

And all of these thoughts gave her just enough strength and will to drag herself the final few blocks to the Shea house, to look for Mickey, to throw herself into his arms, to be rescued by him just as he had promised.

She entered the house, music blaring, finding Eugene in the kitchen.

"Where's Mick?" she asked.

Eugene gave her a big hug. "I'm glad you're here. Mick was worried to death where you were."

"Where is he?" she yelled over the music.

"He's gone for a walk, he's tipsy again."

"Where?"

"Up on the boardwalk, but wait here. It's too cold. He'll be back in a minute, I'm sure."

But she could not wait another minute and ran out of the house, down the two blocks to the boardwalk, calling for him, "Mick, oh Mick, it's me Terri. I'm here! I've made it!"

She ran onto the boardwalk, standing in the freezing ocean breeze, feeling adrenaline in her veins for the first time in hours, knowing that he was near.

She looked in one direction, then the other, but could see no sign of him. She squinted her eyes and looked hard into the distance, out over the beach. *Where is he?*

257

She then saw someone, lying under a street lamp out on the boardwalk, not a hundred feet away, not where one would expect a person to be lying. *My God, it's him, he's passed out.* She ran to him, dropping to her knees, grabbing his hand, looking at his face. His eyes were open, staring but not seeing, and his lips… slightly blue, and his hand felt… cool … limp, terribly so. She reached down, placing her hand on his chest, over the place where she liked to feel his heart beat. His chest felt strangely empty and still, like winter earth, and… nothing. She felt nothing at all.

She grabbed his head, pulling it up into her lap, kissing him, but his lips… passive, and his eyes… staring but not seeing, not seeing her at all. She felt confused, panic creeping up into her throat. She twisted his head around, yelling to him, "Mick! Mick, it's me Terri! I'm here! I made it!" But he did not react, did not respond. Then she absorbed it. Then she understood. It cut right into her heart like a frozen razor blade and she knew that she really was completely dead now, not half dead, not a ghost, no, she was not even a ghost anymore. He had gone, gone… gone… now nothing at all was left for her on this earth… nothing she cared for… nothing she wanted… no joy no warmth no solace no happiness no peace no smiles no Christmastimes no Easters no Thanksgivings no summer vacations no sunlight no ice cream… no hugs… it had all gone with him, gone away to that other place beyond this miserable life.

She fell on him, consumed in a powerful vortex of despair… suddenly feeling a ferocity that she had never known … desolate… a black, infinite anger… a swirling hurricane of fire within her. Her eyes drilled out over the spectral ocean and she knew deep inside that Mickey's spirit was there… out there floating over the moonlit sea… calling to her… waiting for her. '*I'm coming Mickey,*' she called to him desperately in her mind…. *I'm coming, I'm coming and don't you go dare go without me, don't you dare go….* She looked up, turning one way and the other, looking down the boardwalk, her eyes wild with rage. They were alone.

She reached underneath him to his back pocket. *It's there!* With great effort, she wrenched his buck knife from his jeans, and held it up in the light from the street lamp. She opened it with a wild fascination, inspecting the sharp, enormous blade as it gleamed in the lamp's light; indeed, it sparkled just like the diamond he had given her.

She knew exactly how she would do it now. She stood up in the freezing ocean wind, undressing, tearing off her shirt and bra so she could feel his skin on hers. He was cold as the bleached December moonlight, yet she remained ferocious, knowing exactly what she wanted. *Nothing will stop me, nothing.* She would feel him one last time and then would drown him in the love that coursed in her veins. She would die right on top of him, right over him, her steaming red life completely spilling from her wounds and covering both of them, warming them both. He was out there, and she knew that in the moment of her death she would feel his magnificent spirit, his brave, strong and humorous soul wrap himself around her, inflame her, rescue her, carry her away to Maine just as he had promised.

She straddled him in the bitter winter shadows so they were together just as they had been the night they made love, when she had felt that incredible shudder run through her body and soul. She saw that the skin over her heart was just like the skin they had broken that night… a flimsy piece of nothing… when she cut through it she would bleed and it would hurt… but then they would be joined for all eternity, and they would have their child with them too, in that other world beyond this great misery called Earth.

"God forgive me," she said, with her left hand lifting his head, and with her right hand holding his blade over her heart. She kissed the blue petals of his lips, holding his forehead against hers, staring into his dead eyes, whispering softly and fiercely, *"Michael Shea, I love you, I love you more than my life, I love you more than my God…. Happy dagger, this… is… thy… sheath."* Then she drove his brutal buck knife home into her broken heart in one terrible, impassioned thrust, just as she had driven him into her when they had made love. And it was *exactly* as she had thought it would be. It *hurt…* it *hurt…* it *hurt…* but then the pain faded… and her flaming pulse, the river of her very soul rushed out in a pool between them… and she felt his powerful spirit arms catch and wrap around her as she fell, lifting her, raising her up toward the heavens, his soul embracing hers in an everlasting kiss. She died on top of him, just as if they had been loving each other, feeling tender and complete, feeling peace beyond all understanding, knowing that she would never again be apart from him, her one true love, having bathed him now, and swam with him, in all of her bodily fluids: vomit, saliva, snot, tears, urine, arousal, blood.

CHAPTER 23

The Dead

Looking for Mickey, Nando found the duffel bag with the cash, bag of heroin, needle, and gun, and Mariel, face down on the bed. He tried to rouse her. She flopped over strangely, eyes open and fixed. His heart pounded as a serpent of panic twisted through his gut. Pulling her to the floor, he started CPR, pressing first on her chest, then putting his mouth to her cold blue lips, blowing gently but firmly, the way he had learned as a Boy Scout. After five desperate minutes, he put his ear to her chest. Nothing.

Kneeling beside her, he remembered the day that she had come home from Beekman Hospital three years earlier, after the brutal assault at PS 13. Playing stoopball, he had watched them come in, her father and brother helping her into the house, her head covered in a pale blue scarf. After a few minutes, she came out and sat near her top step.

He had been so nervous, as though having swallowed a bag of jumping beans, but wanted to tell her how sorry he felt.

As he approached, she smiled warmly.

"Hi Mariel."

"Hi yourself."

"You're back."

"Yeah," she smiled, rocking a little, something she did to calm herself.

They both spoke at once, then she paused to let him start.

"Mariel, I'm so, so sorry about what happened. I wish… I just wish I had stopped them."

She sat quietly, as if holding a fragile glass figurine inside her, seeming to think about what he had said.

"You did. You did stop them."

"No, I mean… before, before they… hurt you."

She looked at him blankly and he could see that she either did not remember or did not know how he had waited and paused for that moment on the roof. He wanted her to forgive him, but there was nothing to forgive. He struggled, knowing that it was *his* regret to carry, not hers.

"I wish… I just wish I could… kill him… Mariel."

She nodded, her eyes welling up as she fought to control the pain inside. Reaching toward him, she touched the cut on his chin, almost healed. He took her hand in his, sitting down next to her on the step.

"Do you want to see the stitches?" she asked, as though revealing a strange insect inside a box.

Taken aback, he nodded.

She pulled back the scarf on her right temple. They were scary, so many, like a centipede crawling lengthwise down her face.

"Do you want to touch them?" she asked. "I'll let you. You're the only one I'll let." He could feel the pain underneath her smile, like blood pooled beneath a healing wound.

He did not want to, but knew that it would help her if he did. Putting his hand to her cheek, he gently ran his finger along the thread, then down the side where the skin still appeared pink and swollen.

"Wow… they're cool."

She pulled off her scarf.

"I don't like wearing this."

They were silent for a while.

"You don't have to. It's OK."

She reached over, grabbing his hand again and squeezing it in hers. Leaning over, she kissed him on the cheek, smiling again.

"Mariel?"

"Yeah?"

"Do you wanna get an ice cream or something?"

She looked at him in her perfect way, vulnerable and beautiful and sad, but still smiling bravely. He knew then that she loved him.

Kneeling beside her dead body, the blue in her fingernails and lips became the blue at the bottom of a flame that had ignited inside him. He burned... at her, at Mickey, at this world that could let her die like this, at God who could stand by doing nothing, and at himself. Most of all, himself. He remembered their last encounter, his evasive refusal to see her. He felt a river of rage wash over his heart, flooding his eyes, ears and mouth, making him want to scream so his chest would explode. He had to leave, to find Mickey right now. *Mick, that fucking bastard. Mick had given it to her. Mick had killed her with his drugs. Helen was right: He was deadly.*

Seeking a weapon, he grabbed Mickey's .38, staring at it, feeling violent, on fire with loathing. He wanted something that could kill; he shoved the gun into his waistband then ran downstairs, finding Eugene.

"Where's Mick? Where was he going?" asked Nando.

"Towards the boardwalk."

Nando ran from the house.

Mickey was like his brother, closer to Nando than to anyone, even his own father and mother. But what if his brother were a killer? Mickey had saved his life once but now he had killed Mariel, angelic little Mariel, beautiful little Mariel with her scar so unfair, the most unfairness he had ever witnessed.

At the boardwalk he saw them immediately, but froze, confused. What was Mickey doing to her? Was he fucking her in the middle of the cold ocean breeze, in the middle of the boardwalk, exposed for everyone to see, while Mariel lay dead in his bedroom?

He approached slowly. They lay still on the boardwalk, like a sculpture. Only their hair moved, his curly strands and her long, gold brown tresses, blowing silently in the icy breeze. Stripped to the waist, she lay over him, his face and chest covered with her and... with blood. Her hand touched his chin, her fingers upon his lips, also smeared with blood, but with a blue tinge that showed through. His eyes were fixed, his pupils enormous, hollow, as if he had stared beyond the farthest stars.

Terri was gone, her cheeks like white gauze, her eyes scrunched in pain. Her right hand clutched to her chest, she held the hilt of Mick's buck knife in her little palm.

Kneeling next to them, his face close to Mickey's, he whispered, "You stupid fuck-up. What did you do...? What did you do to yourself...? Why...? What's wrong with you, you fuckin' asshole? Did God give you a brain? Where's your fuckin' brain?"

As he stared at Mickey's face, which looked exactly like Mariel's, he suddenly knew what had happened. He wanted to cry but the tears would not come; finding no release, his sadness poured like gasoline onto the fury burning inside him.

He got up and paced away from them, his head spinning, his world unraveling. He strode toward the house, dizzy and sick. It had all been a tragic mistake, a wrong turn that had started back in that schoolyard, the day Dingo had cut her. It was all a bad dream: the play, Mickey with Terri, his feelings for Helen. Now death had come to correct it all; death had come for Mariel, for Mickey, for Terri, and now it would come for him. He *wanted* it. He wanted death to come for him, too.

As he approached the house, he started to shake inside, as if all the imaginary poison he had drunk as Romeo was taking effect and would finally kill him now. The ice flowed through his arms and legs into the blood vessels in his head, and he could feel it closing in on his heart.

He then saw Dingo in his leather waistcoat and stupid leather hat, Dingo who had scarred Mariel, Dingo who had paid Mickey to get the poison. He did not hesitate. He took the .38 from his waistband, cocking the hammer.

His consciousness rocketed forward into the moment, taking thousands of pictures per second, strangely slowing time to a psychotic crawl, like a strobe light sickeningly flickering on a dance floor. He saw Dingo turn toward him, finding his eyes. He wanted to believe that Dingo recognized him, but in his heart he knew better. He followed through, aiming steadily at the star tattoo on Dingo's neck, the muzzle not five inches away, while the instant seemed to linger a hundred years, as though captured in an oil painting hung in a forgotten museum. But as he pulled the trigger, the moment detonated, rocketing Dingo backward off his feet onto the street.

Nando stood over him, watching intently as Dingo clutched his gashed throat. Nando leaned over him, looking deeply into his eyes, wanting him to know his killer, but Dingo did not understand what had happened. He tried to talk, but could only utter silence. Blood spouted through his fingers while his eyes went wild, staring in all directions, then suddenly stopped sharply, seemingly riveted upon death's sweeping approach. His pupils rolled back as he shuddered, flailing like prey being devoured alive. At last he lay completely dead: motionless, pinpointed in time, no longer in the river of life but now frozen on its bank, fixed forever in the past with Mickey. With Terri. With Mariel.

CHAPTER 24

Soliloquy

D ecember 9, 2008. *Thirty years have passed since that night. Some memories remain so clear, as if I were looking through an open window. The pictures linger there, close, like the breeze on my skin, like the breath in my throat. Others have drifted away, so remote from me now. Like driving at dusk on an obscure dirt road, through a place I've never been.... I'm not sure where anything stands, what the signs mean, where they lead.*

I've never spoken about it. People know, but not from me, never from me. They don't know what I remember.

Mom and Dad... gone now. James too. Seven years and five months ago. I imagine him in heaven on a cloud lovingly telling of his own tragic death that September morning; even more so, the tale of that singular night after the play. James would never dare to speak of it in my presence. Steven and Colleen were too young to remember the truth of it. To them, it's a sad story from long ago, like a legend told from a stained-glass window, as though it didn't really happen. We didn't speak of it as a family. Ever.

Last week I walked in Sunnyside, past Queen of Angels. Stopped to light a candle, say a prayer. Then to the Boulevard and down 46th Street. The little apartment is gone now... turned into luxury condominiums. All the way, I could feel her with me.

Not a single day passes, almost not a single moment, without my thinking of her. That seems hard to explain, how she could stay so near after so long. Like she's here, like I could turn the corner and find her waiting for me, could wake up and find her at my kitchen table. Why?

She visits in my dreams, vivid and exactly the same every time. I remember the day I first dreamed of her...

It had been the most important accomplishment of my life, but Terri had somehow taken it away, because Mom, Dad and all the others were focused on her instead of me.

Dad said we had to go straight home. Mom whispered to me what had happened before they left Sunnyside, all about the dreadful fight, how Terri was in pieces. I remember asking myself—it's a painful, selfish thought to me now—couldn't she have waited one more day to tell her secret?

Anger rose inside me. How could she have been so stupid? Why hadn't she told me? I felt angry with Mick for... doing it... to her, with her. Like a wolf stalking a lamb, he had separated her from us. I remember Dad, his eyes narrow, his mouth slack, heartbreak scrawled over his brow. I wish... I wish that he had wanted to go back home just to wipe her tears away, wish he had wanted to soothe her, to hold her hand, to tell her it would be all right. But Dad was cold and hard, wasn't he? A rigid man, his life full of toil and frustration. He never hugged us before bed, never told us the sun would rise tomorrow. A faithful man, honest. But a comfort? Not at all. He was a man to give you a sharp dose of shame and fear.

After the play, I sat next to James in the subway car rattling back to Queens, feeling ill. My whole life had been poured onto that stage, my heart emptied. Watching my reflection in the train window, lost in my imagination, I remember thinking of Ferdinand. I wanted him near, wished I could find a way out of this family of mine. I felt trapped among these people, my own flesh and blood. Love and hate twisted together inside me, especially at that moment.

When we got to Sunnyside, Mom stopped Dad, pulling him near the curb of the street. After speaking in hushed tones, they sent me to Maggie Mae's to see my Uncle Sean. Good for me. I didn't want to watch our family drama. Mom said James would fetch me when their difficult talk had finished. Smiling, squeezing my arm, she winked at me, whispering in my ear that I was the best Juliet. She never smiled that way again—never in a way to say, 'We're together.'

Behind the bar at Maggie's, Uncle Sean laughed, pouring the rounds. My Aunt Karen, Dad's sister, stopped in. She'd seen the play that night. "You've a celebrity here at your bar," she told them all in her brogue. Sean made me a great big Long Island Iced Tea, and they made a fuss over me, cheering me up. No one knew Terri's problem. It was family business, and I wanted attention to myself.

Hours passed. I remember feeling drunk, staring into my glass, thinking about her, worrying for the first time. How strange for Terri to be a mother before me... I'm ashamed to say I felt a twinge of envy that she would have a baby first. I thought about Mickey, bothering to myself whether all this meant we'd be related, wincing to think of him as family, sitting in the kitchen with us at breakfast.

The next part... I can barely tell it now, even after 30 years. It plays in my head, jerky, like an amateur video of a street crime.

Perched at the corner of the bar, I turned to face the street. James walked past the picture window toward Maggie Mae's entrance. I knew right away that something unspeakable lay inside him. James always carried himself in a conscious way, you see... he imagined how other people saw him, feared what he looked and sounded like. When he walked, he did it for other people to notice, filled with attitude, tough as the pavement under his feet, as if he wanted to say, 'Here, I'm James,' with every step. I knew something awful lay in his heart, because he walked past the window like a child, the way he'd walked at age 7 or 8, before he had a sense of himself, as though he didn't care what he looked like or what anyone thought of him now.

He seemed to burst into the bar, coming straight to me. I said, "James, what is it? What's wrong?"

His first words... something like: "She's gone, Helen. She did it just like you. In the play."

At first I didn't know that he meant Terri. He kept on through the noise of the tavern... 'My God,' I thought, 'he's talking about our sister.' I said, "What are you saying, James? What are you saying?"

This I remember clearly as if he had just whispered it. It still takes away my breath. He put his lips to my ear, amid all the tavern music and raised voices. "Helen, our Terri is dead. She stabbed herself just like your Juliet."

Your Juliet. As though Juliet belonged to me.

A coarse chill ran through me, as though God had drilled a mineshaft through my heart. What happened next? I wanted to get away, pushing him from me, punching and slapping him. I didn't believe it. My mind wouldn't accept it; I planned to make it false just by refusing to hear it. How dare anyone cut me with these words, a message to drain my own blood.

I ran from Maggie's, stood in the middle of traffic on Queens Boulevard, right in the center of the road, cars whizzing past, feeling the freezing wind on my forehead, my ears burning... my thoughts arrested. I didn't want to think because where would my thoughts go if they roamed? Then a strange feeling set upon me, rippled through me, that she was there, all around me, listening. 'How could she be gone?' I thought. 'How, when she's right here, right here, now, inside my head?' But then... 'Maybe she's in my head like this because she really is gone.'

It seems that I knew then, standing in the middle of Queens Boulevard... Mickey had died. I knew she'd never have taken her life while he lived.

Uncle Sean followed me. Breathless and steaming in the bitter winter air, he chased and called me, crying out my name in the traffic teaming beneath the wailing trains. I didn't have any money, but went up on the subway platform where the trains ride above the Boulevard. I flashed my pass at the token man. He didn't care; he would have let me by without it. I couldn't go home. Going home would make it all true. I had to keep it away, couldn't let it become real.

I went downtown to the Village near Xavier, first sitting there stunned on the train, empty of sense, then pacing the streets, staring ahead, saying to myself over and over and over: 'This can't be, God, please... don't let it be.'

Wandering in Washington Square, past vagrants and drug dealers and delinquents, a truth seemed to rise slowly from within me: Terri had played Juliet through me. She held the living heart, the spirit, inside my Juliet. What was I? Her costume… Terri had put me on and played the part through me, as if I were nothing but a medium to the character she had made.

I wanted to talk with her, to ask her. I felt that she could hear me, but why couldn't she respond? I could feel her presence but not hear her voice. I feared going mad right there in the street. And swore never to go home. Never.

Then my mind flooded with him. A wave of Ferdinand, his face, his voice, his body, the feel of his hands and lips. I knew somehow that Mick was gone and Terri was… she seemed hurt, not dead, but sick and wounded… and my heart believed that Ferdinand faced deadly trouble as well. I had tangled him with Romeo, spliced them together like two ends of rope. I, Helen—not Juliet— loved Romeo. I wanted Ferdinand to remain Romeo. Part of me wanted to return, to go back into the play, be closed within it forever… to die with him on the stage…. Why couldn't I have died with him that night, so that I never would have known any of this?

Standing in the middle of Broadway and 25th, outside Madison Park, I pulled the room key out of my pocket. Room 353. The metal of it flashed in the dim light of the street. Again, I felt myself long for death. But I knew inside that I couldn't do what Juliet had done, what Terri had done, because I lacked the courage. I walked into the park, sitting there alone on a filthy bench in the shadows, trying to decide.

He was there, in room 353 of the Curragh, waiting for me. I knew it. He was solid, focused like the sharpest spotlight on the blackest stage. That's what I remember of him most, the way he fully directed himself to me, like I was the sun itself, and he, a planet in my gravity. He didn't just hear my words; he listened beyond them into what I felt and meant. He didn't just see my face and body; he looked within me to what I hid inside, like his eyes were there within my heart. He knew me completely. We had been lovers in our dreams, over and over again. It was a love without truth… but this love, conjured in our shared imagination, opened unlimited before us, clear as the empty horizon. I trusted him in my soul, felt utterly safe with him, more than with Charlie or anyone. The way he looked right into my eyes… something about his calmness. I have never known it since. Mick was the raging tempest; Ferdinand, the center, the storm's eye, still and steady.

I looked up at the Flatiron Building, so strange, long and thin, with its triangular prow jutting toward the Square, seeming to point at the hotel. I thought it looked like a giant canoe making its voyage down Broadway. I wondered, 'Where is it going, that canoe? To where does the river run?'

My heart beat fast in my temples; my palms wet with fear. Room 353 might be my tomb. And his. Would that be the last door I passed through in my short life? I felt scared for myself but also for him. I don't know why… but I believed we were to die there… in room 353.

I don't remember entering, nor opening the door. He lay sideways on the bed, stripped to the waist, knees to his chest, curled like an animal with a mortal wound. I studied him, his dark, curly hair spilling over his pale skin. A gun lay in his hand. Did he live?

I sat softly next to him, quietly watching for a long while, till I could see he was breathing, asleep. And I could feel her presence… the Angel of Death. She had come there with us, deciding what to do. Regal… tranquil… warm… strangely comforting, yet her presence was also brutal, indifferent. How many times had we ended of our imaginary lives, he and I, in our mock dance with sovereign death? The beauty of our shared suicide terrified me in that moment. For the first time, I thought to myself what a twisted play it was, Romeo and Juliet, with lovers killing themselves in a meaningless turn of fate, poisoning and stabbing their hearts instead of kissing and loving one another. I thought it was evil, how the poetry made you love death, how it made you want to die instead of to live.

The Black Angel upon my shoulder… I put my hand out, gently running my fingers through his thick hair to wake him. Stirring, he opened his eyes, looking up at me, at first dazed. His gaze upon me… searching, tentative, lost… his heart in an empty dark ocean, barely afloat… going under. I whispered, "Please, Nando, tell me it's not true… tell me. I can't bear for this to be so."

The Angel's storm descended, her suffocating blanket sweeping over, tucking us in as though we lay inside a cozy casket at the bottom of a grave, the black earth falling in upon us.

I had to stop Death.

I denied her. "No more, Death. No more," I whispered to the Angel. "Let us live… set us free…."

I didn't want to be Juliet anymore… didn't want him to be Romeo, ever again.

In that moment, I felt my Teresa lead me by the hand toward him, and I heard her whispering. "Love him," she urged. I knew, just like Romeo and Juliet, this would be the only night we would ever spend, only this one, because of all the torment. Yet I knew this one night would be enough. Teresa told me that this was the point. She whispered to me: "Now seize love."

I touched Ferdinand's face tenderly, kissing him on the lips. He still held the gun, but he laid it down, grasping my two hands, folding my gaze into his own.

Together, we took our lives, we took them back: We wrenched them away from Death. We rolled and pushed that dark Angel from the room, closing the pages of Romeo and Juliet, snapping it shut, putting it away….

He kissed me in return and I could feel his longing, his absolute hunger, the flame of life itself inside him. We made love in that bed in room 353, innocent first love. Naked for the first time, we lay together without clothes or words between us… wearing nothing, saying nothing, not about Terri and Mick or the play or Finnegan or Charlie or Mariel. We let that room be our whole universe, as though we were the last creatures left in heaven and earth, forgetting who we were, what families we came from, what city we were in, forgetting language itself, without a care for what the world was, or why it had come to be. Loving each other, we pushed Death away.

Then we slept. Encircled in his arms, I dream…

I see a field of pure snow beneath a mountain peak, and the black raven circling, soaring above.

Mickey. Naked and cold and dead, with ice-blue lips and clouded, frozen eyes, laid out in the white, sprawled on his back. A sheer red shroud covers him; head to foot, the gauze lays over him, the color of blood but wispy and thin, so his bare body beneath shows through. Over his chest, on top of the red, a sword lays down flat on his sternum, the hilt pointing to his chin and the blade running down his center, past the dark triangle of his loins.

Teresa. Naked and dead, she lies on his chest, face down, legs wrapped round his hips, clutching the sword to her breast so it rests between them. The hilt of the sword, a crucifix.

Her face is drawn in pain and despair, with her golden hair flowing around her chin, swimming over Mickey's shrouded head and chest. Below his bloodless lips, her cheek rests on the cross.

The snow around them slowly begins to thaw, trickles of clear water running down the hilltop like a thousand sparkling teardrops. Green grass starts to show through, the vanishing snow revealing a mountain meadow. All around them wild flowers appear… yellow, blue, red and white petals among the grass blades, green and gold, as a warm mountain sunshine bathes them both.

Teresa's face relaxes… suddenly she breathes in, sharp and full, a miraculous great gasp of air like a baby's first breath, like Eve when God first touched her, made her quick. Her eyes open; she's startled.

Seeing Mickey, her face floods with love and worry, with passion. As she looks at him, the red shroud evaporates into the air, so she's lying right upon him, her warm skin against his. She takes his chin in her hand, kissing him, pale and parched, and as she does, blood flows from her kiss into his lips, down through his face, his body slowly growing pink with life.

His eyes opening in wonder, then he kisses her in return. Their lips part and they smile, each one to the other, their gazes entangled. The sword between them becomes a glimmering gold cross hanging around Mickey's neck, shining in the crisp air, in the clear sun.

He stands, flashing me a broad, forgiving beam, full of optimism and with glister in his eye. As he turns and moves, striding easily toward the summit, I feel his wild spirit.

And last is my own Teresa, my younger sister, my heart, my soul, her blood in my veins. Sitting on the ground, she looks up at me. She's older now, a woman in full, brimming with beauty and confidence. Eyes clear and full of mirth, feisty and bold, sexy and frank, she's not smiling, but about to smile, about to crack her devilish grin. I know she will follow him. Her long glance overflows with meaning and truth. She will not release me. Time endless upon her face, she is the future.

ABOUT THE AUTHOR

David Castro is a graduate of Haverford College (1983) and the University of Pennsylvania Law School (1986). In 1993, following a successful career both in private practice and as chief assistant district attorney in Philadelphia, David was awarded a Kellogg Foundation National Leadership Program Fellowship. As a Kellogg Fellow, he studied community leadership and its relation to improving quality of life. Based upon this work, collaborating with his mentor and colleague Lynne Abraham, in 1995 David founded I-LEAD, Inc., a school for community leadership development that has served several thousand emerging leaders across Pennsylvania through its affiliation with Pennsylvania Weed and Seed (a program that addresses violent crime, drug abuse and gang activity), and the development of an accredited Associate's degree program in leadership. David is also one of the founders of I-LEAD Charter School, a high school that combines leadership development with academic remediation serving at-risk high-school age youth in the economically challenged city of Reading, Pennsylvania. In 2002, in recognition of David's work on behalf of Pennsylvania communities, he was awarded an Eisenhower Fellowship, which he used to study leadership and its impact on economic and community development in Turkey. In 2009, in light of David's work in community leadership and education, he was named an Ashoka Fellow by the Ashoka Global Funds for Social Change. Ashoka is an international community of the world's leading social entrepreneurs. David is a teacher at heart, frequently consulted as a speaker, serving on panel discussions and contributing regularly via blogs and articles posted through the Ashoka network, the Kellogg Leadership Alliance and the Philadelphia Social Innovations Journal. David is the author of *Genership 1.0: Beyond Leadership Toward Liberating the Creative Soul,* now available in print and e-book formats. He is also a host of Innovate, a biweekly podcast featuring dialogue with key leaders, social entrepreneurs, creative visionaries and researchers engaged in transformative thinking, action and creative collaboration. Innovate has featured renowned guests such as Kailash Satyarthi, winner of the 2014 Nobel Peace Prize. Innovate is sponsored by Ashoka, the Kellogg Fellows Leadership Alliance, the Philadelphia Social Innovations Journal and I-LEAD, and produced by Arch Street Press. David lives in Bryn Mawr, Pennsylvania, with his wife, Julia, and their four children.

CPSIA information can be obtained at www.ICGtesting.com
Printed in the USA
BVOW08s0028010816

457273BV00002B/3/P